DIRECT STRIKE

"Eagle One! Eagle One!" The two helicopters were trying to establish communication, their radios screeching. Moving toward the midpoint of the bridge from either end, they drew close to the scene of battle.

Facing away from the bridge, two more of Yazarinsky's men emerged from the shadows, each carrying a sleek, dark green cylinder containing a deadly Stinger surface-to-air missile. There was a *thud* and a cloud of smoke as each was fired, and a gray streak pointed upward.

"Look out! Something's coming at you!" squawked the helicopter radio. But it was too late. The infrared heat-seeking missiles locked onto the choppers' exhaust pipes, both Stingers found their marks, and simultaneously the helicopters were blown out of the sky in a flash and a thunder, leaving only a shower of debris.

BLACK GHOSTS

VICTOR OSTROVSKY

BERKLEY BOOKS, NEW YORK

THE BERKLEY PUBLISHING GROUP
Published by the Penguin Group
Penguin Group (USA) Inc.
375 Hudson Street, New York, New York 10014, USA
Penguin Group (Canada), 90 Eglinton Avenue East, Suite 700, Toronto, Ontario M4P 2Y3, Canada
(a division of Pearson Penguin Canada Inc.)
Penguin Books Ltd., 80 Strand, London WC2R 0RL, England
Penguin Group Ireland, 25 St. Stephen's Green, Dublin 2, Ireland (a division of Penguin Books Ltd.)
Penguin Group (Australia), 250 Camberwell Road, Camberwell, Victoria 3124, Australia
(a division of Pearson Australia Group Pty. Ltd.)
Penguin Books India Pvt. Ltd., 11 Community Centre, Panchsheel Park, New Delhi—110 017, India
Penguin Group (NZ), 67 Apollo Drive, Rosedale, Auckland 0632, New Zealand
(a division of Pearson New Zealand Ltd.)
Penguin Books (South Africa) (Pty.) Ltd., 24 Sturdee Avenue, Rosebank, Johannesburg 2196,
South Africa

Penguin Books Ltd., Registered Offices: 80 Strand, London WC2R 0RL, England

This is a work of fiction. Names, characters, places, and incidents either are the product of the author's imagination or are used fictitiously, and any resemblance to actual persons, living or dead, business establishments, events, or locales is entirely coincidental. The publisher does not have any control over and does not assume any responsibility for author or third-party websites or their content.

BLACK GHOSTS

A Berkley Book / published by arrangement with the author

PRINTING HISTORY
Wilshire Press trade paperback edition / April 2001
Berkley premium edition / May 2011

ISBN: 978-0-425-24146-2

BERKLEY®
Berkley Books are published by The Berkley Publishing Group,
a division of Penguin Group (USA) Inc.,
375 Hudson Street, New York, New York 10014.
BERKLEY® is a registered trademark of Penguin Group (USA) Inc.
The "B" design is a trademark of Penguin Group (USA) Inc.

PRINTED IN THE UNITED STATES OF AMERICA

10   9   8   7   6   5   4   3   2   1

To Bella.
I love you, babe!

In memory of Adash Silverberg, Bella's uncle. A wonderful young man who didn't survive the Holocaust.

CHAPTER 1

Peter Ivanovich Rogov expected all hell to break loose, and he was well aware of the fact that any deviation from the plan could render him dead. Either way, he regarded it as a gamble worth taking. No matter what happened he would be free from this frozen abyss. After six years in this barren scrap of purgatory, the chance of freedom, no matter how slim, was worth taking.

Few places on Earth were as inhospitable as Prison Colony No. 5—or, as the prisoners referred to it, "the grave"—on a winter morning. Little, if anything, ever changed in the grave, except perhaps the weather, and that was always for the worse. Peter raised his frayed coat collar, shielding his face from the freezing wind that howled across the desolate, color-starved valley, pushing clouds of swirling snow in its wake through the razor wire and electric fences.

The prison colony was perched on a hill overlooking the nuclear bomb factory known as Tomsk-7. Guard towers rose high on solid timber stilts and loomed over the rectangular prison compound. Powerful spotlights and heavy Gurianov machine guns mounted on each tower probed the grounds day and night. The prison administration building and guards' barracks were outside the fence, beyond a deep moat surrounding the camp like an ugly scar. Except for the shrinking food rations and a decline in the guards' discipline, which manifested itself in their sloppy attire and rowdy behavior, the prison was a living monument to a dead regime.

Peter, found guilty of treason for his part in the failed coup against then-President Mikhail Gorbachev, had been sentenced to life with hard labor. He found it ironic that he, a devoted guardian of the revolution, was called a traitor, while those who sold out the motherland, aiding in the collapse of an empire, were honored. That, he vowed, he would soon change.

He heard a truck grinding its gears in the distance. He squinted his pale blue eyes in an attempt to catch a glimpse of it through the arctic veil of blowing snow. His thin lips twitched in what the few who knew him would call a smile.

"Lev!" Peter hissed to the frail man beside him who was busy stomping his feet to keep his meager body from freezing. "It's time."

"Yes, sir," the little man muttered, his breath icing up his sparse mustache.

"Tell the others to get ready!" Peter commanded.

Lev nodded and headed for the inmates' quarters.

Drawing one last puff from his yellow, foul-smelling cigarette, Peter watched Lev hobble across the central yard. As soon as Lev entered the first in a row of dilapidated barracks, Peter flicked the smoldering cigarette butt to the ground and headed to the long woodshed at the other end of the camp, passing a row of prisoners huddled by the kitchen exhaust shaft, attempting to draw some heat from it. They stood with their backs to the wind, waiting for what the camp administration cynically referred to as breakfast. They were too busy keeping themselves from freezing while protecting their place in line to even notice him.

Although Peter wore the same tattered gray uniform and coat as the other inmates, he stood out, shoulders pulled back, chin forward in defiance, unmistakably a general, the kind men fear and admire, an ex-KGB brigadier general eager to make his comeback.

A guard entered the latrine just as Peter had approached it. Peter stopped a few feet from the filthy door and made a futile attempt to light another cigarette against the wind. Precious moments were being lost, but there was nothing to do but wait. When the guard finally straddled out, still battling his fly with his heavy mitten, Peter slipped in. The stench almost overwhelmed him as he headed for the second stall from the end. He could hear the old truck rumbling in the distance; his ticket to freedom was making its way down the road. The only consolation in that dark, foul latrine was the refuge it offered from the wind, providing an illusion of warmth.

Peter leaned against the outer wall and waited, listening intensely for sounds as he tried to visualize his plan unfolding a mile and a half down the windswept road.

The old ten-wheel Zeel truck stopped at the gate cut in the high wall surrounding the nuclear complex. The sleepy guard in a glass booth put down his cup of hot tea and leaned forward, wiping the condensation off the glass to get a better view of the truck and its driver. He recognized the new deliveryman, two weeks on the job. His predecessor had a close encounter with a military truck in Omsk, they said. Poor man, the guard thought, but then that's life: One moment you're here, the next you're under a truck.

According to regulations, he was required to check the truck before letting it in, but as Peter had predicted, he didn't want to leave the warmth of his booth. Instead, he glanced back into the yard to make sure the duty officer wasn't on rounds. Then he pressed the green button and waved the truck in as the loud screeching gate slowly moved along its track.

The gate log would read: *6:50—delivery truck arrived, checked and found clean. Entry permitted.*

The old diesel engine revved and the truck slowly gained speed, making its way into the calm of the inner courtyard, moving down a narrow winding path wedged between the wall and a row of concrete silos that extended into the murky sky. Once out of the guard's sight, the truck made a brief stop.

"Now!" the driver shouted through the window separating the cabin from the back. Three men, two in guards' uniforms and one in a black diver's wet suit, jumped out the back as the truck continued on its way to the kitchen.

Within seconds, the three men had cut the lock on a metal hatch at the bottom of the third silo. For months, they had practiced this on a mock-up. Moving quickly, they entered what was probably the most dangerous and unstable environment in the world. A reinforced steel tank, forty feet wide and thirty feet high, occupied the interior of the concrete silo, leaving a narrow corridor around it. The tank was filled to the brim with water. An electric grid along its inner wall kept the contents at 34 degrees F.

The two uniformed men carried a large black duffel bag. Their mission had to be completed before the truck returned. They had come to release Lucifer from his steel bottle.

The diver climbed a rusting ladder bolted to the tank wall. Once at the top he opened a round hatch and slipped into the water. Descending, he turned on a powerful flashlight strapped to the side of his head. A series of shiny cylinders made of a titanium alloy were neatly stacked on the tank floor, each with a red valve at its end. They contained radioactive acid, a lethal and volatile byproduct of the bomb factory. The water kept their temperature steady, as a fluctuation of more than three degrees could prove lethal.

Hovering over the cylinders, the diver hesitated only briefly before he carefully connected explosive devices, which he had removed from his belt, to two of them, each one positioned several inches from the red valve. A series of small suction cups held the devices in place. The detonators were equipped with electronic timers, on which a diminishing row of LEDs reminded him that time was running out.

There was just enough C-4 explosive in each device to blow off the security valve, releasing the deadly toxins into the water. The other two men were placing a second set of explosives on the outside wall of the tank, intending to blow a hole in its base, allowing the contaminated water to spill out of the containment area.

The timers were synchronized to create a single blast rather than a series of explosions, which could suggest sabotage. Peter knew that if sabotage was even suspected in the early stages, he would have to contend with a total shutdown of all entry and exit points in the entire region. It had to look like an accident if he was going to get away.

Standing in the stall, Peter counted the seconds, tapping his finger on the grimy wall. They should be just about done, he thought. They're closing the hatch. Tap, tap, two ninety-nine, three hundred, three o one. Back on the truck, three o six, three o seven . . .

He closed his eyes. Three twenty-two. The truck should be at the gate of the nuclear complex—three twenty-four, three twenty-five—now! He stopped breathing, aching to hear the gate open. "Now," he whispered, pleading through clenched teeth, "open the goddamned gate." He felt stiff, the veins bulging in his forehead. Peter had no god to pray to, no one to whom he could promise repentance if things went well. He was all alone in that miserable latrine, knowing every moment of silence drew him that much further away from freedom. He was as focused as a man could be on an object so far out of reach, pushing at the gate with his tortured mind, trying to pry it open.

Finally, like the sound of water to a thirsty man, he heard the gate open, then the truck moving. He slapped one hand against the wall, sending his other fist skyward. Then he stepped on the toilet seat and reached to the overhead ceramic water tank. Pushing the cover to one side, he pulled out a wet plastic bag. Anxiously he ripped it open and unfolded a guard's uniform. Now that he knew the team was out of the complex, he could put on his disguise.

He covered the filthy floor with his threadbare gray coat, placing the brown uniform in one corner and hurriedly tearing off his prison garb.

The sensation of the clean, ironed cotton against his skin was something he had long forgotten. He felt the coolness of the starched collar on his grimy neck. The fullness and warmth of the overcoat felt good. He looked at the prison uniform bundled on the floor, thinking he would rather die than wear it again.

The wind had subsided to an icy hiss. Peter could hear the Zeel changing gears as it approached the prison gates. The well-oiled electric gate slid open just enough for the truck to pass. Peter knew the guards would not bother to check the vehicle as it entered, but they would pick it clean on the way out.

Peter's heart pounded hard against his chest, sweat broke out on his forehead, and he felt a numbness in his knees. There was nothing for him to do but wait, a passenger on the brittle wings of fate. His gas mask was in his hand, ready.

The sudden blast cut through the cold air like the crack of a whip, shaking the entire camp. All eyes turned in fear toward the complex down the road.

Peter pulled the black gas mask over his face, waiting for the alarm. Time seemed to have stopped. Then, with a monstrous shriek, the siren began to howl. Peter stepped out into the blinding white cold. What he saw reminded him of Bruegel's vision of hell. Armed guards in green coats and black gas masks, like warriors from another world, were herding rows of thin, pale men in tattered gray uniforms onto dark green trucks. In the distance, an ominous gray pillar of smoke capped by a black, swirling toxic cloud slowly leaned away, toggled by the wind, like a giant contorted mushroom.

The prison colony's proximity to the nuclear complex was no coincidence. The inmates were regarded as disposable labor, to be used on cleanup details in the event of an accident. No great loss, as far as the designers of the facility were concerned.

In fact, the prisoners had been drilled for such an occasion as this. Now they were being rounded up to be trucked to the facility that was spewing clouds of deadly black smoke. The guards' assignment was to deliver as many prisoners in the shortest time possible into the hands of the security cleanup team at the nuclear complex.

Peter made his way to the last truck in the convoy that was about to leave for the accident site. He climbed into the cabin and sat next to the driver. In back, his block-mates were shackled with leg irons to the truck floor, guarded by four men in guards' uniforms and gas masks. The last guard to board the truck signaled Peter with a thumbs-up. It would be hours before anyone would find the four real guards who had been on kitchen duty, their throats slashed, stacked in the corner of the walk-in freezer like so many slabs of beef.

Soon he would be free. Suddenly his blood froze in his veins as an officer tapped on his window, signaling him to roll it down. What had gone wrong? Options were rushing through his head. He looked at the truck's rearview mirror and could see one of his rescue team cocking a gun. His men had their orders: "If something goes wrong, open fire and we'll try to fight our way out." It would be a futile attempt, but Peter was getting out of this place, one way or the other.

The officer looked directly into Peter's eyes. Peter recognized the man and was sure the recognition was mutual.

"Here," the officer said finally, reaching through the window and handing Peter a key on a short chain. Peter nodded and palmed the key. The officer turned and walked away from the edge of his grave, never realizing how close to it he had been. Peter had forgotten that although his face was known, no one would be likely to recognize him behind his gas mask.

It was the key to the prisoners' shackles. The role of the truck guard was to hand the key over to the security man at the complex. Now Peter had the key, and some of the inmates in the back knew this was their final trip out of this damned place. The driver, who'd been paid handsomely by Peter's colleagues for his cooperation, turned the ignition and followed the convoy on its way out.

The camp's commandant stood by the guard's booth, pressing his stopwatch as he waved the last truck on its way. He was pleased at the record time in which he had managed to mobilize the work crews. Grinning, he walked back toward one of his lieutenants and held the stopwatch above his head.

The concrete bridge halfway between the camp and the nuclear complex came into sight. "Slow down," Peter ordered, pointing at the truck ahead. "Put more distance between us." By the time they reached the bridge, the truck in front of them was out of sight.

"Stop," said Peter, and the driver slammed on the brakes. The truck skidded closer to the edge of the bridge. They could hear thuds from the back as some of the inmates were tossed to the floor. The driver sat silently, a worried look on his face, like a thief on his first job. His eyes scanned the end of the road.

Getting out of the prison camp was only half of Peter's problem. Tomsk-7 was a vast, well-guarded territory, a fenced-in county. Peter estimated that the other trucks would have reached the smoldering nuclear facility by now and would be unloading their prisoners before heading back for a second batch.

"You wait here," Peter ordered the driver. "I'll be right back." He got out of the truck and walked to the rear. His four-man rescue team jumped off the truck. Three of them ran toward a fork in the road and down a narrow trail leading away from the bend. The fourth, a giant of a man, nodded to Peter and moved around the side of the truck toward the cab on the driver's side.

The prisoners sat motionless, staring at Peter through the opening. Some of them, Peter's close friends, were smiling. They had served him faithfully over the last six years and were about to collect their reward. Peter raised his hand to them, dangling the key that could unlock their leg irons.

"A few more minutes," he said, "you'll be free."

They nodded anxiously. Peter headed back to the cab. He opened the passenger door with one hand, heaving himself onto the wide running board.

"Okay," he said to the driver, "let's move her over there." He pointed to the center of the bridge. The driver put the truck in gear; seconds later, he came to a stop at the exact spot Peter had designated. He took it out of gear and pulled the hand brake. The driver turned to face Peter, smiling uncertainly. Without warning, his door violently swung open. The giant moved swiftly. He grabbed the driver, placing one hand on the man's chin, the other on the back of his head. With a single sharp tug, he turned the head around, snapping the neck with a loud popping sound like the breaking of a dry twig.

The driver's head was now facing in the wrong direction, still wearing the same uncertain smile.

"Goodbye, comrade," Peter muttered, returning to the back of the truck. He glanced into the dark interior. Slowly, hesitantly, his comrades got up. Grinning, they held forth their leg irons for him to unlock. Peter did not move. Then they heard the truck's ignition fire again.

"Come on, hurry up," said one.

"Quick, unlock the bloody chains," shouted another.

Peter stood there, a hint of a smile on his face. When the truck started moving, the prisoners turned to one another, baffled. Some tumbled to the floor, pushing others with them. Lev, near the door, pulled furiously on his chain, cursing at Peter. The truck gathered speed as it rolled toward the rotting wooden railing.

Peter could not make out what Lev was yelling, his voice drowned out by the screams of the others. The railing gave way and the truck plunged twenty feet, crashing through the frozen crust. It slowly began to sink in the icy river, its rear wheels still turning.

Peter moved closer to the edge to see the men he had sacrificed for his freedom. They were still screaming, fighting their chains as the truck slowly slid under. He turned to the giant who stood next to him, hypnotized by the sight. "Let's go."

"Yes, sir," the big man said.

They followed the trail from the fork in the road to where a military ambulance was waiting. Peter lay on a gurney, and his face was bandaged so he would not be recognized. They settled down to wait.

A few minutes later, a string of military ambulances passed them on the way to the accident, sirens wailing. As the last one cleared the turn, they drove onto the road. Its siren blaring, the ambulance sped in the opposite direction, heading for the main entrance to Tomsk-7. No one even thought to stop them.

Twenty minutes later, they reached the airfield, a lonely stretch of frozen asphalt barely visible under the blowing snow. It extended from an igloo-shaped hangar across a field. A large green snowplow was racing from the end of the runway to where a white twin-engine executive jet was waiting for them, engines humming.

"We need to take off as soon as the strip is clear," said one of the general's men as they got out of the ambulance. "If we wait, the snow will cover the runway and we'll be trapped until they can clear it again."

"How long does it take to clear it?" the general asked, unwinding the bandages from his face.

"Couple of hours." The big man pointed at the snowplow. "He's been working since before we left."

The general nodded toward the gleaming jet, then turned to the big man standing beside him. "Where did this come from?"

The big man shrugged. "Colonel Yazarinsky asked me to inform you that this was a gift from your American friend. He said the man was keeping his promise."

The general's face twitched slightly. "Remarkable," he said, "a Westerner who keeps his promise."

"Sir?"

"A Westerner's promise," the general said in a lecturing

manner, "could be written in the wind or running water, my boy." The men headed to the plane. "Our American friend is not keeping his promise, he's placing a bet. I wonder how much he has placed on the other side?"

CG Command Bunker, outside Moscow
February 17
16:40 hours

If the unthinkable were to happen, and there were to be an invasion and occupation of Soviet soil, it would be expedient to have a resistance already in place, a KGB general once thought at the height of the Cold War. It would be an armed faction within occupied territory that could help reclaim it for the Soviet Union. With Stalin's approval, the general established a network of like-minded allies within the Soviet army and KGB, and before long he had created a shadow secret army known as the *Chornia Gostia*. "Black Ghosts."

Once activated, the Black Ghosts would be a force to be reckoned with. They consisted of some twenty tank and mechanized battalions, several nuclear sites, and thousands of dedicated men, most but not all of whom were drawn from the ranks of the KGB. There were also several Russian army officers at various ranks, who could be counted on to shift their allegiance to the Black Ghosts if the current leadership of Russia, which the Ghosts regarded as weak, unprincipled, and unpatriotic, were to veer too far in the direction of appeasement of the West.

General Vladimir Kozov, according to his special designation in times of emergency, was the new official commander of the Black Ghosts. He was bent on being their last commander and the one who would disband them for good. Although he understood the fears that had brought about their creation, he believed them to be outdated. Given the fact that the Russian president was on the path of peace, Kozov assumed, as did the rest of the Russian high command, that the Black Ghosts' three underground command posts located in Vladivostok, Novosibirsk, and Moscow were a sealed relic of a bygone era, to be dealt with at a later date.

In order to prevent the activation of the Black Ghosts by any unauthorized personnel, new sophisticated security systems had been installed in all three command posts. The Moscow command bunker was protected by a new Iris Identification Scanner, which prevented anyone but General Kozov from powering up the mobilization computer, without which the units were only an imaginary army, fragmented and unreachable. The computer was at the heart of the Black Ghosts' call-up mechanism and held all the activation codes.

General Kozov had advocated that the Black Ghosts be disbanded altogether, but the presidential decree dissolving the units was slow in coming. Meanwhile, General Kozov had to content himself with the promise that the IIS was fail-safe.

If tampered with, the IIS worked as an explosive lock, instantly destroying all information stored in the computer. The only way to unlock it was for Kozov to have the device scan his eye and compare the image of his iris to a previous scan. Without that image, no one could unleash the fury of the Black Ghosts.

The career of Kozov's predecessor as commander of the Black Ghosts was less auspicious. Implicated in the 1988 coup attempt against Gorbachev, he had been exiled to a prison colony in Siberia and was now presumed dead, a victim of the horrific accident at the nuclear facility adjacent to where he was incarcerated.

Peter, however, was sitting in the Combat Information Center of the Black Ghosts' underground command bunker outside Moscow. He was well rested and felt comfortable in his tailored black uniform, with gold general's shoulder braids. His legs were raised on the dark wooden desk, his chair tilted back. In these surroundings—the familiar charts, screens, the smell of fresh paint, a staple of underground military bunkers—Peter felt at home. It was almost as if the years at the prison colony had never happened. But they had, and for that Peter was about to tear his revenge from the living tissue of his adversaries.

"Operation Czar is on schedule, sir," said Colonel Sokolov, a tall, slim man with a sophisticated aura about him.

Peter lit a cigarette. "And the communication array?" His eyes were like two slits scanning Sokolov's face.

"Most of it has been delivered, sir. The rest should arrive any day."

"How about installation?"

"On schedule, sir."

"What is the status of the prisoners?"

Before Peter had arrived at the bunker, his men had found a small maintenance crew and a contingent of guards. They'd been quickly overrun and taken prisoner.

"They were interrogated, sir. Colonel Yazarinsky handled that."

"And?"

Sokolov's face showed his distaste for his fellow colonel. "He disposed of them, sir."

"I see." The general leaned back in his chair and gazed for several seconds at the darkened computer screens on the walls of the control room. Except for the yellowish glow of the emergency lights, nothing was on. The only system that worked was the life-support system for the skeleton maintenance crews. "Any progress on breaking the lock on the computer?"

Sokolov looked uncomfortable. "Not very much, sir. The technician said we might have to find an alternative to the computer."

"An alternative?" Peter was about to pour out all his anger on the slim officer standing to attention on the other side of his desk. But he reconsidered. Still staring at the blank screen, Peter seemed to reach some kind of decision. There was a hint of a smile on his face.

"Get Colonel Yazarinsky in here now," he said absently. "I have a little job for him."

CHAPTER 2

Grantsville, Utah
February 17
06:05 hours

Dawn cautiously probed the winter sky, dragging the valley from under the shadows of the jagged snow-covered peaks to the east.

"Le Bistro" was located in an old converted warehouse at the west end of Grantsville, where Main Street bends northwest, joining up with Highway 138 on its way from Salt Lake City. The restaurant was the source of a mouth-watering aroma of fresh-baked croissants that lingered in the cold air. Using a recipe he picked up in the south of France, Edward baked an increasing number of the crescent-shaped rolls every morning. He now removed the last sizzling tray from the oven, placing it in a tall metal rack.

Whistling a tune only he could have recognized, Edward attended to his favorite part of the morning: preparing a hearty, somewhat oversized breakfast for himself. His staff was not due in for another hour, which gave him all the time he needed.

He had begun this routine the day after he opened ten months ago, and since then he had guarded it as a sacred rite. For someone who had dragged himself through some of the bloodiest gutters the world had to offer, as an officer with Alpha 27, a highly specialized and extremely covert operation unit of U.S. Military Intelligence, this was as close to heaven as it could get.

Edward had just poured himself a cup of hot black Colombian coffee and set his loaded plate—three eggs over easy, six crispy strips of bacon, and a basket of fresh croissants—on the counter separating the open kitchen from the bistro's main seating area, when he heard a knock at the door. It was the door leading from the kitchen into a back alley.

Edward glanced quickly at the neon Michelob clock on the wall above the cash register. It was ten past six. The road in front of the restaurant was empty, and large, fluffy snowflakes descended gently through the fading yellow glow of the street lamp.

The second knock was stronger, more vigorous. Edward felt the hairs bristle on the back of his neck: In his book, surprises were rarely pleasant. All his senses were now alert. Moving fast, he reached under the counter and drew a .357 Magnum Ruger revolver from a secret compartment.

"Just a minute," he called out, moving closer to the door. Through the spy hole, Edward got a fish-eye view of the back alley and the woman standing at the door.

Clumps of wet snow clung to her coat and to the knitted black cap pulled over her ears. She was alone, her arms folded across her chest, trying to keep warm.

"We open at seven," he said through the door. "What do you want?"

"I'm looking for Edward." The woman's voice was barely audible. "Larry Collins sent me."

Larry Collins was not a name that would come up in casual conversation. Larry was CIA, one of the few friends who knew where Edward could be found. They had met on a job about ten years ago, in the Middle East, and had become friends—not common in the murky province of covert activity. The work they had done together was usually referred to in the inner circle of the intelligence community as an INHAP OP—It Never Happened Operation—giving the politicians their precious plausible deniability. Therefore, on the record, Larry and Edward had never met, which was exactly the reason they could be friends without endangering each other.

Edward pulled the latch and moved a few feet back. "It's open." He stood with his back to the wall, the gun cocked.

The fact that it was a woman behind the door and not some gorilla made no difference to him. During his career, he had witnessed more than one incident when a tough, well-trained combat grunt had been blown to bits by a small, innocent-looking girl. Aside from that, saying "Larry sent me" didn't necessarily make it so. For now he had only her word for it.

It took her a moment to push the door open, as it

had frozen to the jamb. A burst of cold air carrying her gentle scent reached him almost the instant she entered.

"Hi," she said, closing the door behind her, a brief apologetic smile touching her pale face. She seemed to be in a hurry, restless, catching her breath. She stamped her feet to get the slush off her boots and then dusted the melting snow from her shoulders. By the time she pulled off her black cap, releasing a splash of disheveled blond hair, she was standing in a small puddle of melted snow.

"What can I do for you?" He lowered the gun slightly.

"Are you Edward?" She stared at the menacing Magnum bore. The smile was gone. Even in her big, bulky coat, she seemed graceful, fragile. Edward thought she was very beautiful, and very tense, as though she expected something terrible to happen.

"Yes. And you are—?"

"Natalie," she responded quickly. "I work with Larry." She stepped forward, extending her hand.

Edward raised the gun. "Let's not be hasty," he said.

She froze, her hand hanging in midair. "Right. Listen—"

"Where's Larry?"

"He's wounded, he's in the van. We must hurry," she pleaded.

Edward felt a knot form in his gut. A friend was in peril, but he didn't let it show.

"How do I know this isn't a trick to get me out there?"

"Larry said you owed him a bottle of scotch—Navy Cut."

"That's rum. Navy Cut's a rum, not a scotch."

"He said you'd say that. Now can we go?" She pulled her cap back on and turned to leave.

It was a joke between Larry and him, having to do with payment for a shot of illicit booze they had enjoyed together in Saudi Arabia, after a successful incursion into Iraq. Edward reached for a brown leather coat on the rack by the door and stuck the gun into his belt. "What happened?"

"He's been shot." She opened the door. "The van's a couple of blocks from here."

"Who shot him?" Edward followed her out, closing the door behind him.

"Look, mister," she said coldly and impatiently, "what goddamn difference does it make who shot him? He said you'd help."

"Why didn't you park here?"

"I wanted to be sure the place was safe before I brought him here. Things are not what they appear to be lately."

It stopped snowing, but the day was still very cold. By the time they had reached the end of the alley and turned onto Main Street, Edward could feel the chill penetrating his coat, and his ears were smarting. He put his hands deeper into his coat pockets, envying the woman in her black cap.

At the corner of Apple and Hale he saw the dark blue van parked across the street from the small town hall building. The exhaust was emitting a white cloud, indicating the engine was running.

"You drive," she said as she entered the back seat.

Edward moved fast. Grantsville was not a place with a night life, but that was not to say everybody was asleep. A parked van with its engine running at this hour of the morning was bound to draw attention. This was a place where people would sit up and complain if a bird was chirping out of tune. He opened the driver's-side door and looked into the back seat. Larry was wrapped in a gray blanket soaked in blood. His head was slumped to one side, leaning against the fogged-up window. Edward could hear him wheezing and gasping for air. It didn't look good.

The sight of Larry all bloodied and helpless angered him. He couldn't tell whether he was angry with whoever had done this or with Larry himself for making him deal with this sort of thing again.

"How long ago did this happen?" Edward asked.

"A couple of hours." She put her arms around the unconscious man, gently lifting his head from the cold glass and leaning it on her shoulder. Larry opened his eyes briefly, trying to focus and muttering something. Then his eyes closed again.

"What did he say?" Edward asked.

"He's delirious." She lifted the blanket and looked underneath. "He's losing blood. We need to get him inside, change his dressings."

"We'll get him to a hospital. There's one down the road in Tooele." Edward put the van in gear and eased out of the parking spot.

"No," she said sharply, tugging on his shoulder. "Drive to your place."

"He needs medical attention," Edward reasoned, looking at her in the rearview mirror.

"They'll nail him if we take him to a hospital."

"Who's they?"

"FBI, CIA, whoever."

"Oh, great," muttered Edward. Things were going from bad to worse. "How close are they?"

"We shot at the ones who came for us."

"Came for you? What do you mean?"

"Larry called for backup and they came."

"Larry's backup did this?" Edward was starting to realize the magnitude of the problem. From what she had told him, it was very possible they had just killed some CIA agents. If that was true, it would not be long before they would have the National Guard on their case, and not just the kids from Tooele.

"Do they know you?"

"What do you mean?"

"I mean, do Larry's so-called friends know you?"

"No."

Edward thought fast. They had to get Larry out of sight as quickly as possible. If, however, he was already being tailed, it was game over.

"What about this van?"

"What about it?"

"Is it clean?" Edward could see in the rearview mirror that she was staring blankly at him, obviously confused by the situation. "Who rented it?" he pressed.

"Shit," she said in frustration. "He did."

Edward had to think fast. He couldn't dump the van,

not with blood all over it. God only knew what the sheriff might do if he found it abandoned in that condition. Edward had no time to clean it up. He decided to park it in the old warehouse. There was a closed-off section he had been planning to turn into another seating area for the bistro. Edward turned down Main Street, back the way they had come.

"Why are they after him?" Edward asked as he pulled into the alley behind the bistro.

"He stumbled on something big, and they want him silenced."

"And how do you fit in?"

"It's a long story. I'm a friend of a friend."

"Okay," Edward said as the van came to a stop. "Let's get him in."

"Is there a drugstore around here?"

"There's a medical clinic; you were just parked by it." Edward got out and opened the back door to the kitchen, then returned to get Larry. Together, he and Natalie slid him out of the van, and Edward carried him in his arms.

Momentarily revived by the cold air, Larry opened his eyes and looked at Edward. He seemed to want to say something, then his head slumped back and he was out again.

Natalie held the kitchen door open and followed Edward in.

"Open that green door over there." Edward nodded to a door leading into a hallway at one end of which was an office area and at the other the staircase to his private apartment.

Carrying Larry up the stairs took everything Edward had. Larry was not a big man, and Edward was six-foot-one and totally out of shape, not to mention his bad back. At this particular juncture, it would not be prudent to aggravate the old Army wound he had suffered during a night jump into El Salvador. It could render him as helpless as Larry.

Edward passed through the living room and into the bedroom, where he carefully lowered his unconscious friend onto the bed. Exhausted and catching his breath, he sat next to Larry.

"Excuse the mess," he said when Natalie entered. "I wasn't expecting company."

"Looks okay to me." There was a patronizing tone in her voice. She turned her attention to Larry. "He started bleeding again. We need to change his dressings. Where did you say that clinic was?"

"Not a good idea, especially if they know he's wounded."

"I'm not sure. I mean, if they're dead they don't know. But I can't be sure about that." She sounded anxious, frightened, needing reassurance that all would be well.

"Calm down. We'll figure something out." He couldn't bring himself to tell her it would be all right because he couldn't see how. For all he knew, they—whoever they were—could be breaking his door down any minute, and there was absolutely nothing he could do about it.

Edward reached under the bed and pulled out a large black attaché case. "Here, my emergency first-aid kit. Somewhat larger than a conventional kit, but then I always expect the worst." He smiled at her, trying to reassure her, hoping she couldn't see through him. "You'll find everything you need in there. I'll go take care of the van. I'll be right back." He stopped at the door. "Is there something you need from the van?"

She thought for a minute, staring at the floor and running her long fingers through her hair. "There's a blue duffel bag behind the back seat, if you could bring it." She sounded tired.

"Anything else?"

She shook her head. Edward went down to the vacant portion of the warehouse, swung open the double doors, and backed the van in. By the time he returned, Natalie had dressed Larry's chest wound, and he was resting comfortably.

"He took a bullet to the chest," she said, her voice quavering. "I think it's still in there."

"We'll have to get him to a doctor," said Edward. He handed her the duffel bag. She took out a green woolen sweater and pulled it on.

Natalie chewed her lip thoughtfully. "Maybe if they don't find him by tomorrow, they'll think he's back in Washington or somewhere. Then we could get him to a doctor."

Edward knew Larry wouldn't make it until tomorrow, not with that bullet in him and his fever the way it was. He also knew she was right about not taking him to the hospital.

From beneath his feet, Edward could hear the sounds

of the bistro coming to life. "I'll be back shortly," he said. "I've got to make sure everything's fine downstairs." He left her sitting on the end of the bed, her eyes fixed on Larry. Her mind seemed to drift away.

In the living room he stopped by the phone to make a quick call to a number in New Jersey. It was an emergency number, the kind veterans from the battlefields of the Cold War carry etched into the tissues of their minds. Larry needed help, and fast.

The call, as usual, was answered almost immediately. "Yes?" said a rasping voice.

"It's Edward." There was no need for secret code names. No one was listening; no one cared. "I need a doctor."

"What's up? You sick?"

"Not me. A friend. Bullet in the chest."

There was a momentary silence. "You're in Utah, right?"

"Right. How about someone from the hospital in Tooele?" Edward could hear the computer keys as his friend was searching.

"No, sorry, we have no one there. I don't even know if we have a doctor out there at all." There was a pause, then the voice came back on again. "I can get you a medic."

"That will have to do."

"Okay. I'll have him call you."

"Hurry up, man. My friend is running out of time."

"Peace," rasped the voice, and the line went dead.

Edward knew, as he hung up, that you couldn't always get what you wanted from this network of abandoned souls, but it didn't hurt to ask. It was a comfort to know he wasn't alone, that there was someone out there who would at least try to help.

The bistro was in full swing. The first wave of customers was pouring in. Edward's breakfast, which he prepared so diligently, had long since been consigned to the trash. Kelly, Edward's manager, came rushing from the main seating area into the kitchen. Her round face was shining with sweat.

"What's with you?" she asked on her way to the large dishwasher, where she was about to give the new gofer a hand, seeing that the stream of clean cups was slowing to a trickle. "Is something wrong? You look as if you got hit by a truck."

"No, I'm fine. Could you please get me some breakfast for two?"

A knowing look came into her eyes as she smiled at him. "For two? Yes, sir!" She saluted mockingly and turned to the burly man in a long white apron who was pouring perfect flapjacks on the wide black griddle. "Two Napoleons for the boss," she called out. Then she turned back to Edward, her eyes curious. "Want me to bring it up t'ya?"

"No, I'll come down for it."

"Okay, no problema." She turned back to her tasks. Edward would have to be careful about that curiosity of hers: For the moment, Larry was a stowaway.

When he got upstairs, Natalie was where he had left her. He sat in the chair by the window. After a few minutes of silence, he realized she had no intention of starting a conversation.

"I need you to tell me what's going on," he said.

"I don't know. Larry didn't tell me much."

Edward sensed she was lying. She had a wary look in her eye, like that of a hunted animal. He wondered how deep her involvement with Larry was. Could she just be a friend to whom Larry had turned in an hour of need?

"At least tell me what happened."

She turned to face him, leaning on the bed's brass footboard. "Larry wanted to replace some electronic device he said was about to be stolen from Hill Air Force Base with a fake one."

"Just like that?" he interrupted.

"No, he'd been working on this for quite some time now. He knew someone was going to steal it, so he wanted to get in there and replace the real deal with a fake." She seemed like she was about to cry, but she swallowed hard and kept on talking. "We drove over there—it's on the other side of Salt Lake City." She paused, moving on the bed carefully so as not to disturb Larry. "We got there about midnight and Larry parked by the base fence near a large hangar. He cut a hole in the fence and entered the base on foot. He told me to wait for him there."

"When was all this?"

"I told you, last night around twelve."

"He went in alone?"

"He expected to meet with the backup from his office when we got there. They were not there when we arrived. He wanted me to wait for them at the fence."

"CIA?"

"No, Larry's been out of the CIA for over a year—well, not really out, he was loaned to the National Security Council."

Edward was stunned. He had seen Larry several months earlier and was told nothing. Why would Larry keep this from him? Larry, working for the NSC? "Go on."

"He told me to wait for them. If they arrived before he got back, I was to tell them to wait. Well, I got scared sitting alone in the middle of nowhere, so I hid behind the hangar and watched the road. From where I was, I could see the van and the hole in the fence. He left me a gun, just in case. After about half an hour, a black car stopped across the road from the van. Three men got out; one walked over to the van and looked in. Then he walked back to the other two."

"Weren't you supposed to ask them to wait?"

"Yes, but there was something about them." She shrugged. "I don't know—call it woman's intuition. Something didn't smell right. So I stayed behind the hangar. One of them got a rifle out of the trunk and hid in the bushes. The other two got back in the car and drove down the road. I couldn't see the car, but I could see by their headlights that they had stopped and turned around."

"What about the guy in the bushes?"

"I couldn't see him, it was too dark. It was around four when Larry came out of the base. He saw me behind the hangar and came over to me. Then the car pulled up behind the van and stopped. Larry asked me why I wasn't waiting in the van and I told him I was worried.

I told him about the man in the grove with the rifle and how they came and left and now had returned.

"He said it was okay. They were just following procedure in positioning themselves that way. I told him I didn't trust them." She started crying. "Larry told me to stay out of sight—he would go meet with them himself. He said he got the electronic device and was going to give it to them. He had it, wrapped in blue bubble wrap. I kneeled down as he walked towards them."

She shook her head. "I knew something bad was going to happen, I just knew it." She wiped the tears with the back of her hand. Edward leaned over to the large pine dresser for a box of tissues and handed it to her.

She smiled, drew a tissue, and dried her eyes. She cleared her throat and went on. "He walked towards them, they got out of the car and waited for him. That's when I saw the man in the grove suddenly stand up and aim his rifle at Larry. I yelled out to Larry and fired my gun at the man. Larry turned in my direction. One of the men standing by the car drew a gun and shot him. Larry fell back. I ran towards them, firing my gun until there was no more bullets. Larry also shot at them from where he was on the ground."

"Did you get them?"

"I think so, because they'd stopped shooting when I got to Larry. Anyway, I grabbed him and dragged him into the van. He said I should get the circuit board—he dropped it when he was shot. I went back and got it, and took off as fast as I could. Before he passed out he said that I should try and get to your place. After a while, I pulled off the road. I dressed his wound as best I could, just to stop the bleeding, and then found my way over here."

"Were you followed?"

"I don't think so. If they were after me they could have killed us both when I stopped to take care of him."

Edward knew she was right. He also realized she was not as fragile as she looked. There was quite a woman under that beautiful outer shell.

"So what is this circuit board, anyway?"

"You'll have to ask him when he comes to." From her expression, he knew she was not going to say any more.

"Edward!" Kelly called from the bottom of the staircase. "The Napoleons are ready!"

Kelly had left coffee and the croissants stuffed with smoked Canadian bacon and melted Swiss cheese at the end of the counter by the door.

"Breakfast," Edward called when he returned, placing the tray on the living-room table.

Edward lost his appetite. He took a bite out of the croissant but his knotted stomach seemed unwilling to accept the offering. He washed it down with the hot coffee. Natalie, on the other hand, wolfed down the croissant and poured herself a second cup of coffee.

"That was good," she said, stretching her arms. "It's been a long night. Mind if I lie down for a while?" She seemed to have been transformed, shrugging off the frightened, vulnerable woman.

"Go ahead." Edward waved her toward the sofa. Soon she was asleep.

Pushing away his unfinished plate, Edward realized the shelter he had created for himself was disintegrating around him, a house of cards about to be knocked down by a breeze from the past. He was back in the wilderness of mirrors, where nothing is real except death.

He quietly went into the bedroom. Larry had not moved, although his wheezing appeared to have lessened some. Edward took a wool blanket from the dresser and covered Natalie with it, moving gently so as not to wake her. She looked so vulnerable lying there, hair tousled, mouth slightly open, showing the gleaming edge of her perfect teeth.

For the moment, there was nothing he could do for Larry: Sleep was his best ally. Leaning his chair back against the wall, Edward looked out the narrow opening between the blind and the window frame. He spent a few minutes pondering the situation and idly watching the passers-by in the street below.

Two men wearing light green trench coats and close-cropped hair crossed the street from the motel. Suddenly all Edward's senses were alert. The men stood out like a sore thumb in the colorful carnival atmosphere of holiday skiers milling through the streets. Stepping onto the sidewalk, the taller man stopped by the newspaper dispenser, searching his pockets for change. Up the street from the bistro, the other man approached a parked blue Chevrolet Caprice, which Edward hadn't noticed before. Putting one hand on the roof of the car, the man leaned by the front passenger window. He talked for a minute, pointing in several directions, then he stopped and nodded. Edward knew the trench-coat was getting instructions from someone in the car, but he couldn't see who it was because of the car's tinted windows. Still nodding, the trench-coat glanced in the direction of the general store, then at the bistro. From the looks of it, they were conducting a thorough search of the town.

Finally the trench-coat straightened up and headed toward the general store. His friend, who still hadn't managed to find change, joined him.

Because an experienced operative can determine a lot about who he's dealing with by observing them perform their job, Edward wanted to get a closer look. It was clear from the start that these were Americans: No foreign agency would be bold enough to behave so casually in the U.S. They would be more discreet, as would Americans working abroad. It was a fault of law enforcement and intelligence agencies the world over to execute their job far less graciously when on their own turf.

Edward went downstairs to the kitchen, looking out across the counter at the dining area and the front windows. Within minutes the taller man, who had finally managed to purchase a paper, emerged from the store. He stood outside the bistro, his hands deep in his pockets, coat collar raised, the paper folded neatly and tucked under his arm.

His partner walked in, standing momentarily in the doorway, then stepping out of the way to one side, slowly scanning the seating area. He seemed thorough, like a fox picking the fattest chicken in a coop. He examined the noisy crowd one table at a time. Occasionally he sneaked a brief look down at something in his palm.

Edward would wager anything the man was looking at a photo of Larry. There was no doubt the man was a professional. It was obvious they had to bring in reinforcements, people who had never seen Larry in person, which meant they were searching not only this town, but a much larger area. That also meant they had no idea where he was but were hoping to get lucky.

With a nonchalant expression on his square face, the trench-coat crossed the room and stopped by the door leading to the washrooms. Edward knew his kind only too well: young, arrogant know-it-alls. Over the years, Edward had run into these types in Indochina, South America, and the Middle East. Every time, they spelled nothing but trouble. It was during the fighting near Bong Son in 'Nam, when Edward was a sergeant with the 173rd Airborne Brigade and about to complete his second tour of duty, that he had run into them for the first time. They all looked alike, clones of the same B-movie stand-in: neatly suited jerks, popping out of nowhere in the middle of the bush, accompanied by translators to "interrogate" the Viet Cong prisoners, eager to recruit dim-witted, innocent, patriotic fools for just one special mission. He had no idea what he was getting himself into when they signed him up. By the time he came out the other end, he had worked enough to last a lifetime, and all he had to show for it were the kills etched on the butt of his gun and a deep well of loneliness where his heart used to be.

Edward headed for the brass-and-chrome espresso machine, staying out of the kitchen staff's way as plates loaded with lentils and ham—a lunch specialty—zipped across the Formica counter on their way to the hungry crowd. He busied himself loading up the machine with fine-ground coffee. As expected, the trench-coated spook disappeared into the washroom. Seconds later he emerged, walking briskly to the front door and out on the street. After a short verbal exchange with his partner, he pointed up the street and the two walked away. No one in the bistro seemed to have noticed their brief encounter with America's "most secret." It had always seemed to Edward that intelligence activity, no matter how bold, was taking place in a different dimension from the rest of the world around it.

From the way the search had been conducted, Edward concluded they were unaware of how seriously Larry was injured. Natalie's hope, that they'd assume Larry had made it out of the area, was not so far-fetched as he might have thought earlier. They didn't ask any questions, which could only mean they were keeping a low profile, hoping to get a handle on things without letting whatever it was Larry had uncovered spill out. Nor were they involving the local authorities, which meant that once they were gone, Larry and Natalie were in the clear.

Edward poured an espresso for himself and a cappuccino for Natalie. She might be awake now, he thought.

She was, holding the blanket up to her chin. "Is everything okay?" There was a quiver in her voice.

Edward nodded. "I brought you a cappuccino."

She began to get up, still holding on to the blanket. Then, as if suddenly aware, she glanced toward the bedroom, a worried look in her eyes. "What time is it?"

"Two thirty." Edward handed her the large coffee bowl. "I'll check on Larry. Here, this should warm you up."

"Ooh, cappuccino." She sat, letting the blanket drop.

Pleased at having pegged her as a cappuccino person, Edward went into the bedroom. Larry was still unconscious but his breathing was now steady and silent. The wheezing was all but gone. Edward knew that was a temporary state and that things would soon take a turn for the worse if he was not treated.

"He's fine for now," Edward said as Natalie sipped the steaming brew, holding the bowl in both hands. He watched her, trying to figure her out. After a while, she licked away the foam mustache left by the cappuccino and put the empty bowl on the end table. She pulled her legs to her chest, leaning her chin on her knees.

"Natalie," he said, sitting next to her on the sofa, "you have to tell me more. I need to know what's going on."

"Larry didn't tell me much."

"I want to hear what he did tell you. Come on, Natalie, I know the guy, he wouldn't keep you totally in the dark." Edward got up again and went over to the window, peeking out. "They were just here, a few minutes ago," he said as casually as he could.

Her eyes widened in fear. "Who?" She nervously ran her fingers through her hair.

"A couple of bloodhounds. They're gone for now, but they'll be back. I need to know."

She was silent for a moment, her eyes focused on the empty space in front of her. She looked like a diver about to plunge into a dark river, wondering how deep it was.

"I'll tell you as much as . . . as much as I can. For the rest, you'll have to wait until Larry comes around."

"Fair enough."

She began slowly, her voice hesitant. "I told you, Larry was on loan to the NSC—working for some guy in Washington. He was investigating some kind of infiltration of American intelligence by some secret organization based in London. He had a source in London who told him that the organization was stealing components of a classified communications system." She sniffled. "That's all I can tell you, I'm sorry." She seemed close to tears, like a little girl who had dropped her ice cream.

"Where were you staying?" He wanted to keep her mind working, to control the emotions that were building up inside her. For years he had managed to survive in the shadow of death due to his attention to detail. Now he had to verify that Natalie and Larry hadn't left any loose ends that would come back to haunt them.

"A hotel in Salt Lake City."

"Under what names?"

"We registered separately. It's a big hotel. No one made a connection between us, I'm sure of that."

"How about people from the Agency? Or Larry's new place? Were you in contact with them at all?"

"No, just Larry."

"Did he ever take you to Langley, or to one of the other CIA offices?"

"No. I told you, it was only me and him."

"What about a photo? Did you give him a photo of yourself?"

"No. He said that since I would use my real identity, he didn't need to get any documents prepared. So he didn't need a photo."

"What about the background check? Didn't he do a background check on you when he hired you?"

"Yes, but he only used my social security number for that."

"Good. With any luck, they don't have your photo on file."

The phone rang. Edward grabbed the receiver.

"Yeah?"

"Edward?" The man on the phone sounded young.

"Yes."

"Joe said you needed help."

"I do. How fast can you get here?"

"Where's here?"

Edward gave him directions. The young man was a medic at a ski resort thirty minutes away. He had access to the required medications, and as a veteran of the Delta Force, he had ample experience in dealing with bullet wounds.

"On my way," the man said and hung up. Edward went downstairs and told Kelly he was expecting a friend and asked that she send him up when he arrived.

Back in the apartment, he told Natalie that help for

Larry was on its way. He asked that she stay out of sight when the medic arrived. "You can never be too careful."

Then he went into the bedroom. Larry was sweating, he mumbled something, and then he gave another choking cough.

"Hang on, buddy. Help is on the way. Just hang in there, man." Larry's body relaxed again, his eyes closed.

Edward returned to the living room, where Natalie was sitting, wrapped in the blanket.

"Do you know to whom Larry reported?"

"Didn't tell me," she replied. "He only said it was someone high up."

"Since when have you been working with him?"

She stared at the ceiling, thinking. "About eight months, maybe nine."

"Doing what?"

"I'm a freelance reporter."

"You're a reporter?" Edward asked in amusement. "How does a reporter get involved in this business? Don't tell me—you're working on a story." His voice had a hint of irony.

"Well," she paused, looking down and tilting her head to one side, "I am, and I'm not. After I graduated from journalism school, there weren't that many jobs. I had this idea that I could go somewhere where things were happening, be a freelancer. I speak Russian, you see, so it was Moscow."

"And that's where you met Larry?"

"No, no, no. I had a roommate who worked for him, and she put me in touch with him. You see, I wasn't doing as well as I had expected, so I asked Sarah—that's my roommate—to see if she could get me some work." She raised her eyes and looked at Edward, a sad smile on her face. "I thought they were also working for some wire service or something. Sarah introduced me to Larry over the phone. Several days later Sarah had an accident." Natalie stared at the floor. "She was killed."

"What happened?"

"She was in this old elevator that was over its capacity. The cable broke and the elevator fell nine floors. Larry asked if I could take over for her. I worked for him for a couple of months, just sending him bits and pieces, looking up odd facts in the library, that kind of thing. Somehow Larry believed there was a Russian connection to this thing he was working on."

"Right."

"Then one day Larry wanted me out of there. He didn't explain much, but I understood it would be better if I left. I got back to the States and worked with him here. When I got to Washington, Larry made it clear that I would work only with him, no one else. I ran all kinds of errands for him. Then he told me we had to come down here." She looked over Edward's shoulder, her eyes glazed, her thoughts seeming to drift away.

"So, when did you find out what he was really doing?"

"When I got back to the States, although I had my suspicions a little before. But when I got back he told me as much as he could and he said that he'd got me out because I was no longer safe in Russia." She paused for a moment. Straightening up, she ran her fingers through her hair again. "How about you? What's your connection with Larry?"

"We go back a long way," said Edward. "We met in hell, I guess . . ." He was interrupted by a shout from Kelly below.

"Your friend's here!"

"Okay," he called back. "Ask him to wait in the office." Edward suggested Natalie get a coffee or a bite to eat in the restaurant. She agreed. He took her downstairs and introduced her to Kelly, who looked her over with a practical eye. Seeming to like what she saw, she took Natalie by the arm and led her into the restaurant. Edward opened the door to the office where the medic was waiting.

Wearing a dark blue rescue team uniform under a bright orange ski jacket, the man looked more like a Boy Scout than a Delta Force veteran. But Edward knew looks can be deceiving. The young man was all business. After a short inspection of Larry's wound, he washed his hands, pulled on a pair of latex gloves, and returned to Larry's side. He cleaned the entry hole which had swollen and turned purple with a reddish ring, oozing pus at the slightest touch. As though it were a daily occurrence for him, the medic used a hypodermic to administer a sedative into Larry's vein. After waiting a few more minutes for the sedative to take hold, he went to work, his poker face remaining sealed.

Using a scalpel and a pair of long tweezers, he extracted the bullet and cut away the dead tissue. Before the hour was up, Larry was stitched, bandaged, and loaded with antibiotics. The medic placed an infusion into Larry's vein and hung the plastic container from a nail in the wall.

"Well?" Edward asked as the young man packed up his things.

"I don't know." The young man tossed his bloodied rubber gloves into a plastic bag that was full of used bandages and the like. "I did what I could. Your friend has lost a lot of blood. He has an infection. I drained the wound and the antibiotics should take care of it now. Just make sure that he's warm, and keep a hot compress on the wound area. That should help." His tone was that of a bored guide in some remote museum, giving the last tour of the day. He took a small cardboard box out of his backpack and placed it on the dresser. "Make sure he keeps getting liquids. Do you know how to change one of these?" He pointed to the intravenous needle in Larry's arm.

"Sure."

"I left you a second bag in that box." He headed for the door. "That's all I have with me. If you need more, call our friends." Edward sensed that he didn't want to get involved.

Edward escorted the man down, letting him out by the back door. Then he went into the dining area, where Natalie was nursing a cup of coffee.

"It's over," he told her. "Now it's up to Larry." They went back upstairs to where Larry lay sleeping.

"Did he get the bullet out?"

"Yes." Edward pointed to the small tray by the bed.

He felt better now that it was out. The entire time the bullet was lodged in Larry's chest, Edward had felt something pressing down on his own.

Natalie seemed relieved too. With a sigh she sat down, pulling off her green sweater. Edward nodded toward the bathroom. "Why don't you go take a shower, you'll feel better."

She slowly got up, picking up her duffel bag on the way. Just before closing the bathroom door, she turned to him, then hesitated for a moment.

"Larry is a remarkable man, to have such friends," she finally said.

Edward shrugged silently.

"Thanks," said Natalie.

"Don't mention it."

The bathroom door closed behind her. Edward cleaned up the place, tossing anything that had any blood on it into the plastic bag the medic had left. This he took downstairs and buried among the half-eaten steaks and cold vegetables of the bistro's refuse.

Edward sat in the bedroom, listening to the water running in the shower and Larry's slow, rhythmic breathing. It had been a long day. Edward tried to analyze his situation, only to realize he was working in a vacuum. Bits and pieces of unrelated information were running through his mind, like frantic rats lost in a maze. There were far more questions than answers, and the questions were of the worst kind: the kind that spawn more questions.

The medic had said there was no guarantee Larry would pull through.

"Goddamn it, Larry," Edward cursed aloud through clenched teeth. "Why didn't you fill me in when you had the chance?"

CHAPTER 3

The motorcade slid through the neon jungle like a giant boa. Two of New York's finest, on gleaming Harley-Davidson electric-light motorcycles, led the way, leaving the UN Secretariat Building on First at 42nd Street, heading north. Three Secret Service escort cars, a black stretch limousine between them, followed the motorcycles. Two more Harleys and two unmarked NYPD squad cars brought up the rear. It was an impressive sight, all that glittering metal and chrome moving in unison, with the arrogant confidence that comes with numbers.

Captain McPhee of the NYPD Seventh Precinct sat in the tail squad car, chewing on a cigar stub as he barked his orders into the microphone. His thick voice with its heavy New York whine filled the cockpits of both Huey police helicopters circling above, on the lookout for unexpected obstacles along the route.

The motorcade slowed as it approached First and 52nd. A black-and-white patrol car had already secured the intersection. McPhee was running three black-and-whites on duty this morning, verifying that one was always at the next intersection as the motorcade approached it.

"So far, so good," McPhee snarled at his driver.

"Yep," answered the driver, unwilling to say anything that could ignite the captain's extremely short fuse. Besides, there was little else to say. It was a standard security operation, and it was proceeding as planned.

McPhee nodded. If it hadn't been for his nagging toothache and that obnoxious little Russian security chief—"call me Boris"—McPhee could easily have graded this morning as okay. But his tooth did ache and Boris—well, Boris was a pain too. He hadn't liked the man from the get-go, he thought, scratching his bull-like neck. Something wasn't quite right about him, not wanting to ride in the limo with the general. Giving that lame excuse about Russian security protocol. Protocol my ass, thought McPhee, the general probably doesn't like him either. McPhee had the misfortune to work with Russians before, but this guy took the cake.

Barely half an hour ago, at 2:30 in the morning, the general's conference had ended. From McPhee's point of view, the timing couldn't have been better. The city that never sleeps was numb, its asphalt arteries not yet clogged by traffic. They could take the Queensboro Bridge on their way out to LaGuardia Airport, rather than using one of the tunnels. McPhee disliked tunnels;

if something went wrong in a tunnel, you were trapped like a rat in a drainpipe. Not that he was expecting anything to go wrong. His cargo, he'd been told, was a popular guy, both here and back in Russia. Still, there were too many agencies involved for McPhee's liking. He preferred to work alone, knowing all the angles. He ran his finger around his neck. The shirt collar was too tight. He loosened his tie. "Fuck 'em," he said, bringing a cautious grin to his driver's face.

General Kozov settled comfortably into the soft leather upholstery of the limousine. Things had turned out very well.

The conference produced most, if not all, of what both sides had expected. President Konyigin had made it very clear to him that neither side wanted total nuclear disarmament. "For a start," the president had said, "safe disposal of nuclear warheads is far more expensive than keeping them poised for action, and not nearly as reassuring." He had talked to the veteran soldier about the "what if" factor: What if some Third World upstart got a hold of a bomb and decided to play cards with the big boys? "No," Kozov could hear the president saying, "disarmament is definitely not an option."

So they came up with the next best thing: trust and verify, as the old Russian proverb went, or as his American counterpart had said, "In God we trust; everybody else pays cash, baby."

What this translated to in practice was the deployment of several hundred Russian technicians who would be seated at computer consoles in all American strategic command posts, such as the Strategic Air Command Center, known simply as SAC, near Omaha, Nebraska. The technicians would be keeping a lookout for any targeting changes for the intercontinental ballistic missiles, referred to as ICBMs in the tedious documents the general had to read over the last several days. The technicians would be patched into the central computer, and as long as the readout confirmed that no missiles were set to land anywhere on the territory of the Confederation of Independent States, life went on as usual. At three hundred and seven locations, more than a thousand people would keep their eyes open and fixed on the screens, one shift after another, twenty-four hours a day, seven days a week.

Each technician would be connected at all times to the Supreme Command Center of the new Russian army in Kolozny. The telephone line would be a constant open link, emitting an electronic pulse every one-hundredth of a second. If even one of the pulses was missed or out of sync, a state of emergency would be declared.

And, of course, for each Russian technician in the U.S., there would be an American in Russia—not a very fair trade, the general chuckled to himself. Each American would be connected to the Pentagon by a similar pulse line, likewise trusting and verifying.

The general and the American negotiator had concluded the agreement in the early hours. The final text they had arrived at would be the primary document to be signed in less than three weeks' time, when the president of the United States of America would fly to

Moscow for the historic ceremony, "paving the way," as President Konyigin had put it, "for Russia's onward march to peace, prosperity, and a place of honor among the world's democracies." Not to mention, the general thought, the huge American aid package and the boost that the deal would give to both the Russian and American presidents in their respective bids for re-election.

The general was proud of his day's work. The sense of achievement energized him, although he hadn't slept for twenty-one hours. He thought with pleasant anticipation of the journey ahead. First, a brief stop at the hotel to pick up his luggage, already packed by his trusted aides. Then the drive to LaGuardia, the flight toward dawn, and the return to Mother Russia. It had been a very satisfying day indeed.

When it reached the Avenue of the Americas, the motorcade turned right, heading toward Central Park. Two blocks farther, it turned again along Central Park South, and the lights of the Plaza Hotel came into view. They turned in front of the hotel and parked opposite the Pulitzer Memorial Fountain.

The hotel doorman in his gold braided uniform attempted to open the limousine door but was politely and firmly ushered aside by the Secret Service men who bolted out of their cars. The general's aides were waiting in their trench coats and fur hats, unafraid of the winter chill. They quickly loaded the suitcases into the trunk of the limo, then climbed into the spacious interior, sitting side by side on the seat facing the general. Few words were needed; they could see from the general's calm smile and the triumphant gleam in his eye that all had gone well.

The lead motorcycles were revving. When Captain McPhee's terse order came through on their headsets, the two riders edged forward. They wheeled around the fountain, the Secret Service car followed, then the limo and the rest of the motorcade. They headed north again, turning almost immediately onto 59th Street and heading east towards the Queensboro Bridge.

All was quiet on the bridge. A lone car sped across, its driver oblivious to everything except the need to get home to Queens and go to bed. If his eyes had turned to the right, instead of fixing upon the road ahead, he might have noticed the men dressed in all black, their faces obscured beneath the frog eyes and gaping mouth of a gas mask, standing silently, each by one of the massive steel girders that reached skyward along the side of the bridge.

Near the end of the span, between Manhattan and Roosevelt Island, Yazarinsky looked at his watch and listened tensely for the sound of the helicopter. Shouldn't be long now. He had it all planned to the last second, but it was the prey who would spring the trap. His men were in position, twenty-four of them, waiting, their backs pressed against the rivets that held the bridge together.

Yazarinsky was a small man with thick eyebrows and tiny rodent's eyes that barely moved behind the orbs of the gas mask. Under his bulletproof vest and black protective clothing, he was an unremarkable specimen. His somewhat oversized head sat directly on his shoulders, and he tended to tilt his entire body in the direction he was looking. You might even regard him as somewhat comical—until you got to know him. Then you might discover something remarkable about Yazarinsky: his uncommon talent for hurting people, and the enormous pleasure he got from watching them suffer.

Boris had filled him in on the proposed route less than twenty-four hours ago. Good old Boris. Yazarinsky would make sure he received due reward for his efforts.

Now he could hear the helicopter thumping above. The motorcade was on its way. Yazarinsky's men, affectionately referred to by General Rogov as "Yazarinsky's morticians," readied themselves. In order to succeed they must act with split-second precision. No room for error; they knew their foes were not amateurs. When dealing with the American Secret Service, Yazarinsky had told them, there was no middle ground. "We are dealing with people who are mentally prepared to die; we must therefore accommodate them."

At twenty-seven minutes after three, the motorcade turned onto the entry ramp to the Queensboro Bridge, each car sounding a thud as it rolled over the metal mesh. The general heard the motorcycle team changing gears as it slowed slightly on the bridge. Captain McPhee made contact with a new escort team that was waiting for the motorcade to enter Queens. The radio mike thrust against his teeth, he exchanged a word with the helicopter pilot who had by now checked the route all the way through to the Queens Plaza. Somewhere above, the second chopper was circling back.

Yazarinsky leaned out from his niche in the steel girder. He saw the empty pavement of the bridge stretching back to Manhattan. Then, at the mouth of the bridge, the lead motorcyclists came into view, their red and blue lights flashing. Silently, Yazarinsky waited. The motorcade drew closer. He could feel the bridge vibrate beneath his feet. In his mind, he had marked a diagonal line from where he stood to a point on the other side of the road.

The Harley was almost thirty feet from him when it crossed the line. It was time. He stepped out from his shelter, submachine gun tucked hard into his shoulder. When the motorcyclist's white helmet filled his sights, he squeezed the trigger.

That first volley was the signal. Six more figures stepped out from their hiding places as one man, each with a Heckler and Koch MP5 machine gun spitting fire.

The Heckler is a handy little gun; it can discharge a salvo of fifteen 9 mm bullets in one second. Reload, and you can fire another forty-five rounds from the extended cross clip. Because of its light weight, high accuracy, and excellent reliability, the Heckler is the weapon of choice for hostage-rescue work—and for other, more evil activities.

Yazarinsky's armor-piercing bullets exploded the lead motorcyclist's helmet and what was in it. For a moment the bike careened on wildly, lurching across the pavement like a chicken with its head cut off. Then it keeled over and was immediately struck by the second leader bike, now likewise out of action and blocking the road.

The first of the cars—with Boris and the two American Secret Service men in it—veered and skidded to avoid the remains of the motorcycles. Behind it the limo slammed on the brakes, as did the two other Secret Service cars that were following. Stopping was against every bit of training the drivers had ever been given. But to proceed, you need a path, an opening, and Yazarinsky had made sure they had none. As the cars were being hit by one burst of machine-gun fire after another, any of the Secret Service men who were still living rolled out of the cars onto the ground, aiming their weapons at the source of the deadly storm. It was then that the six shooters and Yazarinsky moved back into the safety of the metal girders, as twelve other morticians stepped out with double the firepower, and from a new position down the road, they opened up. The men on the ground didn't have a chance; not one shot had been returned from the motorcade.

Then two more men moving in unison stood out from the bridge's metalwork, aiming Soviet-made rocket-propelled antitank grenade launchers—known in the trade as RPGs—that they carried on their shoulders. The men drew their sights and fired.

From each of the launchers, a rocket hissed through the air, and all the black-clad figures stepped back into the shelter of the steel girders. There was a moment of silence as the RPGs sought their targets. Then they struck. One hit the lead Secret Service car in the front passenger door. The second hit the car following the general's limousine, entering the vehicle through the front windshield. Each car exploded in a ball of fire, blowing off the roof, hood, trunk, and doors, leaving only a burning shell with grotesque smoldering bodies twisted and melted into the hot metal.

The gas escaping from the ruptured tank of the second Secret Service car engulfed the car behind it, which also blew up in flames. The blast sent the two motorcyclists who followed flying backward, one landing with his Harley on the windshield of the first patrol car. Not that the driver minded. As the black hole in his forehead testified, he would never mind anything again.

By this time Yazarinsky's men had stepped out again, firing at anything that still moved, sending a spray of cartridge cases flying upward and rattling against the bridge.

On its way in from Queens, a Volkswagen minibus, filled with bleary-eyed tourists eager for their first sight of New York City, chanced to cross the bridge on the westbound lane. When they saw the flames and the men in their black protective clothing, the astonished passengers thought at first that a movie was being made—until the bullets tore through the side of the bus and ripped into their flesh. The driver died immediately, and the vehicle crashed at full speed into the railing, sending up sparks that ignited its damaged gas tank—a warm New York welcome for the few surviving passengers.

McPhee, still outside the line of fire, hidden by the flaming car ahead of him and the black smoke from the burning tires, had seen enough. He yelled at his driver, "Back it up! Off the fucking bridge! Back, back, back!" The driver slammed the car into reverse and it screeched backward, hardly moving at first, as a hail of bullets bounced and rattled around it. The front windshield shattered into a million tiny bits of glass. From under the dashboard, McPhee looked up at his driver. The man's head was tilted back at an unnatural angle, and McPhee realized he was looking at a dead man. The car was still moving furiously in reverse. Without hesitating, McPhee shouldered the corpse against the driver's-side door, kicked the lifeless foot away from the pedal, reached across to grab the wheel, and struggled to regain control of the vehicle. At the end of the bridge he stopped, picked up the radio mike, and yelled into it.

"Eagle One! Eagle One! What the fuck is this shit! Eagle One! Get me some fucking support! I need backup now!"

Eagle One was approaching the bridge, hovering over the Hudson River on the Queens side.

"Eagle Two! This is Eagle One! What's happening?" The two choppers could not understand McPhee's garbled message.

"This is Eagle Two! I'm going in! Calling for backup!" The helicopter moved forward from its position above the 59th Street interchange to try to make sense of the confusion below.

Like a beached whale, the limo was trapped between the burning shells of the Secret Service cars. Five men from the assault team rushed toward it. They attached a small detonation device to the door and stood aside. Seconds later the blast ripped the door off its hinges, tossing it onto the pavement. Instantly two of the five were facing the limo, firing into the opening. If anyone was still alive by the time the first of the men got inside the vehicle, that life was extinguished immediately. The men worked quickly: They knew what they had to do.

"Eagle One! Eagle One!" The two helicopters were trying to establish communication, their radios screeching. Moving toward the midpoint of the bridge from either end, they drew close to the scene of battle.

"Eagle Two, this is Eagle One. Can you see anything? Over."

"Negative, Eagle One, too much smoke."

"I'm going in closer. Did you get through to McPhee? Over."

"Negative."

Facing away from the bridge, two more of Yazarinsky's men emerged from the shadows, each carrying on his shoulder a sleek, dark green cylinder containing a deadly Stinger surface-to-air missile. There was a thud and a cloud of smoke as each was fired, and a gray streak pointed skyward.

"Look out! Something's coming at you!" squawked the helicopter radio. But it was too late. The infrared heat-seeking missiles locked onto the choppers' exhaust pipes, both Stingers found their marks, and simultaneously the helicopters were blown out of the sky in a flash and a thunder, leaving only a shower of debris.

"Move! Move! Move!" Yazarinsky shouted to his men in the limo. The five ran back, two carrying a metal container, the kind used to house cameras or other delicate equipment.

Down toward the mouth of the bridge, McPhee rolled

out of the car and onto the pavement, gun in hand. He took cover between two of the bridge's girders. The gunfire had stopped and it was ominously quiet, except for the occasional pop of exploding ammunition in the burning cars. He peeked out. The carnage was gruesome. There was no movement other than the flicker of flames and the black smoke billowing from the burning hulks of metal. None of the burnt and mangled bodies littering the bridge was moving. A stench of burnt flesh and rubber stood in the air.

"Where are they?" he said to himself, peeking out from his cover on the other side, along the sidewalk that stretched between the girders and the railing, beyond which was nothing but the East River three hundred feet below. The big man was shaking: For the first time in his life, he knew what fear really was. His movements were frantic—he expected them behind him, blowing him to kingdom come at any second.

He couldn't believe his eyes. Amid the smoke and fire he saw them, all in black, standing on the railing, facing out. And then, as if by a prearranged signal, they all jumped off the bridge and into the black frigid air.

Was this some bizarre kamikaze ritual? Without the benefit of a protective mask, McPhee's eyes stung and watered from the smoke and dust. Nevertheless, he wasn't blind. He knew what he had seen. He moved quickly across the sidewalk, leaving the cover of the steel girders, and leaned over the railing. It was then that he saw the long strands of the bungee cords, stretching down from the railings and disappearing into the darkness.

At the other end of those cords, Yazarinsky and his men floated gently down toward the glimmering black surface of the river. When each man reached the lowest stretch of the cord, a couple of feet from the water's surface, he released the catch on his belt and was left to slide easily into the waves as the bungee snapped back upward, twisting and writhing.

Underneath the bridge, five motor launches were waiting. As soon as the men hit the water, the outboard motors roared into life, and their gray rubber noses edged forward to the heads bobbing in the waves. Soon the men were hauled into the launches, five men to a boat. Special care was taken for the two men who between them bore the metal container, now wrapped in a flotation device. Once Yazarinsky was satisfied, he gave the word and the launches sped downriver.

On the bridge, McPhee was tearing his hair in frustration. He had run back to the car and was trying to raise some backup on the radio.

"They're on the water!" he screamed, not realizing his radio antenna had been blown off in the blast. "In boats! Get after them, you fuckheads!"

Even if he had been heard, it would have made very little difference. No one had expected any of this. They were used to dealing with emergencies on land, and even now a posse of squad cars was assembling at either end of the bridge. Ambulance sirens wailed, although there would be little for the ambulances to do other than put the bodies in bags and take them to the morgue.

McPhee tried to console himself. Nobody could have

dreamed of an attack in midair, halfway across a bridge, and an escape across the water far below. He had been attacked by a circus, he thought. It was a goddamn circus.

"Get me the fucking Coast Guard!" McPhee yelled into his dead radio. "Where are those assholes when you need them! I want those boats stopped!"

He ran back to the railing, leaned over the bridge, and emptied the magazine of his pistol into the black water in a futile gesture of fury. "Don't they know bungeeing off a bridge is illegal in New York!" he shouted into the night.

CHAPTER 4

The antibiotics began to take effect on his friend two days after Edward had found him unconscious in a pool of blood. Still delirious and running a fever, he kept calling out for Natalie and mumbling something or other about the microcircuit. Then his words would trail off into delirium and he'd pass out again.

By the end of the third day, Larry's fever had finally broken. Although still very weak, he was lucid. Edward was coming up from the bistro when he heard voices in the bedroom.

"Are you okay?" Larry's voice trembled.

"Thank God you're awake," said Natalie. "I'm fine, how are you feeling?"

"Like I was hit by a freight train. Where are we?"

"In my castle," Edward said as he entered the room with a smile to greet his old friend back from the edge.

"Hey, buddy!" Larry was glad to see him. "How long have I been here?"

"This is your third day," said Natalie.

Larry's face hardened as if he had just remembered something. "Did you get the microcircuit?"

She nodded, her eyes fixed on him as though afraid he would fall back into a coma if she let him out of her sight.

"Good girl."

"I'm not a girl."

Larry and Edward looked at each other: Neither man could be sure whether she was joking or not. She got up and walked over to the dresser, opened her duffel bag, and pulled out a small package in dark blue bubble wrap. As if it were of no significance, she walked back to the bed and put it casually on the night table.

"Who shot you? And why?" Edward asked, impatient with the small talk.

Larry stared silently at him for several seconds. "Sorry, I'm just trying to figure it out myself. I called for backup and they came, then they shot me."

"I know that part. Natalie told me. Who did you call?"

"I called for backup," Larry said again. He was starting to fade away. His eyes closed and his head rested deeper in the large white pillow.

"I have to take care of some business downstairs," Edward said. "Meantime, we should let him rest."

"Not that we have much of a choice." She arched her brows.

"It waited three days. It can wait a little longer," he said and went downstairs.

Kelly asked him to sign the paychecks, handing him the time sheets and the filled-out checks. He took them into his office, where he pretended to go over them—another of his rituals, this one intended to make his staff think he knew what was going on. The truth was that he had no idea. If Kelly ever wanted to take advantage of him, she would find it extremely easy. He knew that and suspected she knew it too. Yet he was lucky when it came to the people he had working for him, always had been, even in the service. It was the people he worked for who gave him the trouble.

When he returned some hours later, Larry was awake again, his eyes were clearer, and there was color in his cheeks. Edward had no doubt this had something to do with the bowl of chicken soup Natalie had brought him from the kitchen.

"I stink," Larry griped. "How can you stand sitting in the same room with me?"

"It ain't easy," Edward teased.

Larry chuckled, then started to cough. "Don't make me laugh. It hurts when I do. Who patched me up? Frankenstein?"

"We did our best." Edward jokingly threw his hands in the air. "You got the best medical attention a restaurant can offer." His face turned serious. "Now for God's sake tell me, what is this all about?"

Larry began to talk slowly, his voice so low that Edward had to lean closer to the bed.

It had started the previous year. During an economic summit in Paris, the American president was told privately by one of the European leaders that a clandestine organization—a remnant from the Cold War—was active in the United States.

"A remnant of what?" Edward pressed.

"At the height of the Cold War," Larry explained, "NATO chiefs were convinced the Soviets would invade western Europe at any moment. Acting on that assumption, they formed special paramilitary teams in every European country that was a member of the alliance. These units were dubbed 'Patriots' in the Netherlands, or 'Gladiators' in Italy, or simply 'Left-behinds' as was the case in Norway. As the latter name indicates, they were conceived to be a ready-made underground which would stay in occupied Europe and carry out terrorist activity as well as tactical and strategic intelligence gathering. The idea for the 'Patriots' came, in fact, from a shred of intelligence information—never confirmed, mind you—that the Soviets were preparing what amounted to a shadow army, with the intention of activating it behind enemy lines should the Soviet Union or parts of it ever fall under occupation.

"The Patriots were dismantled on a presidential order, with the approval of the entire NATO command some ten years ago. It appeared, however, from the information handed over to the president, that some units remained in place.

"More precisely, the president was told that these units had been activated by some ex-intelligence officers and members of the military-industrial complex, who were offering the services of the Patriots as executors of "dirty work," such as assassinations and other such operations, for the Western intelligence communities whose hands were tied with endless rules and regulatory red tape.

"The president realized that the intelligence community, having come in contact with such a group and used their services, would more than likely be tainted. If a formal investigation were launched, the corrupt elements within the intelligence community would naturally attempt a cover-up. Therefore, the president turned to Richard Townes, the secretary of defense and the president's trusted childhood friend. He instructed Townes to investigate and neutralize the Patriots, in as discreet yet thorough a way as possible.

"Richard Townes called on Bud Hays, a top-level staffer at the National Security Council, and asked him to run the actual operation and report directly to him. Hays, who had no field operatives at his disposal, made a formal request to the CIA, asking for me."

"Did you know this Bud before?" Edward asked.

"We were involved in something together in Honduras and he trusted me. So I was loaned to the NSC. The official reason was that I was to handle an investigation for which my experience was needed. Since the NSC is only an advisory body, this was not an unusual request, and therefore promptly approved.

"I became the head of a one-man task force in charge of uncovering the activities of the Patriots and exposing the links they had created with the intelligence community.

The final objective was to sever such ties, with a minimum of commotion and damage to the community."

Larry paused to take a sip of water. Edward looked at Natalie. She seemed to be listening intently. Edward guessed that she had never heard the full story before.

Larry was briefed by the secretary of defense, in the presence of Bud Hays. He was given access to a bank account which held a well-concealed slush fund for just that sort of activity. He was given almost unlimited credit and as much latitude as he could ask for, as long as he was discreet.

After the first week on the job, Larry found out that the Patriots had a legitimate front in the form of a think tank, based in London, called the Wish Foundation. The name was supposedly derived from its motto: "Wishing for a better world is the first step." The truth was that the name had a much more sinister meaning.

Requests for executive action or other terrorist-style activity would be discussed hypothetically in seminars organized by the Foundation. There would be some tongue-in-cheek negotiations, using such phrases as, "supposing such an action were legal, how much would it cost?" Then, if the subject of the discussion happened to meet with some unfortunate accident, a donation would be made to the Foundation by the agency making the "wish."

Larry got lucky on his first dig into the Foundation's structure, when he realized he had struck gold. An old source he had once worked with in British Intelligence, a gentleman named Herbert Donoven, was now employed in the Foundation. By greasing up the man with a handsome monetary gesture and a promise of more of the same, while reminding him that the illegal activities he had once performed for Larry were still regarded as such by his former employers the British Intelligence, Larry managed to net himself a ready-made mole inside the Foundation. Unfortunately, Donoven was employed at a very low level, as a gofer, a sort of delivery man, which inevitably resulted in information which was of no real value.

It took Larry four months to map out the Foundation's structure. He then suggested Donoven have a minor car accident, hoping he would be moved during his recuperation to a desk job, which would most likely give him access to a computer. And this, Larry pointed out to Donoven, would mean more cash.

The accident was a success and they got their computer. From that point on, things began to fall into place. Even though Larry got most of the information after the fact, he was able to tie the Foundation and its thugs to several assassinations. That in itself would have put most of the Foundation's operatives behind bars for a very long time. What he didn't yet have, however, were the Foundation's friends in the intelligence community. And he realized that unless he could get rid of them, the Foundation would simply find other contractors to do its dirty work.

Then came the big break Larry was hoping for. Donoven learned that the Foundation had been contacted by someone in Russia, someone from the Soviet equivalent of the Patriots, known as the Chornia Gostia, or Black Ghosts. They had been referred to the Foundation by an American.

"How did he know that?" Edward spoke quietly, so as not to overexcite his friend.

"The Russian contact said so in his introductory communication. He also made it very clear that he was not an official with the ruling body and he requested that his contact be kept secret."

"But I thought the Foundation was a legal front."

"It had a legal side to it, but the clandestine activities were also carried out, or rather controlled, from the same location."

"Weren't they concerned about security?"

"When you're doing the dirty work for the intelligence community, you're not gonna be high on their list of targets, now are you?"

Edward nodded. Larry was right. After all, the Foundation was in a way a child of the system, illegitimate but a child nonetheless.

Larry needed an operative in Russia. Because he was working clandestinely, outside the rest of the intelligence community, he was not able to draw from the regular manpower pool of operatives. Instead he called on Sarah Jones, a colleague from CIA research, who he knew was on leave from the Agency, learning Russian on her own in Moscow. She was living with a roommate, an American of Russian descent, a freelance reporter who spoke fluent Russian as well as English.

Larry turned his head slightly, looking at the woman

seated at the end of his bed, hugging her legs, chin placed squarely on her knees. "Her name, as you might have guessed by now, was Natalie. Sarah told me about her and as she was extremely impressed with her abilities. I used her on several occasions to gather small bits of information—she, of course, having no idea we were not in the newspaper business."

A short while later Sarah was killed in an accident when an elevator she was riding crashed. Larry decided to try to get Natalie—who had shown great promise in her work—as a replacement. From his point of view she had several things going for her: She was unknown in intelligence circles, she had a natural knack for gathering information, and she was in desperate need of work.

Edward thought he noticed a veiled grin on her face.

"Now there's a twist," said Edward. "Larry trusting a newspaper reporter."

"You're making me laugh again," Larry coughed, "and I need to go to the washroom."

"I'll get you the bed pan," Edward offered.

Larry looked at Natalie as if he expected her to leave the room.

"Don't look at her like that." Edward grinned. "She changed you more than once during the last few days. And you can rest assured she made sure you didn't piss all over the place."

Larry's complexion changed to a glowing red, a vein in his forehead thickening. His voice hoarse, he finally managed to say, "Just my luck to be out cold when I'm being handled by a beautiful woman."

"On second thought," Edward counseled, "I think it would be good to get him out of bed. The medic said he should get up as soon as possible."

Larry tried to sit up, then swayed and fell back on to the pillow. "Damn," he muttered through clenched teeth.

"Wait." Edward put a hand on his shoulder. "We'll help you." They led him to the bathroom, supporting him on each side. Natalie stayed outside as Edward supported him while he answered nature's call. Then Edward applied a waterproof seal on his chest dressing and sat him under the shower for a while, after which he was put back to bed for a well-deserved nap.

Edward and Natalie, regarded already as an item by the kitchen staff, went downstairs for a bite.

"So tell me," Edward asked as they sat at a corner table, "how did that old war dog get you to work for him? I mean, I heard his story, but what's in it for you?"

"I guess I was in the right place at the right time," replied Natalie, stirring her coffee.

"That's why you got the job. What I want to know is, why did you take it?"

She shrugged. "I guess I didn't have anything better to do."

"Come on, Natalie. We're not talking about waitressing here. You don't do this kind of work just because it's there."

She gazed out at the street, her big blue eyes damp as if she were about to cry. When she turned to face him, her expression had changed. Something was there that wasn't there before, something hard, something that he thought didn't belong.

"He made me an offer," she said. "You know, the kind I couldn't refuse. He said once all this was over, I could write the story, all of it." She leaned closer to him across the small round table, her voice low, yet very intense. "Do you have any idea what something like this could do for my career? With this story as an exclusive, I could write my own future."

"You could also write your own obituary. Larry's a professional. He plays in the big leagues; whatever he's involved in is right up there where lives get traded for policies, and loyalty is just a tool to gain extra leverage. Do you have any idea who you're dealing with?"

Natalie's lip curled. "Don't get all parental with me." Her tone was sarcastic. "Just remember who brought your professional friend in. I can take care of myself. And I would very much appreciate it if you would just get off my case."

Edward leaned back, raising his hands in a mock gesture of surrender. "There I go, sticking my nose where it doesn't belong. I didn't mean to offend you. I'm sorry."

She nodded, a hint of a smile on her lips. She had stood her ground, and he realized it was important for her to do so. She had drawn a line in the sand, a line he would not cross.

"Apology accepted," she said. "Now, are you going to buy me dinner or what?"

"It's on the house," said Edward, laughing in relief. With a single phrase, she had cleared the air, making him feel comfortable again. He couldn't help admiring her beauty. It was almost an uncontrollable need to look at her and, for some reason, to protect her.

Larry was awake when they got back to the apartment. Natalie brought him a glass of water and some painkillers, and soon he was sitting up in bed, ready to carry on where he had left off.

"Where was I?" he asked, trying to put on a brave smile that was no mask for the pain in his voice.

"You talked about the Russian contact and how you got Natalie to take over for . . ." Edward looked to Natalie for help with the name.

"Sarah," she said.

"Right, right. Well, after that I tried for some time to revive various Russian sources I had used in the past, but I kept running into a brick wall. Every time I made contact, the source either dried up or died—it was as though someone was anticipating every move I made. At one point, Donoven informed me that my name had been mentioned in some correspondence. I realized I had been compromised to the Russians, which meant someone on our side had to know about it too."

Edward could hear the anger in Larry's voice as he recounted the events that had followed. In the correspondence Donoven had unearthed, it was clear that Sarah's death was a hit, not an accident. Donoven also told Larry that another woman was being targeted—Sarah's roommate. He realized Natalie was in danger and he decided to get her out of Moscow as fast as possible.

It was about then that more pieces of the puzzle started to fall into place. Donoven, who was being instructed by Larry in the finer points of field intelligence work, was doing very well in the Foundation as a result and had been promoted. That gave him access to more information. What they learned was that the Russians were planning something big, and the Foundation was asked to use the Patriots to help them.

"Help them do what?"

"Steal a high-tech communications system."

"I thought they'd been doing that on their own for some time now," Edward commented ironically.

"They have." Larry's face remained serious. "Except the Russians we are dealing with are not the official Russians. Apparently we are dealing with some rogue element."

"I see. So what were they after?"

"The Federal Emergency Management Agency, or FEMA, developed, in conjunction with STSC at Ogden ALC and—"

"Wait, what's an ALC or STSC? For God's sakes, Larry, don't talk gibberish to me."

Larry smiled. He knew that although his friend had spent most of his adult life in the service, he had usually worked in small units which cared very little for Beltway jargon. "Sorry. Ogden ALC is an Air Force Logistical Center, which is located at the Hill Air Force Base outside Salt Lake City. Actually it's right by Laton."

Edward nodded. He knew the place.

"Well, the STSC is the Software Technology Support Center there and it's all part of the AFMC, which is the Air Force Material Command. Okay?"

"Whatever," Edward said, leaning back and folding his arms across his chest.

"Well, to make a long story short, they had developed a sophisticated communication device." Larry was now choosing his words carefully to get the most out of his limited energy. "It's called the Emergency Total Band Replacement Broadcast Array, or "Barby" for short. It's an emergency broadcast system, meant to override normal communication channels both on TV and radio. If a major emergency—hurricane, flood, earthquake, etc.— were to threaten a wide area or even the entire United States, warnings and rescue communications could be broadcast using the array. It would interrupt and block out normal broadcasts for as long as was necessary to communicate the emergency messages."

"Big brother never sleeps," said Edward.

Larry returned a faint smile. "Big brother is in deep shit. Barby is still in the experimental stages."

He slowly explained that a multitude of components had been built in various parts of the country, and FEMA had brought them all to Hill Air Force Base, where the array would be assembled and tested. According to Donoven, it was the array the Russians wanted.

As far as Larry could figure, based on the communications Donoven had deciphered, the array was already in Russia or on its way there. Yet officially, all was well, and the array assembly and testing would begin shortly. They were only waiting for a final element called a Software Configuration Initializer, or SCI—the electronic key to the whole system. The SCI could only be complete after all the system configurations were known; that is, after all the other components of the system were built. That microcircuit was the key Larry needed to prevent the array from being activated.

Larry knew from a source he had in FEMA that the final element had been ready for several days. It was to have been transferred from the labs at Kirkland Air Force Base in New Mexico to the STS center at Hill Air Force Base. Larry knew he had to get his hands on that device as soon as it came in.

Accompanied by Natalie, Larry made his way to Salt Lake City. He had informed Bud at the NAC of his intentions and, after some protest regarding the method he was about to use to retrieve the unit, he got the man's approval. Larry made arrangements with Bud that he send a backup team to the base, and Bud gave him a rendezvous point where he would hand over the device. He had a nonoperational replica with him which he was going to plant in place of the real device. "There was no reason to let them know we were on to them," he said, reaching for the water. Natalie almost fell off the bed as she jumped to get the glass for him. "It's okay," Larry said, his voice low and hoarse. "I can get it. I guess the painkillers have finally kicked in."

"Should I get you another one?" she asked.

"No, not just now. I'll wait awhile. Really, I'm fine."

Natalie sat on the chair by the window, next to Edward. He could feel her almost touching him.

"So what you're saying is that this guy Bud is a bad apple?"

"It looks that way. He was the one who sent the backup. I was lucky I didn't trust him with Natalie."

"How do you mean?"

"He didn't know about her. He thought I was coming in alone. If it wasn't for her, I'd be dead now." Edward nodded. Natalie smiled.

Larry described the way he got into the base and replaced the unit. Then he repeated the exact story Natalie had told Edward about what happened outside the base. He was a little fuzzy about how he finally got into the car and how she got the circuit, but that was quite understandable considering his condition.

"Well," Edward said, getting up, "I guess that means mission accomplished, after all. Now all you have to do is get back on your feet, get back to Washington, and straighten it all out."

"According to Donoven," Larry said, repositioning himself on the bed, "the Russians were requesting that the Patriots supply them with a cache of weapons in the U.S. They're planning a hit in the United States, and they don't want to be caught smuggling the stuff in."

"That's a smart move. If they can trust these Patriots, that is."

"They can and they do."

"Do you have any idea what they are asking for? I mean if you knew what weapons they are going to be using, you might be able to figure out what or who their target is."

"That I doubt. They were asking mainly for light arms: The target could be anyone, anywhere."

"So you have no idea who the target is? Or could be?"

"Not a clue, except that he's of importance to them. And the hit is supposed to go down any time now."

"Okay," said Edward. "So now what?" He felt a momentary sense of relief that he was not being dragged back into the marshland of intelligence intrigue.

"I should be back on my feet and out of your hair in a couple of days," Larry said bravely.

Edward had to be content with that. But he knew things were never that simple, and he had a feeling it was not over yet. Leaving Larry to rest awhile, he went downstairs. Seating himself at a table by the window, he sipped his coffee and started to prepare tomorrow's menu. Someone had left a newspaper on the opposite seat. A big headline caught his eye: "The Queensboro Bridge Massacre." The subhead read, "Russian envoy dead after bizarre attack in New York City."

He crossed the dining room in a flash on his way to the kitchen. Getting up the stairs to his flat in three giant steps, he rushed into the bedroom, almost out of breath, and handed Larry the newspaper. "Here it is," he said. "Read this."

Larry's eyes flicked rapidly across the page. Soon he was nodding his head. "Yep, sure looks like it." He read the article a second time, a frown creasing his pale fore-head. "We need to know more about this."

Edward gave him a steady look. "We, paleface? I don't even want to know. I—not we. I am me and you are you, and that's the way it's going to stay."

Larry was silent for a moment. "What do you want me to say? Come on, Edward, what would you do in my place?"

"That's just it, I don't want to be in your place."

"Well, you should have turned me away when you had the chance." His voice took on a pleading tone. "Edward, we need to bring these guys down."

Edward knew what Larry was asking. "What does this have to do with me? I'm a restaurateur. I bake croissants."

For the first time since his collision with the bullet, Larry betrayed some real fire. "Come on, Edward! So you've been out of the game for a while. But you've got the contacts, the know-how. Look at me, man. I'm not going anywhere. I need you to help me. As a friend. More than that, your country needs you."

Edward didn't say a word. He turned and went look-ing for Kelly in the bistro. He found her at his desk, in the little office, doing some accounting.

"Listen, Kel, I'm going to New York for a couple of days."

She smiled, her dimples deepened. "Is Natalie going with you?"

"No, she'll stay here. You'll be okay minding the store?"

"Sure, no problem." Kelly clipped some receipts

together, filing them away as they spoke. Something was still bothering Edward.

Larry had Natalie bring him the phone, then she disappeared into the bathroom to take a shower. Soon the sound of running water could be heard. Larry dialed a number, then listened for several seconds. He heard a series of beeps. He punched in a second number, then waited again until someone came on the line. Larry spoke urgently, then listened. As Edward returned, he was just hanging up.

"Who was that?" Edward asked. The fact that Larry was on the phone surprised him.

"I talked to Donoven."

"From here?" Edward looked alarmed.

"Don't worry. I rerouted the call."

"Okay. So what did he say?"

"We were right. That was the hit."

"Does he have anything else?"

"He said he has, but he wants to be paid before he says what."

"Did you ever screw him?"

"No, but that's the kind of guy he is. He's coming to New York; the Foundation is sending him to check for loose ends after the hit. I set up a meeting for you with him."

"You did what?" Edward almost went through the roof. "How could you do that without asking me? What kind of security arrangements did you make? What the hell do you think you're doing, waltzing in and rearranging my life?"

"Calm down, Edward. He was on his way to the airport. I was lucky to get ahold of him. He gave me a phone number where you can reach him in New York. You set up your own security, damn it. What the hell do you take me for? And one more thing, and I will say it only once. If I had any choice it wouldn't be you, okay? However, I don't, and neither do you."

CHAPTER 5

Ritz Hotel, New York City
February 20
14:00 hours

New York no longer tempted Edward; now it bothered him at best. He remembered when the heartbeat of the big city vibrated through him as he walked its marble canyons, blending into the endless streams of mentally cocooned individuals. In no other city or culture had he run into so many people struggling to manifest their individuality, so often compromised by sheer numbers. In those days, he was able to marvel at it all, but now it was just a big apathetic city with an attitude.

He called Robert from his room at the Ritz. Robert King was an old comrade-in-arms from military intelligence. After leaving Alpha 27 he joined the NYPD and rather quickly made detective.

"Look, Edward," the man said, drawling out the words in his Boston accent, which had brought him more than one strange glance in his work. "I wish I could help, but I'm not involved in that investigation."

"I understand." Edward paused for a second. "I don't really care much about the investigation and who did it. I need to find out more about what actually took place, and I don't mean the garbage you guys feed the media."

"Edward, is there something I should know about this thing? Is there something here we should be looking into?"

"Don't turn cop on me, Bob."

"That's what I am, man. If you know something, tell me. We lost some good men on that bridge and I sure would like to nail whoever did that." There was a slight hesitation, then he said, "Edward, I want us to nail the bastards even if they're somehow related to us, do you understand?"

"If I find out something you'll be the first to know," Edward lied. "At the moment I'm still looking. So what can you tell me?"

"Not much, although I heard people talking around the precinct. They say it was gruesome, as you said, much more than was let on to the media. If you want, I can put you in touch with the duty captain, fellow named McPhee. He was on the bridge when it all happened."

"I thought everybody who was on the bridge died."

"Well, everybody except him, and he was running the operation."

"Thanks."

"Don't thank me. You haven't met the guy."

"Why?"

"He's a brute. Lives on raw meat and whiskey. The man thinks G. Gordon Liddy is an intellectual. He never had a good disposition, and since the attack he's practically intolerable. Was in country around the same time you were, Marine. Maybe you guys can swap war stories." Robert chuckled.

"How can I get in touch with him?"

"Where are you?"

"The Ritz," said Edward.

"Under what name?"

"Real name. I told you, this is a favor for a friend. I'm not part of that game anymore."

"Right." Robert sounded doubtful. "I'll have McPhee call you there. Shouldn't be more than a couple hours. You take care now. We should get together before you leave. Call me, you hear?"

"Will do." They both knew it would never happen; it was only lip service. They each had a life, at least Robert did, and reminiscing about the time he was part of a heap of disposable flesh was not tempting.

Edward was disheartened that he had to wait for someone else to dictate a timetable, but there was nothing he could do about that. He counted himself lucky to have found the sole survivor of the attack. He would have to wait until after he'd set up a meeting with the captain before he could move on to the next item on the agenda, which was to try to contact Donoven.

He intended to call Donoven from the Ritz and make all the arrangements by phone from there. At the end of the day, however, after verifying he was not under surveillance, he would take himself to some small, out-of-the-way motel, allowing whoever might be looking for him to wait around an empty room at the Ritz.

After his fourth cup of coffee he was tempted to buy a packet of cigarettes, something he hadn't done for a long time. Now more than ever, he was reminded of the old days, of how it felt to be on an operation. It was the waiting that got to him—hurry up and wait, as the saying went—waiting on the edge of your nerves, ready for anything, doing nothing.

At last, at three minutes past five, the phone rang.

"Yes?"

"Is that Edward?"

"Right."

"McPhee here," said a voice like gravel. "Anthony's Bar and Grill, 28th and 4th. Think you can find it?"

"Sure."

"Six thirty. Tell the girls at the door you're looking for me. They'll bring you over." Then a click. Things were starting to move.

18:28 hours

Anthony's Bar and Grill was in a seedy part of town, sandwiched between a peep show and a massage parlor. Several large loudspeakers were blasting deafening rock music that seemed to entertain no one except the greasy-haired man in the small glass booth in the corner of the cavernous room, seemingly empty at first glance. In another corner Edward saw a naked woman dancing on a small stool in front of two grinning fat men who kept leaning closer and closer to her. A few more men were seated around a long, narrow stage protruding from a curtained doorway in the back wall. A ring of tiny white lights, several of which were defective, edged the stage, making it look like a gaping mouth with missing teeth.

As McPhee had said, once Edward mentioned his name he was ushered to a small booth across from the rhythmless naked lady.

"Goddamnedest thing I ever saw," said McPhee, stubbing out his cigar on the remains of a very rare steak on the plate in front of him. "Twenty guys, jumping off into thin air. Then I saw the bungee cords and I figured it out. Before I could do a thing they were off the bridge and out of my jurisdiction. My radio was all shot up, the helicopters were blown out of the sky. And where is the fucking Coast Guard when you need them?"

"Did they find anything?" said Edward.

"They found the launches the next day, abandoned in different parts of the harbor."

"How many launches were there?"

"Five. One on the Queens side, four in Manhattan. Not a mark on them. We found their gear, too, all of it—well, whatever they didn't leave up on the bridge. Gas masks, bulletproof vests, waterproof coveralls. We figure the bastards just unzipped their coveralls, climbed out in street clothes, and melted into the crowds. They could be anywhere now." He gave Edward a look that mingled boredom and disgust. "You could be one of them, for all the fuck I know."

"Who do you think they were?"

McPhee shrugged, glancing over Edward's shoulder at the dancer now bending over her two patrons. "Search me. I'll tell you one thing, though: These guys were pros. No mistake about that. I tell you, that bridge was a mess, fire everywhere, reminded me when Charlie would target a firebase back in country. They had guns, they had Stingers, they had fucking antitank missiles, for God's sake. They left everything up there—weapons, casings, rocket launchers, everything. The best stuff too. And you know what? Not a mark on it, any of it. Not a serial number, not a fingerprint, not a hair. Forensically spotless. Untraceable. Fuckin' incredible."

"What about the bungee cords?"

"Good thinking. The FBI traced them to Australia. The outfit there said they were stolen just a few days ago." McPhee lit another cigar. He was a one-man smoking section.

"Twenty-eight goddamn corpses up on that bridge. Twenty-eight! I was lucky not to be one of them."

"Any other survivors?"

McPhee's mood seemed to shift from surly to belligerent. "Who are you, anyway?"

"Didn't Bob tell you?"

"I asked you."

"Just a guy looking for answers."

"Are you a fucking reporter?"

"No, this is a favor for a friend, that's all."

McPhee shrugged apathetically. "Who cares, anyway? There was one more survivor, a guy from the motorcycle detail. He was laying on the ground, dead still, but he had his eyes open. He died at the hospital a couple of hours ago."

"Did he see anything?"

"Matter of fact he did. He said that after they'd trashed everything, the general's limo was still standing there, like they were keeping the best for last, you know? He saw a bunch of them blow their way into the limo, shooting everything that moved. Then there was nothing for about three minutes. He couldn't see what they were doing in there, but whatever it was, it was keeping them pretty busy. Then he hears somebody yelling something, the bugger thinks it was in Russian, but who knows what you hear when you're half-fried and your backbone is in pieces. Then they get out of the limo, blood trailing everywhere. And two of them were carrying a metal container, like a big aluminum camera case."

"Any idea what was in it?"

McPhee chewed his cigar and shot Edward a speculative glance.

"I wouldn't like to say," he said. "But you can figure it out for yourself."

"How come?"

"Later, when the forensic boys went into the limo, underneath the blood they found four corpses, a lotta bullets, and a wire handsaw."

"A handsaw?"

"That's right. Oh, and one other thing I forgot to mention. They found the general, sitting there with his stars and braids and medals. Only his head was missing."

20:15 hours

Back at the Ritz, Edward called Donoven's hotel, only to be told the man was out. He left a message that he would call back at nine. Then he ordered a club sandwich from room service. It came with a huge salad made of a variety of colored lettuce, and only after taking the first bite did he realize how hungry he actually was. A few minutes after nine he called Donoven again. This time the man was in.

"Donoven here," said a stiff, cold, very English-sounding voice.

"Hi, I'm Edward."

"You are a friend of Larry's, am I right?"

"Yes."

"I understand you have something for me."

"I do," said Edward. "When can we meet?"

"Tomorrow, at the bar of the Plaza Hotel, at precisely two o'clock. I expect you to be punctual."

"Okay. Is that the one on Central Park South?"

"That' the one."

"How will I know you?"

"I'll be wearing a gray raincoat. How will I identify you?"

"I'll be wearing a cowboy hat."

"Wouldn't that be rather conspicuous?"

"Don't worry about that, just be there."

Edward hung up, chuckling to himself at the prim, stuffy voice that had insisted on punctuality. It went well with a gray raincoat. He couldn't help himself with the part about the cowboy hat, but since he had no intention of meeting Donoven at the rendezvous, it really made no difference.

February 21
13:55 hours

Leaning on the stone fence of Central Park across the street from the Plaza Hotel, Edward saw the nervous-looking man in the gray raincoat entering the bar at precisely two o'clock. Through the window, he could see the pink, bald head looking around at the people seated in the plush bar. Edward smiled; he knew Donoven was looking for a cowboy hat—not something you would readily find in this part of Manhattan. Edward dialed the hotel on his cellular phone and asked for the bar. He told the barman that his friend, a Mr. Donoven, had just come in wearing a gray raincoat. Could he be called to the phone? Edward watched through the window as the barman dispatched a waitress, who carried a mobile phone on a silver tray to Donoven's table.

"Who's this?" said Donoven, taking the phone and looking around him in suspicion. This was not what he had expected, nor what he had planned for. But Edward knew Donoven was not going to give up what Larry had promised him, surely not for a mere technicality.

"It's your cowboy. I hope I haven't kept you waiting too long."

"I've only just got here. Where are you?"

"I'll tell you where to go and we'll meet there."

"What's wrong with meeting here?"

"I don't like the service at that place. Besides, it would be better for you if I knew you were clean before we met, don't you think?"

Donoven hesitated, then said quietly, "Where, then?"

"Walk over to Madison. You know where that is?"

"Yes, I turn right outside here."

"Right. On Madison take a right and walk down to 53rd. Then go right on Lexington until you reach 50th. You got that?"

"Is there much more?"

"No, just turn left on 50th. There's a hotel there called the Kimberly. Wait for me in the lobby. If I'm not there five minutes after you get there, I'm not coming and you are in deep shit."

"Not funny, old chap." The man sounded annoyed. "See you soon, then." He was trying to put up a brave front, but Edward, like a good hunter, could sense the fear.

"Walk normally, don't rush, and don't look for a tail. I'll handle that. If you have a tail, we don't want to scare them off, do we?"

Edward took up position on 59th Street between Madison and Park. From there he could see Donoven's pink face and gray raincoat approaching. He could easily have spotted a tail had there been one. When Donoven turned on Madison, Edward quickened his pace and headed down Park, arriving in plenty of time to see Donoven turn on 53rd, heading for Lexington. Edward knew that if he was clean here, everything was fine.

Edward let him enter the hotel. Then he dialed the lobby and had the desk clerk call Donoven to the phone. He told him to come across the street to a small diner next to the San Carlos Hotel.

"So we finally meet," said Edward, extending a hand and a smile to the man standing by the door.

"Edward?" said Donoven, looking somewhat lost.

"Yes, yes. Come and sit down."

It was clear from his expression that Donoven was not expecting such a welcome, not after all the running around he'd been made to do. "Sorry to have dragged you all over the place," Edward said as they sat at a sticky table to the rear of the establishment.

"I must say, that was quite a walk. I'm quite out of breath."

"So, what do you have for me?" Edward dived right into the subject matter.

"And you for me?"

"Mine is a payment for yours, so let's have it, pal. We both have other things to do."

For the next twenty minutes Donoven talked, leaning

across the table, his voice low. Edward felt like offering the man a breath freshener, but since he had no intention of meeting him again, he decided to suffer through Donoven's halitosis. He took notes and occasionally dropped a question. Donoven was not reluctant to give him the answers. As Edward was showing no sign of being ready to pay him, he kept talking. There were still some details missing, but Donoven, who was now sweating more than he had after his short walk, promised to get them.

"When?"

"When I get back, most of what you need should be waiting on my desk. It will, however, cost you."

"Not me. It will be Larry who will deal with you then. I'm just helping out for the moment." Edward took the envelope out of his coat pocket. As he was about to hand it over, he said, "One more thing. Why did they kill this General Kozov, or whatever his name was?"

"He was the commander of the Black Ghosts."

"So why kill him?"

"I don't know. Perhaps they didn't like him. It would seem rather stupid, though."

"Why is that?"

"Well you see, only he can, or rather could, activate their computer. It has a security system in place that scans the general's iris to verify it's him before they can get access to the system. Without that, if activated the system self-destructs."

Edward handed Donoven the envelope. The man

tore off the end and peeked inside at the bundle of one-hundred-dollar bills. His pudgy pink face beamed. Without another word Edward got up and walked out of the diner. He was starting to get the picture, and it was not a pretty one.

CHAPTER 6

The White House, the Oval Office, Washington, D.C.
February 21
10:55 hours

The most powerful man in the world reached into his desk drawer and pulled out a small tube of Rolaids. He crunched up two of the chalky white tablets, hoping they would calm his stomach, which had been acting up intermittently since breakfast. He made a special effort not to let the minor pain show on his face. He knew for a fact that if one of the two men in his office at that time were to notice, it would only be a matter of minutes before his personal physician would be notified and he would face a tedious battery of tests over at Bethesda Medical Center. And he was in no mood for that.

James Fenton, the senior Secret Service officer in charge of the presidential detachment, was one of the two. He was about to leave, the president having just signed his forty-eight-hour schedule update. The other was Terry Kay, personal secretary to the president.

"The call from Moscow should be coming through in half an hour," said Kay. "The briefing is scheduled for eleven."

The president looked at his watch. It was five to eleven.

In the west wing of the White House, Bud Hays was also looking at his watch. He had three minutes to deliver the briefing note to his boss. The president's National Security Council staff adviser was scheduled to present it at the briefing in the Oval Office.

The National Security Council, or NSC, is an executive council formed in 1947 to coordinate the defense and foreign policy of the United States. The principal members of the NSC are the president, the vice president, the secretary of state, and the secretary of defense. Their special advisers are the chairman of the Joint Chiefs of Staff, as part of the defense department, and the DCI—the director of the Central Intelligence Agency.

Various other members of the NSC are drawn from the intelligence community at large when their particular expertise is called for, such as the head of the Defense Intelligence Agency, the central coordinator of the various arms of defense intelligence which include Army, Naval, Marine Corps and Air Force intelligence, or, on occasion, the head of the National Security Agency, the highly secretive and extremely powerful organization in charge of U.S. communications security activities.

Bud Hays was middle age, of less than average height, and with a spare tire around the middle. No one would guess, from looking at him, that he was one of the key players in the U.S. intelligence game.

Bud looked again at his watch. Angela, his secretary, was busy at her workstation, inputting the final changes to the briefing note. She was a perfectionist when it came to her work and her hair, and she had no intention of letting one of the girls under her botch a paper that was going into the Oval Office. The note dealt with some new developments in Russian terrorist activity emanating from the troubled region of Chechnya. The topic was rather sensitive, due to the active sources that provided the information and the pending arms verification treaty. The Russians had insisted time and again that the region was finally under control, but the facts contained in the document were somewhat different. Bud had decided on several last-minute changes to the briefing note, in order to downplay the seriousness of the terrorist threat. After all, there was no sense in upsetting the apple cart, not while everything was going so well—as he'd been told by someone who was going to see to it that he had a great future after he left government service.

Having been in the business for more then ten years, Bud knew that the politicians who came and went through the corridors of the White House could only digest things that were relayed to them in bite-sized pieces, while the only outcome they really cared about was the one that played itself out on TV.

He had made the changes by hand and had given them to Angela just a few minutes ago. Fortunately, he thought, looking again at his watch, she was very good at her job. And that's not all she was good at. Angela noticed his stare and returned a warm smile, filling him with pride and lust.

However, Angela's feelings were at odds with her expression. She thought Bud was a little weasel and could barely stand to let his sweaty hands touch her. But she also knew that his sexual satisfaction was her ladder to bigger and better things—neither of which, she thought, should be hard to find in his case.

The printer hummed into life, running off the remaining pages.

"It's done," she said, slipping the papers into a green file.

"Thanks." Bud grabbed the file and took it to his boss's office.

"Come in, Bud," said Jeff Millner, head of the NSC and Bud's boss. "You know Secretary Townes." He indicated the tall, well-dressed man standing by his desk. Bud nodded his surprise. The last person he had been expecting to see here was Richard Townes, the secretary of defense.

"Yes, of course, Mr. Secretary."

Townes shook Bud's extended hand, smiling at the little man. "How have you been, Bud?"

"Very well, thank you, sir."

Bud had no way of knowing whether the secretary of defense had told Millner about the operation Bud was carrying out for him. As far as he had understood his instructions, Bud was not to say a word to anyone and report directly to Townes. He had no doubt that if this were to come out he would be in hot water with his boss. Not that the operation was illegal—it was only the small matter of personal loyalty that his boss might have a problem with.

He decided to say nothing, especially since Larry had gone missing and he wanted to be the one to get to him first—if the son of a bitch was still alive, that is.

"The secretary here will be presenting the brief to the president." Jeff Millner's wide smile did not hide his disappointment that the matter was being taken out of his hands by the secretary of state.

"Sure," Bud said and handed Townes the green file he had brought with him. The secretary stuffed it into his briefcase and immediately set off down the hall toward the center block.

When Townes arrived at the Oval Office, the DCI, a sophisticated-looking, white-haired man named Charles Bouver, was already seated opposite the president at the massive oak desk. President Bradshawe smiled at Townes, and with a broad gesture he waved his old friend over to the third chair.

"Are you okay, Mr. President?" asked the secretary of defense, noting that the president looked somewhat pale. Townes addressed his old high school buddy in the proper fashion. He would call him Jim when they were alone, but with anyone else present it was always Mr. President.

"Just fine, Rich, nothing a couple of Rolaids can't cure. Just keep it down. We don't want Murray to rush in here and drag me over to Bethesda." The three men laughed.

Richard Townes took his place by the president's desk.

"Well, Rich," the president asked, "where do we stand, now that the chief Russian negotiator on the disarmament treaty has managed to get himself killed?"

"The agreement stands, Mr. President. I've talked to Konyigin in Moscow, unofficially of course, and he said they are as keen as ever to sign the treaty. They want this thing to fly."

"I'd expect that much," said the president. "So you don't think they're going to try and renegotiate any of the terms?"

Townes shook his head. "Not a chance, Mr. President. It was all finalized before the incident. The documents went through their embassy via diplomatic pouch. Nothing was lost."

"Except a heck of a lot of face," growled the president. "How did that happen, anyway?" He was now addressing the DCI.

Bouver scratched his chin, looking faintly embarrassed.

"We're going over all the leads we have outside the country, Mr. President. Don't forget, it did take place outside our jurisdiction. I mean, it was in the hands of the Secret Service."

"Come on, Charles, don't give me that crap. I need to know who is behind this thing," the president growled.

"From what I can gather, sir, very few people knew the route, and there is no doubt that such an operation had to be planned at least a few days ahead. That's the way we see it, and so do the people over at the Bureau." He knew the president had more respect for the FBI than for the CIA, which was the reason Bouver referred to them whenever he had them on his side. "They've narrowed the leak down to a couple of options. There's the duty captain—he's kind of a loose cannon."

"Why him?" The president's eyes narrowed.

"He's the only one who survived the attack. Then there's the Russian security officer. We can't talk to him, obviously."

The president glared at him. "And what am I supposed to tell Konyigin?"

"Blame it on the Russian security officer," Townes said immediately. He turned to the DCI. "You get the Bureau to work on it, check his contacts and so on . . . make it look like it was their fault."

Bouver was less sure. "Don't forget, Mr. President, you're going to Moscow yourself soon. We don't want this to become a diplomatic incident. Let's just say it's under investigation and the perpetrators will be brought to justice."

Townes slammed his hand on the table. "No! We can't afford to sound defensive! We've got to make them responsible, let them feel the heat . . . Come on, what are the chances it's the cop?"

"But we don't know enough yet to—" began Bouver.

"All right, enough." The president held up his hands. His stomach was still bothering him, and the bickering was starting to give him a headache. "I'll handle Konyigin my way. Now, about the signing ceremony. Is there anything you gentlemen think we need to inform our Russian colleagues about?" He looked at Townes again. "We'll have the entire world watching us. We don't need any screw-ups. Let me remind you this is an election year."

"Nothing in particular, Mr. President," replied Townes, taking from his briefcase the file Bud had given him just before the meeting, "Whatever information we thought they could use, we passed along to them." He ran his eyes quickly over the page. "Here's something that just came in, regarding some terrorist element from Chechnya. The report says it's nothing significant, but I suggest we keep an eye on things."

"Should we mention it to the Russians?"

"Probably not. Not yet, anyway."

"Good. What about you, Charles?"

"Nothing new, Mr. President," said the DCI. "The report the secretary just gave you is based on information we brought in. I myself would tend to think they are not yet in control of these people. You never know where one of them might just show up."

"So you think those guys on the bridge might be connected somehow to that?"

"I couldn't say, but it is possible."

"Do you think we'll ever catch them?" asked the president, fixing his eyes on the DCI.

"Not very likely, sir. We're dealing with a highly sophisticated group here. They haven't left a trail of any sort." He paused and took a deep breath. "That doesn't mean we won't keep trying."

"You do that, and keep me informed."

"I will, Mr. President." The DCI closed his folder and got up. It was understood that his part of the meeting was over. "If you will excuse me . . ."

"Thank you for coming over, Charles. I have a few more points I want to go over with you after I talk to Konyigin."

"I'll be in my office, Mr. President." The DCI nodded to both men and walked across the room, letting himself out.

As the door shut, the president asked, "What about our special project? Have you heard anything from your man?"

"No," said Townes, looking worried. "Bud Hays said he dropped out of sight. I gather a call came into my office from him while I was out, but he left no message. He hasn't called Bud or myself since."

"Do you have any idea what he's up to?"

"Last we heard, he was somewhere in Utah. We're not working through regular channels, as you know, which makes things awkward, to say the least."

"What do you intend to do?"

"Well, Jim, there isn't much I can do. Unless you want to get the whole community involved, we just have to sit tight and wait. He's a good man, I'm told. He knows his stuff. We just have to give him some time."

There was a knock on the door and Terry Kay came in again. "Any minute now," he said, pointing to the red phone on the president's desk.

As if on cue, the telephone began to ring. Kay picked it up on the second ring and handed it to the president.

"Hello?" the president said, knowing full well who was on the other end.

"Hello, my friend. How are we today?" the Russian president said.

"Very well, Mr. Konyigin, and you?"

"I have had better days."

"May I express my condolences to the families of your officers and diplomats who were killed while visiting my country."

"Of course, James. That is understood. Have you caught the killers yet?"

"No, but you can rest assured that we will. I hope, however, that despite this unfortunate incident, we can conclude the treaty as planned."

"Of course, of course. This I hope also. The treaty will be for both of us a feather in the tail, no?"

"Cap. You mean a feather in our caps."

"You can put it where you like," said the Russian president, laughing immoderately. "We both know how important is this treaty. We need it very much, if we want to continue these pleasant conversations we have, no?"

"Quite so, Mr. Konyigin. I look forward to seeing you in Moscow next month."

"And I you. My wife has already begun preparing the dacha. We will have a splendid party. Oh, and by the way, James."

"Yes?"

"I wonder if you would be so kind. I am a great admirer of your American bourbon, your famous Tennessee sour mash. Could you manage to bring a case of it with you? Now that we are a democracy, I cannot ask my people at the embassy to do anything for me without they say I'm corrupt." He laughed again, enjoying his own joke.

President Bradshawe rolled his eyes in disbelief, shaking his head. "Will one case be enough?"

The Russian roared with laughter again. "See you in Moskva," he said.

As the president hung up, the two men looked at him expectantly.

"Business as usual," the president said glumly.

CHAPTER 7

Peter Ivanovich Rogov sat at his wide wooden desk, reveling in the sense of renewed power this room gave him. He could almost hear the drumbeat of destiny fulfilling itself. His exile in Siberia had been an aberration, a glitch in the smooth, powerful flow of his life. He regarded himself as being in the saddle. A throne was but a chair; a saddle was power, and power would take him places, now that he held the reins.

Interrupting his mental ride into the near future, the intercom buzzed sharply. He reached over and pressed the winking button. "Colonel Yazarinsky has arrived," said the anonymous voice.

"Send him in," barked Peter, impatient for the next phase of the operation to get under way.

Yazarinsky's uniform and jackboots made him look

comical, too small and runtish to be a proper soldier. But there was nothing comical about his sallow face and cold eyes. He clicked his heels.

"Welcome back. Everything went well, I see," said Peter, indicating the soundless wall of televisions, each in its dark wooden frame, each displaying a different channel.

"America's underbelly is as soft as ever." Yazarinsky's voice was monotonous. "They were quite powerless to stop us."

"And Boris?"

Yazarinsky chuckled. "Ah, yes, dear Boris. He played his part well. A noble man, he made the ultimate sacrifice for his country."

Peter's eyes twinkled. Yazarinsky's ruthlessness amused him, much as the innocent antics of a young child amuse a world-weary parent, "And General Kozov?"

"The general caught his flight as planned, sir. He's waiting for you downstairs."

"Very good. Shall we go?"

Outside Peter's quarters, a junior officer stood waiting. When the general emerged from his office, the young officer opened a metal door leading to a spiral staircase. The three walked down without a word. Only the sound of their leather heels echoed down the long shaft. The young officer stood holding the door again as Rogov and Yazarinsky entered the CIC room, which was still deserted and lifeless. The blank computer monitors stared at them defiantly. The eye of the Iris Identification Scanner gleamed expectantly.

A metal container, the kind used to transfer photographic equipment, sat on the table. Peter nodded to Yazarinsky, who opened the container. His face betrayed no emotion as he pulled out the grotesque, dripping, bloody thing that had once been connected to Kozov's body. The junior officer had brought a towel and a waterproof sheet, on which the head was placed. From a first-aid kit he took a cotton swab and a small bottle of surgical alcohol, and as if it were something he did every day, he proceeded to wipe the coagulated blood from around the head's right eye. When he was done, Yazarinsky picked up the head by its hair and brought it over to the scanner, the junior officer supporting the head from below with the towel. Together the two men positioned the head carefully, and at a nod from Yazarinsky, Peter typed the code into the keyboard next to him, activating the scanner.

A pencil beam of light came forth from the scanner's eye. Yazarinsky and the junior officer repositioned the head so the beam bore directly into the dead eye.

Peter held his breath. His entire future was now in the hands of American ingenuity, since it was an American device that had been used to prevent electronic trespassing in the Ghosts' headquarters. The last time Kozov's eye had looked into the Very High Speed Integrated Circuit Signal Processor was when he was very much alive and visiting Rome Laboratories in Doral Air Force Base. It was then that they had scanned the general's eye and entered his code. Now, if all went well, the machine would recognize the dead eye and unlock the computer system. If it didn't, Operation Czar was over before it had really gotten started.

The scanner buzzed and hummed for a few seconds, and then a green light glowed on the console. Immediately the room burst into life. Thirty-two monitors glowed, flickered, and produced images. Some showed military installations, others showed systems diagnostics and menus. Across one wall, nine large computer-generated maps appeared on gigantic screens, showing color codes that indicated the locations of military installations, arsenals, airfields, and naval bases. One showed a computer-enhanced view of Russia from an orbiting satellite.

"Get this garbage cleaned up," snapped Peter, flicking his hand at the bloodied head that now lay on its side on the table. The junior officer hurried to do his bidding.

Peter sat at a keyboard and typed a second password. The command center menu appeared. Peter nodded, satisfied. Then he went to the intercom and pressed the button.

"Sir!" said the anonymous voice.

"There'll be a briefing session in ten minutes. I want everyone here."

Ten minutes later, a half dozen officers were seated around the conference table in the glass cubicle at the far end of the CIC room. Peter stood at the head of the table.

"Colonel Yakov," he said to a squat, mustachioed officer to his left. "We need a few more strikes by your people."

"We have two more attacks planned, sir. Should we still make it look like the work of the Chechen resistance?"

Peter thought for a moment. "We should increase the

circle. We want them to raise the level of their alert to at least code blue. That will enable us to get our troops into position right under their noses."

"Who, then?" asked the officer.

"Make it anonymous. After all, who is not angry in Russia today?"

A grin appeared on all the faces around the table. Heads nodded in agreement.

"Make sure there are enough casualties that they can't brush it under the carpet," continued Peter. He raised his hand. "But at the same time, we don't want them to overreact."

"I understand, sir."

"When you're ready, bring me the final plans for approval."

"Yes, sir." The young officer looked relieved that the general was going to give the final approval; the responsibility wasn't going to fall on his own shoulders.

"We need to get ready to mobilize. Once they declare code blue, they will start moving their forces, and we will not have too much time. I want the Second Armored Brigade from Sverdlovsk with the T-72s . . ."

For over an hour, the six officers watched and listened intently as Peter spoke and pointed at the maps on the wall behind him. Then he sent each of them by turns on his separate way, until only Colonel Sokolov remained.

"So, Andrei," said Peter, looking intently at the tall, slim man in his immaculate black uniform. "What are your thoughts?"

"The operation is proceeding as planned," said Sokolov. "We are still missing one piece of the communication array."

"How soon will it arrive?"

"Very soon. We're working on it now."

Peter was glad to have Sokolov on board. He knew the colonel was as dedicated as he to restoring Russia to her former glory, and as realistic as he in acknowledging the only way that could be achieved was through strong, aggressive leadership. Russia was not made for democracy; she was built through the might and terror of the czars and would survive and prosper only under a new generation of czars, of which he, Peter, would be the first. Sokolov knew this better than anyone. Nevertheless, Peter was conscious of a slight area of tension between them, no doubt due to the colonel's being overly concerned with sticking to procedure. The man was brilliant, Peter thought, but too inclined to focus on details, and lacking the necessary vision to see the big picture.

Sokolov cleared his throat. "General, may I speak candidly?"

"Yes, Andrei, what's on your mind?"

"There is one aspect of the plan which still troubles me, and that is the final phase."

Peter smiled indulgently. "Do not worry. I have given it considerable thought."

"I strongly advise against the course of action you propose."

"I remind you, Colonel Sokolov, that I am not proposing. I am ordering."

"Of course, General." Sokolov got to his feet and saluted.

"Carry on, Colonel. Oh, and could you have Colonel Yazarinsky come and see me in my quarters?"

"Yes, sir."

"Remember, my boy, Russians are at their best when they are afraid."

A few minutes later, Peter was again seated at his desk in his private office. The intercom announced Yazarinsky's presence outside, and then the door opened and the small man moved like a crab across the carpet.

"Any news of our American friend?" asked Peter.

Yazarinsky sat in the high-backed leather chair opposite Peter's. "It seems there was a leak."

"What did he find out?"

"That we had a contract with them that involved a communications array and that the death of General Kozov is related to this affair."

"Where did he come by that information?"

"From someone in London."

"Any idea who?"

"Yes, I have a name. He's from the London office of the Foundation, an ex-MI5 operative named Donoven."

"I see. And where is this Mr. Donoven now?"

"He was sent to New York to clean up after the assassination. He'll be checking that the equipment we left behind is clean, and that nothing went wrong."

"I see. When he returns from that laudable task, I think you two should have a little chat?"

Yazarinsky's eyes did not blink. "Understood, General. And the American?"

"Do you know where he is?"

"Yes, of course."

"We'll leave him for now. He has no one to pass that information to and he may yet prove to be useful to us."

CHAPTER 8

Grantsville, Utah
February 22
10:15 hours

The United Airlines Boeing 737 began its gradual descent into Salt Lake City International Airport. In obedience to the tiny sign above his seat, Edward buckled up. He was hoping that by the time he got back to Grantsville, Larry would be ready to take over. All he wanted was to get back to his gently mind-numbing routine of baking croissants, eating, and sleeping. All this activity was causing him to think, and thinking meant remembering. And there were too many things he wanted to forget.

He could feel the dull pain he had lived with for so long creeping back into his chest. The kind of pain that comes from sadness, the kind you can only numb but never cure. It was almost like meeting an old confidant he had painstakingly managed to elude. The guilt that he normally kept so deeply buried was stabbing at him as sharply as ever. He would now have to start forgetting all over again, but he didn't know how anymore. The last time he had tried, he hadn't used any kind of system—he had just tossed himself into the wind, hoping never to land.

No matter what anybody said, he knew he was responsible for their deaths. It had started out as a simple enough operation that turned unexpectedly nasty. A drug kingpin who had enjoyed the luxury of the CIA's pampering, in return for his contacts in the Eastern bloc, had become expendable. His arrogance and tenacity, which had previously made him an invaluable asset, had overnight turned him into an embarrassment. He was no longer of use to the Agency, so it was unilaterally decided to end the relationship. The man would be paid off not with the fulfillment of his expectations of refuge and glory, but rather with a few ounces of lead. It was Edward's mission to deliver the lead to the awaiting target.

Edward and thirty other men disembarked from low-flying Black Hawk helicopters several miles from the man's residence in the thick, mountainous jungle of Colombia. Several hours later, like a dark cloud in the small hours of the night, they descended on his residence and made their deadly delivery. His guards and cronies were so utterly surprised, the operation was as easy as a simulated exercise and extremely successful. They managed to liquidate the man and all his cronies, or so they believed. Almost a year later, Edward learned that two of the man's brothers were still alive and out for vengeance. They managed to lure their brother's CIA contact man in Bogota into a trap. After several days of intense torture, and just before they granted his final wish and killed him, they got him to give them a name. Not long after that, they caught up with one of Edward's men, and as every man can be made to talk in the end, they got the names of the other unit members, including Edward. He was at Fort Bragg when they called him the first time. They made him listen to his man's cries as they took their revenge upon him. Edward could remember standing there, unable to hang up, listening. After what seemed like eternity, the callers informed him the man was dead, and they said they would call back. Several weeks later they did, and then again and again.

It was all coming back: the sights, the sounds, the anger. He resigned from the service and spent the next ten months tracking them down. They had captured and tortured seven of his men before he finally caught up with them, ending their careers and their lives.

By then he was attached to his bottle and on a long fall into the darkness of self-blame and depression. His wife told him it was her or the bottle, and when he chose the latter, she walked out. For months he drifted aimlessly from one bar stool to another, until one night he found himself beaten, robbed, and lying facedown, almost drowning in a six-inch-deep puddle of water outside a roadside bar near Grantsville, Utah.

He could remember the gentle hands that helped him up, the look of worry on the faces that seemed to belong in a generation past. It was then that he realized there was still decency in the land of the free, and it was time to start over.

Grantsville was as good a place as any, and more remote than most, which suited him just fine. For the first few months he still had to drink himself to sleep, but as time went by and he slipped into the comfort of his routine, he began to calm down. He kept the past well buried inside him, putting off dealing with it as long as he could. Fortunately, the bistro gave him plenty of things to keep his mind occupied.

Now it all came back. For the first time since coming to in that puddle, he felt an overwhelming need, a need he knew could never be satisfied. He wanted a drink to dull the pain, to help him face the emptiness of his life.

It was midmorning when Edward arrived. Natalie was out shopping. Larry had borrowed some of Edward's clothing and looked like a little boy wearing his father's suit, but he was able to walk a few steps around the apartment. Edward suggested coffee and croissants, to which Larry consented gladly. They sat upstairs and munched in silence for a few minutes. Edward was a little disturbed to note that the croissants were as delicious as ever, even though it was not he but the burly short-order cook who had prepared them. Perhaps, Edward reflected ruefully, I'm not as indispensable to this place as I thought.

Having satisfied his hunger, Edward briefed Larry on what he had learned on his visit to the Big Apple. He tried to sound uninterested, as if none of this really had anything to do with him. When he had finished, he handed Larry his notes.

"The details are here," he said, "as much as Donoven claimed to know."

Larry looked the documents over. "You still write the best goddamn reports I ever read. I guess you don't much like Donoven, do you?"

"Not really."

"Well, I guess we have us a situation here."

"You mean you have a situation."

Ignoring this remark, Larry continued his thoughtful perusal of the report. "So they mobilize their special units under the veil of a general state of alert as a result of the increased numbers of terrorist attacks. Then, once in position and with the communication array active, they take over. The perfect coup d'état. We've seen that happen before, in Weimar—a fledgling democracy falling prey to a nationalistic, militaristic, lunatic fringe. Except this time the fringe is everywhere. Too bad we don't have any idea of the timetable."

"Well, that is what Donoven's supposed to get for you when he gets back to London. My feeling is that things could start happening very soon."

"I guess you're right."

"Time for you to call your boss again, Larry." Edward shrugged. "Good luck."

"Edward . . ." Larry hesitated. "I'm going to need your help on this one."

"No way. I did what I could. Now it's back to you."

"Edward, you've got to understand . . . I cannot afford a mistake at this point. There's too much at stake. I have no one I can trust but you. I'm out of the CIA—and who knows which side they're on in this, anyway? My own boss is probably the one who set me up, or someone close to him. Then there's those spooks you saw the other day. They sure weren't going to inquire after my health. They probably think I'm public enemy number one. I'm on my own, Edward. I can't stop this thing alone. I need you."

"Larry," Edward said in a soothing voice. "I think the antibiotics got to you. Look at the big picture, my friend. It doesn't make any sense. Why would anyone in the United States want to help a coup in Russia that could very well bring back the Cold War? Maybe this time it might not be that cold, either."

"Don't you see?" said Larry, looking strained. "The military industry is dying off with this peace. The metal-eaters survive on conflict. As far as they can see, conflict is good for the economy—it stops unwanted immigration, it creates a lot of new jobs, and stops the strain on the financial markets due to the endless aid packages the Eastern bloc countries are receiving. They want the old world order, when you knew who your enemy was and could buy your friends."

"Come to think of it, old buddy, it doesn't sound that bad."

"It's not funny, Edward. This could turn the whole world into one big Bosnia."

There was silence. Edward began to think of various lines of argument as to why he could not possibly get involved, but deep down he knew he was licked.

"All right, but only until you can get your act together."

"Agreed," said Larry. He shakily went back to bed.

Edward took his report and sat behind a small desk in the corner of the bedroom to go over it again.

The door opened and Natalie came in. She seemed pleased to see Edward. Bending to him, she gave him a kiss on the cheek. Edward wanted to hold on to her. It was a nice welcome back from the cold, hard city.

Natalie opened her packages on the bed, showing them what she had bought. An innocent smile on her face, she was like a little girl showing off her toys. She had bought some new clothes for Larry "so he can get out of that circus tent he's wearing." Turning to Edward again, she asked, "So what's new?"

"Edward's agreed to help us," said Larry. She smiled, clearly happy with the news.

Edward didn't say anything, but her closeness and her sweet scent squeezed the knot in his stomach.

Downstairs, he closed himself in his office and again went over the information Donoven had given him. He needed to understand it better. Now he was no longer just a messenger, but an active player.

After some hours of doodling and drawing up little charts, he had a plan. He knew it was a crazy plan that could probably never be pulled off. But in this situation, he knew if anything could work, it would have to be crazy. The odds dictated that. He went back to talk it over with Larry.

"It's gonna take a lot of money," said Edward.

"Money is no problem."

"And I'm going to need some help."

"All I can offer you is myself and Natalie."

Edward could hear the shower running, which gave away Natalie's whereabouts. "Could you ask her to meet me downstairs when she's through?" he said. "I have something for her to do."

"You got it."

Edward went across the street to the convenience store, where he picked up a copy of Real Estate Weekly, a bulky tabloid-format newspaper with nationwide listings. Sitting at his table in the bistro, he thumbed through it until he found the pages for Long Island. While he searched the columns of print and the small photos, Natalie came in and sat opposite him. He looked up and smiled. Then he circled a couple of property listings for sale or rent in Bay Shore, outside New York. Both were for large suburban properties in their own grounds, with adequate shelter and privacy afforded by trees and fences.

"Here," he said. "I need you to go to New York and rent one of these places. Fit it up to house at least fifteen people." She noticed the change in his tone of voice; he clearly knew what he wanted and was taking charge. "Get furnishings, food, linen, everything. We want our guests to be comfortable. We'll also need a couple of small cars and a pickup truck—rented, ready, and waiting. If anybody asks, you're setting it up for a wealthy couple that likes to party."

"Where's the money coming from?"

"Larry will arrange that, as much as you need. It's not the expense that matters, it's the time. How soon do you think you can get it set up?"

Natalie pushed out her lips in thought. "Four, five days should cover it."

"Good." Edward appreciated her businesslike manner. "How soon can you leave?"

Natalie shrugged. "Ten minutes?"

"I'll drive you to the airport."

After he had dropped off Natalie, Edward drove back to Grantsville, thinking what else and who else he would need if his plan was to have a prayer. The list was long and getting longer with every passing minute.

Back at the apartment, while Larry slept, Edward dialed the number he had used when Larry had first been wounded.

The ringer tone sounded four, five times. Come on, Joe, where are you? Normally, he knew, Joe had a phone within reach all the time.

At last the ringing stopped and a voice answered. "Joe Falco."

"Joe? It's Edward."

"Edward! Sorry to keep you, I was in the can." Joe laughed cheerfully. Impatient though Edward was, he forgave him. Ever since he had stepped on a mine while on patrol with the Fifth Marines in Hue during the Tet Offensive in 1968, Joe had been in a wheelchair. He had a veteran's pension and a disability pension, and his father had left him some money. Joe spent his days in a modest bungalow in New Jersey, surrounded by computers, radios, televisions, telephones, and the best hi-fi system money could buy. He spent hours at the computer, surfing the Internet, keeping in touch with other veterans and anyone whom, for whatever reason, he found interesting.

"How did that medic I sent you work out?" Joe asked.

"Fine. He did a very professional job."

"Hey, would I send you an amateur?"

"Joe, I got another little problem, and it's going to take more than a medic to fix. I have a few other requirements here, if you know what I mean."

"Fire away."

"I need some grunts for a dirty job." There was no point in trying to paint a pretty picture; honesty was mostly what veterans had left between them. "I have no idea how long this may take, although something tells me it won't take very long."

"Okay. Who do you need?"

"I need about fifteen to twenty combat vets—you know, Green Berets, SAS, whoever you can get your hands on and trust."

"Sounds interesting."

"Joe, I need the best."

"Relax, Edward. It's understood."

"Okay. I also need two pilots, fixed wing, not choppers. I also need a communications expert, someone who can remember every goddamn radio frequency there ever was, and what played on it. Someone who can look at any piece of telecommunications equipment, old or new, and tell me exactly what it can and can't do. Someone who also knows computers inside out. You read me?"

"I read you," Joe said slowly. "I know a guy in Philly, but I think he's out of the country. I'll look into it."

"What ever happened to Monty?"

"Who?"

"Used to be a Sparky on the carriers. Guy's a genius, got a photographic memory. He was in my unit for a short time just before I left. Hell, the guy practically had radio antennas coming out his ears."

"You mean Montgomery Houston?"

"Yah, that's the one."

Joe chuckled. "I had a feeling his name would come up. But Edward, there's a problem. I can't reach him."

"How come?"

"He ain't on the phone, he has no street address or post office box, and he doesn't keep homing pigeons."

"Where the hell is he? The North Pole?"

"Nope. He's in New York. But you'll never find him."

"Why not?"

"Seems like Houston always had a problem, you know, upstairs? He was never quite all there. I guess there's a name for that."

"Yeah: human."

"Well, some of these people who are, you know, that way, if anything bad happens to them, they get worse?"

"And is that what happened to Houston?"

"I don't know what happened exactly. Just that he couldn't keep his act together. He kept saying everybody was out to kill him. He wound up on the street, panhandling, hustling, whatever. He could be dead by now."

"Damn!"

"Last I heard, someone saw him asleep in a doorway in the Village. That was about six months ago."

"Where was the doorway?"

"Hey, you ain't planning to go look for him, are you?"

"I might."

Joe laughed. "Still the same old Edward. Okay, I'll try to find out. What else?"

"I guess that's it for now."

"What do you want me to tell these people?"

"Tell them I need them. It's a big job. Anybody who owes me one, I'm calling the debt in now, and we'll be even. But they have to come through for me. It's a once in a lifetime thing."

"What is this, a heist or something?"

"No, it's legitimate business. But we could all get into deep shit because of it."

"So why go through with it?"

"Because we'll be in deeper shit if we don't."

"What the hell is it?"

"Trust me, Joe, I'll tell you as soon as I can. It's just I don't want anyone who isn't in to know anything about it. You read me?"

"I hate when people ask me to trust them, whatever. Give me a couple of days. I'll get back to you. Okay?"

"Okay. See ya, Joey."

It was nail-biting time again, nothing to do but wait and think. Two days later, Natalie reported in. She had rented the safe house and was in the process of fitting it out. She already had the phone hooked up—she was in the living room when she called—and the furniture was on its way. That afternoon, she was taking the rented pickup to Wal-Mart to fill it with food.

"What kind of food do you eat?" she asked Edward.

"A lot," he replied.

"A lot of what?" she murmured.

"Everything," said Edward, "just get lots of everything."

Later that day, Joe Falco called back. He had identified players for all the roles on Edward's list. They all were ready, willing, and able to hear what Edward had to offer them. All he had to do was say where and when. Edward gave Joe the address and phone number in Long Island.

"Tell them to call me there or just show up the day after tomorrow."

"Okay. Listen, I found out some more about Montgomery Houston. Apparently it was his wife, woman named Hannah. He was already pretty shaky when he got out of the Navy, found her in bed with his best friend. That's what did it to him. Funny thing is, she was killed in a car crash couple of months ago. Houston probably doesn't even know it. He was last seen wandering around the Lower East Side of New York. I figured he's out of the picture so I found someone else—the guy in Philly."

"Is he as good as Houston?"

"No, but still good."

"Bring him in."

"Okay," said Joe. "Say, Edward, is this deal something I could help you with too? I mean, I don't get around much, but this sounds like something I'd like to get involved in."

"You're involved already, Joe. I need you right where you are. You're my gatekeeper."

"Thanks, Edward."

"Thank you, Joe."

Edward still had an important detail to get straight: the bistro. He had a long talk with Kelly in the back office, explaining that he had some family problems he must attend to.

"I didn't know you had a family," she said.

"There's a lot you don't know." He told her he was going to take a few weeks to handle the situation. Meanwhile, could she look after things here? No problema, she told him. Edward also explained that his friend upstairs would be sticking around and would handle any personal calls. He'd just had an operation, Edward explained, so his staying in the apartment while Edward was gone suited everybody.

The next morning, Edward packed a few belongings into a suitcase and took a flight to New York.

CHAPTER 9

Holborn office building, London
February 26
17:03 hours

The revolving door at the Holborn offices of the Wish Foundation spun around, spitting Donoven out and into a dull, wet London street. The sidewalks were swarming with men in hats and raincoats, carbon copies of one another, moving silently in streams, never colliding. Tired secretaries, their femininity squashed into suits and sensible shoes, hurried to get out of the rain.

Donoven turned up his raincoat collar and sank his head deeper between his shoulders. He turned north, walking briskly along Kingsway. He was upset that an importunate clerk had delayed his departure from the office. The stupid bloke, Donoven said to himself. He hated when people tried to strike up meaningless conversations with him, especially when he was on his way out the door. He hated himself for being too polite, for not just brushing them off the way he wanted to. One day, when he had enough money stashed away, he would tell them all where to go. The idiot had kept him talking a full two minutes.

Trying to make up for lost time, Donoven quickened his pace. It was not that he had an appointment or someone waiting. As a sworn bachelor, he had no reason to be punctual in arriving home, except that it was in his nature. He derived a certain satisfaction from getting somewhere on time, even if he was the only one there.

He looked forward to returning to his flat in Russell Square at precisely the usual time. He would heat up the snack his housekeeper had prepared yesterday—today was her day off—and then he planned to spend the early part of the evening as he usually did, reading newspapers he subscribed to from around the world and taking notes. Having worked for so many years in the intelligence field, first for the British Secret Intelligence Service and then for himself, he could spot an event that had the intelligence signature on it. He believed he had a pretty good picture of what was going on in the world, even without the inside track his position at the Foundation gave him.

Later, after having salved his conscience with a sufficient amount of work, Donoven would spend some of the money he had received from Edward in New York. Donoven thought Edward to be an arrogant bastard. In fact, he decided that if Larry asked him to meet with Edward again, he would refuse.

From experience, Donoven knew that money was in most cases the downfall of otherwise very good agents.

He was not going to let that happen to him. He kept Larry's money hidden in a stash in his flat, keeping it for a rainy day, using it only for the extras that didn't drag a paper trail behind them. Tonight he planned to spend some of it on a very beautiful, very expensive professional call girl. Thinking about this, he quickened his step again.

Passing the crowds of people that poured into the entrance of Holborn tube station, Donoven reached High Holborn and crossed on the red light, risking immolation by a taxi that appeared from nowhere. With no room to spare he dodged to one side, cursing the rain that had speckled his glasses, turning his field of vision into a web of dancing lights. The spray from the taxi's wheels had soaked his trousers through to the skin. The whole world was going down the drain, he thought. Reaching Southampton Row he cut through Sicilian Avenue, as he always did, heading toward Bloomsbury Square. At first he didn't notice the small man in a large, thick coat standing halfway up the street.

When the man blocked his way, Donoven moved to one side, trying to avoid the obstruction, which was as insignificant to him as the puddle he had just stepped in. The man moved, blocking Donoven's path again. Assuming it to be a coincidence, Donoven tilted to the other side to pass the man, who was becoming a nuisance.

"Mr. Donoven," the man said finally as he moved to block Donoven, this time making eye contact. "How was New York?"

Donoven froze. Slowly, he took off his glasses and

stared directly at the man. He saw a pale face with bushy eyebrows and cold, steady eyes.

"Who are you?" He tried unsuccessfully to sound stern. "What do you want?" Donoven was trying hard not to panic.

"Just a messenger. Why don't we find a pub and have a drink out of the rain?"

"I'm sorry, but I don't have time." Donoven tried to move past the man, only to find his way blocked again. This time the man grabbed his arm. His grip was tight.

"I insist," the man said in a heavy Eastern European accent, his tone unchanged.

Donoven tried in vain to pull his arm out of the grip.

"Mr. Donoven, why not just hear me out? Then you can be on your way."

Donoven nodded dumbly. Lost time was no longer his concern. He let the man lead him to the Railway Tavern. Once inside, the man finally loosened his grip on Donoven's arm as they made for an opening at the bar.

"What do you drink?" the man asked, facing Donoven, one hand resting on the bar.

"Gin," Donoven mumbled quickly. He cleared his throat. "Gin and tonic," he said over the man's head to the barman, who was leaning in their direction, trying to hear the order over the loud chatter of the other patrons. Donoven looked nervously around the room, asking himself, why this place? Was the small man alone or were there others with him?

"Make that two," Donoven's escort said.

Donoven was still wondering who this diminutive

stranger could be. Then, in a shattering revelation, he suddenly knew who it was. How much does he know? Donoven thought frantically. What will they do with me? Where will they take me? Donoven could not come up with an answer that made him feel better.

"Come," said Yazarinsky, picking up the two glasses. "Let us sit."

Donoven could feel the weakness in his knees as they headed for the cubicles at the back of the room. Yazarinsky stopped and indicated one. Donoven slid in, facing the back wall and the passage that led to the cigarette machines and washrooms. Yazarinsky set the two glasses on the rough wooden table. Then, instead of sitting on the opposite bench as Donoven had expected, he squeezed in beside him.

"Now would you please tell me what it is you want?" Donoven's voice trembled.

"Did you talk to Larry in New York?" said Yazarinsky, coming straight to the point.

"Who's Larry?" Donoven made a feeble attempt to sound convincing. He looked at the drinks on the table and had a sudden urge to down them both as quickly as he could. Tiny beads of sweat were developing on his upper lip and his bald head. He reached for the glass, his hand shaking visibly, causing the ice to rattle against the glass. He licked his lips nervously.

"This is no time to play guessing games with me, Mr. Donoven." The man's head seemed to be welded rigidly to his shoulders without the benefit of a neck. When he turned to look at Donoven, his whole upper torso moved with his head. "I ask the questions, you answer the questions. We keep it simple. Now one more time, did you meet Larry in New York?"

Donoven thought quickly, the wheels of his mind spinning, digging him deeper into the quicksand of fear. He considered jumping up and calling for help; he would have a lot to offer the police in exchange for his personal safety. But he was sure the place was full of Yazarinsky's people, and doing so would only prove to them that he was not going to be cooperative and should therefore be terminated. "Terminated"—now that it applied to him, he hated the word. He had written and said it so many times over the years, never realizing its gravity until this very moment.

"No," said Donoven. He had decided there was no point in beating around the bush. "I spoke to him before I left for New York." Should he tell the little man about Edward too? Perhaps not right now. It was unlikely they knew about Edward. Donoven would keep him for later. He had no doubt Yazarinsky was going to escort him to some safe house where the treatment wouldn't be so gentle. He wanted to have ammunition for then, something he could offer, bargain with. "I'm supposed to call him today," he finally said.

"Do you have a number to call?"

Donoven nodded.

Yazarinsky drew a pen and a small notebook from his pocket, pushing them on the table toward Donoven. A cold smile appeared on his face. Donoven took that as a sign of hope. He wrote down the number.

"And where is this place?"

"I believe it's in Utah, a restaurant of some sort where he gets his messages."

"Thank you, Mr. Donoven. You have been very cooperative."

Donoven didn't dare look at the man's face again. "What now?" he whispered.

"Don't worry, Englishman. I have something for you. It's a gift from the general, for your cooperation." Yazarinsky placed his right hand inside the front of his greatcoat. The silencer barely coughed. The first bullet passed through the side of Yazarinsky's coat, through the thinner material of Donoven's jacket and shirt, and into the pink, hairless flesh. Traveling at an upward angle, it tore through Donoven's liver and entered his heart, rupturing the aorta. From there it passed out of his body near the left shoulder blade and, with a low thud, lodged in the wood of the cubicle.

Donoven blinked. The thought of finishing his gin and tonic was still in his mind, even as his life drained away. The silencer coughed again, and the second bullet sliced into Donoven's spinal chord, where it remained caught between two shattered vertebrae.

Donoven's eyes remained open, his hand holding on to the base of his glass, as his body slumped slightly downward.

"Cheers," said Yazarinsky. He clinked his glass against Donoven's, downed the contents in a single draft, then got up and left the room, alone. It was not until seven minutes later that a librarian from the British Museum, returning from the men's room, saw the figure with the glazed look slumped in the cubicle and called for help. But help, at this point, was not something Donoven could use.

The White House, Washington, D.C.
February 26
17:45 hours

Bud Hays called his wife to say that, once again, he would be held up at the office. It was an emergency meeting, he explained. He would be home for supper about eight. She didn't complain; she liked being part of the Washington inner circle and knew there was a price to pay.

Bud already had on his jacket and overcoat as he hung up the phone. Fifteen minutes later he entered the underground parking garage of the Lexington apartment building on Q Street. Even though he had a key to Angela's apartment, he allowed his executive secretary the courtesy of opening the door for him. He rang the door and waited while the light in the spy hole was momentarily obscured. Then the deadbolt clicked open.

She opened the door wide, standing still for a few seconds. Bud caught his breath. The thin, semitransparent nightgown she was wearing accentuated everything that was beautiful in her full, voluptuous body. Her skin glowed milky white with a hint of rose. She knew unmistakably the full power of her sexuality.

Without a word, she linked her little finger into the front of his belt, turned, and led him through the apartment to the bedroom. He followed silently, knowing she was about to scorch into his gray brain tissue another memory that would cause him discomfort every time she passed by him in the office.

In the dim light she swayed to the sound of the soft big-band music coming from the stereo system in the next room. Like a cat, she was rubbing her smell on him, claiming him as her territory. She knew it would be all over as soon as he'd had his fun, but still her female instinct claimed its prey. His nostrils flared and his heart pumped ever more blood to his oxygen-starved muscles as she helped him undress.

At that moment it was worth more than anything: His career, his family, his position in life—he would risk all that and more if he had to for this glorious stolen moment. He felt alive, vibrant, as he came in a great shuddering gasp that was quickly followed by a wave of guilt. As they lay silently together, he wanted to escape.

The light was too dim. Her smell, which only moments before had intoxicated him, now seemed heavy, cloying, and cheap. He stared at the ceiling, knowing this strange feeling of revulsion would dissipate as soon as she aroused him again.

He told himself he deserved these secret meetings, that they were the reward for the extreme pressure he was under. They were good for his work, and Bud believed in his work. He enjoyed it and he put everything he had into it. But one aspect of his work was bothering him.

It was not the daily pressure of decisions, deadlines, politics—that he could cope with, always had. It was that time was running out on him. There was a phone call he had to make. He'd been putting it off for some time now. He had planned to make the call from a pay phone, but then he thought Angela's phone would be as good as any. There was no reason for it to be monitored, and if it had been, he would be the first to know.

"I have to make a call," he said.

"Now?" She sounded disappointed.

"Sorry, you know how it is."

She got out of bed and headed for the bathroom. "Okay, you can use the phone in the living room." She stopped and turned to face him, stark naked. He could feel his heart start pounding again. "Don't be too long, okay?"

He put on his underwear and went into the living room. The phone was answered on the third ring. "The Singleton residence," said a British-sounding voice. "How may I help you?"

"Mr. Singleton, please."

"And whom may I say is calling?"

"Just tell him it's a friend."

"Very well, sir. Please hold."

He waited, feeling slightly cold in his underwear. There was no sound coming from the bedroom. He wanted to get back there as soon as he could. This call was not going to be pleasant. He knew Singleton well enough to know that he would not appreciate a blunder.

"Singleton here." The man's voice was deep and full of authority. It seemed to suggest that everybody else belonged among the little people—and it did mean everybody.

"Hello, sir." Bud was hoping Singleton would recognize his voice; he did not like saying his name on calls such as these.

"Hays, is that you?"

"Well, I'd prefer . . ."

"I don't care what you'd prefer. In a perfect world I wouldn't have my own people spying on me."

"What! Who's spying on you?"

"You are, you little twit. Or are you so stupid that you didn't even know?"

"What are you talking about?"

"Your man Larry Williams had a mole in the Wish Foundation."

"Are you sure? He never told me . . ."

"Where did you think he was getting his information?"

"He never told me. We were working on a need-to-know basis only," Bud said stiffly. This conversation was not going the way he had planned.

"I see. Well, what you needed to know—but obviously didn't—was that he was getting very close to the communication array."

"I did know that. He called me—he told me he'd found out about the array being stolen. He figured that if he could get his hands on the array's activation device, no one could use it. He was going into Hill to make a switch and he asked me to send in some backup. So I sent the backup over. He was supposed to hand over the component, which I was then going to pass on to you."

"And? Can you get to the point? I have guests here."

Bud found that his next words did not come easy. "Something went wrong. He killed two of my people and the third was wounded. I understand that Larry was hit, too, but he had a woman with him who got him out of there and they took the component with them."

"I see," Singleton said again. "Tell me, Hays, why did you get this guy to work for you in the first place? You were supposed to get some jerk who would stumble all over himself. From what I hear, this guy is good. He should be working for me."

"Well, he's regarded as somewhat of a loose canon in the Agency. They were quite surprised I asked for him. The good thing about him is that if we try and make him look dirty, they'll buy it in a minute."

"So where do we stand now?"

"If we can't get the activation device, the whole array is useless. We should let the buyers know. I mean, if your clients try to use it they will be a very disappointed bunch, whoever they are."

"I'll handle that. They don't need to know. The array is only one component of their operation. Once they're committed, array or not, they have to take it to the end."

"So what do you want me to do about the mole in the Foundation? I could get our British friends to pick him up."

"He's already been taken care of. I don't think he will give us any more trouble. Keep me informed about Larry Williams. I want to know as soon as you get him." There was a short silence on the line. "You are trying to get him?"

"Yes, sir, we sure are. I have the Agency and the Bureau out looking for him. He's regarded as armed and dangerous. They've been told that he stole and was trying to sell advanced technology that could help some third-world dictator build a weapon of mass destruction."

"Did you come up with that all on your own?" Singleton said, mockingly. "Just get the guy, okay? Otherwise I will not be pleased, Hays."

"I understand, sir."

"Keep me in the picture." The phone went dead.

Bud sat there for a few more seconds. He knew that this private sideline to his official duties could turn bad on him at any moment. He also knew that if he could pull it off and stay clean, he was destined to be a very rich man. Nothing else mattered now. He had to get his hands on Larry, if the man was still alive.

"What's up, honey?" said Angela, startling him as she appeared in the doorway. She was wearing a loose terry-cloth robe. Apparently she had taken a shower, and now she looked ready for a second round. She came in and sat beside him on the sofa. "You look kinda preoccupied."

"It's nothing," he said, reaching for a cigarette.

"That can wait," she said. Laughing, she began to caress him, her fingers moving lightly over his body until he was fully aroused again.

Later, as he drove home, Bud again thought about Larry. The irony of Bud's having been picked to run Larry was not making him laugh anymore. He was no longer sure he was so lucky. Now it was Larry or himself.

First thing in the morning he would have to brief the secretary of defense. He would make sure Townes knew Larry was a bad apple. Then they would have to admit to the president they had screwed up by picking the wrong man for the job. He would take full responsibility. Bud's mood was improving. After all, who could blame him? If you can't trust a veteran from the CIA, whom can you trust?

CHAPTER 10

New York City
February 28
10:00 hours

Edward looked shabby in his old coat, worn sneakers, and wrinkled T-shirt. The fact that he had not shaved for three days, or washed for that matter, added considerably to the strength of his cover. Before going on the streets, he had burnt a cigarette hole in the sleeve of his coat and rubbed ash into the T-shirt to give it that lived-in look. But after the second day, he not only looked the part, he also smelled it. He knew that when people are cast or fall into the gutter of life and are regarded as non-persons by the rest of society, they have to adapt in order to survive. It's a caveman existence on the rim of civilization. All the rules change, and there are no milestones to mark the path. Once he started to look for ways to clean up rather than look bad, he knew they would accept him.

The only way to get information from people who had nowhere to go was to listen. If you asked questions beyond the immediate needs of survival you had to pay for the answers, and what you got for your money was usually not worth much.

Edward thought he might find what he was looking for here. He left his car where he had parked it, on 34th Street, and headed down on foot to 32nd. Underneath the bridge, invisible to all but their own kind, were a few faded figures, blending into the heaps of garbage and discarded appliances. They were gathered around a black oil barrel from which the open end spewed black smoke and a few orange flames. He moved toward them. Thrusting his hands into his coat pockets, he could feel the small transistor radio he had bought from a pawnbroker on 37th Street the previous morning.

Already it seemed a long time since Edward had left the so-called civilized world, although in fact he was only forty hours into the grime.

"What can you tell me about street people?" he had asked Robert, his buddy from the NYPD, before starting his descent into the underworld.

Robert made a face. "What do you want to know? They're everywhere—can't get away from them. Most of them smell bad. What else can I tell you?"

"If I was looking for one guy in particular . . ."

"Good luck. There's a thousand of the suckers in New York City alone. Where you gonna start?"

"That's what I'm hoping you'll tell me."

Robert looked at him. "You're serious, aren't you? Okay, let me think." Robert chewed his toast for a minute, took a drink of coffee, and looked to the ceiling, his brow wrinkled. "Okay. Who is this guy? Who was he before he became a street person?"

"He was a radio operator in the Navy."

"Name?"

"Montgomery Houston."

"Ever use a nickname?"

"Monty, I guess. Why?"

"A lot of them are only known to other street people by a nickname. Okay, what else? Joined the Navy. Likes the sea. You could try the waterfront, for a place to start. Be careful, though. They are very protective of themselves. They know we don't give a shit about them, so they can get tough."

There was something about Montgomery Houston that Edward just couldn't turn away from. He had no doubt that whomever else the gatekeeper had found for him would do just fine, but he wanted Houston. It was very possible, as Joe Falco had said, that even if they found him he might not be in the kind of shape they could use. But Edward knew that he was looking for part of himself out there. He needed to try to bring the man back, to let him know that even if he was no longer useful they still owed him. They owed them all, but Edward was going to try to pay one back, even if the debt wasn't his.

Edward approached the ragged group of people around the fire. One was a tough man in a brown trench coat. His hair showed random bald spots, as though someone had given him a haircut with a machete. He had a mad, vicious look in his eyes. Next to him was an old-timer with a dirty gray beard. He looked as if he was waiting to pass away where he stood in peace. Between them stood a black woman who mumbled, chanted, and sang like a person in the throes of religious ecstasy and spoke in tongues. The two men ignored her.

Edward moved closer, stretching his arms to take some of the fire's heat as he took his place in the circle. He said nothing and just stood there for a while.

"How ya doin'?" the old-timer said morosely, as if he had just emerged from a deep sleep and noticed a guest in his house. Edward nodded noncommittally.

"Fuck off," said the tough man. "Fuck off or I'll kill ya." He remained in place, shifting his weight from one leg to the other, as if waiting for the old man to send him to rip Edward apart.

"No you won't," said Edward.

The tough man stared insanely into Edward's eyes. Then, seeing something there that frightened him, he looked back at the fire, his head lowered.

Edward took the radio from his pocket. "See this? It's broke. Know anyone can fix it?" The black woman stopped her singsong mumbling and looked at the device. So did the old-timer. The tough man kept his eyes fixed on the fire. Edward spun the dial. "See? I'm looking for someone who can make it work."

The black woman looked at Edward. "Sparky knows," she said. It took a moment for the coin to drop. "Where can I find Sparky?"

She turned her head toward the foot of the bridge, where it touched the gray river.

Edward couldn't see a thing at first, but as he came closer he saw the wet cardboard box and the figure huddled inside, staring blankly at the water, the faint ghost of a person Edward had once known.

"Sparky?" said Edward, keeping his voice down, not wanting to startle the man. The face was pale and expressionless. When he turned to look at Edward, his eyes were vacant. "I need to talk to you," Edward said as he drew level.

"Why?" said the man, turning back and staring at the water.

"Do you know who I am?"

Sparky blinked his eyes. "What if I do?"

"I need your help."

The pale man in the cardboard box looked at Edward. Then he shrugged his shoulders. "Me? You want me to help you? Do what?"

"Why don't we go get something to eat and we'll talk?"

The bundle of rags reached his filthy hand into his pocket and took out a half-eaten sandwich wrapped in newspaper. "Here, we can share this."

Edward suddenly remembered that to Sparky he must seem just as miserable as Sparky himself. "Come on," he said, reaching out to the man.

Sparky shrank deeper into his box.

"Have you heard from Hannah?" Edward asked.

Suddenly there was anger in the eyes that, seconds

before, had been dead. Sparky sat up. "What do you want from me?"

"I need your help, man. What is so hard to understand about that?"

"What can you tell me about Hannah?" said Sparky, his voice quiet.

Edward breathed a sigh of relief. He knew it would be all right now.

"Let's get out of this place, buddy," he said. "When was the last time you slept in a bed?"

Sparky scratched at the stubble on his angular jaw. "Let's go," he said.

Safe house, Long Island, New York
March 1
15:30 hours

At first glance, it would be difficult for any outside observer to find anything that might link the dozen men seated around the spacious living room, except maybe for the fact that they were congregated, listening intently to Edward.

At a more thorough glance, one might notice a certain look, a somewhat weary expression on all of their faces. Edward knew that look well: He saw it every time he shaved. All of them together had seen enough anguish to last a generation. The two pilots looked like clean-cut Americans—until you noticed the tattoos on one and the scars on the other. Apart from Sparky, who sat in a corner looking lost, the rest were combat grunts. Seven were from the Green Berets—America's finest except, perhaps, for the two SEALs who sat next to them. There was one man from the British Special Air Services, known simply as the SAS, who'd been brought along by his friends, two Canadian veterans of the famous Airborne Regiment of Petawawa.

Already Edward could feel their particular energy starting to build. There was enough experience in this room to topple a government or save a nation. If only he could harness all that energy and experience, there was a good chance that even his hair-raising plan might succeed. They had the advantage of surprise on their side. Even if the odds were stacked heavily against them in every other aspect, surprise had a price of its own.

"So who are the bad guys in this thing?" asked a man named Tom, lighting a cigarette and automatically handing the pack to the person next to him.

"The Black Ghosts are the enemy." Edward paused. "Well, they are the visible enemy. As far as we know, there are also people on our side that are helping them achieve their goal."

"You mean Americans?" said Jeremy, a bearded man in a leather biker jacket with a large snake and dagger tattooed on his thick arm.

"Yep, they are Americans, all right. You know the kind: They sent us all to hell and didn't want us to come back and tell the rest of the people what jerks they were.

They work behind the scenes, turning a profit from every drop of blood we have ever shed."

"Who are we working with?" asked one of the Canadians, a tall, blond man with a hint of a French accent.

"We're on our own. We trust no one and work with no one but ourselves."

"Who the fuck are we doing this for?" asked one of the SEALs, a thin man in a black turtleneck.

"And why?" asked the other SEAL, a man named Vern. "So they can kick our butts again? Who gives a shit anymore?"

"Okay, okay." Edward could feel the reins slipping out of his hands. "We all have our reasons for being bitter, but this is bigger than that. If we don't do this, everything we stood for doesn't mean shit. Everybody that died gave his life for nothing, everybody. We all need to take one last shot at trying to get it right." He stared back at Vern. "Why? Because I asked you to, because I believe it's important we do this, because there is no one else that is willing or able to do it."

Edward picked up the cigarette pack from the coffee table and drew one. The thin man in the black turtleneck tossed him a Bic lighter. After he'd lit up, Edward tossed the pack back on the table. His voice was now low, calmer. "The reason we ended up in 'Nam was the Cold War. We couldn't fight the Soviets, and the same went for the Chinese, so we got stuck in that bloody mess. We couldn't win, they wouldn't let us, and now it's the same people who want to bring that same shit back.

They want to make a profit from another generation they can put through the meat grinder of war."

He turned to face the men on the sofa, raising his hand in irony. "Limited war, of course, so they can control the expenses and make it worthwhile. They're just aching to start pumping out those damn body bags again, and the only thing standing between them and their goal is us."

There was a mumble in the room. "Aren't we trying to bite off more than we can chew?" asked Dan, the well-tailored pilot.

"Probably." Edward smiled at him. "But since when did that bother you?"

Everybody started laughing—a short, nervous laugh, but it broke the ice. They all knew they were in for the long haul, whatever it was Edward wanted them for. They also knew that once Edward had set his mind on something, no one could change it.

"I'm getting hungry," said Tom, a huge man in a dark blue training suit. "How about we grab some chow?"

There was a rumble of agreement.

"Okay," said Edward. "We'll take a break. Afterwards I'll fill you in on what the other side has planned and what I think we can do about it."

The men got up and headed for the large, open kitchen. Edward stayed behind and sat down next to Sparky, who was still staring vacantly, seemingly oblivious to his surroundings. Edward was beginning to have some doubts about him now. He wasn't going to let Sparky slide back into the gutter where he had found him, but was it fair to the others to take him along? Edward was in command again, and the responsibility for the lives of others brought with it a whole new way of thinking. He hadn't thought he still had it in him and was surprised at how easily it all came back.

"Sparky," he said, once the last man was out of the room. "Are you here?"

The sunken eyes slowly moved, but other than that, Sparky's face was lifeless for a long time. Then, in a very low voice, he said, "I am here, Skipper, but I'm not sure if this is all real. Is it?"

"It's real, all right."

"How can I be sure? I had dreams where everything would be starting to go well, then I'd wake up back under the bridge." He looked away. "It's cold under the bridge, you know. I like it better here. Tell me, please, is this real?"

Edward was not sure what to say. He had seen it before—they called it some syndrome or other. Too much pressure, and then something inside goes "click," and it's all over. Joe Falco had warned him to expect this. He had said that sometimes people build this shield against reality, and if things stay right for some time they can climb back out. Edward was hoping it would work that way for Sparky. He could remember how the man was before—he would have trusted Sparky with his life without a second thought. Now he wasn't sure if he could leave him alone in the room. It was possible that this was only a temporary stage. But if it wasn't, he needed someone who could do the job. Edward decided he would have to call his gatekeeper and get a backup.

"I'll get you something to eat, buddy," he said and headed for the kitchen.

"Yeah, get me something, man." It was as if someone else was speaking and Sparky was just moving his lips.

Men who serve long tours in the field don't spend much time on eating. It's not that they don't eat a lot, Edward thought, it's just that it doesn't take them long to eat it. Soon all the men had finished their food and were back in the living room, each with a bottle or a tall glass of beer. Edward could sure use one now, but that was one wagon he wasn't falling off. The cigarettes were bad enough.

They were seated almost the same way as before. Edward lit another cigarette. "By the way," he began, "if there's anything you people want while you're here—food or whatever—give me a list. We're not here for a diet." His remark seemed to put everybody in a good mood.

"Okay. Let me just fill you in on what the other side is planning. As I said, we still don't have the full picture. What we know is that the Black Ghosts have already started to execute terrorist activities across Russia and are planning more. They are blaming the attacks on various anti-government underground, such as the Chechen resistance front and others. The reason for that is that they want to raise the level of alert in the Russian army. Eventually, this will cause the government to request the army to take positions and protect key installations and posts against further attacks. The Black Ghosts, who are well integrated into the army and in fact control elements of it, will put their own units in place under the cover of the emergency situation."

"I still don't get it," said Mario, a balding former sergeant in the Green Berets. "What do we care what happens over there? It's not like they're going to attack us or something."

"If the military industry and sections of our own intelligence are backing this thing, it just can't be good for the rest of us. But it's not just that. The people behind this coup are crazy. They want to bring back the evil empire. They don't like us much. They stole the array from us, they murdered one of their generals on a bridge in New York . . ."

"I heard about that," said Doug Findley, the British SAS man. "That was only, what, a week or so ago?"

"Right, and they killed a bunch of NYPD cops and Secret Service men. They really don't care much about who they kill. What they are really worried about—and this will tell you quite a bit about their intentions—is the upcoming disarmament summit. They want to strike before the nuclear arms are out of their control. At the same time, the Russian president is sure to keep his security beef-up as secret as he can. You see, he's very eager to get the treaty signed, because it will bring with it a large financial aid package to Russia, without which their fledgling democracy will not last.

"From what we know, the Black Ghosts will stage the coup when the president of the United States arrives for the summit. They will also block all radio and television communication as well as any other broadcast ability, using a device designed and created for the Federal Emergency Management Agency, which was stolen for the Russians by their American friends."

"I'd like to get my hands on the bastard who stole it for them," the sergeant said with an expression of disgust.

"Yeah, me too," said Jeremy, one of the Green Berets who had served with Edward on loan to the military intelligence special unit. "I could spend some time with him, teach him a thing or two about skinning a cat." His smile could send a shiver down anyone's spine.

"We might get that opportunity," said Edward, "although I doubt it. Let's get this straight from the start: We might manage to stop what they are doing, but I'm very doubtful we'll actually nail them all. We are dealing here with the kind of people that never pay for their deeds."

The room fell silent. Edward went on. "Activating the Barby will prevent the Russian people and the world at large from learning what is going on until their general has everything under his control. During the broadcast blackout, the mechanized and armored units of the Black Ghosts will take over the key installations across the country, the same installations they were supposed to protect. At this point, Russia will in effect have a new government. The U.S. president in Moscow will have to deal with Russia's military rulers on their own terms, which are not likely to be very favorable. Before the year is out we will have to stand back and let the new Russian empire devour whole sections of Europe, Africa, and the

Middle East. Or risk a global war to stop them." Edward leaned back against the bar and put his cigarette out in the large crystal ashtray. He then turned back to face his people.

"Edward." The British SAS man stood up. "May I call you Ed?"

"Sure."

"Is there anything in our favor here? I mean aside from the surprise element, which is obviously crucial when an ant is attacking a mad elephant." A low rumble of laughter crossed the room. "Anything—just for the morale?"

"Actually there is something." Edward grinned back. "We have in our possession a component of the array that has in fact rendered it useless. They don't know their system is not operative. We hope that when they find out it will be too late."

"I suppose that changes the picture," the Englishman replied. "I suppose now the whole world will be able to watch us getting slaughtered on the telly." He looked around, as if expecting a round of applause from the chuckling men as he sat down.

"You don't have to come along," Edward responded quickly. "I said from the start that this was not going to be a tea party." The chuckles turned into a roar of laughter.

Now Edward was sure they all knew what they were getting into and that he could count on them. It wouldn't be the first time in their lives they were stepping across the threshold into an abyss of uncertainty. He also knew they all wanted redemption for past actions they had taken beyond the call of duty—things for which medals may have been pinned to their chests but which destroyed a large chunk of their humanity.

"Good. So we can proceed. I've outlined the Black Ghosts' plan. Now let's look at ours . . ."

CHAPTER 11

CG Command Bunker, outside Moscow
March 11
12:20 hours

The dark green flatbed truck bearing a large steel container stopped at the gates, coughing out clouds of brown diesel gunk into the crisp morning air. The guard in the black, well-ironed uniform checked the documents closely, making Corporal Litov, the truck driver, somewhat nervous. The sight of military order and correctness was not what he was used to lately. Ever since Russia's giant step into the new age of democracy, sloppy disobedience was the rule of the day. And even though the sharply dressed guard, the well-painted walls, and the large iron gate with no rust visible seemed out of place and somehow ominous, they also promised a chance of a good meal, like in the good old days. Corporal Litov longed for the old regime, when soldiers belonged and were well taken care of and everybody knew that. It was a time when even he, a nobody driver, was a somebody because people had respect for the uniform of the great Red Army.

"You're late," the guard said, looking at the clipboard in his hand.

"What?" Litov asked in disbelief. Not only had they known he was coming, which was unusual enough these days, but they also knew he was late. Even he didn't know he was late. He'd been sent on his way with little more than a wave and an order to keep quiet. This, however, was neither the time nor the place to tell that story. This was the army, the real army, the way he knew it was meant to be. "I got lost," he said apologetically. "I'm not from this area and this was my first assignment."

The sentry finally handed back the papers, checking something on his clipboard. He signaled toward the steel door at the side of the bunker's mouth, where a second guard, looking through an observation slit in the door, opened the gate.

"Move it," the sentry said with a stern expression on his face, the kind that gate sentries in every army in the world use to project authority.

Litov, a backup driver with the Ninth Armored Division that had been moved to the outskirts of Moscow for exercises only days before, had received his orders that morning to pick up a container from Sheremetyevo-2 Airport north of Moscow and deliver it to this location. He was more than an hour late in picking it up, as he had taken the wrong exit off the Moscow Ring Road. Due to a lack of signs and the fact that his destination was not marked on his map, things had gotten a little hairy for him. But now he was no longer in a rush. His commander back at division had told him to gather his personal belongings for this trip as he was reassigned to his new destination.

The container had arrived by plane from London that morning, bearing the tags and bordereau of a diplomatic delivery. The bordereau had been signed by an assistant to the military attaché, an FSK man, at the Russian Embassy in London. He believed he was signing for a consignment of office furniture and filing cabinets.

Twenty minutes after Donoven's thoughts had been interrupted by Yazarinsky's bullets, the police had arrived at the pub. It had taken them another ten minutes to identify the body. A couple of detectives were sent to the deceased's flat, only to find it empty: There was not a stick of furniture, not a light bulb anywhere to be found. Where hours earlier there had been a man's life, there was nothing—not even, as the detectives soon found to their amazement, a single fingerprint. A neighbor had seen the movers arrive that morning but found nothing unusual in what they were doing. It wasn't the first time people had moved in or out of the building without telling him, he said.

Litov drove his truck through the newly painted gateway and parked inside the large garage space.

"The truck has arrived." Yazarinsky's voice crackled over the intercom on Peter's desk.

"Very good. Tell Colonel Sokolov to examine the containers." Peter sat back. This would be the ideal job for the plodding, methodical Sokolov, he thought. He was starting to dislike the man, who seemed to question him on every occasion. It was as if he didn't get the bigger picture; he expected the military takeover Peter had planned for so long to be temporary—until they could get things working again in Russia, Sokolov had said. What a fool, Peter thought. If we get Russia working again, what is the point of handing it back to the miserable people? What have the people ever done for Russia? Stalin, as the czars before him, knew the people needed a leader to fear. They still feared and revered Stalin, and he'd been dead for half a century. Peter wanted them to tremble when they heard his name too. And so they shall, he thought.

A few minutes later, Yazarinsky and Sokolov walked toward Litov's truck, now parked in the underground garage. Yazarinsky explained the situation.

"We have recently acquired the personal effects of one of our operatives in London. We have reason to believe this man has been in touch with American intelligence, in a way that may be detrimental to our mission. He himself is no longer a problem." Yazarinsky permitted himself a rasping, excited giggle before continuing. "We have to find out who his contacts were, and what information he passed to them. General Rogov requested that you personally examine these materials and see what secrets they reveal. We brought you everything except the wallpaper."

"As they say in English," murmured Sokolov, "everything but the kitchen sink."

Yazarinsky's face was impassive, although his voice

sounded slightly worried. "We did not bring the kitchen sink. Would that have been helpful?"

Sokolov did not bother to reply. He regarded Yazarinsky as a barbarian, an illiterate bum in a uniform, a creature whose only talent was to destroy. Unfortunately, he thought, people like him were necessary in times of great upheaval, when to create a new order you first had to destroy the old. Sokolov sighed and continued walking. Yazarinsky's presence, however, increased his doubts regarding the purpose of that new order. He realized that General Rogov had no intention of alleviating the Russian people's suffering. In fact, the man believed their burden should be increased. Sokolov was beginning to wonder if all it would be was a crueler version of the old order. He brushed away the thought, knowing full well he was already committed, and there was nothing to do but push on.

Standing by the truck was a detail of soldiers ready to assist Sokolov in dismantling the container. Giving a courteous thanks to Yazarinsky, who then returned to his post, Sokolov ordered the contents transferred to a storage room deeper inside the bunker, where he began to sift through the belongings of the late Mr. Donoven.

The furniture was easily dealt with. Once Sokolov had determined that they contained no secret hiding places, a sofa, two armchairs, a dining table and chairs, a bed, and a side table were quickly cleared for disposal. A tape deck and cassettes took a little more time. In the background as he worked, Sokolov had to listen to hours of Brahms, a composer he detested, before he could be sure that the tapes contained nothing but music.

The contents of Donoven's study desk were put into a box and labeled, then the desk was taken apart and out of the way. Sokolov was hoping to find some information here, but the drawer had contained nothing but writing paper and envelopes, pens and pencils, erasers and paper clips. To be on the safe side, Sokolov had the papers tested for invisible ink, but nothing came to light other than the fancy watermark of the stationery company.

Donoven had owned large numbers of books. It was Sokolov's job to look through each one to see if there were any papers hidden between the pages, or handwritten markings that may have indicated a code. Most of the books were non-fiction tomes on economics, international finance, and military matters. Clearly, Donoven had taken the public side of his work quite seriously. There were also a number of volumes whose high-quality photos and illustrations indicated that Mr. Donoven had a well-developed taste for sadomasochistic pornography. Sokolov looked at the lurid pictures with mingled disgust and fascination. Although to him they were the corrupt and corrupting product of the decadent West, he also found their frank and explicit sexuality disturbing and exciting. Having determined that the secrets they revealed were not political ones, he filed them in the box marked "personal" and continued his perusal of Donoven's library.

Among the books, he found old letters and postcards, pressed flowers, stubs from concerts and theater visits, all the odds and ends that people accumulate during their lives. To most people other than their owner, they were junk. But to Sokolov, they were clues to riddles he still had to ask, about what their owner was really like, how he thought, who he dealt with.

By early morning, Sokolov still had found nothing that would indicate who Donoven's covert contacts might be. One thing was becoming very clear, however: If Donoven's personal effects revealed anything, it was that he was extremely security conscious and must have used a very sophisticated technique for encrypting whatever data he wished to keep secret. It looked as though it would take some time to extract any useful information from this pile of paper.

One more box of books remained. In it Sokolov found, among the paperback thrillers, something which didn't quite fit with the rest of the puzzle called Donoven: a brown envelope in which were considerable numbers of hundred-dollar bills and twenty-pound notes. This was starting to get interesting.

Next in the pile was a brown, leather-bound volume with no title. Opening it, Sokolov gave a wry smile. He had been wrong about Donoven: Far from being an intelligence sophisticate, the man was an idiot. For the book's pages were filled with notes, handwritten in English, detailing the essentials of the Black Ghosts' plan. And on the last page was a column of names, dates, and phone numbers. The last and most recent entries read:

Larry Williams: (nice guy) U.S. intell.: Leave message at 561-2448

> *Met Edward: (arrogant bastard)—taking over from Larry.*

Sokolov sat back in his chair, his legs resting comfortably on the "in" basket on his desk. He held the book up to the light, searching for a mark of some kind, but there was nothing. Then he closed the book and put it on the table by his legs. He had found what he was looking for, the missing link. His next step would have to be well calculated. If this Donoven person was an amateur or an idiot, that didn't necessarily mean Larry or this fellow Edward were.

Having made up his mind, Sokolov moved quickly. He retyped the column of handwritten entries on several sheets of paper, sorting them by name. These he placed in separate files in his cabinet. The leather-bound volume he consigned to the box marked "personal," along with Donoven's letters, novels and hardcore pornography. Then he went to report to General Kruglak.

Safe house, Long Island, New York
March 12
10:45 hours

It was Natalie's idea to get the men dressed up like a soccer team so they could train in the park without attracting too much attention. Mario Rosili, the former Green Beret who was assigned as the group's sergeant, was taking the training very seriously, as were the rest of the men. By the end of the first day, there were very few muscles they had and were not aware of. With the exception of Sparky, who seemed to be regaining his awareness through the sweat of his brow, no one was complaining. The men were experienced enough to know that the harder the training, the better their chances of making it through this operation alive. They all knew it was sometimes the ability to jump across one more inch of wall in one less second that could make the difference.

Natalie's job in the safe house was done and she was going back to Larry in Utah. Edward was helping her pack when the phone rang.

"Yes?"

"Edward, we have us a problem." Larry sounded down. In fact, he sounded depressed.

"What's up?"

"Donoven was killed."

"When did this happen?"

"Right after he got back from New York. We have nothing now, there's no way we can get the final timetable. I think I may have to chance it with Bud Hays."

"Wasn't he the one who almost got you killed?"

"We can't be sure. It's possible it was someone else who had access to the file, someone working in his office. Look, Edward, what other choice do we have? We have to stop this thing—you know it and I know it. With Donoven dead, we know squat about what the hell is going on. The whole thing can blow up in our faces tomorrow, for all we know. And we won't know about it until we hear it on the eleven o'clock news."

"Wait, let me think this over before you do anything stupid. I didn't put my ass in the sling for you so you'll go out and get yourself killed all over again. When was Donoven hit, exactly?" Edward was looking for clues. He wanted to find another way to deal with this problem. There had to be other sources for the information they needed. You don't take over a country the size of Russia without anyone knowing.

"About two weeks ago. It must have been the twenty-sixth or the twenty-seventh of February. What difference does it make when he died? The bastard is dead and that's that."

Edward thought back to his meeting with Donoven. Was there any clue, any other source that might be unearthed from anything Donoven had said? Edward racked his brains but could think of nothing. "How did you find out he was dead?"

"He was supposed to call me two days ago, I told you, and he didn't. Finally I called his office looking for him. They said he'd been found sitting in a pub, shot twice, very professional job. He sat there for some time, dead, in a bustling pub before anyone realized he wasn't going to finish his drink. Every time I get close to someone they nail him. I'm telling you, either I'm jinxed or they have eyes in the back of their heads."

"Come on, Larry, you know that's not true. Donoven wasn't a pro, you said so yourself. He was a desk jockey at MI5—big deal." Edward knew he had to calm his friend down, get him back onside. "Think, man, think. There must be something you overlooked."

"Like what?"

"I don't know. Did you have a mailbox for him? Something he could leave you a message in? Something, anything."

"I gave him a call number. It's a relay setup. He never used it, though."

"Did you check it?"

"No, what's the point? The man didn't use it when he was alive, why should he use it after he's dead? We're not dealing with Lazarus here, you know."

"What's the number? I'll check it."

"Hold on, I'll get it for you."

Minutes later Larry gave Edward the phone number and the code by which to retrieve the messages. Before hanging up, Edward made Larry promise he would not do anything until Edward got back to him. For the moment, as far as Edward was concerned, everything was to go on as planned.

"What was that all about?" Natalie asked, an expression of concern on her face as she combed her hair away from her forehead with her fingers.

"Donoven was killed, and we have no timetable, we have nothing."

"What are you going to do?"

"I have no idea, but one thing is for sure: I'm not backing off now, not when I know what's at stake, no way."

"Okay, but how will you know when to do what you want to do if you don't know when that is?"

"You could put that to music," Edward said with a hint of a smile. "There is no way they are going to do it just like that. They are going to try and link it to something else, like a magician who waves one hand in the air to draw your attention from what he's really up to. If we could only figure out what that other thing is." He sat in silence for a minute. "I also have this number Larry gave me." He picked up the phone and dialed. "Let's see if dead people can talk."

The phone rang several times, then came a recording. "You have one message. Please enter your access code after the tone. Thank you for using AT&T."

Edward punched in the number and waited. After a second beep, a voice with a Russian accent came on. "This is a message from Mr. Donoven. Meet me at the Grave of the Unknown Soldier, outside the Kremlin. March 18 at 3 p.m., Moscow time. I have the information you need. Also you must have a copy of the Phoenix Gazette." Then came a second voice: "End of new messages. To erase all messages, please press . . ." Edward hung up.

"Well?" Natalie leaned closer to him. "What was it?"

"I just got a message from the grave. Wait a minute." He dialed Larry's number and told him what he had heard, talking to Natalie at the same time. She had become paler than he had ever seen her, and for someone of her complexion, that was very pale.

"It's a trap," Larry insisted. "It's a goddamn trap. Can't you see that?"

Edward was thinking quickly. "But there's a chance it's not. Something in that voice tells me it's not a trap. Think about it, Larry; what's the point of a trap? Donoven's dead, and getting whoever was running him would only be an act of revenge, nothing more. We're dealing with professionals—these people are out to take over an empire. Do you really think they would stop to play games?"

"Can you say for sure they wouldn't?"

"No, but there's only one way to find out—and it isn't sitting in Utah and wringing your hands."

"I don't care what you say, Edward. I know it's a trap. I can feel it."

"It's an offer, Larry—one we are in no position to refuse."

CHAPTER 12

International Airport, Anchorage, Alaska
March 14
12:10 hours

Before parachuting into enemy territory in the dead of night, he used to feel more or less the same way. There was always the concern that the chute might not open, but never had he jumped not knowing if he had a chute at all—not until now, that is. He was about to break the first rule of intelligence activity: "Do not take action without a safety net." Leaps of faith were meant for fools and dead people, not intelligence officers.

Edward was very uncomfortable in the airport departure lounge, not only because he was embarking on a journey into the unknown, but also because he was taking Natalie with him. She had insisted on coming along, and since he could not speak a word of Russian and didn't know the first thing about the country, he could hardly argue. She made it very clear that she knew the risks and was ready to take them. He tried to dissuade her, pointing out that she was already on a Russian hit list and it was only chance and Larry's connections that had gotten her out in one piece. But she was adamant. Also, he knew deep down that, where he was going, he needed her.

They went over all the details in the safe house. Edward helped Natalie conceal inside her portable tape player the array microcircuit that Larry had switched at the Air Force base. Edward's initial plan was for his assault team to bring it along with them so that if they could somehow manage to take control of the array, they might use it themselves to hamper whatever the Black Ghosts were doing. Natalie, however, suggested that she and Edward smuggle it in with them. That way, if the need arose sooner, they could take advantage of it.

Larry had been able to offer Edward one more resource for when he got to Moscow. "There's a guy I used to deal with occasionally, works as a staffer in the British Embassy. I was never too sure how reliable he was—hard to tell which side he's on. But he might come in handy if you need something in a hurry." He gave Edward the man's name and number.

From the information Donoven had given to Larry over time, they knew the Black Ghosts had people working in just about every facet of Russian security, including customs and immigration at the major airports around Moscow. Given the possibility that Donoven had, before his death, given someone Edward's description—and Natalie's being on the hit list to start with—they had ruled out a regular flight into Moscow. With all that in mind, it made more sense to enter Russia by the back door.

"Alaska Air Flight 603 for Vladivostok is now ready for boarding," announced the barely intelligible voice so unique to airports and hospitals. It varied in accent but always had the same sound and apparent echo. "Please have your boarding passes ready. People who need assistance in boarding, please notify the attendant at the gate."

With very little pomp and ceremony, they were soon high above the Bering Sea in the McDonnell Douglas 80. The uniformly cold air made for a very smooth flight. The meal was the usual bland airline fare: The steward's description of the matter on the plate was the best way to find out what it was meant to be. Edward leafed through a magazine from the pouch in front of his seat while Natalie dozed, her head resting on his shoulder. Once again, he was struck by how she managed to make a perfectly natural action seem full of intimacy and promise. He was amazed at her ability to relax while on her way to what could very well be her doom. On every flight into battle there was always that one person who fell asleep, no matter how dangerous the mission, no matter how slim the chances of survival. Edward had often wondered whether it was stupidity or a phenomenal ability to suppress one's feelings.

"We are now crossing the Island of Sakhalin," the pilot announced with the hint of a Southern twang, almost two hours into the flight. Edward, in the aisle seat, could barely see the land below. He was not going to wake up Natalie for that. From thirty thousand feet, most places had a tendency to look alike. Someone once told him that they blamed the map makers for all the problems this world had. If they would only separate the countries by lines and not paint each country in a different color, it wouldn't take people long to realize how stupid borders were in the first place. Even though he found that speech—which had been made with some pathos and a large amount of brandy—to be rather simplistic, it had a point.

Before long they approached mainland Russia and the administrative district of Khabarovsk. The plane veered slightly to the left, giving Edward a brief first glimpse of Russian soil. He vowed to tread very carefully until that shoreline was moving in the opposite direction. He felt like a blind man entering a bear's den and sitting himself on the bear's paw. No matter how friendly that bear may have become, it was still a bear.

The plane angled gently down and the announcement came that they were starting their decent into Vladivostok. Natalie stirred, murmured something warm and incomprehensible in Edward's ear, like a soft, purring cat. Then she awoke fully. Moving automatically, she drew a small powder case from her handbag and a lipstick, which she started to apply while staring into the small mirror in the case. With a jolt and a rumble of undercarriage, the plane touched down.

At first the sight was like that of any other insignificant airport where Edward had landed during his lengthy travels, until he saw the almost endless line of gleaming Ilyushin II-86 planes with the Russian flag painted on their tails. The big, wide-bodied aircraft looked like overstuffed Boeing 707s. Further down,

Edward could see the Ilyushin II-76 transport planes. He recalled how, during the Cold War, these aircraft had been code-named "Candide" in Western intelligence reports, and getting this close to them meant you were in deep trouble. Things haven't changed much, he thought. Seeing their ominous silhouettes in the evening light, he was reminded again of the urgency of his mission. It was very possible, he thought, that because the war had not been fought and won on the battlefield but rather in the weary minds of politicians and on the backs of their own people, not everyone was aware that it was in fact over. It would take very little effort to turn the tide, making what was now an airline fleet back into an airborne armada.

Clearing customs in Vladivostok seemed to take forever. A stout bureaucrat in an unimpressive uniform examined each of their documents in turn, applying rubber stamps, initials, and signatures that probably served no real purpose except guaranteeing his children an employed parent. Unlike many of its former satellite states, Russia does not allow foreigners complete freedom of movement within its borders. Fortunately, Joe Falco had found the right person to help them, and Edward's visa and other documentation had come through very quickly. Natalie already had a visa from her stint as a reporter in Moscow, which was still not officially over.

Once the surly official was done with them, they rechecked their baggage aboard Aeroflot Flight 219 to Novosibirsk and settled once again into the uncomfortable seats to wait. There was nothing to do in that giant complex but sit and stare at the huge murals of the workers and peasants, all smiling with joy as they brought the abundant fruits of their labors to be shared by all, under the warm glowing sun and the red flag with its golden hammer and sickle. Edward couldn't shake the feeling that he was in enemy territory. And indeed, the enemy was here, although not in power—for the moment.

Central train station, Novosibirsk, Russia
March 15
09:40 hours

Along with several hundred other people who looked almost like refugees with all their belongings, they waited on the platform of the Novosibirsk train station at the foot of a huge bridge that spanned the Ob River. The train was late. It seemed to Edward that, over the last few days, most of his time had been spent waiting. Natalie sat on the bench beside him, reading a paperback novel. Since they had started this trip, a relaxed, silent relationship had developed between them, which Edward found so much easier than having to make conversation all the time.

In the distance, a train whistle blew. The people on the platform began to get to their feet and busy themselves with bags and bundles and the occasional suitcase that had undoubtedly seen better times. Several minutes later, the Trans-Siberian Express moved with agonizing slowness into view at the end of the long stretch of rail.

The electric engine rumbled into the station, pulling behind it a motley collection of different-colored cars, like a dance troupe in perfect step but out of costume.

Natalie translated the silver Cyrillic lettering on the sides of the cars: "Moscow-Vladivostok. Here, this is ours." She pointed to the gray car, third from the front of the train.

They had been lucky to get a berth on the train, luckier still that it was a first-class cabin with twin bunks and a shower. Taking the train had been Natalie's suggestion: Although their visas were good, the rest of the extensive travel documentation needed for the trip might not stand up to close scrutiny, and security on the train was lax. Unless you looked or sounded like a Chechen or someone from the Caucasus, she explained, no one bothered you.

With some people still on the platform loading their baggage into the crowded cars, the heavy iron wheels clinked on the tracks and the train began to move forward.

Edward lay on his bunk. Within a few minutes the rocking motion of the train had lulled him into a gentle sleep, which came as a sweet relief after the hours of waiting.

On the bunk below, Natalie lay awake, looking out the window as the taiga, the endless forest of the Russian hinterland, slipped by. This train, she felt, was like Russia itself, hurtling forward into the night, guided by the immutable, inexorable steel rails of destiny, taking its passengers whither it would, callously indifferent to their own wishes and hopes for what lay in store at journey's end.

The clinking of the wheels and the rhythmic movement of the car echoed her thoughts with every mile the train covered. At last she sighed, resting her head on the pillow, and she, too, slept.

By 7 a.m. the train had reached Sverdlovsk. They had decided to stay on board, even though the stop was to last three hours. Many of the passengers who could barely afford the ride and could not bear the cost of meals on board got off to purchase food. They saw them coming back an hour or two later with a few pieces of fruit or loaves of bread.

At 10 sharp, after almost two full minutes of deafening whistle blowing, the train continued westward toward Perm and Kirov. Edward and Natalie spent their time watching the monotonous view, reading and sitting in the train's modest dining car, eating food that made Edward sorry he hadn't finished his meal on the plane. There was no coffee, so they made do with lukewarm, diluted hot chocolate. With the help of the phrase book, Natalie also gave Edward some coaching in Russian.

By the end of the first day, their conversation started taking on a much more personal tone. Being alone in the crowd, and she his only link short of hand signals, seemed to strengthen a bond between them. She told him more about her life and gently questioned him about his.

She had been born in St. Petersburg when it was still called Leningrad. When she was four, her father, a diplomat, received a posting to Washington. A few months after they arrived, he was called back to Moscow. Natalie stayed behind with her mother who, as was the case with most Soviet diplomats' families, also had a job at the embassy. They didn't hear from him for a few weeks. Then her mother was informed that her father had a medical problem and that the family should return to Russia. Suspecting the reason her husband had been called back and not heard from since was that he had been involved with an American woman who was working for a U.S. intelligence agency, Natalie's mother knew she would be returning to a very unsure future, both for herself and her daughter. After they had packed all their meager belongings, and less than an hour before the car from the embassy was to pick them up and drive them to the airport, Natalie's mother, leaving everything behind, called a cab. Then, from a pay phone across the street from the White House, she contacted the State Department and requested assistance to defect.

After more than a month spent in a hotel in Miami, where the mother was extensively debriefed, the State Department finalized their status and helped them relocate to Nebraska.

"Years later," she said, her voice quavering, her eyes filled with moisture, "we found out that he was imprisoned, interrogated, and executed within a few days of arriving back in Moscow. When they told us to go back, my father was already dead." She looked away through the window. The Ural Mountains slid past, indifferent to the train and its cargo. Edward moved closer and gently took her hand. After a short pause, she continued her story.

Her mother remarried, allying herself with a wealthy

cattle rancher. Natalie was sent to a private school in New Hampshire and later to Columbia University, where she studied journalism. After graduating, she had gone back to Omaha for a while, gathering experience working on a local paper, doing odd jobs. She wanted to get a job on her own merit and not have one bought for her with her stepfather's name and money. But that turned out to be more difficult than she had expected. She had the talent; all she needed was a break. As she had never exchanged a word of English with her mother, even though they both spoke it fluently, her Russian was flawless.

Edward listened with increasing fascination. In the forced intimacy of their shared quarters, they had at first been excessively polite and circumspect. Then they had broken that barrier and developed a cheerful, almost boisterous camaraderie that alleviated the boredom of the journey. Looking at her now, in her long, oversized T-shirt and dark blue jeans, Edward gradually became acutely aware of how much he desired her. He wondered idly how this would affect their operational effectiveness.

Train station, Kirov
March 17
08:10 hours

Natalie was asleep on the lower bunk when the train pulled into Kirov. Edward knew there would be a four-hour stopover here. The fact that she was asleep worked to his advantage as he wanted to pay someone a visit, alone. He moved about very quietly. Since they had spent most of the night talking, she was not likely to wake up yet. He left a note on the washstand before leaving, saying he should be back shortly.

Joe Falco had given him the address. There was no phone number—this was strictly face-to-face business. The address was of a Russian veteran of Afghanistan, a counterpart to the Vietnam vets in the States. Joe had gotten in touch with him through a friend who used to fly for Air America in its heyday, when it was the semi-official airline of the CIA. The pilot had been flying supplies in to the Mujahedeen rebels fighting the Soviet-backed puppet government in Kabul.

The pilot had introduced Falco to some Soviets who were searching for their "Missing In Action," or MIAs for short, very much the same way the Americans were looking for their MIAs in Vietnam. The two organizations—if the Russian one could be regarded as an organization—provided each other with any assistance they could.

Joe had tried to help some American families trace their vanished sons by putting them in touch with Vietnamese agencies through his new Russian friends, even if such actions were regarded as unpatriotic. A Russian veteran living in Kirov, introduced to Joe through his pilot friend, had been doing the same type of work with the Mujahedeen. The man, known only as Gregor, had been eager to make contacts in the West—not for the good of mother Russia, but because he saw a distinct possibility of economic gain for himself, in addition to helping some lost soul find better permanent accommodation.

Edward hired the lone taxi waiting outside the station, a beat-up vehicle which was a Russian replica of a '57 Chevy. Only when it started to move did he realize that they had probably saved a bundle on the shocks. He read the address out loud to the driver, repeating it several times until the driver, with a sonorous "Da, da, okay," indicated that he knew the way.

As they drove through the streets of Kirov, Edward searched the Russian phrase book he carried in his pocket. He realized it would have been smarter to bring Natalie with him on this excursion, but it was too late to worry about that now. Besides, Gregor had indicated that he was to come alone. They reached their destination, an apartment building in an undistinguished suburb. It seemed that the only difference between the various buildings was their height and the color of the laundry hanging from the front porches. Edward had the impression there was one basic plan for an apartment building which had been approved by the Supreme Soviet and then replicated over and over throughout Russia.

Edward wanted to be sure that the taxi driver would wait for him. The only thing he could think of was to tear up a ten-dollar bill and hand the driver half. There was no doubt in his mind that the man would be there when he came back out.

Time was running like sand from a broken hourglass. Not knowing the man he was about to meet, in an unknown city with a train that for all he knew might leave before the scheduled time because some business-man slipped a few rubles to the engineer, Edward climbed the staircase three at a time to the fifth floor, smelling a variety of dishes on his way up. He finally arrived at his destination and rang the bell. A big, morose-looking man opened the door a crack, leaving the chain on.

"Gregor?" said Edward.

"Da?" the man asked suspiciously.

"Speak English?" asked Edward. The man's face soft-ened a little. "American? Pazhahlsta, come." He closed the door, unhooked the chain, then opened it wide.

They sat in the living room, which was simple and sparse in its furnishings and decoration. The air was stale with heavy body odor. It took Edward some time to explain who he was and why he was there. It appeared Gregor was waiting to verify that he was talking to the real Edward, the one his American friend had told him to expect.

Edward wasn't sure at first how far he could trust this man, but realizing he was still alive and free, he decided he had nothing to lose. Gregor listened. Edward explained that there was a conspiracy between Ameri-cans and Russians to bring back the good old days when everybody was killing everybody else and the military industry was making money. When he had finished, Gregor scratched his chin thoughtfully. Then he stood up. "Okay, we take drink," he said, opening a dresser and pulling out a plain bottle with no label.

Edward shook his head. "I can't drink, my friend."

The Russian opened his eyes wide. "Can't? What mean, can't? You mean not want."

"I want more than you can imagine," Edward said with a grin. "I'm on the bloody wagon."

"What?"

"I'm an alcoholic." The words were still hard to say.

"Me too! I love alcohol, good reason to drink." He handed Edward the bottle.

"When I start, I can't stop." Edward pushed the bottle back gently, hoping his host would understand.

"Not to worry. I have much bottles, drink how much you want."

"Thanks, but no. I'm sick, you see. If I drink I can't do anything."

"Okay, I give bottle na rodny, for road."

Edward nodded with relief. He had passed the test again.

Gregor, it turned out, didn't mind drinking alone. He poured Edward a glass of water from the tap and settled down with the vodka bottle on the table in front of him. By now, he was beaming and talking volubly in his heavy, halting English.

"America wonderful country. I like go there. When I be rich man." He laughed loudly. "Maybe you help I be rich man. We do business, good money, yes?"

Edward sipped his water and nodded noncommittally. Gregor was suddenly morose again, gazing through the window at a gray landscape of apartment buildings. "Ah, Rassia, what could be if you know how." He turned his mournful eyes back to Edward. "We have problems. But we learn. We need vremya, you know, how say, time. Slowly, slowly." He poured more vodka. "Now. You go to Moscva. What will you do in Moscva?"

"Gather information, mostly."

"And what you do with information?"

"Try and stop a military coup."

"Why you do this? You not Russian?"

"It's good for my country that your country is democratic. We don't want another war."

Gregor's eyes widened. "Good. I help you. I have friends in Moscva." He fetched a small brown notebook, from which he copied a name, address, and phone number on a scrap of paper, which he handed to Edward. "Here. This my friend. You need something, legal, no legal, he help."

Edward looked at the paper. He took out his pen and a small notepad and coded the information for himself into what seemed a simple address in New York, then he handed the note back to Gregor.

"No. You take." Gregor tried to push the paper into Edward's hand. "For you."

"No need," said Edward, "thank you."

Gregor smiled. "Ah, professional. I like. My friends like. Good."

Gregor drank more, saluting everything American he could name, from McDonald's to Cadillacs and then some, until Edward took his leave. As a parting gift of goodwill, Gregor presented him with a flask-shaped bottle of vodka that slipped easily into Edward's inside coat pocket. They shook hands and the big Russian hugged

Edward and slapped him on the back, knocking the air out of his lungs. Gregor stood at the top of the staircase until Edward got to the bottom, where he could hear the big man cry after him, "Dus vidaniah, Tavasrish," which by now Edward knew to mean "goodbye, my friend." Outside, the taxi was waiting for him. Or, to be more exact, for the other half of the bill.

Back on the train, Edward went straight to the cabin. Natalie was standing by the wash basin, wearing her oversized T-shirt and, as far as Edward could see, not much else. She had an odd look in her eye that Edward could not quite fathom.

"Where were you?" she shot at him.

"I had to see someone." Edward realized she was angry.

"Why didn't you tell me?"

"Everything's fine. You were asleep and I didn't want to wake you."

"For God's sake, Edward. I'm not a little baby. You should have told me what you were doing."

Edward was stuck for words. He stared at her for several seconds, then he said in a low but firm tone, "Let's get one thing straight here, Natalie. When it comes to the operational side of this journey, I tell you what you need to know, when you need to know it. This is not an operation run by a committee, we don't take a vote on things or make mutual decisions, and I don't have to explain myself to you, or anybody else for that matter. Is that clear?"

Natalie sat on the bunk, looking away from him.

She burst into tears. "I thought something terrible had happened."

He sat next to her on the bunk and took her in his arms. "I was so worried about you," she sobbed. He pulled her closer to him, stroking her back, trying to soothe away the tears. She buried her face in his neck, and he breathed the warm fresh scent of her hair. He felt a tightness in his groin and a pleasant weakness in his chest. But he could do nothing about it. His role here was that of comforter, not seducer.

Natalie lifted her head and sniffed. Seen like this, her face streaked with tears, she looked even more beautiful.

"I'm sorry I cried. It's not like me," she said finally.

"It's okay." He leaned his head on hers. For a long time they sat there in each other's arms, until the Trans-Siberian started rolling again. She turned her head and watched as the station house and the deserted platform slowly moved away, clearing the view for more of Russia's endless forests.

Natalie slid a cold hand under Edward's shirt and slowly ran her hand across his chest. Rolling to one side, she lifted her leg across his thigh, her T-shirt riding up. He realized he was right: She had nothing under the shirt but herself. He drew her closer to him, searching with his lips for hers, his hand pressing against the small of her back. Slowly, bit by bit, she helped him off with his clothes, kissing every part as it was exposed. He, in turn, ran his lips over her soft skin, breathing in her scent, drinking it, feeling his head drift with it. Then, as though in a slow dance through a perfumed dream, they were naked, swaying on the narrow bunk. Her slim, soft body motioned slowly in his arms. Kissing his chest she coiled slowly, sliding down his body like a gentle wave, teasing him to the point of ecstasy.

Then, kissing her way back, she lifted herself gradually, standing as high as the upper bunk would allow before returning to unite with him. He felt the smooth warmth as she slowly took him in, seating herself on him, letting the gentle motion of the train dictate the rhythm as it rolled onward to Moscow.

CHAPTER 13

Moscow
March 18
11:15 hours

The taxi sped through the broad, frozen streets of the big city. Although Natalie was curled up close to him on the car seat, Edward had an empty feeling of loneliness, an underlying anxiety about the unknown that was gaining on him with every passing minute. This could very well be his last encounter with freedom for a very long time—or even his last day alive. Not knowing who was waiting for him, and why, was taking its toll. At first glance, Moscow was extremely reserved, lacking the friendly bustle of a Western city. The wide streets seemed distant and formidable.

Automatically, before he even realized it, he had snapped into operational mode, his attention focused on every detail that might affect his survival. He was learning the terrain, familiarizing himself with the rhythm of the place. His emotions were compressed into a tiny knot somewhere in his guts. It was that which caused the loneliness. As experience and training had taught him, the only person you could count on to get you out of trouble was yourself. But it wasn't only himself he had to look out for.

Edward was glad of Natalie's company, of the intimacy they had shared, and he was hopeful it would continue. If he could only leave her in a safe place and keep her there while he took care of the business at hand. He felt something for her. He wasn't quite sure yet what it was, but he liked it. Still, there was something odd about her that he just could not put his finger on. She was like a moon rock, the kind children used to get out of Cracker Jack boxes, changing colors almost to fit with his moods.

Natalie still had her apartment out on the Kalinina Prospekt, in the western part of the city, but they had decided against using it. There was no way to know if it was still under surveillance by the people who had wanted her dead.

They checked into the Hotel Metropole, a large, old-fashioned monument to what Russia could have been if it had only been allowed. In contrast to its welcoming glow and old imperial charm of gilded mirrors and marble columns, the clerk behind the oak counter under the sign reading "Registration" had a bored, sullen look, and although Edward couldn't understand what he was saying, his tone was obviously less than cordial, At last, after many surly looks and irritable remarks, he handed them their key and turned away with an insolent air to stare at the wall.

"What was that all about?" Edward asked as they made their way up to the room.

"Nothing much. It's par for the course around here."

"How come?"

"These people haven't had to be polite to their guests for seventy years. It's going to take a while for them to change their ways, and there's very few who can teach them how."

The room was clean and airy. The en suite bathroom was spacious and exhibited a sunken bath. When she saw it, Natalie's eyes lit up. She turned on one of the brass taps, and after a short cacophony of coughing air, it finally issued gushes of cold water which gradually turned steaming hot.

"Check this out," she said, looking at Edward with laughing eyes. "After four days on that lousy train, I'm ready for this." Before he could say anything she was naked and testing the steaming water with her toe. There was a mischievous expression on her face. "Care to join me?"

Edward was as clean as could be by the time they were dressed for dinner. He felt he was in the eye of the storm, where the quiet and serenity were temporary. He had a sensation that he was being watched but, not giving way to the constant enemy of covert activity, paranoia, he dismissed it. No one knew which hotel they were going to stay at, and he had not yet made contact with anyone. Considering these two facts, there was no possible way for him to be under surveillance unless their entire operation leaked badly. And that was not an option he could check out at the moment. Nevertheless, he knew he would feel more secure if he had a weapon. Bringing his snub-nosed revolver through Russian customs, of course, had been out of the question. He decided to make use of Larry's contact from the British Embassy. He called the number Larry had given him.

"I can get you a Luger at very short notice," said a British-accented voice when Edward had explained who he was and what he wanted. "Would that do?"

They agreed to meet in the ground-floor washroom of the Metropole at eleven. Edward would bring the five hundred dollars, and the man named Smythe—he had sternly corrected Edward when the latter had called him "Smith"—would bring the gun. Feeling reassured by this arrangement, Edward announced to Natalie that he was ready for dinner.

The hotel's Russkaya Chainaya restaurant boasted traditional Russian cuisine, as well as a selection of Western dishes, including omelets and hamburgers. The smell of cooking in the place was appetizing, even if the dishes they were presented with were far less so. Natalie ordered traditional Russian dishes: fish soup, rasstegai pies, and a small bottle of Georgian wine. Edward was more careful. Tomorrow was his rendezvous at the Grave of the Unknown Soldier, and the last thing he wanted was a bad stomach. He stuck to buns and butter and some cooked vegetables.

After dinner they returned to their suite. Natalie settled down with her paperback, but Edward was too restless to sit still. He prowled around the suite, looking out the window, checking his watch, waiting for eleven to come around. At last it was time.

"You'll be okay?" said Natalie.

"No problem." He took the elevator down to the

ground floor and went directly into the washroom, where a man was standing by the mirror, trimming his beard with a small, thin pair of scissors.

"Smythe?" said Edward, taking care to get the pronunciation right.

"End cubicle," the man said quickly.

Edward went down the row of tan painted doors, opened the last one and shut himself inside. He heard the door of the next cubicle being locked.

"Money," said Smythe.

Edward put his hand, clutching a fistful of fifties, through the gap between the cubicle wall and the floor.

"All right," said Smythe's voice. "Here."

As soon as he saw the pistol, Edward loosened his grasp on the bills. They were quickly removed from his hand. The toilet flushed, and Smythe left the washroom. Edward gave him a couple of minutes, then went back upstairs.

Natalie was in bed already. Edward sat by the small table and took the gun apart. It was not enough to have a gun; he had to make sure it would work. Then, satisfied it was all in order, he placed it under the pillow and got in beside her.

Moscow
March 19
10:05 hours

The Federal Express office was located on Kalanchovskaya Street, not far from the Ostrovsky Theater. Edward picked up the parcel first thing in the morning. The waybill described the contents as "documents." In fact, the parcel consisted of a large carton filled with books, as Edward confirmed when he got it back to the Hotel Metropole. He searched a couple of paperback volumes before he found what he was looking for: a large book in which the inside pages had been cut a square hollow, large enough to conceal two thick piles of bank notes. In that book alone, there were two hundred bills worth one hundred each.

The parcel contained a total of over forty books, all but the first few of which contained similar hidden compartments. Edward counted the bills with satisfaction. All in all, Larry had sent him nearly half a million dollars.

Edward put some of the money into an attaché case. The rest he placed in a special belt he had brought with him for this purpose, which he then strapped around his waist, beneath his shirt and pants. It made him look a little overweight around the middle, but he wasn't worried about that. He was more concerned that the money might not be enough. He still had only a vague idea of what he would spend it on, but he was certain that none of the items that were likely to wind up on his shopping list would come cheap.

He and Natalie put their coats on and went down into the street. It was a fine day, and their destination was not far off, so they decided to walk.

The Tomb of the Unknown Soldier, at the foot of the Kremlin's Armory Tower, south of the large square at the end of Karl Marx Avenue, appears humble enough at first glance. But as you come closer to it you realize its impact: a large granite platform with a slightly sunken section, in the middle of which an eternal flame burns at the center of a five-pointed bronze star with an inscription in Russian. Closer to the wall, behind the star, is a large granite sarcophagus draped with the Soviet flag in polished brass, and a larger-than-life Russian helmet with the star emblazoned on its front. Behind the sarcophagus, on each side of which stands a ceremonial guard, is a row of pine trees glowing green against the red stone of the Kremlin wall, over which tower the yellow walls of the former Arsenal Building.

Occasionally someone stopped and placed a bouquet of flowers at the foot of the inscription. Edward knew the look in their eyes; he had seen it many times at marble and granite pillars where names were not marked. There was the hope and the frustration of not being sure, which differed from the agony of those who knew all too well where their dear ones rested.

Edward looked at his watch. The rendezvous was set for eleven; it was two minutes to. Arm in arm with Natalie, he stood in front of the brown granite tomb. Together they looked like any tourists, except maybe for the copy of the Phoenix Gazette sticking out of Edward's coat pocket.

A woman walked up and laid a bouquet of red tulips among the others at foot of the tomb. She stood there for a minute and looked at the effect, then stooped again and moved it a little closer to where Edward was standing. "Toriste?"

He nodded.

"You speak English?" she asked.

Edward nodded again.

"Such beautiful flowers, yes?" she said, standing again, smiling. Edward nodded indifferently, wishing she would go away.

"You see here," said the woman, pointing to the inscription on the granite tombstone. "You know what says? I will translate." And she read: "'Your name is unknown, what you have done is immortal.' Beautiful, yes?" Edward nodded again, trying to walk the fine line between keeping his distance and being outright rude to the woman. At last, as if sensing that these tourists were not friendly, she walked away. Edward looked at his watch again. It was one minute past eleven. If something was going to happen, it would happen now. Edward watched the second hand ticking on his watch, then his eye was caught by the white card that was attached to the bouquet the woman had left. On it was written one word: *Larry.*

Edward bent down and busied himself with untying and retying his shoelace. Before standing up, he palmed the white card. Written on the other side were the words: *Restaurant. Hotel Intourist. Alone.*

Edward slipped the card into his pocket. Natalie had not noticed a thing. He waited for a couple more minutes, then he looked at his watch again. "I don't like the way this is turning out. Something's wrong. Go back to the hotel and wait for me there. If you don't hear from me within three hours, leave the hotel. Contact Larry, he'll get you out of here." He handed her the attaché case. "There's at least a hundred and fifty grand in there. Use it if you need it."

"What happened? Why the sudden change?"

"I don't know, it's just a hunch. But I want you to be safe. I'll probably be back shortly. It's just a precaution. Don't argue with me. Please, just do as I say."

"Okay. If I'm not in the hotel I'll be at my apartment."

"That might not be smart. They might still have it under surveillance."

"I mean if you don't come back right away. For now I'll wait for you at the hotel. Don't worry, I can take care of myself. You just watch out. Don't be a hero, okay?" She flicked her fingers at the monument. "This is what heroes get—a hole in the ground." She looked into his eyes. There was a strength in her look.

"Okay. If you don't hear from me soon, don't hang around. Get the hell out of this place."

She leaned over and kissed his lips. "I love you," she said and turned to walk away. He had nothing to tell her, nothing that would sound as clear as her statement.

Sokolov had the tinted window of his car rolled down a couple of inches. He waited until the woman who had come with the American walked away. Then, once he was sure his target was moving in the direction of the hotel as instructed, he ordered his driver to head to their second position. As he passed by the Hotel Intourist, he signaled a man waiting outside. The signal meant the target's on the way and all is clear.

Sokolov had to come up with the card trick at the last minute. He had no idea who the woman was, and he wasn't about to find out during the operation. As Rogov had said to him over and over again, do not compromise your plan and you minimize your risk.

CHAPTER 14

11:05 hours

Edward walked through the Alexandrovsky Gardens, across the Square to Gorky Street. He soon identified the Hotel Intourist and went inside to find the restaurant. The menu was posted on a board outside, and he stood there reading it for a minute or two. A man approached and stood by him. "See anything that whets your appetite?"

"Not really," Edward replied truthfully.

"There is a bakery on Pushkin Street. Perhaps you'll find what you're looking for there."

"Perhaps I will."

"Left on Gorky," said the man, pointing at the main entrance. "Take the first right, then the first left. It'll be on your right." Then he turned away as if they had never met and wandered off into the restaurant.

Edward followed the directions. He knew they were

testing to see if he was bringing a tail with him or leading his contact into a trap. The method was well known and used by every intelligence agency worth its salt, and yet it was foolproof. The counter-surveillance team would consist of at least five people and two cars, as well as whomever he was to meet with. The fact that they were taking precautions made him feel better; if this were a trap, none of it would be necessary.

Edward walked at an easy pace, trying to look inconspicuous. The buildings along Pushkin Street were all quite anonymous, with few signs to say what they were, not that he could have read the signs had there been any. He wondered how easy it was going to be to find a bakery. He thought he should be looking for a shop with a line of people outside. Weren't Russians supposed to have to line up for everything? But there were no lines of people anywhere in sight. He kept walking.

In the end it was the smell that gave it away. He was passing a blank storefront when he caught the unmistakable aroma of fresh-baked bread, which reminded him tantalizingly of the bistro in Utah. He stopped, looked in the building's darkened windows and saw rows of desks with office staff seated at them. He glanced up and down the street. A couple of doors back the way he had come, he saw someone staring at him. From the man's intense expression, it was obvious that this was Edward's contact. He slowly walked up to him.

"Looking for what?" the man asked.

"A bakery."

"The bakery is closed today. But I can recommend

another one, by the statue of Prince Dologurky in Soviet Square." The man pointed up the street, in the direction Edward had been walking. "Take the first left, then turn right on Gorky Street." Abruptly the man turned and walked away. Soon Edward was back on Gorky Street, heading north toward Soviet Square. Cars sped past on his left. He was vaguely aware of a car that had slowed at the curb behind him. A statue came into view, of a man bearing a shield and riding on a horse. That must be Prince Dologurky, he thought.

Suddenly things started happening very quickly. The car which had been trailing him overtook him, then slowed to a halt five feet ahead. The rear passenger door opened and a large man got out. Holding the door open, he gestured to Edward to enter. At that moment, another man walking behind Edward caught up with him and, pressing him in the back, guided him to the car. As he bent to enter, Edward felt himself being expertly frisked. Then he felt the man's hand on his head, pushing him quickly and efficiently into the car's back seat. He found himself seated next to a tall, thin man on the far side, and then the man who had frisked him got in beside him. The one holding the door slammed it shut and jumped into the front passenger seat. The car gathered speed. The entire capture, as they call it in trade lingo, had taken five seconds or less, and it would have taken a trained observer to notice that it was anything more than just a question of offering a friend a ride.

Edward recognized the technique. He had done it many times and had filled just about every one of the team's positions, including that of host—which in this case must be the role of the tall, slim man on his left. The man who had climbed in after Edward held a gun to his ribs. He said something in Russian to the slim man.

"He asks that you put your hands where he can see them. He said you're wearing some sort of belt. And that you have, or rather had, a gun."

"It's a money belt."

More words were exchanged in Russian, and the gun stopped pressing against him. The slim man extended his hand. "My name is Sokolov. It is a pleasure to finally meet you, Larry."

Edward shook the proffered hand, wondering in a flash if he should reveal his true identity. He decided he would. If this Sokolov was on his side, then he should know who he was dealing with. If not, then Edward was already dead.

"Larry couldn't make it. My name is Edward."

"Da, da," the man said, nodding. "I learned from our friend Mr. Donoven that you had taken Larry's place."

"Did you kill Donoven?" Edward asked, unsure whether the mention of the man's name was a veiled threat of some kind.

"No, one of my associates in the CG did."

"So you are with the Black Ghosts?"

"Indeed, indeed I am. I am a colonel in the armored divisions and my emergency posting is with the Black Ghosts." Then he lapsed into silence.

Edward tried to fathom what this silence meant. Was there a hint of wistfulness in the colonel's voice, indicating that he was less than happy with his role in the Black Ghosts? Or did he remain silent simply because there is nothing much to say to a man who is already dead? Playing for time, Edward said he nearly hadn't made the rendezvous because of almost missing his contact at the bakery. "I was looking for people lining up for their bread," he said.

Sokolov smiled sadly. "You see what Russia has become. We used to wait in the queue for our bread. Now there are no queues, but there is no bread either. This is called progress."

"Where are we going?" Edward asked as the car turned a corner.

"Nowhere special," said Sokolov. "In fact, nowhere at all. The safest place for us to talk is right here in this car. Our companions are my most trusted allies. If we are not safe with them, we are safe with nobody. We are going to ride around the city for a while, then we will drop you at your hotel. Is that a satisfactory arrangement?"

"Suits me, as long as I get my gun back," Edward said with cautious optimism. So far, he hadn't felt any more threatened than is natural when you are riding around a foreign city with four strangers, some or all of whom are certainly armed.

"Of course, that goes without saying. Now to business," said Sokolov. "You want to know why I called this meeting."

"I'm here, aren't I?"

"Quite so. Donoven informed you, so I understand,

about the plan of the Black Ghosts. I, for better or worse, am part of that plan. Why, you may ask? The answer is that I am patriotic. I believe in a strong and powerful Russia, for the good of the Russian people and their neighbors. What we have now is a repetition of history, a weak government like the German Weimar government, run by corrupt politicians who are lining their pockets. They live like czars while our people starve. What Russia needs is a strong central leadership. This, at least, we had under communism, whatever the many faults of that system. In the absence of such leadership, Russia has crumbled into anarchy. Too much freedom . . ."

"Save your breath," Edward interjected. "You won't convince me there is such a thing as too much freedom. I'm an American, remember."

"Precisely, and I'm a Russian, which is not the same. We cannot have what you spent two hundred years building handed to us overnight. Everything you have, you earned. Our people are like children: They were taken care of first by the czars and then by the Communist Party."

"I'd rather be an orphan." Edward grimaced.

"They are orphans now. Russian law has always been lenient, but its implementation has been stringent. What we have now is what you call a free-for-all, where the only ones that prosper are the criminals and parasites. The police state is the only alternative. Democracy does not work here; it's foreign to our nature. Russia was built by the czars and will return to her former glory only when the czars, or some other kind of benign dictatorship, return to take up the scepter. General Rogov's plan is a means to that end."

"Then we are on opposite sides," said Edward.

"Yes and no. I agree with what General Rogov says. However, I have learned that our esteemed leader, whom I revered as precisely the powerful dictator Russia needs, has become corrupted by his power. In fact, it is not an exaggeration to say that our general has become power-mad. He spent six years in a Siberian gulag and is no longer the man I knew when he first went there."

"Power corrupts," said Edward.

Sokolov frowned. "That axiom is not one that I personally accept. However, in this particular case, I am afraid it does fit the facts. I have come to the conclusion that, for the good of Russia, Rogov must be stopped. This is where I am hoping you might be able to help".

"Well, that's what I'm here for. Us Americans, as you know, we aim to please," said Edward.

"I do know. I got a degree in political science at Berkeley." Sokolov smiled for the first time. Edward liked what he saw. He could get to like this guy, he thought.

"Listen, we already have the basic outline of Rogov's plan. What we need is precise dates, times, locations. Only then can we plan any kind of response."

"That will not be easy. General Rogov is a secretive man. He has revealed only the bare outline of the plan, giving precise details only as and when they are needed. Nevertheless, there are a few details I can give you now, and I will keep you informed as soon as anything new comes to light."

"By the way, if Donoven told your people about me, won't they be looking for me?"

"No, he didn't tell anyone about you. I found out from his papers. I kept them to myself, along with the contact numbers to Larry and a few other things. I turned in all the money he had, which proved to the general that I'm trustworthy."

"Okay. So bring me up to date, then."

"The operation in fact started some time ago. Through the use of several commando units and the bought help of the local Mafia, we carried out terrorist acts under the name of the Chechen freedom fighters and other undergrounds. That created a need for heightened security around key installations. The Supreme Command has called for the deployment of infantry units and tank battalions with artillery support to carry out the so-called reinforcement of civil stability. We, I mean the CG, have people in almost every level of the military. We have managed to assign units whose commanders and part of their command staff are members of the CG for the job. So as of now we are either in position or about to take position around all vital installations."

"So it's the government that you are out to topple who are in fact putting you in a position to do just that."

"Precisely." There was an aura of pride on Sokolov's face which worried Edward.

"Are you sure you know what you're doing?" he asked. "You seem to be extremely proud of your former alliance. I mean, you are aware that if we do succeed it will be the end of the so-called CG. That is what I'm going to try and bring about. If you're going to change your mind on me, do it now, before I get any of my men into harm's way. You are an officer, you know what I mean."

Sokolov smiled. "I'm sorry. You are one hundred percent right. But you must understand that what I'm now trying to stop I did help to put together. And you must admit it's a very good plan."

"It is indeed. The more I hear about it, the more I realize that without you we would not be able to do much."

"That's what I was afraid of." Sokolov drew a silver cigarette case from his inner jacket pocket and offered one to Edward. "Have one, they're French. They know how to make cigarettes that you know will kill you." After lighting up he went on. "The main operation will start just before the arrival of your president for the signing of the Mutual Verification Treaty on the twenty-eighth of March."

"Aha," Edward said, as if he had just hooked a big fish.

"What?"

"Nothing, I just knew it had to coincide with something big. It's the nature of conspiracies to ride on the tail of some other event."

"Right. The more secure President Konyigin thinks he is," Sokolov explained, "the stronger Rogov will be, since all the troops brought in as reinforcements will be Rogov's. By the time the U.S. president lands, Sheremetyevo Airport will be secured by the CG, as will the Kremlin itself.

"With the U.S. president held hostage on the tarmac at Sheremetyevo, Moscow will be safe from Western attack. The Russian president will be taken prisoner in the Kremlin, from which the new ruler's orders will emanate all across the country. We have already set up the communications array we stole from the U.S. It requires one more piece, the computer card that houses the activating codes, without which the entire structure is just so much scrap metal. Once the card is in place, the array will be used to block all media broadcasts to and from Russia, and instead to provide disinformation as required. And eventually to declare a new government, a new military regime, a new world order, a new czar."

At that point Edward decided he was not yet ready to tell the man that the card they were about to receive would make no difference.

Meanwhile, as Sokolov explained, troops loyal to the CG would be taking over cities all across Russia, from Murmansk on the Barents Sea to Sevastopol on the Black Sea, from St. Petersburg on the Gulf of Finland to Vladivostok on the Sea of Japan.

"You must understand one thing about Russia," said Sokolov. "There is no need to subjugate the entire country. There are peasants in Russia who still think Stalin is in power. I'll bet there are even those who still think the czar is in power. They were hungry before, they are hungry now, they will go on being hungry. It makes no difference to them who is in power. It is in the cities that decisions are made, and Rogov will have the cities in a stranglehold. There will be several more bombings in Moscow before the week is out, so we can move even more troops into position. The beauty of the plan is that every troop mobilization, every military action will have a logical, legitimate explanation, so no one will realize what is really happening until it is too late. Even the troops that are not part of the CG, who sincerely believe they are doing the will of President Konyigin, may end up marching to Rogov's beat."

"How many loyal troops are there?" asked Edward.

"It is impossible to say. No one except Rogov himself knows the extent to which the Ghosts have infiltrated the Russian army and the FSK, who are the KGB's successors. So I have no way of knowing who is a foe or a potential ally. The Black Ghosts are well named; nobody knows their faces. I am one of the very few who even know what their leader looks like. So if I am to stop this insane plan I have nowhere to turn—except to you, the Americans."

Edward didn't say anything. He didn't want to admit that he had the same problem. He, too, was in the dark about who his allies were—in America. He realized that the Russian situation was a mirror image of that in the U.S.: nobody knew which way to turn. The situation was more acute than he had realized before. It was up to him, and this tall, thin Russian colonel sitting next to him, to do it all themselves.

The car's telephone rang. The man in the front passenger seat answered and then handed it to the colonel.

"Sokolov," he said and listened for a moment, his expression changing to one of increasing concern.

"Da," then a pause. "Da," he said again. "Harasho." He handed back the receiver and turned to Edward.

"That was one of my comrades from the CG Command Bunker. I have been ordered to place your hotel under surveillance. It seems that someone has informed us you are here."

"How?"

"I don't know who provided the information. But they are aware that you are armed."

Smythe, thought Edward. The bearded Englishman had been just a little too cooperative in coming up with the Luger at such short notice. Damn it, Larry, why did you give me a contact who wasn't reliable? "I know how they found out," he said.

"That, my friend," said Sokolov, "is something you will have to sort out at your end. Meanwhile, I strongly suggest that you not return to the hotel. Do you have any other place where you can remain in safety? I cannot help you. I wish I could."

"I understand," Edward said. Abandoning the hotel would mean leaving behind his passport. Worst of all, it would mean abandoning Natalie. But he had prepared her for that. She was to contact Larry if anything went wrong, so she had an escape route. And hadn't she said all along that she could take care of herself? He could not afford to jeopardize the entire operation on the assumption that she couldn't.

"Were you also told to observe a woman? Or was it just me?"

"No, just you. There was no mention of a woman."

Edward had no choice but to follow Sokolov's advice. He decided to make use of the phone number Gregor had given him in Kirov and throw himself upon the mercy of the Russian Mafia.

"Do you need a ride?" asked Sokolov.

"Yes, I do," he said. "Can you drop me somewhere near a telephone, away from the city center? The northeast of the city would be ideal."

Sokolov gave some instructions to the driver in Russian, and the car headed out past the Garden Ring, along the Peace Prospect toward the area in which Gregor's friend lived. Sokolov had his man return the gun, and he handed Edward a card. "This is a phone number where you can reach me. If you find out where your leak is, please let me know. Now that we have met, you have in a way tainted me. If Rogov ever found out, dying would be my best option."

"I assure you that I will. How soon will the hotel surveillance begin?" asked Edward.

"Within the hour," said Sokolov. That meant Edward had an hour to get word to Natalie of where he was.

The car came to a stop by a large, official-looking building. There seemed to be a fairly large number of people in uniform on the streets, but Sokolov assured Edward that this was not at all out of the ordinary.

Sokolov told Edward how to make his call from what was known in Moscow as a trunk-call office, which was no more than a house phone with a meter in an office building. They said goodbye and Edward was dropped off at a deserted street corner. He found the trunk-phone in the building across the street as Sokolov had said. He handed several rubles in advance to the clerk, whom he first took to be stoned, only to realize that boredom also had that effect on people's expressions.

He dialed the number, hoping that whoever answered would understand English. The phone rang and rang. Edward was about to hang up when a gruff voice spoke.

"Da?"

"My name is Edward. I'm a friend of Gregor's."

"Ah, American. Cool. We heard you was hitting town. How are you doing, man?" The accent was definitely Russian, but the diction was anything but. Edward tried in vain to picture the face that went with this voice.

"I'm okay. But I need help. I need somewhere to stay for a few days, out of sight. Somewhere safe."

"No problem. Where you at now?"

"I'm not quite sure." From the glass-paneled front wall, Edward could see a couple of street signs but they were in Russian, which wasn't much help to him.

"No problem, dude. You see a sign with a big M on it?"

Across the street he could see the sign above what looked like a staircase leading into a subway. Of course—that had to be the Metro. "Yes, there's one across the street."

"Good man, take the Chattanooga Choo-choo to Krasnosel Kaja. There you go up on the street. We'll pick you up. You can crash here, man."

Edward hung up. He called the hotel but Natalie was not there, and leaving a message with the desk clerk was out of the question. He was now on his own, at the mercy of a Russian yahoo who sounded like he was on a trip of some sort. Things were not looking good.

CHAPTER 15

McDonald's restaurant, Moscow
March 19
12:45 hours

"Bolshoi Mac, fries ea Shokolada milkshake," Anna Vilosova called into the small microphone, some three miles from where Edward stood waiting for whom he thought of as the Russian from Woodstock to show up. Anna turned back to face her customers.

"Hamburger, fries, and a shake coming right up, sir," she said in the bright, cheerful voice she had been taught to use, and the young soldier on the other side of the counter smiled his thanks.

Anna had just completed her training, and today was her first day on the job. So far, she liked it just fine. The pace was tough, especially now that the lunchtime rush was in full swing, but she didn't mind. She had always wanted to work with people, and this job gave her plenty of opportunity for just that. It also allowed her to use her pretty smile and her quick, efficient skill at handling cash. She was happy because she could work in Russian, as McDonald's was the only Western fast-food outlet that accepted rubles, which meant that not only tourists and black marketers but also ordinary Russians could eat there. Not to mention the fact that when coming to work she felt as if she were crossing an invisible border to the United States.

The young soldier paid and collected his food. He glanced at her again. Perhaps he found her attractive. She didn't mind; he was quite attractive himself, and she'd always had a thing for men in uniform.

Outside on the street, a middle-aged American couple vacationing from Cedar Rapids, Iowa, stopped in front of the restaurant's glass doors. They were there on an organized tour and this was their day off.

"Look, Harry," said the wife, holding on to her husband's arm. "A McDonald's, just like back home. Let's go in. I'm dying for a burger." They entered and made their way to the counter. "I don't believe this," the wife said in a loud, squawking voice. "It's just like the one in Cedar Rapids!"

"It looks even bigger, dear," Harry nodded, although privately he thought the women behind the counter were older, more mature, and far more attractive than the chirpy youngsters he was used to back home.

Anna took their order with a smile. Two gray-looking men parked a black car just outside the glass doors, an act that did not seem unusual to her. No one in the crowded restaurant paid any attention to the two men, who didn't enter but walked briskly down the street.

Harry and his wife took their meals and sat down in the front of the restaurant by the window. Harry found his burger and fries well up to standard, and he believed he was an expert, but his wife complained that hers was too greasy.

"I have to disagree with you, dear," he said, to her amazement. It must have been the weather; after twenty-five years of marriage, this was the first time he had dared to voice a dissenting opinion.

The small hand was missing on the old-fashioned alarm clock ticking away in the trunk of the car parked just outside the front door of the restaurant.

"Doesn't that look like the Dodge I once had?" Harry asked his wife, who was still getting over their previous conversation.

"I do so think it's greasy, dear," she said as the big hand reached twelve and activated the alarm. The bell hammer slammed against the chime, closing the electric circuit that sent a spark along a three-foot electric wire connected to a fuse. The fuse exploded inside a small TN cylinder embedded in a block of TNT. Before Harry could take another bite from his burger or Anna Vilosova could smile again, the parked car exploded, blowing out the front glass wall of the restaurant and turning what only seconds before had been a happy, colorful place into a helter-skelter of burning plastic, shattered glass, and torn flesh, a charred and smoldering corner of hell.

Tiny leaflets reading "Chechnya for the Chechens" scattered with the wind down the street, greeting the wailing emergency trucks as they arrived.

The White House, Washington, D.C.
March 20
11:25 hours

President Bradshawe sat halfway along the oval mahogany conference table. Behind him was the white marble fireplace decorated with a potted fern that had outlasted many presidents before him and would probably outlast many to follow—that is, if he didn't screw up in the meantime, as his predecessor had once said somewhat jokingly. That small remark had weighed heavily on his shoulders, representing more vividly to him than anything before the gravity of his office. More than once at times of crisis he stared at that fern, already wanting to pass it on, along with the responsibility that guarding it brought.

The president was breaking with his habit of meeting separately with various members of the National Security Council. Events had dictated that he bring them all in to share the responsibility. He knew very well that such sharing was only formal; the responsibility was his to bear alone. Rarely was a member of the Council remembered for a stupid suggestion he had made; it was always the fault of the president who took it. Bradshawe had no quarrel with that. It also allowed him to make the final decision, giving him the ultimate power that comes as a manifestation of years of campaigning, begging, and bending.

Norman Conley, the vice president, was seated across from him. Next to the VP sat Richard Townes, the secretary of defense, whose long face was not a good sign, Bradshawe concluded. The secretary of state was his usual nonchalant self, while the chairman of the Joint Chiefs of Staff and the director of Central Intelligence were busy handing each other sheets of paper that Bradshawe had probably received himself but had not yet got around to reading. He also had no doubt that they would make him admit that.

At either end of the table were representatives of the president's Foreign Intelligence Advisory Board and the Defense Intelligence Agency, as well as Bud Hays of the National Security Council staff.

The topic on the table was the worsening security situation in Russia and its implications for the upcoming presidential visit. There had been news reports of terrorist attacks close to Moscow, and Army Intelligence had supplied Rick Hansen of the Defense Intelligence Agency with information about several car-bombing incidents, including the one everyone had seen on CNN the day before, outside the McDonald's restaurant, which had caused several fatalities, including the deaths of two American citizens.

"Let's get this show on the road," President Bradshawe said, rubbing his hands together. "I'm sure my in-basket is full of your reports, gentlemen, but I prefer to hear things firsthand. So, assuming you all remember what you wrote, let's get started. Mr. Bouver, if you would care to speak first."

The DCI closed the leather folder with its large gold emblem of the CIA on the desk in front of him.

"Mr. President, from what we can gather, the situation in Russia at the moment is extremely volatile. The Chechen rebels seem to have taken the fighting out of their republic and dumped it on the streets of Moscow. The Russian military is very much in control; in fact, their presence around major installations and the Kremlin has been beefed up. Still, the terrorist cells seem to be able to outsmart and outmaneuver the army."

"Have they made any demands?" Bradshawe asked.

"Well, sir, there is a problem there." He hesitated for a moment, then opened his folder again and took out a document. "We have a source inside the Chechen resistance, and from what he's telling us, they don't know anything about this terrorist campaign in Moscow."

"What are you saying?" The president leaned back in his chair, his brow wrinkled.

"It appears that the rebels' central command, if you could call it that, is not behind the attacks. We believe it might be a secondary underground that wants the Russians out but is not part of the existing power structure. That is not unusual; we have seen it before in South America and Africa."

"What if it's someone who just doesn't want the treaty signed?" interrupted the secretary of state, who suddenly appeared interested in what was being said.

"It's a possibility, sir. However, a remote one, in our opinion."

"And why is that?" the secretary of state pressed.

"The campaign doesn't seem to be consistent with such a theory."

"They are hitting American targets," interjected Townes, turning to one of the young men at the end of the table. "Hansen, could you please repeat the stuff you ran by me before?"

The young man started to stand up.

"No need to stand, young man," the president smiled, "just tell us."

"Well, Mr. President . . ." The young man flushed, then attempted to control the nervousness in his voice. "It seems they are targeting us, sir. There was a car bomb five days ago outside the Pan-Am building at Sheremetyevo Airport." The president nodded. "Then a device was found planted near our embassy in Moscow."

"Who found it?" The president turned to the DCI.

"The security people at the embassy. They have instructions to check parked vehicles for several blocks around the embassy. We implemented some systems developed by the Israeli Shaback."

The president turned back to Hansen. "Go on."

"Then there was the McDonald's thing, sir. So far, that caused the only American fatalities. But the intention is clear."

"Thank you, Hansen," said Townes, the defense secretary. "Mr. President, I would ask that you change the venue of the summit to some safer place like Geneva or Vancouver. To go into Moscow now looks like a recipe for disaster."

The president thought about this. Then he turned to the DCI on his right.

"Bouver, what's your view on this?"

Charles Bouver removed his glasses, revealing eyes of startling blue clarity. "I don't think there is cause for undue concern. I believe that as a result of what has already taken place, the security around Moscow will be greater than under any other circumstances. Unless you plan to go jogging in Red Square, sir, I see no problem."

"What does the Secret Service recommend, Mr. President?" Townes was not giving up yet.

"You know them, Richy. They would prefer to keep me locked in the basement of the White House if they could. Their job is to protect me, not tell me what to do."

"Sir, I must insist that you change the venue." Townes' face was tense.

"Out of the question, Richard. Unless there is a real threat, and by real I mean proof of a plot to kill me, I'm going. Is that clear? We are looking at a significant political achievement and I will not have it said in the upcoming campaign that the president chickened out because some half-assed terrorist might have a few plans. Besides," he smiled at his old friend, "you will be there to protect me, and I promise we will not stay the night. We'll be going in and out the same day."

"It looks like Konyigin has the situation under control," the DCI said as though he'd never been interrupted. "I think an unexpected about-face on our part would cause the Russians to doubt our sincerity on the disarmament issue, which could worsen, not improve, the security situation." He turned to the secretary of defense. "With all due respect, Mr. Townes, my recommendation is that the visit proceed as planned."

Townes broke in angrily. "How can you say that? We have no way of knowing whether Konyigin can really get this situation under control. Given some of the things that have happened over there recently, I would say it's quite likely that he cannot. In which case, going ahead means looking for trouble. And any trouble at this stage would be far more prejudicial to the disarmament agenda than a change of venue for the official signing of the treaty."

"How about you?" The president turned to Bud Hays. "I saw a memo from you just this morning regarding the situation."

"It's only in the preliminary stages, sir."

"What isn't?" The president raised his hands questioningly. He was trying to break the circle of anger that he knew could damage the effective operation of the executive branch. He had no intention of allowing the various members to enter into a feud that could bring down the entire administration.

Bud Hays turned the pages of the file in front of him on the table. "The NSA has intercepted a number of covert communications between various elements of the Russian security forces, the FSK, the army, and the Ministry of Internal Affairs." He turned a page and cleared his throat. Everyone was looking at him. It was moments like this that he treasured. "It seems that the terrorist attacks are the work of a Mafia group headed by a former member of the Supreme Soviet. The attacks are politically motivated only inasmuch as they represent an attempt by this man to assert its power at the local level, kind of a warning to the security forces to let him continue his various racketeering operations unimpeded. According to FSK reports that we have also intercepted, the arrest of the group's leader and his associates is imminent, and his operation will be shut down entirely within a few days."

"That's news to me," said the DCI. "How come we never got wind of that?"

"I have sent you a memo, sir," Bud said somewhat apologetically. "But I was keeping it under wraps as much as I could. You see, it was just a hunch that I had. It only started to pay off yesterday."

"Well." The president was beaming. "I don't think the United States is going to be intimidated by a bunch of thugs from Moscow's underworld, do you?"

The defense secretary burst in again. "Wait a minute. How reliable—?" The president cut him off with a wave of his hand.

"Nobody ever said being president was a safe job. I'm willing to take the risk. Your job is to minimize it."

The meeting adjourned. As the men left the conference room, Townes called to Bud Hays. "I need to see you in your office."

Bud knew the interview was not going to be a pleasant one. The secretary of defense would explode in his face for not telling him about this new information ahead of time. There was little Bud could do, except to tell him that the information had been confirmed only this morning and that he had sent him an urgent note about it.

Enduring Townes' wrath would not be difficult. Bud was rejoicing that his presentation of the information had produced the desired effect—averting the cancellation of the president's visit to Moscow.

The information had been obtained through the National Security Agency's computerized search system. Not all of the countless numbers of radio and telephone communications intercepted by the NSA around the world could be stored indefinitely, for reasons of their sheer numbers. So once the contents of each intercepted message had been digitized, it was run through a series of searches using several thousand key words that the agency kept on file. If any of the key words were present in the message, then that message would be sent to a file name in the appropriate group, and the intelligence agency that had requested that particular key word would receive a copy.

As a staff member of the National Security Council, Bud had free access to the system and could request a search whenever he wanted. He had no idea how Singleton had known the particular key words to look for. But if he had learned anything in Washington, it was that you don't argue with success.

As expected, Townes turned on Bud the moment he had closed the door to his office. "Why wasn't I briefed about that communications report?"

"There wasn't time," said Bud. "I tried to reach you, and if you check you'll find my memo in your office. I tried not to bring it up, but the president . . ."

"Okay, okay. You don't have to tell me the whole story. I was there, remember. Do you believe the information is good?"

"It seems like it is." Bud's face expressed a certain awkward regret. "I didn't intend for it to have the effect it did. I'm not crazy about this presidential visit myself. Something just doesn't smell right."

"Damn it, Bud." Townes' voice was tight with angry frustration. "Couldn't you have come up with some useful intelligence for a change?"

"I wish I could. But, hey, if it ain't there, I can't go inventing it, can I?"

"No, I guess not. By the way, have you heard anything from our friend Larry?"

"No, and I have a bad feeling about that too."

"What do you mean?"

"I'm still checking it out, so I don't want to jump to conclusions, but there is a good possibility we picked the wrong man."

CG Command Bunker, outside Moscow
14:12 hours

"Da," answered General Rogov when his aide handed him the phone in the CIC room. He was in the middle of dictating an order to the 502nd Mechanized Mountain Brigade that was to take position around Bykovo Airport in a few days.

"I will only say this once, general." Rogov knew the

deep voice on the other end of the line. He had done business with the man and probably owed him his freedom, but he had never met him. He knew he was one of the few people on the planet who played with politicians and generals like some play chess, and no matter which side won, in whatever conflict, he would be collecting the prizes. Peter knew him as Singleton.

"Go on, I'm listening."

"If you want the visitor to visit, you better tell your friends to stop breaking windows."

"But I thought we had that straightened out with the communications you asked for."

"It worked for now, but if this goes on they will cancel the visit, trust me." The line went dead.

CHAPTER 16

Safe house, Moscow
07:45 hours

"Drink this," said Igor, setting the chipped mug on the floor next to the sofa where Edward lay. His whole body was sore from sleeping on the short sofa, with a hard lump pressing against the small of his back. Edward slowly rolled over and stared at the mug, which contained the bitter, brown, odorous liquid that he had, in the eighteen hours since they brought him here, come to know as tea. He reached for it and was pleased to note that his hand obeyed his instructions and picked up the mug.

Sipping the hot, rank liquid, Edward began to piece together the events of the previous day. He had stood for a long time by the Metro station at Krasnosel Kaja, waiting for Gregor's friends to pick him up. Finally they had arrived in an old, battered Volkswagen van, into the back of which he was summarily hoisted and laid to rest on a piece of foul-smelling carpet.

There were two of them. Igor, the older one, was a square, squat man with thick black hair and a permanent five o'clock shadow. The other was Alexi, a younger man whose gruff voice and odd choice of words Edward had noticed over the phone. Alexi had apparently learned his English from Hollywood and from recordings of sixties and seventies rock music—which he referred to as golden oldies. He had found that necessary after ending his brief career in the KGB in favor of the more lucrative Moscow underworld, never having completed the English course the agency had enrolled him in. "Al," Edward heard him saying as he extended his hand from the driver's seat. "Like Al Capone." He gave a treacly chuckle. "Al Caponeski, that's me."

They had brought Edward to what might be termed a safe house, although as Alexi had pointed out with a leering grin, safety was a relative thing. It was a large flat that used to house several families before Igor and Alexi "bought" them out, keeping their meager furniture and letting them leave, as Al had put it, alive. In fact, it was two flats separated by a stairwell, one on the second floor, the other adjacent to it but one floor higher. The second-floor flat was used for storage. It was filled to the ceiling with cardboard cartons which contained, Igor explained, a consignment of contraband Korean computer monitors that had been "diverted" in Siberia and now were awaiting distribution via the alternative market—which turned out to be his euphemism for the black market.

The other apartment had a small kitchen and two or

three even smaller bedrooms. In the living room was the stereo system, the sofa on which Edward now lay, a television and VCR with an extensive collection of pornographic videos, and a telephone on an old carved oak desk.

This was Igor's office. It was from here that he had made the calls, sometime last night, that would arrange the rapid deployment of his inventory of computer monitors. While Igor was on the phone, Alexi had gone out to make a few small purchases and had returned with what he called "the lifeblood of Russia," three bottles of Magosty vodka. From then on, it had been downhill all the way. At first they seemed disappointed at their guest's refusal to drink with them, but after a short conversation in speedy Russian in which they had probably reached the simple conclusion that it meant all the more for them, they embarked on their journey into oblivion.

Igor, it turned out, was a lover of classical music. He forced Edward to listen to numerous noisy orchestral works by Glinka and Mussorgsky, and as his memory dwindled with the rise of his blood alcohol level, he had played them again and again, especially a piece by Borodin that Edward knew better as "Stranger in Paradise." If this is paradise, Edward thought to himself late in the evening, it sure is a strange one.

Finishing his tea with a gulp, Edward hauled himself into a standing position and staggered off to find the bathroom. After taking a shower, he went to find Igor, who was with Alexi in the kitchen.

"Igor," Edward said. "We need to talk."

"Is okay, you want something to eat, drink?"

"No, I'm fine. I didn't come here for a vacation. How well connected are you?"

"Connected, what you mean connected?"

Alexi said something in Russian to his friend, then Igor smiled. "I am okay connected."

"Lay it on us, baby." Alexi grinned.

"I need a military unit." Edward had a plan in mind but wasn't quite sure how to get these two clowns to help him put the pieces together. Should he just lay it out for them, in which case they might sell him out to the highest bidder? He decided to use the piecemeal approach. One thing at a time, at a good price.

The two Russians looked at each other, then Igor asked, "What you call military unit, is this . . ." He thought for a moment. "What is this?"

"Soldiers. I need some two hundred soldiers, in uniforms, with weapons."

"This will cost much money," Igor said, totally unmoved by the request.

"What's fair is fair." Edward nodded. "Can you get them?"

"What this for?"

"Didn't Gregor tell you?"

"He say there is going to be military coup and you want to stop. We want to help because if military come and win, we out of business. Military, they much bigger Mafia. But we not stupid, we want to know what need soldiers for. If for fighting, we get from one place. If only for decoratsia, we get from another. You understand?"

"I need them mainly for show, but they have to look real."

"What they must know?" Igor pressed.

"As little as possible."

"So what we tell them?"

Edward had thought about that point all night and he had a solution. "You tell them we're making a movie. We need them as extras."

Alexi's constant smile broadened. "I always wanted to be in the movies. Hollywood here I come, no business like show business."

"Shut up," Igor barked. He was getting serious now that actual deals were being discussed. "I call someone, we do this for you, it going to be much money. You have?"

"I'll get you as much as you need, within reason."

"Reason is, you need what we have."

They went into the other room. Igor picked up the receiver and dialed. Edward watched him and memorized the number. He knew things like that could come in handy, especially since he had no doubt that this small-time criminal he was dealing with was now turning to a higher echelon. What Edward had requested was clearly out of Igor's league.

After a few minutes of fast-paced Russian on the line, Igor put his hand over the mouthpiece and turned to Edward. "When and where?"

"In Moscow. In one week."

Igor went on talking on the phone, explaining things with large hand gestures, as if he were talking to someone who could see him. When he got off the line, he said something to Alexi in Russian. Then, as they both smiled at him, Edward asked, "Well, can you do it?"

"Sure. We get real soldiers. We tell them we make movie. They happy for we pay them good, fifty bucks a day. Good Ukrainians."

"Ukrainians? I need Russians."

"Until not long ago, same thing. Not to worry."

"They would have to have Russian army uniforms, though."

"Uniforms can get. Which division you need?"

"I don't know yet."

"We get tags for you."

"Okay. One question. How we gonna get two hundred Ukrainian soldiers in Russian uniforms from wherever to Moscow?"

"They come from Kiev. We need transport plane. It costs more, but we take care of that."

Alexi went into the other room and came back with a couple of loaves of bread, some jellied fish, and a chunk of white cheese. The three of them sat at the table and had an impromptu brunch, washed down with more of the strong, bitter tea.

If they're coming by air, they will have to come aboard a military transport," Edward said. "Ilyushins or something."

"Ilyushins are not available at bargain price," said Igor, munching on a bread crust.

"Does that mean you can't help me?"

"No. It means we have to borrow one."

"You mean steal."

"We not steal anything. Under communism they say it all belongs to us. Now they say not, so we borrow. You pay. With enough dollars anything can be borrowed in Russia."

After they had finished eating, Igor offered him his chair at the carved oak desk where the telephone was, and Edward got to work.

He contemplated trying to reach Natalie at the hotel again but decided against it. If she was still there, she would certainly be under surveillance and the phone line would be bugged. He had no qualms about calls from the phone in the apartment being traced back to him; Al had explained that they had rigged the phone to show outgoing calls as originating from the Kremlin. They joked at the ease in which the connection had been made. "There is nothing you cannot get in Moscow for a few dollars," said Igor.

The problem was that if he did reach her, it would confirm her involvement with him, and that might be enough to get her into very deep trouble. Edward was hoping that by now she would have made arrangements to leave. She hadn't yet called Larry, as he had found out last night when he finally managed to reach him.

Edward decided to call Larry back. He was still in bed, it being just after dawn in Utah.

"Has Natalie called?" Edward asked.

"No. Did you try the hotel again?"

"No. It would be safer if you do it. She might have decided to split. If not, and you talk to her, get her out of here."

"I'll get her out of there, don't worry. Consider it arranged."

"Good. What have you heard from the men?"

"They're waiting for your orders. I called the safe house right after you called me and told them to be ready. So fill me in on that new friend of yours, the colonel."

Edward brought him up to date on his meeting with Colonel Sokolov. He also passed on to Larry a list of arms they would need. Larry would have to make sure the men all knew how to operate them, if he was up to traveling to New York. "How are you feeling now?"

"I'm on the mend. Kelly's been real nice, bringing me food and all. But I wish there was more for me to do."

"I have something for you to do."

"What?" Larry sounded enthusiastic. He was clearly getting better, and Edward suspected from the way he talked about Kelly that something was going on between them.

"We need a plane," said Edward. "It has to be a Boeing 747-300."

"What do we need it for?"

"What do you think? To get the men over here. We can't have fifteen or twenty heavily armed tough guys flying in on Pan-Am."

"Okay. You want me to buy one?"

"No. This has to be unknown, invisible. If anyone in the intelligence community hears about this, we're dead. So we can't buy one. We have to"—he smiled to himself—"borrow one."

"How do you propose we do that?"

"Here's how." Edward gave Larry all the ideas that had been cooking in his mind since his conversation with Sokolov. "Are you sure you're up to it?"

"I was only shot, not castrated," said Larry, sounding hurt. "Give me a break. It's you who had retired, remember?"

Edward made Larry promise to keep on Natalie's case, and once he got through to her, to let him know that she was okay. After hanging up, he found it difficult not to grab one of the vodka bottles strewn around the flat and down it to dull the ache. Even though he knew there was nothing more he could do, he felt as if he had abandoned her.

CHAPTER 17

New York City
March 21
17:20 hours

An undistinguished brownstone on 24th Street and 27th Avenue—offering low-rent accommodation to businesses hanging on for dear life—housed on its third floor a nonprofit organization dedicated to awakening public awareness to the plight of some Amazon tribe about to be run over by civilization, and Icon Air, a small charter airline that like many of its kind sprung up in the wake of President Ronald Reagan's deregulation of air transport and was now feeling the economic squeeze of reality. The rest of the third floor was vacant except for one suite, situated next to the airline, which had been rented to some entrepreneur that same day.

The landlords couldn't care less what their new tenant was up to, as long as his rent came in on time. And this one had paid three months in advance.

Larry had chosen that building because of the airline.

They were the proud owners—or at least were still paying the giant mortgage—of two jumbo jets and several DC-9 transport planes. At the close of the seventies they only had the two DC-9s and business was great. Then came deregulation and business became phenomenal. They had moved into a large suite of offices at the twin towers and money was literally falling from the sky. By now they owned five DC-9s, several Dash 8s, and the jewels in their crown—the two 747-300 jumbo jets delivered to them in 1989. But after only five charter flights, their house of cards collapsed. Within a year they were haggling over rent in this fleabag they called home. Icon Air was now down to two operational DC-9s, and the 747s were on mothballs in Arizona, eating up their savings with storage fees and interest payments on what they called the two killer whales—which was why Larry had rented the office space in the first place.

Larry was well aware of all that, and he found out much more as he listened for several hours to just about everything that was said in the airline's office. His team had entered the building right after Edward had instructed them and Larry had located the company address. Sparky installed the bugs, allowing them to hear not only what was said over the airline's phones, but also every word uttered in any corner of the office suite, even the washrooms, men's and women's.

Now that they were sure the Boeings were going to stay in one place for some time, and they had the access they needed through the suite Larry had rented, it was time to get to work.

They had been coming in and out of the brownstone all day, loading building materials into the office suite. Their cover story, should anyone ask, was that they were renovating the suite for use as a television production studio, which would explain the large quantities of electronic equipment they were bringing in. But no one asked. At one point Larry contemplated knocking on the airline's door and telling them the cover story just so no questions would arise later. But at the last minute he decided against it.

At 6:30, Mr. Schmidt, the sorry owner and chief executive of Icon Air, left the building. A few minutes later, his secretary, who had been working late, decided to call it a night as well. That would leave the third floor deserted except for the longhair who seemed to spend most of his waking life trying to save that Amazon tribe. So it was decided that Dan, one of the two pilots, would have the job of getting the man out of the building for that evening. Playing the part of a philanthropist looking for a worthy cause to spend his money on, Dan suggested to the longhair that he explain the workings of the organization to him over a beer at the corner tavern. The young man was only too happy to oblige and, of course, one beer led to another.

At 6:39, Vern, the ex-SEAL, phoned in that the secretary had boarded her bus and the building was clear. Tom, the pride of the Green Berets, was watching the back entrance while Jeremy, also from the Green Berets, was inside the stairwell watching for pedestrians, as he had disabled the elevator for the time being.

"Let's go," said Larry, and his team headed down the

corridor to the airline offices. They had slightly under two hours before the cleaning people would show up. They were not to interfere with any of the building's normal activities. No one was to even suspect that something was going on. Jean-Pierre, the tall, blond Quebecer from the Canadian Airborne, knelt at the door and within twenty seconds it was swinging inward. Larry raised his Polaroid camera and took a picture, placing it on the table by the door. He kept on taking pictures as he moved deeper in, placing each on or near the object he had just captured on film. On their way out, they would use those pictures to verify that they had returned everything to its original location.

Sparky, who had been in the office before, lost no time and headed straight for a large computer console stationed on a desk in the corner of the front office. He opened a small tool kit wrapped in black tarp and started to remove the back of the computer tower. "This is the server," he said, grinning. "We get inside this one and we got it all."

"Where do you want this?" Doug, the SAS man, asked Sparky in his strong British accent, holding up a small metal briefcase.

"Here." Sparky pointed to the table by the computer, without looking away from what he was doing.

Jean-Pierre removed the metal grille of an air return vent beneath the table Sparky was working on.

"Hi, Sparky," Mario called from the door leading into an inner office off the main hall.

"What is it, Sarge? I'm busy now."

"I just tagged the one phone you didn't get to last time. We need to have them covered one hundred percent."

"I'll get to it right after I finish here."

"Right," said Mario, and he returned to the office.

Larry sat behind a large, scruffy metal desk, leaning back on the soft, expensive-looking leather chair that had probably made it out of the twin towers just before someone foreclosed on the airline's offices there. He was watching the team work. He realized how lucky he was to have been able to call on Edward for help. The man was in Moscow, yet his presence in the room was so strong that Larry would not have been at all surprised if he'd suddenly heard him giving instructions.

Jean-Pierre dialed a number on his cell phone, and after the first ring Joe Falco answered. He was in the next suite with the rest of the team, getting all the surveillance equipment ready for hookup. "Yes?"

"What's up?"

"We're ready on this side," Joe Falco said.

The return air duct that served the airline's suite was the same one that opened into the suite Larry had leased next door. It was far too narrow for anyone to crawl through, and it turned and twisted, but Larry had come up with a way around that. Once Sparky was through with the computer connections, they would move on to Phase Two.

Sparky opened the briefcase and took out a small laptop computer. He attached a coaxial cable from the back of the laptop to the airline's computer hard drive. Doug Findley was now standing by him, looking over his shoulder. "Are you uploading or downloading?"

"I'm changing their configuration," Sparky answered,

his head halfway inside the computer casing. "Whenever they do something on their computer it will be redirected through our computer in our office."

"Won't that make their computer work slower?"

"Not really. Our processor is faster than theirs, so it will compensate. Actually, I'll have to slow it even more."

"That's neat. So they'll really be working through our computer."

"Right." Sparky took his head out and grinned at Doug. "I'm downloading all their information now. You can start with the cable. By the time you fish it through, I'll have the thing wrapped up."

"Where are you going now?" Doug sounded worried as he watched Sparky walk away, leaving the open, gutted computer and his laptop which now displayed a series of flying toasters chasing slices of brown toast.

"It's going to take some time to download. It's a monster memory. I'll install the bug in that phone for the sergeant in the meantime. Don't worry, if you don't piss on it nothing will go wrong."

"Good thing you told me," Doug said, and everybody laughed. Larry could still feel that pain in his chest when he laughed, but he figured there were times when it was worth it. Seeing Sparky the way he was now was one of those times.

Doug opened a large cardboard box they had brought with them and took out a blazing red remote-controlled toy jeep. It had thick, corrugated tires and a tiny video camera mounted where a driver would be expected to sit. In the box there was a monitor connected via a thin wire to the camera in the jeep. Doug handed the car to Jean-Pierre, who tied a cord to the back bumper.

"Who's going to drive this thing?" Doug asked, holding up the remote control.

"I will," came Mario's thick voice.

Doug handed him the unit and a blueprint of the duct system. "You enter here," he said, pointing to a spot on the sheet. "You try to come out here."

The sergeant headed for the duct opening. "No," said Jean-Pierre, "you sit over there and watch the monitor. I'll get the thing in place. I'll tell you when it's ready." He picked up the toy jeep and placed it in the hole, facing in the direction it was supposed to go. "Can you see anything on the monitor?" he asked.

"Nothing," the sergeant replied, "fucking nada."

"Ah, merde," Jean-Pierre exclaimed, "anyone got a flashlight?"

"I have one back in the office," Larry said, moving in the direction of the door.

"I'll get it," said Doug. "If we wait for you we'll be here all night."

"It's on the shelf by the large receiver. Oh, and thanks for the vote of confidence."

"Anytime," Doug said, already in the hall. It wasn't long before the light was taped to the car's hood and the toy returned to the cavity in the wall.

"It's all yours," Jean-Pierre said, moving away from the wall to stand by the sergeant and watch the monitor. Doug stayed by the opening and was feeding the cables to make sure they didn't snag. Staring at the blueprint while keeping his eye on the screen, the sergeant piloted the car along the duct.

"There's the third-world branch," Jean-Pierre said as the car reached a junction in the duct. "Keep to the left." The journey continued. The entire section of tubing had all but disappeared when the car came to a halt opposite another junction within the duct.

"They can see the lights about nine feet away," Jean-Pierre announced, keeping an open cell line with Joe Falco in the other suite.

"Can't they grab it?" asked the sergeant.

"The duct is too narrow. You'll have to bring it right up to them."

Several minutes later, the jeep made it through, to the cheers of all present. They put everything back into place, hoping that no one would decide to move the desk with the server computer away from the wall. Larry was backing up, collecting the Polaroids he had left and taking his time to verify that all was in place. They finished twenty minutes ahead of schedule and were back in their suite with ample time to spare before the office cleaners arrived. Tomorrow their efforts would be put to the test.

Greenfield, Arizona
March 22
10:00 hours

The telephone at the world's largest airplane parking lot, in Greenfield, Arizona, rang twice before it was answered. Nothing was rushed at the former CIA airport since the agency had stopped supplying arms to the Nicaraguan Contras. Now it was more of a graveyard for mummified relics of a better age. It was hard to believe, looking at the hundreds of commercial airplanes lined in neat gleaming rows, some with their cockpits covered, some partially cannibalized, that not long ago they were all hauling passengers at full capacity. It was in places like this that the full extent of the recession that had hit the air transport industry could be realized.

"Greenfield," Nancy said finally, after having slowly moved the receiver from its cradle to her ear, making sure not to strain any muscles unnecessarily.

"This is Icon Air. We're going to pick up X34v231 the day after tomorrow, if that's okay with you."

"I'll need your clearance code, items one to five on your release list, and a payment in full. Just a moment, please." She typed on her screen the registration number the caller had given her. A small red symbol blinked next to the name Icon Air. "We will need the payment via certified checks and a prepayment for the fuel."

"Sure," said the voice at the other end. "Can you please fax us the exact amounts so we could get it all in order for you?"

"Sure."

Several minutes later, a request for verification came through the computer modem in the office Larry had rented. The people in Icon Air's real office never even knew it came, nor did they have any inkling of the fax that was sent to them but printed out in the office next door. They were about to be short one jumbo jet. They had no idea that their company's mothballed 747-300L, one of only 46 that were ever produced, was about to make history.

When Edward called around noon he was informed that everything had gone smoothly. The only problem was where to put the beast.

"I can get it to Tucson," said Larry. "I know someone who could let us hold it in a hangar for a few days. He'll think he's doing it for the agency. I worked with him before and he'll keep his mouth shut. But what do we do with it after that?"

"You just get it there and get it ready, like I told you. I'll give you the rest of the information later."

There was little said after that. Larry didn't have the news Edward wanted to hear about Natalie. Larry knew the agony Edward was going through. But he also knew he would do what had to be done, no matter what.

CHAPTER 18

Vinigrad office building, Moscow
11:10 hours

Sergei Pozharsky was one of the new cadre of Russian entrepreneurs. Seated in a soft leather armchair in his luxurious office less than a mile from the Kremlin walls, he pondered his empire. His company had been in existence for only a couple of years and already recorded an annual turnover in excess of two hundred million dollars, with profits to match. However, no mission statement hung on the walls, no employee-of-the-month prizes were ever distributed, and the company's financial records were hard to obtain, if in fact they existed at all outside his head. Indeed, the exact nature of Sergei's business was never quite defined, for the simple reason that his company would do almost anything requested of it, provided the profits outweighed the risks.

The previous year, when electrical power shortages were endemic in parts of Africa, Sergei's company had offered to supply the Ivory Coast with a nuclear submarine so they could use the reactor as a source of electricity for the entire country. The deal had been scratched at the last minute, when some environmentalist activists had found out about the plan and tried to put it under the media spotlight. The Russian submarine fleet did not enjoy a very good security record, so the whole plan was scuttled. A couple of newspaper articles had mentioned rumors of the plan, but it had died there, as nothing more than a rumor. It was like most of Sergei's business ventures that did come to fruition: To his satisfaction, most of them remained nothing more than rumors to the world at large. But they were extremely lucrative and occasionally deadly.

The two men who had planted the bomb outside McDonald's and then vanished into the Moscow crowds were on Sergei's payroll. He had realized a tidy profit for the series of terrorist attacks he had undertaken for an anonymous client. Unfortunately, the client had ordered an end to the campaign, saying the situation was becoming too risky. Sergei didn't mind; there were plenty of other ways of making money. At present he was negotiating with the leader of a Japanese fringe religious sect for the sale of a Buran Space Shuttle now in storage at the crumbling Baikonur Cosmodrome in Kazakhstan. Strictly speaking, the spacecraft was not Sergei's to sell, but he had never let that stop him in the past, and if the determined but unpredictable Japanese charismatic stuck to his guns, Sergei would make a killing.

This morning, however, he had more mundane things

on his mind. One of his lieutenants had called with a request for an Ilyushin transport plane. It was a routine matter; Sergei had been leasing the Russian army transport planes for some time, through a company based in New Zealand that was his legal cover.

The man had explained that he was in negotiations with an American movie producer who, in addition to the plane, needed two hundred soldiers who would be used as extras in the movie he was making. His lieutenant wanted to know how much to charge for the plane; he said he had already closed a price of thirty dollars a day per head for the soldiers. Ten thousand American a day for the plane, Sergei said. The whole deal, Sergei knew, would hardly cover his caviar bill for the month, but he liked to keep his men busy, and not every deal could be worth millions. He knew his lieutenant was already making money above and beyond what Sergei would pay him, but if Sergei ever needed someone's dirty job handled well or someone killed on short notice, he knew he could count on Igor and Alexi, and that was worth all the money in the world.

Later, back at the house, Edward listened while Igor explained the details of the deal to him. He had twenty-four hours to come up with a large deposit, but then the plane and the soldiers could be delivered to the airport of his choice. A full flight crew was included in the deal.

"One question," said Edward. "How much is the plane going to cost me?"

Alexi and Igor exchanged a few words in Russian, and

then Igor said, "The standard rate is fifteen thousand U.S. dollars per day."

Very reasonable, Edward thought, especially since it wasn't his money. Nevertheless, he would have given anything to have had Natalie there to tell him what these Russian gangsters were saying to each other in their native tongue. Had he known, a rough translation of what Alexi had said to Igor was: "Never give a sucker an even break."

Zagorsk, Russia
March 23
06:00 hours

The order to mobilize was received early in the morning. The Third Mechanized Battalion of the Sixth Armored Brigade, consisting of T-82 tanks, artillery, troop transports, and support equipment, stirred into life like a slumbering monster of the deep. Orders were shouted in the darkness. A thick smell of diesel oil permeated the chilly air. Truck engines kicked in and revved with a sound like distant thunder.

Their treads biting into the frozen ground, the tanks moved "on foot" toward the waiting trailer carriers. Like giant slugs, they crawled on the trailers, the metal of their tracks clanking ominously. It was still dark when the division began moving out of base. Their military police escort closed off traffic ahead of them on the main highway to Moscow, some seventy kilometers to the south.

With the lights of the city in view, they fanned out

to the west. Their orders were to secure the plain north of Moscow, including the two Sheremetyevo airports, from unauthorized movements of any kind: cars, trucks, or women on bicycles. The rules of engagement for this operation were simple and harsh: Open fire at any intruders in their security zone. In a short speech their commander had made to them over the base speaker system, he explained that the future of Russia was in their hands. They were entrusted with the security of a strategic zone for the upcoming visit by the president of the United States, and security had to be absolute. The eyes of the world would be on them.

The trailers unloaded the tanks in the lee of a ridge that swept east and west across the plain. Their positioning was such that no silhouette of their sinister bulk would be seen on the horizon to provide a target for an antitank missile attack.

Morale was high among the troops who jumped out of the transport trucks to take their positions. They were glad to be doing something, glad to be showing their muscle, glad to get out of the base for a while. Tents, field kitchens, and a command post were quickly set up. By dawn, they could see the Ninety-eighth Mechanized Mountain Brigade positioned on their western flank and the Second Mechanized to their east. As Moscow and its suburbs got ready for another day, the entire plain was secured by a ring of steel.

Inside the command post, Major Lermontov spoke to his radio operator.

"What frequency are you on?"

"Seventy-four point three eight."

"It has been changed," said Lermontov. "You will now use frequency eighty-nine point seven one."

"Yes, sir." As the operator adjusted the settings there was a crackle of static, then communication was established.

"It's done, sir."

Lermontov took the receiver in his hand and pressed the button as he spoke. "Lima Zulu Alpha, this is Tiger Five. Come in, over."

After a short pause and a static crackle the answer came. "This is Lima Zulu Alpha, go ahead Tiger Five. Over."

"We are at point Tango Five Nine Two, over."

"Tiger Five, this is Lima Zulu Alpha, reading you loud and clear. Vortex One sends his greetings. Over and out."

CG Command Bunker, outside Moscow
06:20 hours

Lermontov's voice crackled over the radio speaker. As he reeled off the series of codes that verified he was in control of his section, officers and soldiers cheered. The atmosphere in the bunker was of joyful optimism. Everything was moving according to schedule. Every time a commander called in his position, it was clear to the people in the bunker that another stretch of strategic real estate had been occupied without a fight.

A soldier at a console by the radio who had read the preceded message back to Lermontov was already receiving another incoming message. If there was any deviation from what he had expected in the incoming messages he was to contact the duty officer. Otherwise he was to give the standard answer and enter the positioning of the unit in question into the central computer. With each set of coordinates that was entered, new lights appeared on the illuminated map of Moscow on the wall in the CIC room. Around the northern end of the city, a ring of red lights indicated that the Black Ghosts' hold on Sheremetyevo Airport and the main highways was virtually total.

At a second workstation, similar information was being received and posted from another radio. These coordinates were fed into a map showing the entire region from the Baltic to the Urals, and from the Barents Sea to the Black Sea. Here, too, red lights began to spring up around all the major cities, indicating the range and depth of the Black Ghosts' power.

The third workstation was connected to the large map that spanned the entire continent. Anywhere that mattered, from Novosibirsk to Vladivostok, red dots were beginning to appear.

Colonel Yakov walked down from the control room to General Rogov's private office. He knocked at the door. After stepping in, he stood to attention and saluted. He had been working with the general for several weeks on a daily basis, but still he couldn't shake the sense of awe he felt in the man's presence.

"Well?" said Peter, waiting for the officer to speak.

"You asked that I inform you once we had closed the ring around Moscow."

"And?"

"Moscow is practically ours. We have secured the two northern airports, and all the main roads are also under our control."

"What about the other airports?"

"Vnukovo and Bykovo are secure, sir."

"And Domodedovo?"

"Domodedovo Airport is guarded by the Fourth Armored Brigade, sir, under the command of Lieutenant-Colonel Orlov. He's not one of us. Orlov was a close friend of General Kozov's, sir."

"As long as he stays at Domodedovo, it's fine. The American president will land in Sheremetyevo. Are you sure we have control there?"

"Yes, sir, it's safely in our hands."

"Good, good. And how are the regions progressing?"

"We have reports coming in from Leningrad, Gorky, and Saratov. All will be under our control by nightfall. Sverdlovsk and Chelyabinsk should be reporting soon."

"Any reaction from the Supreme Command?"

"We should know by tonight. So far, our sources indicate that the military suspects nothing. Their exercises are blending perfectly with our operation."

"No questions asked?"

"Apparently not." Colonel Yakov permitted himself a cautious smile. "To the Supreme Command, it is only logical that the best, most strongly motivated units be deployed. And the best units are ours, sir."

"Of course, of course," nodded Peter. "Now. What is the status of the communication array?"

"Fully assembled, sir."

"Carry on, Colonel." Peter dismissed him with a wave of his hand.

Hertzen Street, Moscow
10:20 hours

Yazarinksy leaned on the driving wheel, his eyes still, his head slowly moving from one side to the other like a shark searching for its prey, scanning the crowds that filled the sidewalks outside the TASS Building. He was parked near the corner of Hertzen Street and the Boulevard Ring, in full view of the round-cornered windows from which Russian media people have looked to the world for the last fifty years. He could still remember the good old days, not so long ago, when the news was made inside that building rather then collected outside. A much more efficient and positive system, he thought.

A young, attractive woman caught his eye, her light brown hair blowing in the chilly air as she walked briskly down the street. Yazarinsky leaned over and was about to open the door when he realized as she came closer that it wasn't the woman he was waiting for. He let her pass by unmolested.

He did not mistake her a second time. There she was, walking directly toward him. He opened the passenger door and the woman got in beside him.

"Greetings, Major Androva," he said, his mouth dry. He was not very accustomed to talking to women, especially women as beautiful as this one. Young boys whom he could easily impress were his preference.

"Greetings, Colonel," she said, her tone neutral. She did not like Yazarinsky and preferred to deal with him as little as possible. She was not particularly pleased that it was he who had been sent to pick her up. Surely the general had other men at his disposal.

Perhaps reading her mind, Yazarinksy spoke carefully. "Owing to the sensitivity of your mission, General Rogov asked me personally to come and ensure your safety."

"Delighted, I'm sure," murmured Major Androva. Yazarinksy did not miss her ironic tone. Although she was technically his junior, he felt a need to impress her, to gain her favor.

"The general has expressed his appreciation for what you have done for us."

"I'm so very pleased. I believe we shouldn't keep the general waiting." There was silence.

Abandoning all attempts at conversation, Yazarinsky concentrated on driving. Within an hour they had cleared the confines of the city and were speeding eastward along a country road.

CG Command Bunker, outside Moscow
13:10 hours

The intercom on Peter's desk buzzed. "Colonel Yazarinksy and Major Androva have arrived, sir."

"Send Major Androva in immediately. Yazarinsky can wait."

He had barely finished his sentence when the door opened and Major Androva stepped into the general's private quarters. Peter got up and walked around the desk to greet her, hands outstretched, a twitch to his lip that passed for a smile.

"Kalinka," he said.

She smiled at this use of her childhood nickname, the one her father, the general's best friend, had always used. Her father had been a diplomat. For several years he was head of the KGB station at the Soviet Embassy in Washington, and Major Androva had spent a good part of her childhood there. Her father and the general had been friends since before she was born. It was at the veterans hospital in Gorky, where he was dying of cancer, that he had told his daughter of his plans for the Black Ghosts and had Rogov promise to take care of her and find her a place in the new world order when the time came.

Looking at her, Peter realized he had not seen a finer-looking woman in a very long time. Perhaps, if things went well . . . But this was not the time to be thinking about that. He brought his mind back to the business in hand. "Was your mission successful?"

"Very much so."

"Please, have a seat. Did you bring the component?"

"Yes," said Androva. She reached inside her blue duffel bag and pulled out a small integrated circuit board, which she handed to the general. When he saw it, his eyes lit up.

"Just a minute." He pressed the intercom.

"Yes, general," came a metallic voice.

"Is Nazirov from communications there?"

"Yes, sir."

"Send him in."

A tall, jittery man entered. He stood at an awkward attention, saluting with some effort to avoid tilting over.

"Okay, Nazirov," said the general. "That's enough pageantry for one day." He handed him the circuit board. "Here. Install this in the communication array."

"Sir." The man took the component and looked at it closely. "We already have this component in place, sir. What is this for?"

"The one you have is no good, it's a fake." The general's voice was without passion. "This one will work."

"Yes, sir." The man tried to salute again and left the room.

"What do they call them in the West, nerds?" said Peter. "He could probably get you a line to the moon using a sardine can, but he can't stand up straight." They both laughed.

"Well done, Kalinka. I think this calls for a little celebration." Peter opened his desk drawer and took out a bottle of vodka and two glasses which he placed on the table, filling them to the brim with the clear liquid.

"Major Androva," said Peter, raising his glass, "what you have done will be written in the history books of Russia. I can assure you of that. To Russia!"

"To Russia!" Androva said with a grin, and they finished off their glasses in a single draft.

"Another?" said Peter.

"In a moment."

"As you wish. Now, tell me, what of our American friend?"

"I'm afraid I can tell you nothing. I lost contact with him at the Grave of the Unknown Soldier. I have no idea where he is now. Did you not have him under surveillance?"

Peter sighed. "We tried, but by the time Colonel Sokolov's men got to his hotel, he had vanished. A most regrettable situation. Do you have any idea of who it was that he was supposed to meet at the Grave of the Unknown Soldier?"

"None whatsoever. But it seems certain that it was someone from our organization."

"Dammit," said Peter, banging his fist on the table. "We have to find out who is the traitor among us."

Major Androva smiled sweetly. "We still can. I'm sure Edward will be getting in touch with me soon. After all, to him I'm still Natalie."

CHAPTER 19

"Okay, Richy, let's hear it," President Bradshawe said to his old friend.

"Well, Jim, I must say I feel much better about the situation in Russia than I did before."

"And what, may I ask, brought about this new perspective?"

"These," said Townes, placing a folder on the president's desk. The two men were alone in the Oval Office, a tray of coffee and Danish on the table between them.

"What's in there?"

"Satellite photos of Western Russia. And a series of shots of Moscow. I wanted to bring them over myself the moment they came in."

"What's in them that we didn't know before?"

"I wasn't sure whether Konyigin could get the army to do what he wants. He said he was going to take special precautions before the summit and . . . well, we both know the man's a pathological liar—he'd say anything to get his way. But this time I believe he came through." Townes leaned over the desk and opened the file. "Look," he said, pointing to red markings on the glossy satellite photos. "I had the analysts mark them. You can see. If I didn't know better, I'd say the army was taking over. But the boys over at Langley said they have read communiqués coming out of the Kremlin, positioning every single unit to where it's deployed."

"I guess the terrorist activity really lit a fire under Konyigin. The bastard obviously knows how to get things done when he wants to." The president was satisfied. "So I take it you're no longer opposed to this trip?"

"I'd still prefer if he was coming here, Jim. But under the circumstances, I guess we're going to Moscow."

"I'm glad you see it that way, Richy. There was no way this trip was going to be canceled, but having you onside means a lot to me."

After a brief internal battle with himself, the president took another pastry from the tray. He bit into it, depositing a small amount of strawberry jelly in the corner of his mouth.

"Who else is coming along?" Townes asked, returning the photos to the file.

"Everybody, I guess. You know how that is, Richy. If you're in Washington during a summit, it means you're out of the loop."

"Are we bringing any civilians along?"

"Sure, we'll have some business people, make it look

like whatever we'll be giving the Russians is from private pockets. Besides, we need to let the metal-eaters have first pick at the Russian market—after all, they're the ones who lost the most out of this peace. If they have to shoulder the so-called peace dividend, we should at least let them plunder the other side's natural resources."

"So I take it Hubert Austin and his associates will be along."

"Don't forget I owe him."

"How come?"

"He's my biggest contributor. If it wasn't for him and some of his friends, I don't think I would have made it to New Hampshire, never mind the White House."

"I don't like him. He gives me the willies."

"Well, Richy, as long as he keeps giving me the dough, you will learn to like him."

"Are we going to stop in London?"

"I guess we have to," said the president. "A courtesy visit, if nothing else. Not that the Brits have been very courteous to us lately."

"Why bother, then?"

"Habit, I guess." The president shrugged philosophically. "If they want to kid themselves they are an important part of the new world order, we have nothing to lose by humoring them."

He reached into his pocket for the tube of Rolaids. "By the way," he said, washing down the tablets with the last of his coffee, "any more developments on our special project?"

Townes' face darkened. "I was getting to that. Jim,

things have turned out rather badly, I'm afraid. The person we had on the job screwed up. I don't know how, exactly, but we've lost contact with him. It could be that he himself is one of the Patriots."

President Bradshawe's face wore an angry frown. "Richy, I told you we needed your best people on this. I was counting on you. What the hell went wrong?"

Townes shifted in his seat, embarrassed. "I don't know. But I'm going to find out, don't you worry. As soon as we've finished dealing with the Russians, I can promise you that the Patriot problem will be solved once and for all."

11:15 hours

"The London stop is no problem," James Fenton, the head of the president's Secret Service detail, said to Terry Kay, the president's personal secretary. "It'll be the usual routine. Hourglass lands at Heathrow, from there to No. 10, then Chequers for the night. Then Heathrow first thing. That should put us out of there by 8 a.m."

"So we land in Moscow when?"

Fenton leafed through his papers. "Around eleven. That gives us about an hour to get to the Kremlin for the official reception at twelve noon."

"What's that in New York time?"

"Ah, 4 a.m., I believe."

"So no live news coverage. Too bad." Kay's mouth turned downward.

Fenton was still less happy about the situation. All intelligence reports stated that terrorist activity in Russia had been quelled, and that Moscow itself was heavily fortified with Russian troops and mechanized divisions. Still, he had worked for too long in the shadow of the Cold War to feel comfortable about large concentrations of Russian troops, even if they were allies now and there to defend his president.

Fenton had requested that a company of U.S. Marines be allowed to take positions around Sheremetyevo Airport. But the Russians had balked at that. They said they were perfectly capable of assuring the security of the president and his entourage, and that the presence of American soldiers on Russian soil would not only be completely unnecessary, but also a veiled insult to Russia, implying that Russian soldiers were too weak to do the job properly themselves.

Fenton had to admit they had a point. He couldn't imagine a company of Russian soldiers, except perhaps a ceremonial guard of honor or military band, being allowed to goose-step their way across the tarmac of Dulles International Airport. So why should the Russians allow GIs into Sheremetyevo? Still, he would have felt much better if those Marines could be there, instead of Russian troops.

Leaving these difficulties aside, things could have been worse. The Moscow detail of the Secret Service, working out of the U.S. Embassy, reported that they were getting full cooperation from the Russian military and special security forces, which was something, at least. And Fenton had ensured that the itinerary and schedule were cast iron and watertight.

"We'll have four identical limos backed up to where the president comes out of the plane," he explained to Kay. "There'll be a minimal reception at the airport—the Russian foreign minister, a couple of other dignitaries, that's all. A very quick handshake, no fanfare, and then into the limo. I personally will decide which limo he gets into as we land. We go straight to the Kremlin. The Russian security people have explained that they will have the Kremlin guarded by a crack airborne elite corps, which will be put in place shortly before we land. I tell you, I'm not going to feel safe until we have the president safely inside the Kremlin, with President Konyigin."

"So our media people are where?" said Kay. In a normal operation of this kind, the president and his immediate entourage would travel in Air Force One, followed or preceded by a second identical plane, in which media people and other logistical and support crews would travel. On occasions there would be a Galaxy transport plane that would bring the president's limousine along. However, Kay was beginning to understand that this was not a normal operation.

"They'll be sent in ahead of time," said Fenton. "To the Kremlin. That's where the big photo-op will be. There'll be a few people at the airport, mostly just taping the arrival. I don't want a lot of media jerks hanging around there."

CHAPTER 20

The telephone message was short and to the point. "Bakery. Pushkin Street. Two o'clock."

The caller did not identify himself. Edward, however, knew Sokolov's voice by now and was relieved.

He asked Alexi, who seemed quite content to hang around the safe house not doing much, if he would drive him downtown. Alexi was only too happy to please, looking at Edward as the goose that laid the proverbial golden egg. He got them to the bakery on Pushkin Street with a few moments to spare. The rain had reduced to a slight drizzle.

"Want me to wait?" asked Alexi.

"Better not. I'll call you if I need a ride back."

"Okay." Alexi nodded and sped off with a screech of tires.

The aroma of baking hung in the air. Edward was

beginning to think Sokolov picked the meeting places just to taunt him, reminding him of his other life, which now seemed to exist in another dimension. But then Sokolov couldn't know about that.

After a few moments of waiting, and still no sign of Sokolov or any of his people, Edward began feeling conspicuous and exposed. He wished the colonel had picked a more discreet rendezvous. The familiar knot of tension in his stomach was tightening.

Edward was worried about Natalie. He had not spoken to her since they had said goodbye at the Grave of the Unknown Soldier. He assumed she had followed Larry's advice and gone to her apartment. He tried to call her a few times but was unable to get her, either at the apartment or at the Hotel Metropole. He didn't dare go to the apartment himself, in case it was under surveillance. He could only hope she was safe. The fear that the Black Ghosts may have gotten to her tore at his insides. He began to devise a plan, resolving to put it into operation as soon as he finished his meeting with Sokolov.

He could feel the tension grow inside him with every passing minute he was made to stand alone on the street. Looking at his watch, he realized he'd been there for less than seven minutes, yet Sokolov was already five minutes late. Even though the "hurry up and wait" rule was almost the motto of the intelligence world, lateness for a clandestine meeting was never a good sign. Edward had just decided to give the man five more minutes and then leave, hoping he would try to contact him again later, when a pale green Lada came to a stop across the street.

This time, the lean-faced colonel was alone, except for the driver. Edward got in, realizing his hair was soaking wet.

"Sorry you had to wait," Sokolov said. "I had to take precautions to be sure I was not being tailed."

"I see. I was starting to worry. Five more minutes and I was out of here."

"I know, but I had to be sure. Otherwise we'd both be sorry."

"Right," Edward said, his mood as dreary as the gray streets through which they were driving.

Sokolov spoke with a note of urgency. "Rogov has managed to get his own elite corps to be selected as the Kremlin Guard. President Konyigin will have a nasty surprise when he realizes the troops that have secured the Kremlin are loyal to the Black Ghosts."

"When will those troops be sent in?" asked Edward.

"Early on the morning of the American president's visit. They'll be flown in to Sheremetyevo and then taken by truck to the Kremlin."

"Who will command them?"

"I'm to command them."

"Then we don't really have a problem, do we?"

"What do you mean?"

"If you're in command, just put them in some back section of the Kremlin and lock them up."

"It's not that simple. My duty is to coordinate the takeover of the command from the regular Kremlin Guard. The special units have their own commanders who have already been briefed on the operation. If they suspect any deviation from the original plan they will not hesitate to eliminate me."

"Oh shit, that's just great. This Rogov guy seems to be a smart son of a bitch." Edward stared out at the depressing streets. "How about the rest of the operation? Is there any change of plan?"

"Not really. That could be Rogov's only fault."

"What?"

"His almost religious devotion to his plan. He hates changes and regards them as a manifestation of error. As I've told you, the final stages of the plan will be executed when your president's plane is on the tarmac at Sheremetyevo Airport. The troops that are supposedly guarding the airport will surround the plane and hold him hostage. At that time they will activate the communication array, shutting down all normal media broadcasts during this part of the operation. Then he will come to the Kremlin and issue a statement declaring himself president, or possibly the new czar of Russia."

"What will he do with Konyigin?"

"He will be unceremoniously shot. As for your president, I don't know what General Rogov has planned for him. But I doubt it will be anything pleasant."

"Are you telling me that this lunatic might kill the president of the United States?"

"Certainly Rogov is capable of this. He even suggested it at one point, although I think I managed to persuade him to change his mind. But as much as he likes to stick to his plan, he is also extremely unpredictable. At the slightest provocation he could lash back in a way that, well, let's just say that anything could happen."

"What about the other airports? Are they in Rogov's hands too?"

"All except Domodedovo. The forces there are under the command of a Lieutenant-Colonel Orlov. I know him, a good man. His loyalty to President Konyigin is unquestionable."

"If we can persuade the president to land at Domodedovo instead, that would buy us some time."

"Undoubtedly. But can you do that? From what I understand of your situation, you are operating on your own."

"We are," Edward said bitterly. "Still, we've got nothing to lose by trying." He sat in silence for a moment, his mind racing. Already he could see how his own plan would have to be modified.

"Listen," he told Sokolov. "I'm going to need a car and a driver. I've been using the people at the safe house where I'm staying, but things are going to get pretty hairy, and I'll need all the help I can get."

"I will send Anton," he gestured toward the driver, "as soon as I can."

"I need to know where the Black Ghosts' command center is."

Sokolov had come prepared for that. He opened his briefcase and took out a map. "You see this marking here?"

"Yes." Edward leaned forward.

"That's where the bunker is."

"And the communication array?" asked Edward.

"It's housed in the bunker."

"Have they tried to operate it yet?"

"I don't know," said Sokolov. "General Rogov is very secretive about it. But I understand that just a few days ago they took delivery of the final part of it, some sort of circuit board."

"Well, we have a few secrets of our own," said Edward.

"What exactly does that mean?"

"Back in the States, Larry switched the activating circuit board with another one. What you have received is in fact what you could call a poison pill. If they activate the array, they destroy it."

"So much the better," said Sokolov, finally smiling. "So there is light at the end of the tunnel."

"Let's just hope it's not an oncoming train," Edward said with a sad grin.

Sokolov turned to the driver and exchanged a few words with him in Russian. In response to Edward's questioning look, he explained. "Anton was making sure we were clean. We can take you to within a few blocks from your safe house."

"No," Edward said. "Just drop me off by one of the subway stations. I'll get there myself."

As they came to a stop, Edward said, "I need a way to get in touch with you. In case of emergency."

"I have an apartment on the Kalinina Prospekt. You can call me there. If I am not there, you can leave a message with whoever answers the phone. It will be quite safe. If you get the answering machine, don't say anything too specific. In fact, if you get the machine, just give a name, say . . . Mikhail. We don't want any messages in English left on my machine."

"Good. And thanks."

"Thanks to you. Anton will meet you here in about two hours."

It took Edward less than twenty minutes to get back to the safe house. If the Russians could only get everything else to work like the subway, Edward thought, they would have no economic problems whatsoever.

At the safe house, Edward found Igor sitting at the oak table. Alexi was lounging in an armchair, smoking an American cigarette and leafing through a dog-eared copy of Playboy. Edward wasted no time.

"Igor, we need to talk."

"Okay, we talk."

"I need an airstrip, my friend."

"What is airstrip?" Igor looked puzzled.

"A place where I can land a plane."

"You mean airport."

"Well, yes, and I need a hangar—you know, where you put airplanes inside."

"I know what hangar is." Igor looked insulted. "How big the hangar?"

"The bigger the better."

"There is an airport, was planned to be for the military outside Moscow. Is near where I grew up. I have uncle who has farm there. There is a big hangar, very big, built for the xxx transport. But I don't know how good the . . ." He gestured with his hand, showing an airplane coming in to land. "I don't know how the road for the airplane to land is any good."

"You mean the runway?"

"Yes. I have to check."

"When will you know?"

"Today. Is that all?" Igor sounded almost disappointed, as though his ability was not being taxed to its fullest.

"Not quite."

"What else then?"

"I need some trucks and weapons."

Alexi looked up from his magazine. A big smile spread across his face. "Now you talkin' baby. What kinda shooter you looking for, cowboy?"

"I'll need light weapons for about twenty men."

"Light like in Kalashnikovs, or M-16?" Igor asked. "You tell me."

"I'll take the AK-47s, with about two thousand rounds per unit. I'll need about six antitank rockets and launchers. Grenades, both attack and defense. Some bungalores, a couple of heavy machine guns . . . What do you have?"

"Anything you want, I get you. This all have to be cash before delivery."

"You get me a price, a list, and then I give you ten percent. When I see the goods, you get the rest."

The man who liked to be called Al Caponesky lowered his head. He said sarcastically, "Why, boy, you not trust mama?"

"No." Edward smiled back. "By the way, what are the chances of this airstrip being secured by the army in the buildup to the president's visit?"

Alexi grinned. "None. The Russian military does as it's told. If the airfield isn't on the list, it doesn't get secured. And since we use it from time to time to bring things we have borrowed in other places, we made sure it wasn't on any list."

"Okay," said Edward. "Let's go for it."

"Okay. I make telephone call." Igor picked up the phone and dialed. From where he sat across the table, Edward could not see the exact number he was dialing, but as far as he could tell, it was the same number he had called the other night.

Igor spoke in Russian. Edward caught the name Sergei, then got lost in the heavy vowels and rasping consonants. But to judge from the cheerful expressions that danced across Igor's mobile features, and the avaricious gleam in his eye, the negotiations were proceeding smoothly.

And so it was. Igor gave Edward the coordinates of the airfield and then left him to get on with the next phase of the operation.

Now that Edward had clear evidence that the president's life was in danger, he knew he at least had to get the Secret Service in on it. Larry's concerns that the entire security system of the United States had been compromised by the infiltration of the Patriots would have to go unanswered. If they had gotten as far as the Secret Service, whose agents were willing if need be to take the bullet, sacrificing their own lives to save the president's, then there was nothing Edward or anyone could do to stop the Black Ghosts.

Gambling that such was not the case, and that there were still a few good men at the disposition of the president, was Edward's only option.

He looked at his watch: 4 p.m. That would make it 8 a.m. in New York. He called the safe house. Joe Falco told him Larry had gone downtown to the office building. It was there that Edward managed to reach him.

"Larry, do you have access to anyone in the Secret Service?"

"Natalie called," Larry said, ignoring Edward's question. "I was about to call you. She said she's waiting at the apartment."

"When did she call?" Edward could feel his heart pounding, a burst of joy overtaking him.

"Not ten minutes ago. I told her to stay put and that you'll find a way to get to her. If you can't, I'll call her and tell her to get out of there."

"No, no. I'll get her out." He felt the burden slowly lifting from his shoulders. She was alive and well, and he was going to see her very soon. "Okay. Now listen, Larry, do you know anyone you can trust in the Secret Service?"

"I may, why?"

"This is not about the Russians anymore, Larry. Now we're talking about the president. We have to stop this goddamn visit."

"That would be great, if I could swing it. If we stopped the visit they would probably cancel the coup."

"No, I think they are committed. The coup will go ahead whether the president comes here or not. The only difference is that we might not have an exact timetable. On the other hand . . ." Edward was thinking aloud. "If they don't know he's not coming, they will go ahead as planned. But then my question is, who cares? I mean, why should we risk our people for them?"

Larry stopped him. "Edward, don't get carried away. For the time being, the president will come. I will have a hard enough time even getting through, not to mention the fact that by now they must think I'm working for the other side anyway. I'll see what I can do, but as far as you're concerned, you know very well that if the bastards take control of Russia, we're all going to be fighting a war."

"What we need," said Edward, lowering his voice, "is to at least persuade the Secret Service to change the destination of the president's plane to Domodedovo. And I need the emergency radio frequency on Air Force One."

"Anything else?" Larry sounded tired and sarcastic. "All right, all right, I'll see what I can do. This isn't going to be easy, you know."

"Why?"

"Why? Because we're dealing with a bunch of bureaucratic . . ."

"No, why should I care how easy it is?"

"Ha, ha," Larry said.

"And Larry, make it quick. Things are going to start happening very soon around here. I need our boys here as quickly as possible."

"Where are you going to land them?"

"We have an abandoned airfield outside Moscow." He gave Larry the coordinates. "How soon can you get them here?"

Larry thought for a moment. "There's still some work to do on the plane. Then it's a twelve-hour flight. Say twenty-four hours. How are they supposed to come in, I mean radar and all that?"

Edward asked to talk to one of the two pilots. He instructed him to find a commercial flight and lose it during the descent. He would have to make it the rest of the way flying very low, but Alexi had assured Edward that there was a radar-free corridor leading up to the airstrip. He gave the pilot the entry point Alexi had given him and asked if what he had said made any sense.

"I read you loud and clear."

"Can you bring a plane that big in without detection?"

"With the information you gave me, I could bring in an aircraft carrier if you could get it to fly."

"Good. See you soon. And Dan, let me talk to Larry again." When Larry was back on the line, Edward said, "Put Sparky on a commercial flight to Moscow right away. I don't want to wait that long for him to get here. I have work for him."

"Where should he go when he arrives? The airfield?"

"No, I'll pick him up. Call me back when you have the flight number and ETA."

"You got it."

Edward hung up, satisfied that, as regards the operation, he had done all he could for the time being. Now he had to get Natalie, and for that he would need help.

He found Alexi slumped in front of one of the stolen televisions, sipping from a chipped teacup. The cup held a clear liquid that obviously was not water.

"Are you interested in making some money on the side?"

"Always. Come to think of it, that's the only way I ever make money," Alexi answered, not taking his eyes off the TV screen.

"It involves a little driving."

Alexi shifted his large, heavy limbs. "No problem."

"Are you sure you're okay to drive?" Edward gestured toward the chipped cup. From where he stood, he could smell the vodka fumes.

Alexi grinned lopsidedly. "Like I said, always."

"Okay. First you drive me to the subway. Then I want you to drive to this address." Edward handed Alexi a paper. "It's an apartment. There'll be a woman there. I need you to bring her here in safety."

"A woman!" said Alexi, leering suggestively. "Is she cute?"

"That's not the point," Edward said impatiently. "The point is, somebody may be watching the apartment."

"I guess she is cute, then," said Alexi, laughing loudly. "Don't worry." Alexi took him by the shoulder, still grinning. "I can help you find your little piece of tail."

Edward took a deep breath. "Okay, fine," he said, his voice calmer. "I said, the apartment may be under surveillance. So here's what I want you to do." As he spoke, the urgency of the situation seemed to increase in Edward's mind. He could imagine the soldiers knocking on the door, dragging Natalie screaming into their truck, pushing her into their interrogation rooms, torture chambers . . . With every passing moment, he could feel the chances increasing that his nightmare might become a reality. Now that he knew where she was and that she was waiting for him to rescue her, not making it in time was unthinkable.

With agonizing slowness, Alexi got to his feet and lumbered to the washroom. Ten minutes later he was ready to depart. At last, with a crash of gears as Alexi maneuvered the Volkswagen out of its parking spot in front of the building, they drove off.

With time to spare, Edward arrived at the subway stop where he was to meet Anton. Alexi drove back to the safe house in the pale green Lada.

Now all Edward could do was wait, again. He sat in an armchair, staring into space, trying to think of nothing, trying to calm his jangling nerves and steel himself for the next part of the operation.

"Hurry up," he said to himself. "Hurry up and wait."

CHAPTER 21

Brownstone office building, West 24th Street, New York City
March 26
08:15 hours

"Easy for you to say," Larry mumbled to himself as he got off the phone with Edward. "I've got the whole of the U.S. intelligence community out to get me, and you want me to walk into the Secret Service and persuade them that I know what's best for the president."

In a universe where no one was where he was supposed to be but wanted you to leave your name and number after the beep and they would get back to you soon, Larry in his precarious situation was somewhat constrained. He had to make direct contact on a personal level with a person he couldn't reach. There was no one he could leave his name and number with, no one he could trust not to send in the crew-cuts to pick him off. As regards all the legitimate channels, Larry was persona non grata.

He had one hope. Years back, he had shared a convivial

evening with an up-and-coming Secret Service operative, his wife, and a few other guests at their home in Silver Spring. James Fenton and Larry had always gotten along well when their professional paths had crossed, something that happened quite frequently after Larry was transferred to headquarters at Langley and saddled with a desk. Larry knew that if the whole damn world went berserk, Fenton would be standing there against all odds, defending his president.

Larry had no phone number and wouldn't have risked it even if he had. But maybe, if he could just remember where the house was . . .

By the time Jean-Pierre had the minibus fueled and ready to go, Mario had already rounded up the platoon, and they were getting ready to move.

Standing in the living room was a group of people who until only days ago had been strangers to one another, with nothing in common except a shared background. They were now a cohesive unit. They could read each other's gestures and had an abundance of the inside jokes that were the fruit of tough training and mutual trust.

Larry opened an attaché case and handed each of them an envelope. "There's a grand apiece," he said. "We're going to the airport together. You're all going to catch the same flight, but you each buy your own ticket. We don't want to attract any attention. You can leave behind whatever you don't need for the operation. It will all be here when you come back."

"If we come back," Doug Findley said.

They all laughed in approval.

"Okay," said Larry, playing along, "if you come back your stuff will be here. If not, we'll have a garage sale, okay?"

Within half an hour, they were on their way to LaGuardia Airport, still telling morbid jokes and laughing. Larry gave them the location of the airfield where the stolen 747 was waiting. One of the pilots was still with the plane, and Larry assured them that once they got to the airfield they would have quite a bit of work to do. "Get some rest on the flight over, and don't get yourselves plastered."

Larry dropped the somewhat rowdy bunch at LaGuardia, reminding them to be on their best behavior as there was no time to bail anyone out of trouble. "If you get yourselves into shit, you're out of this game and on your own."

Next, Larry drove Sparky to JFK Airport, with instructions to call Edward from London with the details of his flight into Moscow. Then he got on the road again, heading southwest.

Traffic was heavy on Highway 95, and it seemed to take much longer than usual to drive to Washington. Larry's chest was aching, and at times he had the feeling he was not going to make it. He would have preferred to fly, but not having any false documents to buy tickets, he wasn't going to risk the registration. Flying from Utah to New York had been a calculated risk, but flying into Washington was asking for trouble. He was too well known on the Beltway to pass unnoticed.

By the time he got to Silver Springs, it was already

midafternoon. Now to find the house. He drove through a maze of suburban streets, following a vague memory and a clear instinct. Almost without conscious effort, he found himself on a quiet street with large, red brick houses nestling in deep green foliage. Which one was it? He remembered asking himself the same question the first time he had come here. Then he remembered that it was the house with the tall pine tree in the front garden. He rang the bell.

When the door opened, she was exactly as he remembered her: brown bob of hair, lots of teeth, a friendly face. It took her a moment to place him, but then she was all smiles.

"Larry! Yes, of course I remember. Come right in. Here, let me take your coat."

She sat in a leather armchair and waved Larry to the sofa.

Larry remained standing. "Sorry I can't stay," he said. "It's business, you see. Is Jim around?"

She frowned slightly.

"I really need to get ahold of him. It's urgent."

Mrs. Fenton made a face. "You just missed him, I'm afraid. He's going to England with you-know-who. He left about a half hour ago."

"I see. Oh, boy."

"Can I help? I mean, what's this all about?"

"Nothing, just business."

"Don't give me that, Larry. Jim doesn't bring his work home. Tell me, maybe I can help."

"I need to talk to him. It has to do with the president."

Her expression became serious. "Why don't you call the office?"

"I don't know who I can trust. It's a long story, but I know I can trust your husband."

"That you can, but you better not be playing games with him, Larry. He can be very mean if you play games with him."

"This is not a game." He walked over to the door, then turned back to face her. "I understand your concern, but you have to trust me. I believe it was your husband who kept saying that good security is ninety percent gut instinct."

She nodded, smiling, as if she enjoyed her husband's sayings even when repeated by others.

"I need to talk to him in person, and not some aide or another. Do you know where he'll be staying in London?"

"Larry, I'm surprised at you. You know I couldn't tell you that, even if I knew. The best I can do is talk to him about you when he calls. If he wants to speak to you, he'll give me a number for you to call."

Larry knew she had an emergency number she could call and reach him. It was one of the few perks of being married to the president's praetorian guard. He also knew she couldn't tell him about it. He decided to play along. "That's great." Larry smiled and gave a little bow. "I would very much appreciate that and will be in your debt forever."

"Don't overdo it, Larry. By the way, is the president in any immediate danger, I mean in the next few hours?"

He realized she'd been around this block more than once. "No, not in the next few hours."

"So call me back later tonight."

"Thanks again." Larry walked out with a degree of hope, which was something.

He headed back to New York, but after an hour of driving he realized it was going to be too much for him. His chest was hurting and he needed to take his medication, which in itself was draining his strength. He checked into a roadside motel and decided it was as good a place as any to while away the time until he could make the call.

By 7:45 he could wait no more. He called back Mrs. Fenton. She had spoken to her husband, who had said he could be reached at the Grosvenor Hotel in London the following day. Larry thanked her again. He set his alarm for 3 a.m. That, he estimated, should give enough time for the president and his entourage, which included Mr. Fenton, to get there. He then grabbed a few hours' sleep.

When the alarm went off, Larry was already awake. His inner clock and the importance of the job in hand combined to make a very potent wake-up call. He showered and got coffee and doughnuts from the all-night diner. Then it was time to call. Using Edward's phone card, he dialed the Grosvenor Hotel in London.

"I believe you have a guest there by the name of James Fenton?"

"Just a moment, sir, I'll check."

Larry thought Richard Townes and Bud Hays were probably along for the trip. He was convinced that at least one of those two men would sooner see him dead than succeed in what he was trying to do. It was still hard for him to believe that someone so close to the president could be working against him. But a question arose from that: Was the man knowingly working against American interests, or did he believe that it was precisely those interests he was working for? Or was it all just money?

Larry's only chance to get something done was Fenton. He had to make the man listen.

The receptionist came back on the line. "We do have a guest by that name, sir, but he's not answering his phone. Would you like to leave a message?"

"No, I'll call back."

By the time dawn broke, Larry was back on the road.

CHAPTER 22

Safe house, Moscow
March 26
18:00 hours

Edward wasn't quite sure of his whereabouts. He was walking out of the jungle in Cambodia right on to a sand dune in Iraq when something started ringing. He looked for his gun but it wasn't there. The ringing persisted and he recognized it as the phone on the oak table at Al Caponeski's house. He opened his eyes. He was up, out of the armchair and running toward the ringing phone even before he was fully awake. But Igor got to it first.

"Da, da. Here, it's Alexi. For you." Igor handed him the receiver.

"Hello?"

"Hi, boss." Alexi sounded pleased. "We're at the pay phone, like you said. And she is very much, how you say, she is woman, she can roar. You want to rap with her?"

"Yes, put her on . . . Hello? Natalie?"

When he heard her voice, it sounded like water

bubbling in a parched desert. "Edward? Thank God, I was so worried about you. What happened? Who is this gorilla? Why didn't you call me?"

"Are you okay?" He wanted to ask her a million questions and apologize, explain that he hadn't abandoned her, that there was a reason for everything he had done . . .

"I'm fine, I guess. But Edward, I miss you."

"Where were you? I tried to call the hotel as soon as I knew I couldn't go back there and . . ."

"I got worried, so I left the hotel and went to stay with some friends. Then I went to see if the apartment was being watched. I checked it several times and when I figured that there was no one there, I went in. I was hoping I'd hear from you. Larry called, and then this . . . thing showed up. Where are you?"

"In a safe house. I want you to come here."

"Now?"

"Yes, I just want to make sure you're not being followed. Go with Alexi. Do what he tells you and we'll be together real soon."

"Okay, I can't wait to see you."

Edward had a few more words to say to Alexi, then he went into the other room to talk to Anton, Sokolov's driver, who was sitting silently and patiently in an armchair. Leaving Igor sitting at the oak table, they left the house.

Their first stop was a bar on Stanislav Street. Edward sat at a table by the window, while Anton sat in the car.

After about ten minutes, Edward saw Natalie and Alexi walking around the corner.

Edward had told Alexi to park the Volkswagen about three blocks away and to walk along the street, turning left when they got to the end. Edward watched the street after they had passed, and so did Anton, only from a different angle. There was no activity behind the two walking figures.

Next Anton drove to Sovietskaya Square, where he parked by the statue of Prince Dolgoruky. As Edward had instructed him, Alexi showed up with Natalie a few minutes later. They passed right in front of the car. Natalie was so close that Edward wanted to clutch her in his arms, and he could almost smell her fragrance. Again the street behind them was free of any tail. Edward could say with some assurance that they were clean.

Anton swung the car out of the square in the direction Alexi and Natalie were heading. They found them waiting a couple of blocks up. Edward gave Alexi the thumbs-up as they passed by the parked Volkswagen, and the two cars drove back to the safe house.

After they had finished the introductions, Edward took Natalie to the small room that had become his bedroom. Alexi was hanging around at the door, a wolfish grin on his face.

"You were right," he said in a stage whisper as they passed him to go into the room, "she's cute." He gave Edward a dig in the ribs, and then Edward shut the door firmly in his face. Natalie threw her coat over the back of a chair, then turned to face Edward, a smile of joyous welcome on her face.

It felt so good to hold her in his arms. She leaned her head on his shoulder. Then she pulled him down on the bed. There was something frantic about the way they undressed each other. It was as though they wanted to reassure themselves that the other was still whole, unharmed. Her smell filled his flared nostrils, the blood pumping hard through his body. Her skin was soft, warm, her hands cool. There was a hunger, a need to please in the way she moved. He could feel a difference in her already: She was more aggressive, more confident.

Afterward, Edward felt a deep sense of peace as they lay quietly in each other's arms, their breathing slow. Whatever the future held, he had this moment, this feeling to remember. He was part of the great rhythm of life, which flowed in and out of him like a breath. It was all he needed. For now, he was content.

"Edward," said Natalie, getting up on one elbow, "you haven't said anything about the operation. How's it going?"

Edward smiled up at her, unwilling to leave behind this moment of tranquillity. "It's fine."

"Good." She smiled, too, settling down beside him and laying her head on his chest. They slept until morning.

When Edward awoke, his mind was working again, only calmer than before and with greater clarity. He could picture the interplay of forces, the variables he had to contend with, like a three-dimensional illuminated model in his mind. He could see the many details that needed settling. Had Larry managed to get a frequency to the president's plane?

"What are you thinking?" asked Natalie, her voice sweetly plaintive.

"About Larry. I told him to try to get them to change the airport the president is going to land at."

"Why?"

"I think they're going to try something at Sheremetyevo. So I told him to switch to Domodedovo."

"Hmm." Natalie snuggled closer to him. He sensed that she understood him, that she knew whatever he was saying was important but could hold it inside her along with all the other stuff, the emotions, the love, the passion.

"And did he?" she said.

"What?"

"Change the airport?"

"I don't know. He didn't get back to me yet."

"What else has been happening? How are the boys?"

"They should be on their way here," he checked his watch, "right about now."

"Really?" Natalie's eyes were wide. "Here, to this house?"

"No. We've got a farmhouse and an airfield."

"Where?"

Edward was trying to remember. "What did he say about it? Oh yeah, it's an . . ." Just then there was a sharp knock at the door, and Alexi came in with two steaming mugs of tea. "I brought some refreshment for our sexual athletes in here," he said, grinning his lecherous grin.

Edward was about to utter a sharp rebuke. The man

was starting to get on his nerves. But Natalie reached up with a smile of gratitude and took one of the mugs. Alexi ogled her exposed breast, and then, under Edward's angry glare, set the other mug down beside the bed, turned and walked back to the door. "Your friend Sparky called," said Alexi. "He's coming 2:05 p.m., Flight 809 from Heathrow."

"Why didn't you let me talk to him?" asked Edward.

"I not want to disturb you sleeping," said Alexi, grinning again. "Or trucking, or whatever," he added significantly.

Edward had to resist the temptation to throw the hot mug at the man's retreating figure. The door closed behind him, leaving them in peace.

Natalie worked herself into a sitting position to drink her tea. "This is good," she said, sipping the hot liquid. "I was getting cold."

Edward reached to the chair and pulled at Natalie's coat. As it fell toward him, a shiny object slithered out of the pocket.

"Ooh, what have we here?" said Edward, picking up the polished steel handle. "Haven't seen one of these in a while." He pressed the switch, and the filed stiletto blade shot out. He tested the edge and the point with his finger. "Sharp too. Where did you get it?"

"Had it for years," said Natalie. "I kept it in the apartment for, well, you know, a single girl in a foreign city . . . When your big ugly bear came to pick me up, I wasn't sure if he was on the up and up, so I just slipped it in my pocket. Seemed like a reasonable precaution." She drank.

"I don't blame you." Edward closed the switchblade

and slipped it under his pillow. "Still, I'm glad you're on my side."

She laughed, setting her mug down. He took her arm and pulled her gently toward him. They kissed. Soon they were united again, bathing their souls in a glowing river of passion. The room was suddenly warm again. Natalie looked serene, and Edward wished he could know what she was thinking behind those big blue eyes.

She smiled: If he only knew. She enjoyed him like a toy. It felt good playing with him one last time before throwing him at Rogov's feet. He was so vulnerable and trusting that it almost made her sick. She knew anyone who was so trusting could never amount to much. He disappointed her; he was no match for her. He lacked the cunning of a real man. He was too gentle, even in the way he made love.

She had contemplated using the blade on him. She knew she could surprise the other men and take them after finishing him off. She had planned the whole thing: showing up at the door naked, calling them in one at a time, stacking their bodies in the corner. But it was better to wait. Now she had useful information to take back to General Rogov. And if she bided her time, she probably could get more. She sighed, stretched, and lay her head down beside his.

The heavy smell of kasha, onions, eggs, and thick, greasy potato pancakes forced its way with a heavy hand into the bedroom, drawing them out like a smoke bomb. Igor had prepared a Russian breakfast and cordon bleu it was not, but it went down well.

From this point on, Edward knew he would have very little rest. He had to pace himself. He was now locked into the general's timetable, and he knew he had only one advantage: the element of surprise.

"I want you to go back to New York," he said to Natalie after they had finished eating.

"Why?" Natalie sounded hurt. "I've come this far with you. Can't I stay and help?"

Edward shook his head. "It's too dangerous."

"I'm not afraid." She fixed Edward with a calm and steady look.

For a moment he was tempted to let her stay with him. "There's no point in putting you in harm's way."

Reluctantly, Natalie agreed. There were more things she wanted to ask, but she knew it would raise his suspicions if she overdid it.

Relieved, Edward said that Anton would drive her to the airport. He was leaving anyway, to pick up Sparky, who was due to arrive soon.

"First I have to go back to my apartment," she said. "I left all my stuff there."

"What stuff?"

"My passport, everything."

Edward looked at his watch. He didn't want Sparky waiting alone at the airport, and there was not time for Anton to go to Natalie's apartment before meeting Sparky's flight.

"We can boogie," said Alexi, who had been sitting in silence, reading the newspaper. "It be pleasure to have such sexy chick in my car." He winked at her.

Edward was about to favor Alexi with a few well-chosen insults, but Natalie, glancing quickly at Alexi and then at the watchful Anton, said, "That would be great. Thank you."

So it was decided. Anton did not apparently speak much English, but with the help of Igor's translation services, he was given a description of Sparky and sent off to meet him.

"I'm ready," she said. "You're not coming to see me off?"

"I can't. I have to wait for Larry to get back to me."

They said goodbye at the door. Edward watched her and Alexi get into the Volkswagen and drive away. Everything was coming together just fine, he thought.

CHAPTER 23

There was bad news waiting for Larry when he got back to the safe house. Joe Falco was sitting in his wheelchair in the living room. On the coffee table was a small metallic object.

"Look what I found," Joe said grimly, pointing at the object.

Larry picked it up. There was no doubt what it was, an electronic listening device.

"Where?" he asked in a low voice, suddenly conscious of the fact that there could be more of them. He looked around the room.

"Right here under the coffee table."

"Did you check the rest of the house?"

"Downstairs, yes. It's clean. Upstairs, I had a problem." He shrugged apologetically. Larry carried him upstairs and then went back for his wheelchair. Together they made a thorough sweep. There were no more bugs.

"Who could have put it there?" asked Larry, half to himself.

"Beats me. Somebody must have got in while we were at the office downtown."

Larry tried to think back to all the discussions they'd had in that room. He had to assume the worst, that every word had been passed on to their enemies by whoever planted the bug. He realized he had better call Edward right away. The man might just be walking straight into a bloody trap.

Moscow
14:00 hours

Natalie wasted no time. Less than five minutes after the Volkswagen left the parking spot in front of the apartment building that contained the safe house, she leaned over to Alexi and unzipped his fly. His eyes opened wide and a broad smirk spread across his face. "Aha," he said. "You want a real man after that American boychik."

She smiled at him balefully. "Just drive." Her voice was soft, seductive. By the time she exposed him he was fully aroused. Then his astonishment turned to terror when her other hand opened the switchblade and placed the cold steel blade in the open fly.

"Listen, you creep," hissed Natalie, "if you don't want to lose it, do exactly as I tell you. Understood?"

Alexi nodded dumbly, his face white. Unconsciously, he took his foot off the gas and the car began to slow down. "Keep driving," snapped Natalie, pressing the blade slightly. "Turn right here."

She directed him along the Leninskij Prospekt toward the outskirts of the city. Within half an hour they were in open country.

Where the hell is this witch taking me? wondered Alexi. And what is she going to do when we get there? Somehow, he suspected it would be nothing very pleasant.

The road skirted a rocky hill. Natalie ordered him to turn on to a track that led from the road to the hillside. Ahead of them, a large trapezium-shaped section, sixty or seventy feet wide and thirty feet high, had been cut into the side of the hill. Across most of it were three dark green metal rolling garage-style doors, tightly closed. At one end was another green door, for personnel, with a small metal viewing slit at eye height. Outside the bunker, a sentry was pacing back and forth in a well-ironed black uniform. When he saw the car approaching, he stopped and readied his machine gun. Natalie told Alexi to stop the car.

"Get out," she said, reaching over to open his door.

Moving gingerly to avoid injuring himself on the stiletto, Alexi slid out. Once clear of the blade, panic overcame him and he ran blindly along the track toward the road. Natalie, or Major Androva as she was known in this place, shouted an order at the sentry, who casually aimed his Kalashnikov and fired a few rounds into Alexi's back. He stopped running, a look of surprise on his face, then he turned a pirouette and fell in a heap. Another burst of fire from the sentry's gun finished him.

"I said stop him, not kill him, you fool!" she shouted at the sentry and ran to where Alexi had fallen. When she reached him, she knew he was not going to answer any of her questions. "Stupid oaf," she said. She turned on her heels and walked briskly into the bunker.

The guard stared at her, fear in his eyes, no longer sure of his future.

A few minutes later, she was in conference with General Rogov in his private office.

"How are you, my dear?"

"Well, thank you, sir. I have some new information for you."

"Ah? Proceed."

"Well, I would have more if our soldiers would listen to orders. I brought a man back who might have had much to say to us, but he was killed just now trying to escape."

"What did you do to scare him so?" The general smiled. "Never mind. What do you have for us?"

"The American is planning an assault of some kind. He is bringing a squad of men into some airfield somewhere."

"You didn't get the exact location?"

Natalie shook her head. "But I can tell you exactly where you can find him." She told Rogov the address of the safe house.

"Good," he said. "We will eliminate him there. His little squad will be no threat without its leader."

"Something else I discovered," said Natalie, accepting Peter's offer of a Sobranie. "They are hoping to divert the president's plane to another airport, to Domodedovo."

"I see." Rogov's face was tense. "What made them choose that particular airport?"

"Edward, that's the American, he has someone inside our ranks who is giving him information. I think they know we do not control that place."

"That is correct." The general clenched his teeth. "We must move quickly. Come."

Peter strode out of his private office and down the corridor to the control room, Natalie following close behind. Peter called to Yazarinsky, who was sitting idly at a computer console, and summoned him to the large illuminated map of the Moscow region. Most of the area was dominated by red lights, indicating the presence of troop divisions whose men, or at least whose commanding officers, were under his command. Significantly, the area around Domodedovo Airport showed only the green lights of troops loyal to President Konyigin.

"Domodedovo must be secured by all possible means," said Peter, pointing at the map. "Colonel Yazarinsky, you will devise a strategy and report to me in half an hour." Peter signaled Colonel Yakov. "Major Androva here will supply you with an address and a description of an American who is becoming a nuisance to us. You will arrest this individual, along with any of his associates, and terminate them. Understood?"

Safe house, Moscow
14:10 hours

It was only a few minutes after Natalie had left that the call came through. Edward's first thought, when Larry told him about the bug, was that the whereabouts of the airfield into which his soldiers were to fly would be known to whoever had planted the bug, which could be anyone including the Black Ghosts themselves. But Larry reminded him that he had been at the office when Edward had given the coordinates, and Larry was sure the office was clean.

"How can you be sure?"

"We had it swept several times."

"What made you do that?"

"We were looking to make sure there were no leaks in the system we had installed. We did a thorough check every morning before the airline people came in. If there was a bug, Falco said we would have found it."

The next concern was the house on Long Island, which obviously was no longer safe. Larry was already in the office and he was not going back until this thing was over.

But that was not all. Edward remembered that he and Natalie had been sitting at the coffee table when she had suggested hiding the array's circuit board in her Walkman. This meant they would know, not only that the circuit board they had been supplied was a poison pill, but that the operational circuit board was now in Natalie's hands.

It hit him like a high-voltage jolt to the stomach. She

had the board with her and she must have hidden it somewhere so they couldn't find it. And he had forgotten all about it. The Black Ghosts needed to get to her in order to get to the board. He had to find her before they did.

He got Igor to call him a taxi and went directly to Natalie's apartment. She should still be there. She was barely fifteen minutes ahead of him. He stood outside for several minutes, then walked around the block. The place was clean; there was no surveillance on the building. Alexi's car was nowhere to be seen. Something was not right. He could feel it. He ran up the stairs and knocked on the door. No answer. He knocked again, louder. The place was as silent as a tomb.

Edward felt a chill run through his body. He went back downstairs.

The janitor's office was on the ground floor. He found a bald man in shirtsleeves sitting in the office, watching television, and spiking his tea with vodka. He tried to talk to him, but it was clear from the man's wondering frown that he did not speak English.

"English," said Edward. "English?"

"Inglish," said the man, shaking his head in puzzlement. Then his expression brightened. "Ah, angliski yaziyk!" He stood up and beckoned Edward out of the office and down the hall. He knocked at one of the badly painted doors and a sour-faced, middle-aged woman answered.

The janitor exchanged a few words with her, then she turned to Edward. "I speak English."

Edward explained to her that he was here to visit a

friend and had reason to believe she had come to some harm inside her apartment. Could the janitor let him in to take a look?

After this message had been translated into Russian and answered, the woman asked Edward which apartment it was. Edward gave her the number and she nodded knowingly, an odd expression flickering across her face. She and the janitor exchanged a few more words. Then she shook her head from side to side very purposefully. "Open apartment is against rules, no." Edward stood there in silence for a moment, wondering what it would take to get inside Natalie's apartment. "Twenty dollar," said the woman, as if reading his mind. "And twenty for me," she added quickly.

Edward handed over the bills, the janitor went to get the keys, and the three of them went upstairs.

The place was deserted. Edward had no way of telling for certain, but he had the strong impression that no one had been in here for some time. There was a staleness in the air.

"Two women living here," said the Russian lady, her expression still wary. "Which one you want?"

"Natalie," said Edward. He remembered that the other woman, Sarah, had died in suspicious circumstances, which probably explained the woman's wary look. He looked around and saw a couple of framed photographs on the mantel. One was of a plump girl with curly brown hair. The other was a photo of Natalie, her blond hair flying, a happy smile on her face. Edward picked it up.

"Here, this is Natalie."

The man and the woman exchanged a few words, then the woman turned her cold eyes back to Edward. "This is not Natalie. We seen this woman come and go. Natalie short and big, not like this one." The woman pointed at the other picture, the one Edward thought must be of Sarah. "That Natalie," the woman said.

The fog lifted and all the pieces came together. The beautiful woman staring at him from the photo, whose body he could still feel and whose scent was deep under his skin, was not, and never had been, Natalie. "Shit," he said aloud. "What a fool, what a bloody fool."

CHAPTER 24

16:00 hours

Edward stood on the street, desperate to get back to the safe house, which now was a death trap. Igor was there, Sparky and Anton would arrive any minute.

Natalie, or whatever her name was, could be anywhere by now. She could be working for anybody. But Edward could only assume the worst—that she was an agent of the Black Ghosts.

He felt sick at heart. He felt responsible. Where was his head? Why hadn't he noticed? There must have been signs, clues. What was the damage? How many lives might be lost if this operation failed? And all because he had let his emotions get in the way of his reason. But he knew he could only have acted as he did, treachery or no treachery. He had done what he thought was right, and now he would live with the consequences.

At last a taxi pulled to the curb. Edward showed him

the paper with the safe house address on it, and they were on their way.

He had the taxi drive straight past the house without stopping. He had to know whether someone had already staked out the place.

They were there, all right. At first he saw two men, one on the corner, one opposite the house. Then when he got out of the cab he noticed the third farther down the street. That meant there were probably more of them on the inside. He couldn't help Igor, who was either dead or on his way there. Sparky and the driver should be arriving any minute, if they were not in there already. There was no sign of the green Lada. He had to assume they had not arrived yet. He was going to give them ten minutes before trying to get into the apartment.

Walking casually past one of the surveillance men, he entered the adjacent building. He was hoping they wouldn't interrogate Igor. If they did, they would learn about the escape route that was in place for such a situation as this. The only problem was that, for it to be of any use, there needed to be plenty of warning. The apartment on the floor below had a second door which led into the stairwell of the adjacent building. Edward was now going to use the escape route backward, making his way in through the second stairwell and the storage apartment.

Once inside, he adjusted the Venetian blinds on the window facing the street so he could see without being seen.

He didn't have long to wait. The pale green Lada

rounded the corner, stopping right in front of the building's main entrance. Edward could see the thin, nervous face of Sparky peering out the front windshield. Beside him in the driver's seat, Anton pointed to the door of the apartment. Sparky, carrying a small tote bag, stepped out of the car. It seemed that after his life on the street, he was used to traveling light. He walked toward the front of the house while Anton parked the Lada in the only available spot, a little way up the street. Edward watched as one of the goons, quickly joined by another, approached the car. One of them went to the driver's side and leaned by the open window, his hand thrust deep in his coat pocket. Edward had no doubt Anton was looking down the barrel of a gun. The other goon raised his hand, signaling across the street to a parked van that Edward had not noticed before. Several uniformed officers jumped out of the back of the van before the man had even finished signaling. They unceremoniously dragged Anton out of his car and threw him kicking and yelling into the van across the street. The few pedestrians tried to stay out of whatever was going on, and they made a special effort to look the other way.

Meanwhile, Edward could hear footsteps on the iron staircase. He ran to the front door and opened it, peeking through the crack. Sparky had already passed his door and was on his way up to the other apartment. Edward didn't dare call out, for fear of alerting whoever was waiting behind the door. He ran silently up the stairs, catching up with Sparky just as he was about to knock on the door. He tapped him on the shoulder.

Sparky turned and saw Edward wide-eyed, his finger to his lips. Sparky opened his mouth to say something, then thought better of it as Edward motioned him urgently downstairs. They slipped quickly into the lower apartment. Only then was it safe to exchange a few words of greeting, and even so, Edward was brief and to the point.

"We've got to get out of here, fast. I'll explain later."

Sparky nodded and the two men left the apartment by the other entrance. They ran down the street. Edward calculated that any minute now, the goons would realize their quarry had escaped and would pursue them. They needed to find a hiding place.

Edward felt naked, hurrying unprotected down the street in broad daylight, with nowhere to go and a gang of armed killers on his tail. If they still were not sure what he looked like, some of them at least had gotten a good look at Sparky.

Every time a car passed them, Edward listened for the slowing of the engine, braced himself for the impact of bullets, and breathed a sigh of relief as the car left them unmolested. He looked in vain for a shop, a bar, any public place that would afford them shelter. But it seemed the neighborhood they were in had been designated for living only, if what the Russians had been doing for the last seventy years could be called that. No fun, no enjoyment, no spending of money—no money to spend, for that matter. And nowhere for them to hide.

They reached the street corner. Edward looked back and saw a pale green car approaching them from the far end of the street. From the looks of it, it was Sokolov's Lada.

"Hurry," he told Sparky as they turned the corner. The poor man was obviously still not in the best physical condition. He was badly winded and his face was racked with pain. "I can't . . . I can't . . ." he was saying.

"Come on, you've got to," Edward yelled, grabbing him by the arm and pulling him along. The Lada would reach the corner at any moment.

Ahead of them, the sidewalk opened into a stone staircase leading down into some dark Russian nether-world. Edward didn't hesitate. Still dragging Sparky by the arm, he went down the steps and into the Moscow subway. He ran to the turnstile and held up two fingers to the man in the glass booth. The man shook his head. Not for the first time that day, Edward found himself reaching into his pocket for his billfold and thrusting greenbacks at someone. As before, it worked. The man issued them two tickets and opened the turnstile. They went through to a large ornate hallway, with railway platforms on either side, separated by colonnades.

Simultaneously, two trains headed in opposite directions entered the station. Edward tried to remember which train went downtown. There were no maps or signposts anywhere. "Kremlin? Kremlin?" he asked a man in a raincoat who had just disembarked.

"Da, da," said the man, nodding toward the train he had emerged from. Edward and Sparky got inside just as the doors were closing. They threw themselves into the upholstered seats and tried to catch their breath.

"Welcome to Moscow," said Edward.

He explained briefly what had happened, why they had made their precipitous exit from the safe house. Sparky accepted his explanation with barely a nod and sat in silence, looking rather lost. Edward realized he was probably in shock.

As the train carried them along, Edward took stock of the situation. He had one of the world's best authorities on telecommunications sitting next to him, he had a platoon of miscellaneous tough guys flying into an airfield somewhere not too far off, and he had a couple of hundred Ukrainian soldiers who thought they were going to be in a movie coming into town tomorrow. Other than that, not too much was going right.

The safe house was gone, its other occupants probably dead by now. Edward had no doubt that the goons who had picked off Anton and probably Igor were working for the Black Ghosts, which meant that if they interrogated Anton, the Black Ghosts would know that their comrade Colonel Sokolov had turned on them. From now on, his life was not worth much.

As for Natalie, Edward didn't even want to think about her. But beyond the cloud of pain and confusion that engulfed him whenever her image strayed into his mind, he could clearly see one result of Natalie's betrayal was that the Ghosts now had a fully operational Barby communications array, meaning they could block out all media communications at any time and substitute their own messages. What use they might make of that over the next twenty-four hours boggled the mind.

The train rolled into a station. Edward had no idea where they were, but he knew he had to act fast, so he grabbed Sparky by the arm and pulled him off the train.

They went upstairs to the street. After walking up the street a little way, Edward realized he was very close to the Hotel Metropole. He found a pay phone and called Sokolov at his apartment.

It was a woman's voice that answered. Edward could only speak to her in English and hope she understood. It turned out she not only understood English but could speak it as well. She told him Colonel Sokolov was not at home.

Edward told her that Sokolov's life might be in danger. He gave her the coordinates of the airfield and told her it was extremely urgent that Sokolov meet him there as soon as possible. Her voice betraying no emotion other than a cool serenity, the woman said she would pass the message on.

So far so good. Now all Edward had to do was get himself there. And he wasn't about to ask directions from strangers on the street. He had to slow down and figure things out. There was no way for him to call Larry. The way the phone system worked in Russia, from what he had seen, he would be lucky enough if he could get a local call through again. He needed a place where he could sit down and think. He also needed a phone and something to eat. And he had to get Sparky off the street.

They would never think he'd return to the Hotel Metropole. He still had a room there, and all he had to do was ask for it at the reception. It would give him a phone and everything else that he needed.

It was as easy as that. Twenty minutes later he was sitting in the hotel room. It was as he had left it, except that Natalie had removed all her belongings. Edward also noted that his passport was missing from the drawer where he had left it.

Sparky lay down on the bed and seemed to fall asleep, although Edward wasn't sure if he really was asleep or back in one of his mental hideouts. It didn't make much difference. Edward ordered some sandwiches from room service and a large jug of coffee. He needed the dark brew, since tea was practically coming out of his ears at that point.

He then asked for an outside line and dialed the number he remembered seeing Igor and Alexi call. A thick Russian voice answered.

"Sergei?" said Edward.

The voice said something incomprehensible. There followed a few moments of shouting in Russian and English, then silence.

"Hello? Hello?" Edward said. Nobody answered, but he could hear distant voices shouting in Russian. Then a new voice came on the line.

"Hello?"

"Is that Sergei?"

"This is he. Who are you?"

Edward explained the situation as best he could, while the voice at the other end of the phone made noises to show its owner was listening. Then came another pause while Russian voices deliberated in the background.

"Where are you now?"

"Hotel Metropole."

"Can you get to the Operetta Theater on Pushkin Street? We'll pick you up there in one hour."

"How will I know you?"

"You will not. I will know you."

Again at the mercy of others, Edward could feel the anger building. He had to keep his cool, he kept telling himself. There was a well-stocked bar in the room and the temptation was greater now than it had ever been in the past. But he had a team that depended on him, people who were willing to risk their lives on his say-so. He was not going to let them down. Not only that, but he was going to complete the job he had come here to do. He could feel a surge of energy take over. Suddenly he had an optimism he had not felt for many years.

The sandwiches finally arrived and he woke Sparky. They were really not worth the wait, and neither was the coffee. It seemed in this country of tea drinkers you couldn't get your hands on a good cup of coffee anywhere.

They hurried through the streets again. Sparky was talking nervously. The time he had spent on the streets may have hardened him in some ways, but it also seemed to have made him suspicious to the point of paranoia. Either that, or the delayed shock of the afternoon's surprises was having its effect. "Why are they sending us to the Operetta Theater?" he said. "Why didn't they just pick us up at the hotel?"

"It's a standard surveillance technique," said Edward, his voice calm and patient. "To make sure we're not being followed." He hoped this was true. So far, the treatment he had received at the hands of the Russian Mafia had been exemplary, but now that he had blown one of their safe houses and probably got two of their people killed, their loyalty might be stretched a bit thin, to say the least. It was possible they could believe he was trying to set them up. He knew that if he were in their shoes, with the little they knew about him, he would certainly come to that conclusion himself.

They waited outside the theater. A few tourists wandered by, but it was too early for the evening performance.

A man pulled up on a moped. Still sitting astride the vehicle and revving the motor noisily, he called to Edward and Sparky. Edward went over to speak to him. Above the noise of the engine, the man asked if he was looking for Sergei. Edward nodded. The man gave him directions. They were to proceed along Pushkin Street, turning right at the first intersection. Then they must turn left on Petrovka and keep going until they came to a small park. They were to go into the park and wait for further instructions. Revving the engine again, the man drove away.

There was nothing for it but to follow his instructions, although Edward was getting somewhat impatient with all this cloak-and-dagger stuff. He kept these thoughts to himself. Sparky, however, gave full expression to what was going on in his mind. "I don't like this, Edward. What if it's a trap?"

"It's not a trap. If they wanted to, they could have killed us ten times already."

It was beginning to get dark by the time they reached the corner of Petrovka Street. Sparky stopped walking. "I'm not going," he said.

"For God's sake, Sparky, what's the matter with you?"

"It's a trap, I can feel it."

"Look, these guys want to help us, they're on our side."

"How do you know that?"

Struggling to control his temper, Edward said, "Listen, Sparky, they want democracy for Russia as much as we do. It's the only way they can hope to stay in business and make some money."

He took Sparky by the arm and pulled him along. Still grumbling, Sparky let himself be led.

They crossed a wide boulevard, on the corner of which was a thickly wooded park. Ignoring Sparky's muttered protests, Edward headed into the park. There was no sign of anyone.

It all happened so fast. Edward sensed a movement behind him and quickly turned around. Some fifteen paces away, under cover of the trees, a man in combat fatigues was grabbing Sparky's hands and pinning them behind him. Sparky screamed as his wrists were handcuffed. A second man pulled a large cloth bag over Sparky's head and shoulders. The bag had a cord around it, which the man pulled tight.

Edward ran toward the shadowy figures, but he had not moved very far when someone grabbed him from behind, immobilizing him. He felt the handcuffs encircling his wrists. Then the cloth bag descended over his head and Edward could see no more. He felt the cord squeeze him, and then he was being hustled to the boulevard. Behind Sparky's muffled screams, he could hear the smooth purring of a powerful automobile engine. Doors were opened, and the two were thrown into the back seat of the car.

Sparky was still screaming. Then he could hear someone say, "Be quiet or I will shoot your head off." Edward could only assume the man had brought a gun to bear on Sparky because the screaming stopped.

"I told you it was a goddamn trap," Sparky said in a low voice, almost a whisper.

"Don't worry," said Edward, trying not to worry himself. "This is routine." He was hoping he was right, but there were too many things that could go wrong. Sergei was only a hunch. He could be working with Natalie, or whatever her name was, for all he knew.

CHAPTER 25

10 Downing Street, London
18:06 hours

The crowd of reporters waited outside the prime minister's house, exchanging gossip and speculation about when the occupants would appear. They had been in there for three hours. A statement had been scheduled for five o'clock, and it was already past six. The official signing of the treaty was to take place in private. The Americans had refused to countenance a public ceremony with TV cameras present, citing security reasons.

In fact, went the word among the reporters huddled outside No. 10 in the persistent rain, the real reason the Americans wanted this to be a low-profile visit was that they wanted to distance themselves slightly from the British, with whom there had been disagreements over the Irish question. It had been suggested in media reports that the British Security Service was up to its old dirty tricks in Ireland, trying to undermine what was thought to be a permanent cease-fire and some very fruitful negotiations that were getting close to a positive conclusion. The prime minister had rolled several senior heads at Whitehall in an effort to show that the actions had been carried out without his approval. The Americans, however, were not buying the story. Nevertheless, some show of solidarity was still in order, hence the statement and photo-op outside.

At last the door opened, and the phalanx of men in suits emerged.

"A great day," said the prime minister, eager to extract the maximum public relations value possible from this rather limited opportunity. "A great day for Britain, and indeed for the world. We are at last coming to the promised land of peace and prosperity for the entire world. Never again will the shadow of a nuclear holocaust be upon us."

Beside him stood President Bradshawe, flanked by the U.S. secretary of defense and some of his aides. There were also several uniformed, well-decorated generals. The president was trying to look enthusiastic, a thin smile of comradeship flitting across his face as he turned and shook the prime minister's hand. Cameras flashed, the moment was recorded for posterity, and then the men went back inside the house, completely ignoring the shouted questions and raised microphones of the reporters.

The crowd in front of the house quickly dispersed. They knew there would be nothing more for them tonight. All in all, it had been a very unsatisfactory afternoon.

Inside the house, preparations were being made for the rest of the visit. The president, his wife, his personal secretary, and a small team of bodyguards were to spend the night at the prime minister's country residence, while James Fenton, Richard Townes, Bud Hays, and the others were heading back to the Grosvenor Hotel for the night.

Fenton's people were already in position at the country residence, and he had the rest of the night off. He was going to take full advantage of his time to sleep, as the rest of the trip promised to be very tense. They would be rejoining the president at Heathrow the following morning, when the entire party would board Air Force One to fly to Moscow.

The Grosvenor party returned in several limousines to the hotel, where they rejoined the support group of secretaries and other lower-level aides. It is a little-known fact that no matter where the president goes, the activity of the White House follows. Even in some completely out-of-the way spot, he still has to take care of the smallest of details, signing documents, talking to people.

There would be an hour's break to "freshen up," and then the entire group was to have dinner in a private dining room.

James Fenton was stretched out on his hotel bed when the call came through. He greeted his old friend warmly. In the short conversation he'd had earlier with his wife, when he had told her to give Larry the name of the hotel, he had no idea what was the matter, only that it was urgent. Somewhere in the shuffle it didn't get through to him that the president's safety was the matter.

He listened carefully as Larry filled him in briefly

on his mission to unmask and neutralize the Patriots, on how the mission had turned sour at Hill Air Force Base in Utah, and on the imminent danger to the president if Air Force One were to fly into Sheremetyevo as planned. Larry implored him to switch the destination to Domodedovo.

"There's something I need to know," said Fenton. "Who were you working with on this mission before it went sour?"

Larry decided he had nothing to lose by telling him.

"Bud Hays. And I guess his secretary took some messages for me, although she didn't have to know what they were about."

"And was he the only person who knew about this?"

"Richard Townes, he was the initiator."

Fenton thought about this. Either one of the men in the suites down the hall was a traitor, or Larry was lying. For now, it didn't matter which. Fenton agreed to switch airports, and he also gave Larry a frequency channel by which a competent radio operator could establish contact with Air Force One. It was a standard frequency, confidential but not top secret. The secret ones, Fenton didn't give out, period.

As for the airport switch, Fenton would determine later whether or not Larry was lying. If it turned out he was, the president would land at Sheremetyevo as planned, and Larry's people, whoever they were, would be none the wiser.

With a promise to get together for a drink once this was all over, the two men said goodbye. Fenton had his work cut out for him. It was Secret Service standard policy never to overlook a warning regarding the safety of the president, or as they code-named him, the Falcon. Since the warning had came from a person whom Fenton personally trusted, even though he would have to take all the procedural steps to verify it, he was putting everyone he could on alert. A gut feeling is the basis for good security work, he always said, and his gut was telling him to take action.

Then, after a moment's further reflection, Fenton put a call through to the maître d'hôtel in the dining room.

Two doors down, Bud Hays was having the time of his life. His secretary, Angela Baines, wearing nothing but black stockings, a lace garter belt, and patent leather high heels, was kneeling in the chair by the dressing table. Bud stood behind her, his pants down around his ankles. She liked the act, feeling someone inside her, his hands running over her body, feeling her breasts, pulling her toward him, entering deeper. This way, she didn't have to see him; she could think of anyone. Today it was that young, handsome bellboy. Then he stopped, she felt anger, he just stopped, she tried to lean back and hold on to him just for one more moment—that's all she would have needed—but he was moving back.

What a great idea it had been to get her along on this trip, he thought, pulling his pants back on. She can never get enough of me, he thought as he moved away from her grip. "Later, honey. We'll get back to it later."

Her face was hidden by a swath of dark hair. If he could have seen it, he might have noticed the anger. For a moment Angela remained standing there, unwilling to accept that it was over.

Bud returned and dropped on the large bed, staring at the ceiling. Angela finished putting her clothes on and sat at the dressing table, taking an especially long time in making up her face.

The phone rang, and Bud picked it up.

"Hays," he said. Then his voice changed. "Yes, thanks for getting back to me." Angela could tell that this was not the tone of voice he normally used for business calls. She applied a dab of lipstick.

"So it's in the best interests of America," Bud said. He listened for a while, then he said, "From the Patriots, you mean?" More silence. Angela decided this was the wrong shade of lipstick. She wiped it off with a paper tissue, then selected another shade from the palette in her traveling vanity case.

"When's it supposed to happen?" asked Bud. More silence while he listened. "So there's nothing to worry about," he finished. "Okay, we'll be in touch." He hung up.

"What was that all about?" asked Angela.

"Nothing much," said Bud. Angela, now fully dressed and made up, picked up her vanity case and walked to the door. "See you at dinner," she said.

Bud lay still for a few more minutes. The call from Singleton had reassured him considerably. He knew the Patriots were involved in something that was supposed to take place in Russia. He'd made it clear to Singleton before leaving Washington the day before that he was willing to help with anything that would bring about a more secure America, but he would not support anything that might smell of treason. If it turned out the Patriots were involved in something that could endanger American interests, he wanted out. Singleton had told him that he knew there was going to be a military coup in Russia after the presidential visit, once the loyal military was taken off alert and sent back to barracks. This he said he had learned from the intelligence the Patriots had gathered. He assured Bud that he was taking whatever precautions he could to ensure the protection of American interests and that if it were not for the Patriots, no one on our side, as he put it, would have learned about this. Therefore, Bud had nothing to worry about. He would be back in Washington, safe and sound. And quite a bit richer too.

He was the last to arrive at the dining room. There were seven round tables set. At one sat the contingent of CEOs from the corporate sector of the military-industrial complex—the metal-eaters. Chief among them was Hubert Austin, who sat with yes-men and would-be business partners on either side. Opposite him was an empty place at the table, to which Bud headed. But the maître d'hôtel blocked his path and directed him firmly over to where Angela sat with James Fenton and Richard Townes. He reluctantly sat down in the empty place. He was in the mood for lighter company than this, but there was nothing he could do about it without appearing rude.

Conversation was somewhat formal and sporadic during dinner. Bud kept trying to catch Angela's eye, to rekindle the wild euphoria of their moment of passion upstairs. But her look was cold, and she ate her dinner mostly in silence, save for a few words of polite conversation with the other two men.

During one of the long silences, Bud caught a snatch of conversation from the other table. Hubert Austin was laying down the law about something or other, his voice raised above the general babble. Bud looked over his shoulder in astonishment at the man: For a moment, the voice had sounded exactly like that of the mysterious, faceless person he knew as Singleton. But no, Bud thought, it couldn't be.

While they were waiting for dessert, Fenton turned to him and said, "By the way, Bud, have you ever heard of the Patriots?"

Bud sipped his wine, unsure of the safest way to answer this question. He looked across at Townes, to see if he could read some clue in the man's eyes. But Townes' face was a blank. He decided that the best thing was to act dumb. "The Patriots? No. What are they?"

"What about you, Richard?" said Fenton.

"I've heard of them," Townes said casually. "They're a neo-Nazi militia, out in Montana somewhere."

"Are they a threat?" said Fenton, looking carefully from one man to the other.

Townes shrugged. "Everyone's a threat. Why do you ask?"

"Oh, something I came across in an intelligence report. About the recent wave of terrorism in Russia. They were rumored to be involved. Do you think it's possible?"

"Anything's possible," said Townes.

The dessert arrived. Angela ate her Baked Alaska in silence. But inwardly she was rejoicing. She had been looking for the next rung on the ladder that would lift her toward her goal, leaving Bud Hays far behind. Now she understood that this was it.

CHAPTER 26

Sergei Pozharsky flicked ash from his cigar into the huge marble ashtray on his desk. "I see," he said, "not a movie, but an armed insurrection. This is most interesting."

Edward sat opposite him. The cloth bag had been removed from his head, but his hands were still cuffed. Next to him sat a large man wearing combat fatigues and carrying a submachine gun. For half an hour Edward had been trying to make Sergei see reason. Without much success, to judge by the cold look on the man's face and the skepticism in his eyes.

"Don't you see?" Edward began again. "If this succeeds, Russia will be worse off than it was before Glasnost and Perestroika. You and your kind will be the first to go. I'm telling you, I'm your best bet, and as you can see it's a goddamn long shot."

Sergei just stared at him, slowly drawing from his

large Havana cigar. Then he placed the Coheiba Numero Uno in the ashtray and got up to walk around the room. "You are telling me that you are here to stop a military coup. I like that. You also tell me that you have just about everything in place. I like that too. But I need to see where I fit into all this, and especially how I'm going to profit from it."

"You will get to keep what you have," Edward blurted.

Sergei raised his hand as if to say, I'm not through. "That is what you are telling me. Two of my people who trusted you are now dead." He turned to face Edward. "Not a very good track record, is it?"

"So what is it you want?" Edward decided to cut to the chase. Time was running out, and if he was going to get out of that place and make it to the airstrip on time he had to get moving. "Is it money? Fine, that can be arranged. Just name your price, but get these stinking cuffs off me and let's get moving. Don't forget, you already owe me quite a bit, the way things are."

"How do you figure that?" The man sounded surprised.

"You got my money from Igor and Alexi. You are supposed to deliver on that. Is this charade your way of trying to get out of the deal?"

He seemed to have finally struck at Sergei's heart, where it mattered. This was a negotiation session like any other. Negotiating was the only thing Sergei knew how to do, and he did it well.

At that moment a second armed man walked into the room. He went up to Sergei and leaned over to whisper something in his ear. Sergei listened and nodded.

He then gave a signal to the man standing guard over Edward. The man unlocked the handcuffs.

"Let me apologize," said Sergei, "for the rather rough treatment you were given by my men. We had to be sure, not only that you were not being followed, but also that you were indeed who you said you were and that your intentions are, shall we say, consistent with our own."

"And are you sure now?" said Edward.

"We are. Some of the things you mentioned have been confirmed. It seems these people you call the Black Ghosts are very upset with you."

"Really?"

"When I informed them I had you, they were ecstatic."

"You did what?"

"This is business, my friend, nothing personal, you understand,"

"So what now?"

"I negotiate."

"I have nothing more to offer you, Sergei, except your own life."

"We should do business one day," Sergei smiled. "You have an honest face. That is good. Now we have to teach you to lie and keep the same face." He chuckled, enjoying himself. "I tell these Black Ghosts I want more money for you. That way we buy time, they will think I'm bluffing and still search for you, but not as hard. They want to catch you very much, which in my book makes you a friend."

Edward massaged his wrists and stood up. The armed guard raised his gun and stood in a ready position. Sergei signaled him to relax. "I'd love to sit and chat," Edward said, "but we have things to do."

"All right, I am no fan of those who occupy the Kremlin at present, but at least they don't interfere in business. We will do all we can to help you."

"Good," said Edward. "I need to use your phone. And where is my friend?"

Sergei stood up and pushed the phone across the wide desk to where Edward stood. "He's fine, don't worry. He is well taken care of."

Edward took Sergei's word for it, for the moment. While he dialed, Sergei paced the carpeted floors of his office suite. Outside, beyond the glass doors, high-heeled secretaries and well-dressed clerks in imported suits milled and circulated, had meetings, did deals, and took notes, despite the lateness of the hour. In this building, business was extremely good.

The headquarters of the Pozharsky Corporation was like any well-heeled office building in the West, except for the large number of uniformed guards who lounged around the lobby downstairs, their Kalashnikovs hanging from their shoulders. Another unusual feature of Sergei's office was the second entrance, private and also heavily guarded, via which Edward and Sparky, handcuffed and blindfolded, had been brought in half an hour earlier.

The first person Edward called was Larry, at the office building in New York.

"Thank God it's you," Larry said. "I've just spoken to Natalie. She's worried as hell. Where are you?"

"When did she call?"

"Less than ten minutes ago. Why?"

"Her name isn't Natalie. I believe the real Natalie is dead. The woman you have been calling Natalie was working for the Black Ghosts all along. No wonder you kept losing every agent you tried to get in Russia."

Larry was silent, trying to digest what he had just heard. "Are you sure?"

"I'm lucky to be alive. What did you tell her?"

"I told her about the airport switch."

"Don't worry, she knew about that from me anyway. Did you tell her the location of the airstrip?"

"No. She asked. She said she wants to go there and team up with you. She said you were separated when the safe house was raided. She wasn't sure if you'd made it."

"So how come you didn't give it to her?"

"I don't have it here. I have one copy at the house and the other I gave to the pilot. Just lucky, I guess. What about your friend the colonel?"

"They got his driver, but I'm hoping he's still out there. He has your number. If he calls you, send him to the airstrip." Edward gave him the directions. This time he was reading it from a map Sergei had placed before him.

Larry gave him the radio frequency to Air Force One that he had gotten from Fenton. "Shit, I just remembered something," he said. "I also gave the frequency to Natalie."

"So get ahold of your friend Fenton and warn him. Tell him that when I call in, I'll identify myself as Dagger One. He is to disregard any other calls on that frequency."

"I hope I can reach him. He might already be on his way. How come I didn't notice a goddamn thing?"

"Forget it, Larry. She was good, very good. You just try and get your man. I have to run now. Stay where you are. I'll be in touch."

Next, Edward tried Sokolov's apartment. There was no answer. That in itself was probably a good sign: It could mean Sokolov had received Edward's message and was on his way to the airfield. On the other hand, it could mean he was dead or in the midst of spilling his guts, giving them the location of the field. Edward had to admit the possibility that his men were heading directly into a trap.

When he had finished phoning, Edward went over to where Sergei was standing by the window, which offered a panoramic view of Moscow. As he gazed at the multitude of lights twinkling in the darkness, Sergei's expression was sorrowful.

"Beautiful, isn't it?" he said morosely. "It would be a shame to turn it back into a prison."

"Yes, indeed." Edward cleared his throat. "Listen, Sergei, I'm going to need a powerful radio transmitter."

Sergei stared at him blankly, a remote look in his eyes. Then he seemed to come to his senses. "Yes, of course. That can be arranged."

"Is there a transmitter at the airfield?" If there were, it would be too good to be true.

Sergei shook his head. "I'm afraid not. But I can get you access to the Brosny radio station. They have the largest transmitter in the country and it's not in use at the moment."

"We'll have to get Sparky over there."

"No problem."

"How will I be able to communicate with him?"

"By phone from the airfield."

Sparky had been hit over the head, not hard enough to knock him out, but enough to keep him quiet in the car. He had been released from his cuffs and allowed to stand up and stretch. Soon he was drinking tea and being made a fuss of by two of the secretaries, who applied a dressing to the bump on his head and soothed him with laughter and soft words that he could not understand but enjoyed listening to anyway.

Edward went into the reception area, where Sparky was still enjoying the company of the two pretty secretaries.

"I hate to drag you away," said Edward, "but we have work to do."

He literally had to pull him by the arm to get him into the office. It seemed to Edward that he had done nothing but drag Sparky by the arm all day long.

Sergei had one of the secretaries go out for some food. She came back a short while later with burgers, fries, and coffee from the newly reopened McDonald's.

Edward put Sparky through a thorough briefing. He provided him with an outline of the overall plan and gave him the radio frequency that would put him in touch with Air Force One. After Sergei had made the necessary arrangements, Sparky, still looking slightly lost, was led away by one of the uniformed guards. Edward could only hope that he knew what he had to do and would get it right when the time came.

Sergei put at Edward's disposal a Jeep Cherokee and a couple of men who would drive him to the airfield. He also provided some useful intelligence. The recent troop movements around the city meant that most of the major highways were now controlled by checkpoints. His men would try to guide Edward away from the most likely locations for roadblocks, but even on the back roads there was no guarantee they wouldn't be stopped and searched. For that reason, the men would be in plain clothes. Edward was advised to carry no arms. Sergei had received information that the police were looking for Edward as a fugitive from justice. It was being said that he was behind one of the recent terrorist acts and was armed and dangerous.

"They have a photo of you." Sergei showed him a photocopy of an enlarged photograph with a Russian inscription underneath.

"My own personal wanted poster," Edward said bitterly, recognizing the photo as the one in his passport which was missing from the hotel. "So what now?"

"Nothing. Just avoid talking to the police. And get out of the city as soon as possible."

Once they arrived at the airfield, a man named Yuri would assist them. Sergei had briefed Yuri by phone and impressed upon him the importance of giving the American every cooperation. He also gave Edward a number and told him to call anytime if there was something Sergei's people could do for him. They shook hands and Edward left.

It was around nine and raining when they got on the

road. Traffic was heavy until they cleared the Sadovoye Koltso, the city's Garden Ring, when it began to thin out. Edward vigilantly watched the road from the back seat. It was going to be a long night.

CHAPTER 27

Grosvenor Hotel, London
20:30 hours

After dinner, James Fenton returned to his suite. He pulled off his tie, undid his shirt collar, and sat in an armchair, pondering the evening's events. Townes had confessed to a passing knowledge of the Patriots but had volunteered no information about an operation to neutralize them. Bud Hays had denied all knowledge of them. That in itself was legitimate. If the Patriot threat was as widespread as Larry had suggested, the operation would have to be kept very discreet.

On the other hand, if what Larry had said was true, then at least one of these men would have a more compelling reason to remain silent about the Patriots. Which was the more likely suspect, Townes, who had casually acknowledged their existence, or Hays, who had not even done that?

At the same time, Fenton had noticed they were

staring at each other, as if looking for answers in each other's face. He knew they were both lying to him, each for his own reason, but it confirmed to him that Larry probably wasn't. He was going to have a chat with the president in the morning. After all, he was the one who had asked for the investigation, according to Larry. For the moment there was nothing else he could do. He had no authority to cancel the trip or he would have done so, as he would with just about every trip the president took, including his daily jogging and the occasional night visit to a fast-food restaurant.

There was a quiet knock at the door. Surprised, Fenton got to his feet and peeked through the spy hole. He was even more surprised when he saw the black hair and pale face of Angela Baines. He opened the door.

"Hi," said Angela, smiling nervously, her voice soft. "Can I come in?"

He opened the door wider, unsure what this unexpected visitor was after.

"It's about what you said at dinner," said Angela.

"I said many things," returned Fenton. "Please have a seat." He pointed to the sofa.

"I'm talking about that thing you asked about the Patriots." She sounded unsure of herself, treading in unfamiliar territory.

"What about them?"

"Well." Angela hesitated. "Bud and I . . . let's say that in the past we've had more than a working relationship. Okay?"

Fenton smiled. "Okay."

"I was in his room earlier. He took a call from somebody. He said something about the Patriots, like he knew what they were."

"Any idea who the call was from?"

"No. But I'd say it wasn't anyone he deals with in his normal line of work. His voice sounded different, somehow."

He leaned forward. "Different how?"

"I don't know." She frowned. "Like he was talking to the president, except he wasn't."

"What exactly did he say?"

"Not too much. He mainly listened and said yes, yes. But then he asked something about the Patriots. He said something about making sure they were in the best interests of America, or something."

This was starting to get interesting, Fenton thought. "Did he say a name?"

"No, he just kept calling the man sir. You know, like he was someone very important?"

"Is there anything else you can remember?"

"No, I just thought you ought to know."

"Thank you, Angela. You've been most helpful. Let's keep it between us. If you hear anything else, I want to know. Okay?"

"Mr. Fenton? Could I ask you something in return?"

"Of course."

"I'm trying to get out of my present position like, I mean, I feel like I'm not going anywhere, like you know?"

Fenton smiled indulgently. "I'll see what I can do," he said.

CG Command Bunker, outside Moscow

General Rogov was feeling better. He had been disconcerted to learn that Yakov's men had failed to capture the American and had succeeded only in killing the occupant of the house he was staying in. They had also retrieved the corpse of a driver who had been in the act of delivering a visitor to the house but who had poisoned himself before he could be interrogated.

The men he was staying with were members of the Moscow underworld and were working for a kingpin he had himself used to do dirty work on occasions. Yakov had made contact with the man and offered him a reward for the American. It was now a matter of negotiating a price, if in fact Pozharsky had the man. That parasite was known to lie when it suited him, and since he was not aware of the new world order that was about to come into being, he thought this was business as usual. If he didn't hand the American over by midnight, the general told Yakov, he was to raid the offices of the Pozharsky Corporation and get the American himself. The time for games was over. He could not afford to have anything stand in his way.

Still, the general was reassured to know that even if Pozharsky did not have him, the American would not be able to do much now. Rogov's elite commando troops were scheduled to fly in early in the morning. Then they were to be driven to the Kremlin, where they were expected, and they would "secure" the place.

Looking at the large video screen depicting the capital,

he could see that virtually all the highways in and out of Moscow were controlled by his checkpoints. They had all been alerted to be on the lookout for the American and had been issued photos of him. It was now a matter of principle for the general, more than a real need to catch the man. If the American tried to leave the city by road, he would not last long.

And as for the airport, Rogov had reviewed Yazarinsky's plan and was confident it would work. Within a matter of hours, the Black Ghosts' control of Moscow's airports would be complete.

Peter felt a surge of energy flow through him. The decisive time was approaching, and Peter was ready to meet his destiny. Within the next eighteen hours, history would be made.

21:00 hours

The jeep cleared a turn in the road. Only when it was too late to turn back or get off the road did they notice the roadblock ahead. Like a fly caught in a spider's web, the jeep slowed to a halt, engulfed by the spotlight that burst into life as they came into sight of the centuries. Edward's heart was pounding. The two men in front exchanged a few words. Edward's ear for Russian was developing to the extent that he could sense the note of alarm in their voices.

If they turned and tried to get away, they would undoubtedly be pursued. The only thing to do was try to ride it out. There were stony-faced soldiers in great-coats all around the jeep. They peered inside, shined flashlights through the windows, and then ordered the three men out. They were made to lean with their hands against the windows of the jeep while the soldiers frisked them.

As long as he had his back to them, Edward was happy. They did not seem to have a copy of his photo or be looking for him in particular. That he could sense almost from the start. From his experience in the military, he knew that soldiers were rarely interested in catching someone. All they probably wanted was to get back to whatever they were doing before the jeep showed up. As if to prove the point, one soldier pointed a flashlight into Edward's face, eyeing him suspiciously. He said something in Russian to Edward's companions, who replied in brief, terse phrases. Then, as though they really couldn't be bothered anymore, the soldiers ordered them back into the jeep and allowed them to drive away.

They drove on for another fifteen minutes, the last five of which were spent jolting down an unpaved track. They ended up at a white farmhouse surrounded by a few trees, beyond which, lit by the ghost of a moon behind the scattered clouds, stretched an open field.

Several vehicles were parked in the front yard. Behind the house, there were piles of scrap metal and pieces of earth-moving equipment. Without the benefit of daylight to show the deep rust on the machinery, it appeared that the work on the airfield had stopped only hours before, to resume the next morning. The house itself, a two-story brick structure, was in darkness. The walls, covered with wilted ivy, only added to the scene of neglect.

Walking closer to the main door, they could hear the sound of laughter from inside the seemingly deserted dwelling. Just as they were about to knock on the door, someone behind them shouted, "Astanaveetyes!"

From the tone in which it was said, Edward could understand he was being ordered to stop. "Rucka na Galava," said a second voice to the right. Looking at his escorts, Edward saw them place their hands on their heads. He did the same, then one of his escorts started to speak. He could hear the name Sergei mentioned, then "amerikanski." It was about then that one of the guards who had stopped them walked up to the door and, leaving them outside with their hands on their heads, went inside. Several seconds later he emerged with a big smile and a very large man by his side. Through the open door, Edward could see the place was filled with men in camouflage outfits. The air was heavy with a stench of cheap cigarette smoke and the stale odor of beer.

"You put hands down, it okay." The big man extended his hand to Edward. "I Yuri. You say what you like, I get." He gestured for them to follow him inside.

The soldiers, some holding a beer, others seated on the floor with their backs to the wall, holding on to their Kalashnikov assault rifles, nodded lazily to the newcomers. Yuri led Edward through to a large kitchen. On the way, he noticed that all the windows had been blacked out with heavy cardboard.

In the middle of the kitchen was a long wooden table, bearing the scars of countless chopping knives, scalding pots and pans, and other signs of use. At the far end of the table sat a tall, slim man with smooth dark hair.

"Good evening, my friend," said Colonel Sokolov. "I thought you'd never get here."

Edward greeted the colonel warmly. "I'm glad to see you. I was wondering if you would manage to get out in time."

"Get out in time?" Sokolov looked puzzled.

Edward told him about the ambush at the safe house. Even if the goons had not recognized Sokolov's car, Anton the driver was probably now in the hands of the Black Ghosts' interrogators. Unless the man was extremely brave or extremely insensitive to pain, he would have revealed that Colonel Sokolov had turned against them.

Sokolov's face was grave. "Neither the car nor the driver were known to the Black Ghosts. As for Anton, all my men carry a cyanide capsule, just in case. We know that talking might get us a quicker end, something we can provide for ourselves. I am afraid that by now he will have had occasion to use it." Sokolov remained silent for a moment. "How did they find out about the safe house?"

Edward explained how Natalie had deceived them.

"Why did you bring Natalie to the safe house, if you didn't need her there? Were you in love with her?"

"No!" said Edward, his teeth clenched. Only now did he realize it was true. He wasn't in love, he was infatuated with her. And his emotional confusion had come back to haunt him. "I'm sorry about your friend."

Sokolov looked at him sternly. "Anton was a soldier, loyal to mother Russia, as I am. We are fighting a war, never forget that."

Edward nodded. "There's another thing," he said. "She knows we're trying to get the president to land at a different airport. So I guess your general knows about that too. Maybe they'll try and take Domodedovo."

Sokolov got to his feet. "I will try to contact Lieutenant-Colonel Orlov and warn him." He strode out, and Edward could hear him talking with the men in the other room. He had a natural command and charisma that some might find arrogant, but Yuri and his men seemed to readily fall in with his wishes. Then he could hear him talking louder on the phone. A few minutes later he came back into the kitchen.

"I hope he will get my message. I had to leave it with one of his lieutenants. Orlov is out on rounds at the moment and could not be reached in person. I will try again later. Now, let us start to make our plans."

CHAPTER 28

CG Command Bunker, outside Moscow
21:10 hours

"Well?" Rogov fixed his eye on Yakov, who remained several feet back from the large desk, like a child frightened of getting too close to an angry teacher. "Do they, or do they not have him?"

"We can't be sure, sir. We can only assume that he's there. We have no one in that organization."

"Why not?"

"Well, sir, like all the rest of the underworld, they were tagged for elimination. Once we have control they will be rounded up and liquidated. And they were never regarded as a threat to us, sir. So there was no point in trying to infiltrate them."

"If I may," Major Androva said, her voice soft and soothing, "the colonel is quite right, but only regarding the gangsters. When it comes to the American, it's a different story. We know he managed to change the landing location of the president's plane. That means he has made contact with someone high enough up to do so. We also know that he has a group of extremely well-trained soldiers coming in on a stolen plane. Their sole purpose in coming here is to stop what we are doing." She turned to look at Yakov. Her voice was still low, but now it was more like the hiss of a snake. "The Americans are a threat; we must stop them all before it is too late."

"And how do you propose we do that?" Yakov asked somewhat sarcastically. "Russia is not a small island. It is fairly easy to get lost here, even if you don't intend to. What we need to do is find this Edward. He's the key. If we get him, they are lost."

"Are you sure of that?"

"Major," the general interrupted, leaning back in his seat, "please get to the point. We have a coup to attend to, and we do not have all night."

"I don't believe Edward would not have some contingency plan for them. If he is eliminated, someone else will be ready to take over. We should find them and eliminate them before they can harm us."

"But how?" Yakov shrugged.

"We know they are coming by plane. We know it's not a scheduled flight, so that eliminates all the regular airports, which we control anyway and they know it. We know they are going to land somewhere outside Moscow." She walked over to a large map of the city on the wall opposite the general's desk. "How many places are there around here where you could land a large plane? Where else could they land? If we can figure that out, we've got them."

Yakov smiled. "Why didn't you get it out of your American when you had him—or were you too busy playing the part?" Before he had finished his sentence, he realized from the general's expression that it was a mistake to say what he did. There was a moment of silence in the room. They both looked at him. Yakov lowered his eyes to look at his boots. "I apologize, Major. That remark was totally uncalled for."

"You are a very lucky man, Yakov," the general said, "but you are also very stupid. I see that you are afraid of me and yet you allow yourself to speak this way to her. If I were you, from now on I would sleep with one eye open."

"I'm sorry," Yakov said, feeling very small.

"My dear," the general said as if nothing had happened, getting up from his seat. "I have a final coordination meeting to attend in the CIC room in five minutes. I want you to take whatever you need and get these men. I'm placing clever little Yakov here under your command." The general again stared at the small man, who was clearly unhappy with what he was hearing. "I want you to get this Edward and his men." He turned to Yakov. "Is that clear?"

"Yes, sir." He snapped to attention. The general walked out, leaving the young colonel and the beautiful woman standing in his office.

"So what do you propose we do?" Yakov asked bitterly.

"We have to handle it on two fronts," she said, seating herself in the general's chair.

Yakov's eyes opened wide, surprised at her audacity. "You will go to the Pozharsky Corporation offices and conduct a raid, even though I doubt very much if the American is there."

"What makes you say that?"

"I did some checking. I found out that the safe house where Edward was hiding belonged to one of Sergei Pozharsky's people. Edward was in with them from the start. He met someone in Kirov, during a train stop on the way to Moscow. When he came here he already had a name."

"So what?"

"Don't you see? The airfield, the safe house, everything he has or is getting comes from Pozharsky, and Pozharsky doesn't give anything away. He does things for money."

Yakov was getting his nerve back, and he chuckled. "What's your point? Pozharsky is a gangster. What did you think he was doing things for?"

"Let me enlighten you, my Muzik," she said, using the word for the lowest form of peasant to offend the small officer. "Edward has a lot of money. He had almost three hundred thousand dollars on him in cash, and could probably get millions if he only wanted to. The man behind him, Larry Williams, has access to as much money as they might need. Now you see why I'm very doubtful Pozharsky will hand him over to you. This is a trick. Edward is probably already at the airfield. And his men should be arriving any minute."

Yakov's face was serious as he walked over to look at the map next to her chair.

"Like I said," she went on, "we have to tackle this thing on two fronts." She stood up and spread her palm over the map and ran it in a circle around the city. "Some-where here there is an airstrip where they are going to land. We must find it and eliminate them before it's too late. You take your men and arrest Pozharsky. If you find the American, just make sure you don't kill him."

"You like the guy?" Yakov smirked.

"Don't start with me again, you fool. I've killed bet-ter men than you for much less, and them I loved. We need him to talk. He made plans when I was not with him. He had someone on the inside working with him. I need to know who. Could it be you, little man?" She sounded tough, angry. Yakov backed off a step. "What are you waiting for? Go get the man. Call me here if you have anything." She looked at the map again. Now her voice was low, as if she was talking to herself. "Where could they land a goddamn plane?" She was still looking at the map as Yakov quietly left the office.

Major Androva walked out of the general's office and made her way to the CIC room. In the glass-paneled office at the corner of the large room, the general was talking to a group of officers gathered around a metal desk. Androva crossed the room to one of the computer operators. "Who handles the radar maps?"

The young man took his headset off one ear. "What did you say, Major?"

"I said, who handles the radar maps?"

"What is it you need?"

"I need to see the radar coverage around the city and then for a larger area." She looked at the map of Russia. "Say, as far as the Baltic."

The young man, very much aware of the woman in the uniform, turned his swivel chair and pointed at a screen on the wall. "I'll put it on that screen for you."

Androva nodded to him. "By the way, is that a live radar reading or just a schematic?"

"Both," said the young man, turning to type something on his keyboard. Several seconds later, the map of Russia's northern coast blacked out and the area Androva was interested in appeared. There were green, blue, and red circles covering almost the entire map, with smaller yellow circles covering the gaps.

"What do the colors represent?" asked Androva.

"Those are the various radar frequencies. X band, Y band, and the combination. Those are the red, green, and blue circles."

"What are the yellow ones?"

"Those are activated only during emergencies. They are mobile radars, mounted on trucks. They are used to close any possible gaps in the coverage."

"Could they be activated now?"

"No. You have to put the mobile units in place first, then activate them."

"So if I had a copy of this map, I could get into Russian airspace without detection?"

"Smugglers do it all the time. Once we're in control, the general plans to close the gaps."

"Yes, but for now?"

"You could very well get in, but only with very small airplanes or big ones that fly very, I mean very, very low."

"Can you show me the Moscow airports on this map?"

He typed another set of codes into the computer and a series of colors lit up the screen. She stared at them for a moment. "Any others?"

"No, not airports."

"What, then?"

"Well, we do have a list of emergency landing strips. You know, parts of highways, areas of flat terrain, and incomplete airfields."

"Put them on." Her voice was tight.

An extensive series of red dots flickered on. She grinned. "There they are," she said. "Only three options." She grabbed a piece of paper from the young man's desk and with his pen wrote down several names, copying from the map.

"Where do we have friendly helicopters?"

"At Zelenograd Airfield, it's a military base—"

"I know what it is." Her voice was harsh. She needed the young man no more. "Get me the officer in charge."

"Yes, Major." After a short and frantic attempt on his part to move fast, he handed her the receiver.

"This is Major Androva."

"What is the status of this call?" asked the voice on the other end of the line.

"Phazar," she answered, using the code name—meaning "blaze"—which was the active code for the final stage of Operation Czar.

"This is Colonel Techyanov. What can I do for you?"

"I need you to send helicopters to check the following locations." She read the names to him.

"I can only spare one 'coper at the moment, Major."

"This is of vital importance."

"I will have him in the air as soon as we hang up."

"I need to be informed immediately once you have found any suspicious activity in any one of those locations."

"I will keep you informed, Major."

35,000 feet over Tallinn, Estonia
22:41 hours

"Tallinn Tower, this is Zebra Tango seven ninety-nine, en route to Gorky, over."

"Zebra Tango seven nine nine, this is Tallinn Tower. Welcome to the Republic of Estonia, keep your heading of 275 at thirty-five thousand feet, routing alpha six nine two."

"Thank you, Tallinn, I will direct through Novograd."

"Zebra Tango, do you want me to raise Novograd for you?"

"No thanks, I will take it from here."

"Have a nice trip."

"What now?" asked Mario, seated behind Dan, the pilot, on board the jumbo that was heading toward Russian airspace at nine hundred kilometers per hour.

"Looks like they're not aware that the real flight to Gorky from Sweden was delayed."

"I guess Larry took care of that. He said he had a friend at the Swedish intelligence who could do just about anything."

"Be great if he could take over this operation," Archie,

the second pilot, remarked with a yawn. "I'm tired, and the hard part is still ahead."

"Six minutes to disconnect," said Dan, becoming very tense. "Taking out of auto." He flicked a series of switches.

"Closing auto," Archie said, reaching down to another set of switches. "Ready?"

"Disconnect."

The plane dropped slightly, swaying from side to side until Dan got full control of it. "Four minutes to range," he said, watching as the small blip on his console radar slowly came closer to the rim.

"Once we get out of their radar range, we drop to tree height and make the rest of the way almost on the ground. From the looks of it, we have enough gas for one round. I hope they have the field ready, because I'm going down whether I can see it or not."

No. 17 Helicopter Squadron, Zelenograd Air Force Base
23:20 hours

"Ivan Four requesting permission for takeoff."

"You are clear for takeoff, Ivan Four."

"Do you have the location plotted?" Captain Oleg, the Mi-8 assault helicopter pilot, asked the navigator sitting in the copilot's seat. These were not the glorious old days when all positions were filled and a full crew meant a full crew. With the cutbacks, Oleg couldn't remember the last time he'd flown with a co-pilot. With the fuel shortages, he couldn't remember the last time he had participated in an exercise. The only thing he got to do these days was fly politicians around, and for some reason there was always enough fuel for that. In protest, he had stopped wearing the pilot's wings he had worked so hard to get, as had many of his friends. We don't need wings to be taxi drivers, they said.

In the last few days, however, things had changed somewhat. They were flying military missions, taking various high-ranking officers from one troop location to another. Oleg couldn't exactly put his finger on it, but there was an excitement in the air. The brass he was flying around seemed cheerful, optimistic. He actually saw officers salute each other with a smile.

And now this order to search for anything he might regard as suspicious. They were leaving to him the decision as to what might look suspicious. They'd given him three locations to check out, and he was going to do exactly that—as fast as he possibly could. Whatever was going on, he was happy about it. Even if he wasn't sure exactly what it was.

"Take heading one nine seven," the navigator said. "We should be there in four minutes. It's a strip of highway just outside of Pushkino. Then we head zero eight two. That's an old military airport which has been closed for years."

"Is that near Klimovsk?"

The navigator looked back at the map, "Yes. About two miles south of the town."

"I trained there many years ago. And the third location?"

"Kolomana. They were building the new airport there when they ran into communication problems."

"Didn't they test the array there?"

"I don't know. I was never there. I just read about it a few weeks ago. They're having an investigation into the money they poured into that place."

Scattered clouds were obscuring sections of the star-filled sky. They were flying at four thousand feet, which was low enough to see just about everything but high enough to stay out of the way of the occasional power line or angry farmer with a shotgun.

"There is our first location," Oleg said. "I'm going in for a better look." The helicopter banked sharply and dived almost three thousand feet, stabilizing over the deserted strip of highway. They flew a circle around the area. Then, just to be sure, Oleg brought the helicopter down, almost touching the road. He turned on his night-vision goggles and searched.

"Nothing," he said finally. Almost at once, he was back at his flight level, heading for the second location. He repeated the procedure over the deserted airbase. When he again saw nothing, he reported back to base that he was now heading for the third location, as the first two were clean. He got the go-ahead and turned his chopper toward Kolomana and the deserted airfield.

Oleg calculated that the flight would take about fifteen minutes, as he wanted to see also if there was anything suspicious on the way. Three minutes in, he heard a rumble, gradually getting louder and louder. Both men looked with their night-vision goggles at the sky around them. The sound was of a big plane with large jet engines, closing in from a distance. But they saw nothing. The sky was clear—until the navigator yelled over the microphone, almost tearing Oleg's eardrum.

"Pasmatry, pasmatry!" he shouted, pointing down. Look, look!

What Oleg saw was something he had never seen before. Almost two thousand feet below them, a giant four-engine monster was hurtling through the air. It seemed to be skimming the tops of the trees.

At first, Oleg couldn't quite make it out. He had never seen such a plane from this angle. Then he recognized the hump on the front section of the fuselage and saw that it was a jumbo jet. As it swept below, opening a larger distance between itself and the helicopter, the first air waves began to shake the chopper. From this angle, Oleg couldn't make out what markings it carried, but as he fought to maintain control of the helicopter, he knew he had definitely seen something very unusual. He would head for the third location, just to check if the plane had landed there. Then he would inform his control tower of what he had seen.

"Boshey moyeh," said the navigator. "What the hell was that?"

"A Boeing seven four seven," said Oleg, sounding like a fisherman who had just made his biggest catch ever.

CHAPTER 29

"Yuri!" Edward called to his big host.

"Da," came the reply as the man appeared in the doorway that suddenly seemed very small with him standing there.

"Could you ask him—" Realizing that Yuri's English left much to be desired, Edward turned to Sokolov for a translation.

"I speak English, no need translate." Yuri sounded offended.

"Very well." Edward turned to face him. "What do you have in the way of defense around this place?"

"Not need defense. No one know this place."

"Still, you had the men that stopped me."

"We have men in hangar, and some in forest." He raised his hand, making a horizontal circle in the air.

"Have people around and on roads. This place we use all time. Sergei make much money in this place."

"Do you have communication with your people?" Edward made a gesture as if bringing a phone to his ear.

Yuri drew a small walkie-talkie from his pocket. "Da, can talk to people." As if to prove the point, he brought the device to his ear, pressed the button and said something in Russian. He then let go of the button and after a short squelching sound the answer came. It was brief. The big man smiled. "No one on road," he said.

"Thanks." Edward felt better. There were so many things he had to do and take care of, he was starting to worry that he might forget some tiny detail or other. This was different from when he was in the service. Then, it was all laid out, the plans were in place, and all he had to do was stick to them. There were sometimes minor deviations, but they were the exception. This operation into which he'd been tossed with little warning was all deviations: The basic plan and proper procedure was the exception. From up close, the enemy looked much stronger and more ominous than it did from a distance. It was everywhere, and in control of everything.

"So in fact," he said to Sokolov after a moment of quick thought, "the Black Ghosts have already won the war. It's only a matter of advertising it."

"That is quite correct." Sokolov nodded.

"A hell of a time to be leaving the ship."

Sokolov smiled sadly. "You are right." After a short pause he said, "You wanted to know about the bunker."

He gave Edward a precise description of the bunker's position and location. It lay, he said, in a hillside area in a shallow, partially wooded valley consisting mostly of farmland. Across the valley, half a mile off, was a small village accessible from a different route, which afforded some opportunities for observing activity in and around the bunker. The tree cover shielded the bunker from closer observation but also provided a possible means to approach it unobserved.

Sokolov advised against attacking the bunker by night. Until General Rogov left with his men and equipment, the bunker would be a stronghold of military might. Sokolov estimated that Rogov would be leaving the bunker about nine the following morning.

He would proceed to the Kremlin. By then, the Elite Guard of Russian troops that was scheduled to secure the Kremlin for the duration of the American president's visit would have arrived at Sheremetyevo, from where it would travel by truck to the center of Moscow. They were indeed the best and most loyal of Russian troops, but their loyalty was to Rogov's version of Russia, not President Konyigin's. "I hate the thought," Sokolov said, "that I'm helping that pig Konyigin in any way. He is the lowest form of life on this planet."

"He's a politician. That's what politicians are. That's what democracy is all about."

"Exactly the reason I think it's the worst idea I ever came across. What's the point if you end up having people like Konyigin run things? This will be the end of Russia."

Edward smiled. He had watched his new friend walk straight into it and not even see it. "In a democracy, my friend, if you don't like the leader, you, the people, can vote for someone else and change him. Then you can change the next one, and so on, until you find one you like. Then you keep him for a while. Better than one jerk, like your General Rogov, in power and be stuck with him for the rest of his life. You were so close to helping him take over, and now here you are fighting against him. Doesn't that tell you something? There is no substitute for democracy, not yet anyway."

Sokolov sat quietly for a long minute. Then, in a low, thoughtful voice, he said, "You have a point. I'm sure there's a flaw in your argument somewhere, but we'll have to pick it up again when this is all over."

"You're on," Edward said, and lit a cigarette.

By the time Rogov arrived at the Kremlin, his troops would already have taken control. As soon as the American president's plane had landed, the communication array would be activated, so all normal communication by radio, television, and satellite would cease, to be replaced by Peter's proclamation of his own ascendancy.

"Do you think you'll have any trouble with the Kremlin security?"

"Kremlin security has only one man who is a member of the Black Ghosts, Colonel Denisov, the chief of the entire unit. That is why Rogov was able to ensure that his troops would be the ones called in to guard the Kremlin. All the rest of the staff are loyal. Remove Denisov and we remove the problem."

"And how do you intend to do that?"

"Simple. He believes I'm the one who has to take control, remember. I shall arrest him."

"Can you make it stick?"

"I'm sorry?" Sokolov was puzzled by this unfamiliar expression.

"Can you convince everyone around him that you are right to arrest him?"

"I am a colonel. I need to convince no one."

Their deliberations were interrupted by Edward's watch sounding its alarm. "It's time," he said, getting up. "They should be arriving here in . . ."—he looked at his watch again—"about ten minutes, give or take five. Yuri?" He called to the big man, who was almost asleep at the table, bored with the fast English that Edward and Sokolov were talking, which to him must have sounded like a loose nut in a fan.

"Da?"

"Can you turn on the runway lights?"

"When?"

"We should be able to hear them coming in. We don't want the lights on for too long."

"The switch is in big hangar. My man is waiting there, but I go myself. Maybe he had too much to warm himself." He made a drinking gesture with his hand.

"And get the hangar doors open; we want the plane in there as quickly as we can."

"What kind of plane?" Yuri asked.

"Jumbo, Boeing seven forty-seven."

"No problem, this place built for it. Here." He handed

Edward the walkie-talkie. "This set for you to talk. You tell when light go on."

"Great." Edward was satisfied. "Did you test the lights?"

"No, no need for that."

There was that detail he had forgotten, Edward thought. He had forgotten to take care of it beforehand, when he'd had the time, and he was not used to working with people who had to be told everything. He needed an alternative plan, and fast. "How many cars do you have?"

"Twelve," said the Russian, puzzled.

"Get your men in the cars and out to the field now." Edward's voice made it clear that things were urgent. "Have them line up the cars on both sides of the runway and turn on the car lights. Have them spread out along the entire length. This is a big plane we have coming in. He needs lights, and if your lights don't work we need a backup."

Yuri got the message. Responding to the urgency in Edward's voice, he got up and began shouting orders. His men responded quickly, to Edward's surprise.

"What's the problem?" Sokolov asked, walking by Edward's side on their way out of the farmhouse.

"The plane has come most of the way taking the place of a chartered flight we managed to get delayed." He turned to face the tall Russian officer. "I hope, that is. I've had no communication with them for some time now. After crossing Estonia, they should have descended to a very low altitude. They have to maintain that low-level flight until they arrive here. They should be almost out of fuel. And this is the only place they can land."

By the time they got outside, the various vehicles, including the one Edward had arrived in, were lining up along the runway on both sides. They then turned to face each other, their headlights throwing pools of illumination on the airstrip. Edward was satisfied. In the darkness, he could see the large door of the hangar slowly open, its grooved runners giving a terrible screech.

Then from far away came a sound that at first could be mistaken for a distant drum roll. It gradually developed into the roar of an approaching jet plane.

Yuri pulled the switch in the hangar. The lights on the runway flickered for a moment and then went out, taking with them the lights in the house, the ones at the end of the hangar, and probably everything else within a ten-mile radius.

"Here they come," Edward said aloud, but there was only the sound getting louder and louder. Nothing was visible in the sky. It was eerie, the thundering sound and the empty sky. Then suddenly the giant plane came into view, hugging the top of the hill to the west, almost perfectly lined up with the airstrip. It was flying with landing gear open, not more than fifty feet above the treetops. Before they had time to blink, it was already touching the end of the runway with a screech of rubber on asphalt.

Then came the roar of engines thrown into reverse, bringing the plane to a full stop. It stood there for several seconds, then started to move again, heading for the open hangar. Edward and Sokolov ran to the car closest to them, Sokolov ordering the driver to head for the large open door.

The plane slowly entered the hangar. What had at first seemed to be a giant structure now appeared almost small in comparison with the vast jet that barely fit inside it. The huge engines fell silent.

But almost immediately another sound was heard. At first it sounded like a motorcycle engine, a ta-ta-ta-ta sound. In a flash Edward recognized it: an approaching helicopter. There was the whistle of the turbo engine. It was somewhere beyond the hill the jumbo had just flown over.

"Can you hear me?" Edward shouted into the walkie-talkie.

"What you want?" came the answer.

"Tell your men to turn off their lights!"

There was a call on the radio and the lights went off one by one.

"There's a helicopter coming in!" Edward shouted into the radio. "Can you shoot it down?"

Oleg's helicopter followed the plane's path over the hill. The airfield came into view, and Oleg saw the tail of the huge plane slowly disappearing behind the closing doors of the giant hangar. The entire place was blacked out, but with his night-vision goggles he could see it all in the green light. There were trucks lined up on both sides of the long runway. Men were getting out of them and looking into the sky.

Up in the helicopter, a flash coming from the house

at the end of the runway caught Oleg's eye. He pulled hard on his stick, trying a maneuver he had learned in Afghanistan to get out of the way of a Stinger antiair-craft rocket. In Afghanistan, he had always been ready for one of those and had managed to avoid a few. Today, however, he was not ready, and the maneuver he took didn't stand a chance. He wanted to say something to his navigator, who at that moment was looking in the other direction. Lucky for him, thought Oleg, he will never know.

The ball of fire lit up the entire area for miles around. Then it was dark again, even darker than before.

"If he reported back, we could have the whole Rus-sian army here in no time," Sokolov said.

"Let's get the team out of the plane. We'll have to stay here for now," Edward replied. "We have to play it as if nothing has changed. We have no choice."

CHAPTER 30

Pozharsky Corporation offices, Moscow
23:22 hours

The three military trucks came to a stop down the block from the shiny glass-and-steel office building. There were no pedestrians at this time of night, and the occasional car that passed by only sped up at the sight of soldiers in dark green combat fatigues, black bulletproof vests and black helmets, armed with Kalashnikov submachine guns, and lined up around the corner.

Yakov signaled one of his lieutenants, placing his hand on his head and pointing to the building's main door. Not a word was said. The officer raised a fist in the air, then brought it down to shoulder height, repeating the motion several times, signaling his men to follow him. Hugging the wall, they waited for several seconds. Then a pale green Lada drove up the street and slammed into a telephone pole. The remote-controlled television camera located over the main entrance to the building turned in the direction of the accident. That was the lieutenant's final signal. He got up from his squatting position and, still keeping close to the wall, ran for the main entrance. Stopping several feet short of the door, he allowed two men carrying large steel hammers to pass him. They slammed the hammers into the doors, shattering the glass, and he threw in two stun grenades. Barely waiting for the flash to die down, he ran in with his men, screaming at the top of his lungs. Whoever was guarding the main entrance would be in total shock.

By the time Sergei Pozharsky's guards realized what had happened, they were riddled with bullets and the best they could do was die.

Following the break-in unit, the rest of the soldiers who had been waiting outside now made their way in, each team taking a predesignated floor.

Sergei, up in his penthouse suite, heard nothing until the large oak doors leading from the main hall came tumbling down, bringing the sweating and breathless soldiers to his bedside. The woman seated on him froze, and he had to push her aside as he tried to get to his gun in the drawer by the bed. A single bullet caught him in the shoulder, throwing him back against the satin-covered headboard. He looked at the wound in amazement, as if he had never seen blood before.

The naked woman screamed and tried to run for the door leading to the bathroom. A short burst from the lieutenant's submachine gun stopped her in her tracks.

Splattering the bathroom door with blood and bits of torn tissue, she folded and fell to the floor.

"What do you want?" Sergei shouted in horror. "Who are you, who are you working for?"

"Russia," said the lieutenant, pushing out his chin. "We serve our country, you bag of shit. We will rid the country of scum like you, we'll cleanse it."

Sergei was trembling, trying to stop the bleeding from his wound with his other hand. "What do you want from me?"

At that moment Yakov walked in. "Where is the American you said you had?"

"I don't know what you're talking about!" Sergei tried to gain ground. Yakov drew a pistol from his holster and without any hesitation aimed it and shot Sergei in his shoulder, through the hand that was trying to stop the bleeding. "Where is the American?" He pointed his gun again.

Sergei was crying. His flabby body, now almost completely covered with blood, heaved as he shrieked loudly. "I don't have him, he's at the airfield."

"What airfield?"

"I have the name in my desk," Sergei said, trying to buy some time. He knew that he was not going to be left alive once these people, whoever they were, got their answers. He knew he had one chance to survive. This situation he was in right now did not come as a total surprise to him. The suddenness of it did, though. The way these people had made it all the way to his suite without his knowing was quite a feat, but he still had a card up his sleeve—even if he had no sleeve.

"Where in the desk?"

"The bottom drawer. There is a small compartment there. Inside that, there's a map with the airport marked on it."

"Up," Yakov said, pointing to the door with his gun. "Come on, move it."

"Please, please, let me get something to stop the bleeding," Sergei gasped. He tried to stand up, only to fall to the floor by the bed. He lay still, trying to pretend he had passed out. "Bring him over," the lieutenant said to two of the soldiers who were still standing exactly where they'd wound up after breaking in.

They grabbed Sergei by the arms and pulled him up. The pain in his shoulder became unbearable and he knew he was about to pass out for real. He had to stay out of his office when they opened that drawer. He made a run for the balcony door. Outside, there was a small hatch that led to a concrete safe room, if he could only reach it. The first bullet got him in the thigh. His body slumped to one side, crashing through the glass door that led to the balcony.

The second bullet hit him in the back as he lay moaning on the floor amid the broken glass, jolting his body forward. He could see the hatch, which was open, and he could also hear the click as the hidden switch in the small compartment of his desk triggered the explosive device underneath. This was meant to happen when he was already in a safe place. The blast blew out the windows of the entire floor, filling the street below with a shower of glass fragments, pieces of furniture, and uniformed body parts. Yakov, too, knew what was coming when he heard the click of the trigger, but there was nothing he could do but utter a curse.

CG Command Bunker, outside Moscow
23:50 hours

"What do you mean, you lost him?" Androva was not even attempting to sound polite. General Rogov was approaching her, having completed his briefing session in the glass-paneled office.

"He informed us," said the voice on the phone, "that the two first locations you wanted checked were clean. He was on his way to the third when we lost him. We can't send out a helicopter to search for him because they are all committed to other tasks. In fact, they are all out already."

"What is it?" Rogov asked.

"I think I know where Edward and his men are."

"Get him," the general spat and walked on.

By now the place was humming with activity. Almost all units were in position and reports on the uncommitted units were coming in. The general had instructed his officers to set up more roadblocks that would curtail the movements of such units and send them off in other directions.

Androva had already assembled a second assault unit.

She decided not to wait to hear from Yakov. That idiot would probably get lost on his way back. Besides, she had no doubts any more about the location of the airfield: It could only be this one.

There was one last thing she wanted to do before she went. She walked over to a small wooden room, the walls of which were lined with patent leather. It was the quiet room. It was used to make phone calls to faraway places when you didn't want any background noise to give away your location. The phone was also equipped to prevent detection of its location.

"Larry?" she said when the phone was answered.

"Who's this?" asked Joe Falco.

"It's Natalie. Is Larry there?"

"Just a minute."

"Natalie! How are you? Where are you?"

"I'm fine. I left my apartment. I think there was a surveillance team on me. I'm on my way to Edward. Did you want me to tell him anything?"

"Do you know where he is?"

"Sure, he told me. He's at the airstrip outside Kolomana."

Larry had to think fast. She had the right place, and he also knew she was calling to confirm and would probably be on her way out there with enough firepower to stop a country. "I don't think he'll be there," he said with no hesitation in his voice. "I forbid you to go there. I want you out of that place and on the first flight back here. Do you hear me?"

"I'm not leaving him behind," she said. "I want to be with him. How come he will not be there?"

"He's supposed to pick up the men there and head for the Domodedovo Airport. You know, where the president is supposed to arrive."

"Are you sure?"

"Sure, I'm sure. He has to be there to connect with the Secret Service people that will get there first thing in the morning to secure the field. It's a safe place there—you should go there too."

"Okay. If you hear from him, tell him I'll be there," she said and hung up. Now she wasn't sure anymore, but she was not going to leave any door unopened. Her future was riding on this coup: If it succeeded she would become the closest thing to a god she could ever hope to be. If it failed, she was better off dead.

Kolomana airstrip
23:59 hours

The remains of the helicopter were still burning in the field by the runway. Several of Yuri's men had reached it with a truck and were now busy putting out the flames with two fire extinguishers. Yuri wanted it out as fast as possible. He was worried that either this chopper was not alone or that someone would start looking for it shortly.

Edward had reached the hangar as the doors finally shut. He stood there staring at the giant fuselage. From the corner of the hangar, a small square cart started towing a large mobile staircase toward the front door of the plane, just behind the cockpit. Someone had powered up the emergency generator, and the interior of the hangar was lit by a weak yellow glow from some bulbs hanging so high in the roof they looked like tiny stars.

The plane's door opened, and Edward could see a figure standing inside, directing the staircase closer. The staircase stopped five feet short, and the men had to make the leap off the plane. One after another, each carrying his small duffel bag, the men of Edward's team took the leap as if it were the most natural thing in the world.

"Sir." The sergeant stood to attention in front of Edward. "We're all here, ready to kick ass, sir."

Edward smiled at Mario and shook his hand. "Good job, Sergeant. How was the flight?"

"Okay. We got to see Russia real close up."

"I bet."

"What were the fireworks about?"

"We had a visitor, an Mi-8 assault helicopter. We'd better get ready. We might have to leave in a hurry."

The platoon was now standing in a circle around them. A few minutes later they were drinking hot cocoa and getting to know their Russian hosts. There was some stiffness at first. After all, these were men who for most of their lives had been trained to regard each other as the enemy, but soon they were exchanging cigarettes and trying out words on each other. A feeling of cautious comradeship began to develop.

Edward asked Yuri for a phone. He got through to an operator and finally, after almost ten minutes, he had Larry on the line. "You better get your ass out of there," Larry said.

"What's the matter?"

"Natalie just called. She knows where the airfield is. I told here you weren't there and had probably gone to Domodedovo Airport, but I can't be sure she bought it."

"Shit, I knew I was right when I said it was good to have her on our side."

"Yeah, it sure would be, but she's not."

"We can't move the plane, not until morning anyway."

"Get out of there now with the team. If they come for the plane, that's just too bad."

"I'll see what we can do. I'd hate to lose the plane. Listen, man, I have to run." Edward hung up and turned to Yuri. "We might not have as much time as I thought. Where are the weapons?"

"Come, I show you," Yuri said.

The Sergeant and Sokolov came along with them. As they reached the large barn opposite the house, Edward turned to Sokolov.

"How long would it take to get here from the command bunker?"

"About two hours, give or take a bit. Why?"

"I think that's all the time we have. The woman I know as Natalie is probably on her way here, and I believe she will not be coming alone."

"So now she wants to fuck you," Sokolov said, his face

serious. Edward felt that the man still held him responsible for his driver's death.

"Not funny," Edward said.

"Not meant to be," Sokolov replied.

"So what we do now?" Yuri asked.

"Do you think you could protect this place?" Edward stopped walking and stared at the man.

"I could maybe hold for some time, but my men are not army, they do this for money. We are like what you call, gang."

"How many people do you have?"

"Thirty."

"If you hold this place until morning and get my plane out of here safely, you will get ten thousand dollars a head."

Yuri's face lit up. "For that money we take back Afghanistan." They shook hands and entered the barn.

Inside it was lit by a single naked bulb hanging from a wire slung over a beam. At one end of the barn was an old Soviet army truck, surrounded by bales of straw. At the other end were a considerable number of wooden packing crates. Yuri opened one of them to reveal a couple of Kalashnikov assault rifles. Edward took one out. It was not the first time he had handled one of these.

Yuri was looking at him, his dark eyes gleaming. "You like, yes?"

"Oh, yes," said Edward, "I like very much."

Yuri opened another case: Inside were pistols. A third case revealed hand grenades. Then there were rows of tin cases containing bullets. Beside them, in a pyramid-shaped pile, were shoulder-carried antitank missiles and another pile with some twelve Stinger missiles. And there was more.

"Sarge," Edward said, "could you get the men in here, please?"

"Yes, sir," Mario said and turned to leave.

CHAPTER 31

"Piece of garbage," said Tom Murphy, weighing the Kalashnikov in his huge hands. "I coulda made a better machine gun myself."

Chico Valdez did not agree. "Beee-utiful!" he drawled, unleashing a burst of fire at the bales of straw at the far end of the barn.

Yuri was smiling from ear to ear. Not only had he just landed the best contract ever for himself and his men, but he liked the Americans. They were not at all what he had expected. They were real men, the kind it wasn't so bad losing a war to, even if it was a cold war. He'd always had an image in his mind of longhaired freaks, high on something, stepping to the noise of some rock band. These men were Russian as far as he was concerned, only they couldn't speak the language. "Edward," he said, "why you come here?"

Edward stared in surprise at Yuri. The question was so unexpected. Until that moment he hadn't realized that the man standing in front of him could exist on a level beyond the immediate. "What do you mean?"

"You do this for money?"

"No, of course not."

"Why, then?"

"Free people must help other free people stay free, or they lose their own freedom in the end."

"I wish I could be in America." Yuri had a somber smile on his large face.

"America is an idea, a state of mind. You can make an America anywhere." Edward noticed that all his men were silent and listening. "Okay, okay, enough with the philosophy," he said, breaking the spell. "Yuri, do you have silencers?"

Yuri looked to Sokolov for a translation of the unfamiliar word. Sokolov said something and Yuri shook his head. "Nyet, nyet. But, come, I show you." He walked over to a large metal trunk and opened it. Inside was an old but still functional crossbow. Edward couldn't help laughing. Then he thought of something else. He asked Yuri if any of his men spoke English, and if so, could Edward borrow one of them for a time? "In case I need someone who speaks Russian," he explained. Yuri introduced him to a tough-looking man in combat fatigues, whose name was Vanya, and explained to the Russian that he was now under Edward's command. Then Yuri went off to position his men around the perimeter, ready to surprise whoever might venture in their direction.

Edward turned to his men. "We'll be leaving this place in forty minutes," he announced. Beckoning one of the pilots, he said, "Dan, we need to talk."

"I figured there was a problem," Dan said grimly. "What is it?"

"You have to make a decision. Where is Archie?"

"He's taking a nap at the house. All this weaponry and stuff is not his bag."

"We're going to be moving out. Yuri and his men will try and protect this place, but I can't guarantee they will manage."

"Where are you guys heading?"

"We'll make for the bunker. We're going to try and cut the general off from his command and communication, put them in disarray. Then comes your part. You know what that is, but I can't make you or Archie do it. Things have changed since we made the plans."

"Forget it, Edward, I didn't come all this way for nothing. We're going ahead with it. Like you said, this is too big a deal to leave it to some bureaucrat to solve."

"Listen, you need to know that there is probably a crack military unit on its way here as we speak. If they get here . . ."

"Edward, like I said, I know the risks. I also know that Archie would kill me if I pulled out. You go do your thing and we'll do ours. And when it's over we'll all have a drink. Now forgive my language, but fuck off."

"Do you need some help with getting the beast out of the hangar?"

"No, it's a fantastic deal they got here. The hangar has doors on the other side and a piece of taxiing runway from there too. I just need the door opened and I can almost fly directly from the hangar."

"By the way, how did it go in Greenfield, Arizona?"

"Man, you should have been there." The pilot's eyes lit up. "It was a piece of cake. We gave them the papers. They had the plane all fueled up and ready to go. All they cared about was that the money went through. It was great, just great."

Each man chose his personal weapon and filled his shoulder pouch with as many rounds of ammunition and grenades as one could possibly carry. Jean-Pierre was assigned the crossbow, while several of the others strapped on grenade launchers or Stinger missiles. The rest of the stuff was loaded on the trucks and they were ready to go.

Sokolov took out a map of the area and spread it over the hood of the jeep. He and Edward pored over it. The colonel pointed out the road leading to the bunker and described the terrain.

"Did you guys load the explosives?" Edward asked the sergeant.

"Yep, they're on that truck. Tom will be driving it. Are we taking the Cherokee too?"

"Yes, we'll take three trucks and the Cherokee," said Edward. "Who's the expert with explosives?"

"Valdez, why?"

"I want him to rig the truck so it can be detonated with a remote."

"How do you want it to be triggered?" asked Valdez, who was standing by the truck.

"Here." Edward handed him the walkie-talkie. "You can use this. Just make sure you don't pick an overused frequency."

"When do you want me to get it set up?"

"Now, on the way. I'll need it ready within about half an hour. Can you do that?"

"You'll hear it if I can't." Valdez smiled, showing his gleaming, pointed teeth.

"Okay! Let's go, let's go!" Edward yelled.

The small convoy set off into the darkness of the Russian night. After twenty minutes of driving, Edward ordered Doug Findley to stop the jeep. Looking all around him, Edward got out and studied the lay of the road. The spot where they had come to a halt was on the side of a gentle slope. On one side the hill rolled down some sixty feet toward a small brook, and on the other side of the road there was a thick pine grove.

"Sarge," Edward said finally, "park the truck with the explosives over there." He pointed to a large boulder on the side of the road near the pine grove. "Get the other trucks down that path." He pointed to a small dirt side road that forked off the main road about seventy feet away.

"Are we ambushing someone?"

"You bet we are."

"Done," the sergeant said and began to shout orders, getting things moving the way Edward wanted.

"What are you up to?" Sokolov asked, climbing out of the jeep.

"We have to spend the night somewhere, might as well get something done." Edward looked in the direction of the truck that was loaded with explosives. Jean-Pierre and Jeremy were standing by it, waiting for instructions. "Tell them," Edward said, pointing at the two men, "how to get to the bunker. I need them in an observation position. Meanwhile, I'll get the others into position here."

Sokolov responded immediately, marching off briskly toward the two men. Edward and the sergeant placed the rest of the men at fifteen-foot intervals on the wooded side of the road. Each man had his designated kill area. Now all they needed was a target.

Sokolov returned to Edward with the two men. "I believe they could get there with no problem."

"You guys take the jeep, and this." Edward handed Jeremy a small radio transceiver, one of the units Larry had sent them on the plane. "We should be getting in range in a couple of hours, as soon as we finish the work we have here."

"Okey-doke," Jeremy said, and Jean-Pierre nodded.

As the jeep moved down the road and out of sight, Edward and Sokolov went into the thick grove, heading toward the sergeant, who was the farthest man from the truck.

"Where is Valdez?" Edward asked.

"Still in the truck. He said he wasn't through yet,

and if he was late to start without him." The sergeant chuckled.

"He better get out of there fast. We don't have that much time left. If my calculations are correct, they should be here any minute—if they're coming at all."

"There," the sergeant said, pointing to the back of the truck. Valdez had just leaped down and was running toward them.

"Colonel Sokolov," said Edward, "if we manage to knock them off, can you try and use their radio, if there still is one, and give them some disinformation?"

"I can try. The question is if they have a direct link or not."

The sound of vehicles changing gears came suddenly from down the road. Even though they were all in place and expecting something to happen, it was still somewhat of a surprise. Valdez handed Edward the walkie-talkie. "You do the honors, sir," he whispered.

Led by a command car, four trucks rumbled along the road. Edward could see the soldiers seated in the back of the trucks: Some were asleep, others were talking and laughing as soldiers do. At that moment the leader, seated in the command car, had noticed the parked truck as he rounded a bend in the road. The car came to a halt. Perfect, Edward thought.

An officer got out of the command car and, accompanied by a soldier, walked over to the truck. He stopped a few feet from the cabin and shouted something. When there was no reply he drew his gun and spoke to the soldier standing next to him, who ran back to the first truck, which had already come to a stop. Soon there were some fifteen soldiers standing by the officer.

Edward pressed the switch on the walkie-talkie. The blast tore into the first of the trees, leaving a clearing thirty feet wide. The command car rolled down the hill, turning over and smashing against the rocks it encountered on the way. The first of the trucks seemed to jump slightly to one side and began to burn. There was no sign of any of the men who had been standing by what was now a large smoldering crater. Before anyone could get off the other two trucks, RPGs hit the vehicles in several places. The burning soldiers who jumped off the back of the trucks were put out of their misery by the men waiting in the darkness of the woods. It was over almost as soon as it had started. No one was heading for the airfield now, Edward thought. Not for the moment anyhow.

"Vern," the sergeant shouted, "go get the radio out of that fucking command car. See if it's working."

The slim man moved quickly down the hill. He stopped for a moment, leveled his submachine gun and fired into a bush. There was a thud of someone falling, and he went on. "I need a hand," he shouted from the bottom of the hill. "It's a big mother. Unless you plan to come down here to use it, I'll need someone to help me get it out."

Before Edward or the sergeant could say anything, Chico Valdez was already on his way.

"If it's working," Sokolov commented, "we should wait until they contact us. That way we'll at least know our own call name."

"Good thinking," Edward replied.

His men were walking among the wreckage, searching for tools they might be able to use—or for someone who might need help in dying.

CHAPTER 32

"Are you sure this thing is working?" Edward asked the sergeant, pointing a finger at the half-smashed radio they had recovered from the command car. It was sitting on the hood of the truck, hot-wired to the truck's battery.

"We tried it on other frequencies and we heard them right. So I have to say it's working."

"I wish Sparky was here," said Edward.

A squawk came from the radio box. Then, amid the static, came a woman's voice. Edward could feel the jolt inside him, like an electric shock. It was her. She was talking Russian and there was a strength to her voice, a strength that he now realized she had worked hard to suppress when they were together. It was that which made her voice seem so strange.

Sokolov grabbed the mike. He now knew the call name. He was hoping that Rogov was not standing anywhere near wherever she was talking from, because he might recognize the voice. This, however, was a chance they had to take.

"Intruder One, this is Intruder Two, over."

"Did you reach the target?" came the question, without any formal communications procedure. She was clearly in a hurry and not willing to spend time on what she thought to be rubbish.

"Yes, Intruder One, have reached the target and met little resistance. We're still mopping up."

"What about the American?"

"I can't be sure. Most of the locals are dead. I will interrogate the survivors."

"Is there a plane there?"

"There was a plane, American made, very big. It is now burning very nicely, Intruder One."

"If you find the American or any of his friends, you will notify me."

"Yes, will do."

Edward put his hand over the microphone. "Ask her where she is."

Sokolov nodded silently. Then he put the microphone close to his mouth again. "If we find him, where do we bring him?"

"I'll be at Domodedovo Airport in the morning. Bring him to the command center at the north end of the airport. Over and out."

Sokolov translated all that was said. Edward was satisfied. It looked as though their luck was coming in one piece at a time, but then, he thought, it is said that good things come in small packages.

Domodedovo Airport, Moscow
06:30 hours

Lieutenant-Colonel Orlov had a problem. Someone he knew vaguely, a certain Colonel Sokolov from the Twenty-ninth Armored Division, had called him with a strange story about a potential takeover of the airport he was guarding. As if that weren't enough, a general from Supreme Command had announced his intention of inspecting Orlov's troops at 07:00 hours that morning. Orlov had never heard of General Lubinsky, but a call to Supreme Command confirmed that such a general did exist. Lubinsky's aide, who had set up the inspection, had also given the correct codes, so Orlov had no reason to doubt his credentials, other than the mysterious call from this Sokolov.

The general was to arrive shortly by helicopter. Was this to be the takeover Sokolov had warned him about? On balance, Orlov doubted it.

At 6:45, he heard the percussive drone of the helicopters. He could see them approaching from where he sat in the command center, three of them, flying in formation. They landed on the tarmac, not fifty yards from where he was, raising a terrible cloud of dust and frigid morning air. Orlov watched as the hatches opened and armed men, which he took to be the general's security entourage, poured out. There was a pause while the guards' NCO called them to attention. Then the general emerged.

Yes, this was him. Looking through his binoculars, Orlov could see the stars and braids. The general and his men moved toward the command post.

But as he approached, Orlov observed that the man didn't quite look like a general. He didn't have that certain something. He was too small somehow, his neck too stiff, his eyes too red and unblinking, like a rat's. Orlov dismissed the thought, attributing the man's general lack of luster to the fact that he was probably a well-climbed bureaucrat who had never tasted war except via a phone line or a nasty letter.

Leaving all but two of his men outside, the general entered the command post. "Lieutenant-Colonel Orlov?" he said in an extremely decisive way. Not waiting for a response, he went on. "I am temporarily relieving you of your command while I inspect this unit."

Orlov saluted. "Very good, sir." The telephone rang. A junior officer informed Orlov that the call was for him.

"With your permission, sir." Orlov took the call. It was from the office of General Lubinsky, in Supreme Command. Wanting to verify the information, Orlov had also placed a second call through army command, asking to speak to the general. By doing that he was circumventing Supreme Command and dealing directly with the general, who for some reason was stationed in Vladivostok. The duty officer in the general's headquarters wanted to inform him that the general was in conference at the moment and was not to be disturbed. He would, however, be willing to deal with whatever it was Orlov wanted later on that day.

"Yes, thank you," said Orlov, replacing the phone carefully. Turning to the small man in the general's uniform who stood looking out the window, quietly waiting for him to finish his telephone conversation, he said, "One thing."

"Yes?" The man turned his whole body to look Orlov in the face.

"You are under arrest," Orlov said, his voice as calm as if he were offering the man a cup of tea, "on a charge of impersonating an officer of the Russian army."

Yazarinsky's expression did not change. "I'm sorry, you are mistaken."

"I have just received confirmation that General Lubinsky is still in Vladivostok," said Orlov.

"But I did not say I was General Lubinsky. I am under his command, that is all."

Orlov hesitated. The whole thing was very suspicious, especially in view of Sokolov's mysterious warning. "Arrest this man!" he said to his men.

But his hesitation cost him dearly. Yazarinsky's men in the hall had seen Orlov's guards reach for their weapons. They were not the kind to hesitate. Yazarinsky's answer to Orlov, which made no sense and was not meant to, had given his team the time they needed to get through the open door.

A single shot was fired by one of Yazarinsky's men. A young officer had managed to raise his gun and was about to shoot when a 762 metal jacket scrambled his thoughts, sending a sizable portion of the back of his head crashing against the wall: Yazarinsky's men had their guns pointed at anything that might move.

Not that anything did, except Yazarinsky's lips. "Lieutenant-Colonel Orlov," he hissed, "I arrest you on charges of insubordination and treason."

Orlov and his junior officers were marched under heavy guard to the airport terminal building, where they were locked into an airport security holding cell. Yazarinsky was now in charge.

Woods south of CG Command Bunker
07:00 hours

Edward was awakened by a gentle tap on his shoulder. Colonel Sokolov, immaculately groomed and dressed in full uniform, was bending over him. Edward sat up. It was cold and every bone in his body hurt. It had been some time since he had slept outside on hard, cold, uneven ground in a thin, smelly sleeping bag. This sort of thing was not meant for human beings beyond a certain age, or even before that. Unless you have company, a sleeping bag is not really meant for sleeping, he thought. "I'll have a coffee, two eggs over easy," he said to the surprised Sokolov.

Ignoring him completely, Sokolov said, "I will be leaving in a few minutes."

Edward got up and rubbed his face. Then he bent down by the creek that passed several feet below where he had slept and washed his face. The icy water shocked him into full awakening. Sokolov, who had followed him, smiled at Edward's gasps and spluttering and handed him a towel to dry his face.

"I wonder if General Rogov's face will look like that when he arrives at the Kremlin and finds that his elite troops are elsewhere?"

"Don't bet on it," Edward said grimly. "He'll be heavily armed. He won't give up without a fight."

"Good luck," said Sokolov. "Don't forget you're not fighting against the Russians, you're fighting for them." They shook hands and said goodbye.

Pulling on his jacket, Edward started getting the men up. Mario, the sergeant, was looking after them like a mother hen. He had already started the coffee. Its aroma cruelly reminded Edward of home. After Natalie, his little place over the bistro seemed awfully lonely.

No one jumped out of his sack ready and eager to go. Edward attributed this to the fact that they were still on New York time. They were being told by their bodies that it was one in the morning, just the hour that most of them were used to hitting the sack.

Grumbling and complaining, they assembled around the small portable gas range, holding the tin cups in both hands to beat the Russian chill. The sergeant broke out some of the food rations they had brought over on the plane. Not much, but enough to get them going.

After breakfast they climbed into the trucks. Now not a word of complaint was heard. They knew that today they had a job to do, and it was a job they took very seriously.

CHAPTER 33

Sheremetyevo-2 Airport, Moscow
08:30 hours

"Get your commanding officer, on the double," Sokolov shot to the guard at a checkpoint on the road leading into Sheremetyevo Airport. The guard saluted the colonel in the car and spoke to his radio for a moment.

"Password?"

"Blaze Delta Fox," said Sokolov. The guard checked a list he had on a clipboard hanging from the end of the temporary barricade. He then read something from his board into the radio. It was a secondary code, known to the commanding officers who were part of the Black Ghosts' network. It not only confirmed that Sokolov was a member of the organization, it also identified him personally. If any of Rogov's people had begun to suspect that Sokolov had turned against them, now would be the moment when he would find out.

The guard listened as he got a response over the

radio, then he leaned closer to the open window. "Major Lermontov will see you, sir." He pointed down the road. "The command post is that way." He straightened up and saluted smartly. Then he signaled a second guard to move the barricade. To this point, it seemed Sokolov's status was intact.

Major Lermontov came out of the command post to greet him with a salute. "Is everything all right, sir?" he asked, unsure of what this unscheduled visit portended.

"Everything is proceeding as planned," said Sokolov. "I am here to supervise the arrival of the special commando units and give them their final orders regarding their taking control of the Kremlin. I require immediate access to the air traffic control tower."

"Of course, sir. Right away."

Lermontov provided two lieutenants to escort Sokolov to the control tower. The air traffic control room was busy and the atmosphere was tense—it was an ordinary business day, as well as being the morning of the American president's arrival. The controllers seated at the desks were uncomfortably aware of the strong military presence in and around the airport—soldiers everywhere, waiting, watching. It was a reminder of the bad old days of the Soviet Union, when every move you made seemed to be watched by someone. Still, the tower staff knew it was in a good cause. No one wanted anything bad to happen, today of all days.

"You wait for me here," he said to his two escorts before entering the control room. Inside, he could see all eyes on him. To his pleasure, not one look was sympathetic.

The chatter was muted, each controller involved with his planes, guiding them to a safe landing at the gigantic airport.

Shortly, though, they knew they would have to start diverting traffic to other destinations because of the impending visit. They were not aware yet that the president's landing location had been changed.

On one side of the control room, overlooking a section of the airport where a large number of military planes were parked, sat a uniformed controller. He was a sergeant of the local air battalion who was the military coordinator for the field.

Sokolov approached him. "Do you have your schedule?" he asked bluntly.

The sergeant looked up at him, dropping his earphones to his neck. "Yes, sir." He handed Sokolov a long yellow sheet of paper.

Sokolov ran his eyes over it. "There is an unscheduled flight on its way here." He drew a pen from his pocket and scribbled something on the yellow sheet. "Raise this flight on that frequency," he said. "I need to speak to the lead pilot."

Several seconds later he was handed the earphones, which had a mouthpiece extending from one side.

"It's the pilot you requested, sir," the sergeant said and leaned back in his seat, giving Sokolov as much privacy as he could without leaving his post.

"Condor One, this is Blaze Delta Fox, can you hear me?"

"This is Condor One, go ahead."

"Code nine nine four seven velochick. Do you read me?"

"Yes, sir, I'm waiting for a new heading, sir."

Sokolov had input the emergency relocation code that had been created to divert the flight of the incoming commandos in the event that the CG did not take control of the airport or if there was some other change of plan. He then relayed a new heading to the pilot and ordered them to observe radio silence after this conversation was over. They were now moving away from Moscow and would land at a secondary location in Gorky. Sokolov would have preferred to send them straight to Siberia, from where there was no chance of their returning in time. But that was something only the general was authorized to do.

He then returned the earphones to the sergeant and wrote a second frequency on the sheet. "Get this one for me."

The sergeant nodded and turned back to his radio. Sokolov looked over his shoulder. One of the lieutenants he left outside had entered the room. He stopped to say a few words to the door guard, who was probably one of his soldiers. Then the young officer walked over to Sokolov, just as the radio operator handed him the headset again.

"I asked that you wait for me outside," Sokolov said, frowning.

"I just need to know about the trucks, sir."

Sokolov ignored what the young man was saying. "I specifically remember asking you to wait outside."

"Sir." The lieutenant was starting to lose his nerve. He lowered his voice. "Sir, I just wanted—"

"Get the hell out of this room," Sokolov interjected, raising his voice. "Now, get out now."

The young man, pale and wobbly, turned and left the room. No one dared look at Sokolov. He put the earphones on. "You have clearance to land," he said. "I am handing you back to air traffic control." The operator took back the microphone.

"Bring him in," Sokolov said to the sergeant. He then walked briskly out of the control room and, turning to the two lieutenants standing outside, said, "Come, we will return to the command post."

They drove back across the tarmac. Inside the command post, Major Lermontov helpfully outlined the troop transfer arrangements. Ten transport trucks and several mobile staircases would approach the planes, which would be directed to taxi to a side section of the airport, away from the passenger area. When all were aboard the trucks, the convoy would set off for the Kremlin.

Sokolov didn't have long to wait. He had been in the command post for less than half an hour when a radio message informed them that the Ilyushins were landing. A few minutes later, both aircraft were on the ground.

"Only two?" said Major Lermontov. "I understood there were to be three of them."

"The third developed engine trouble," said Sokolov, improvising. "So they crowded everybody into two planes."

They went outside. The soldiers were already descending the stairways, moving toward the waiting trucks.

Major Ostinov, the commanding officer of the Ukrainian units, walked jauntily up to where Sokolov and Lermontov stood. Grinning broadly, he gave a mock salute. "Where are the movie cameras?" he asked in Ukrainian.

Sokolov could only gamble that Lermontov would believe they were speaking in code.

"They're hidden, for greater spontaneity. But they're already running." Sokolov saluted again. The man's face went very serious and with slightly exaggerated movements he executed a formal military salute. There was still a gleam of amusement in his eyes. Lermontov, who had been speechless with surprise at the man's lackadaisical approach, now seemed somewhat mollified. He returned the salute, although somewhat hesitantly.

Still speaking in Ukrainian, Sokolov ordered Major Ostinov to board one of the waiting trucks. "I will join you in a moment," he said. He took his leave of Lermontov, then climbed into the cab of the nearest truck. As the convoy pulled out of the airport, Sokolov could see Lermontov standing on the tarmac, still with a look of vague puzzlement on his face.

CHAPTER 34

Heathrow Airport, London
09:00 hours

The Boeing 747 taxied gently to the end of the runway. For several moments, the white plane with its chrome underbelly and blue stripe running its length and converging over the cockpit and the inscription "United States of America" just stood there, as the pilots and the ground control exchanged the last procedural bits of information.

With a roar of jet engines, Air Force One began its sudden, urgent acceleration along the runway. The fuselage shook gently, the wheels rumbled, and then like a gigantic hippo leaping into the air, the plane took off. It banked at a steep angle, and President Bradshawe kept his eyes tightly closed. Only when the slope of the floor had leveled off, and the seat-belt sign had winked out, did he release his grip on the chair's armrests and open his eyes. Below him was the chaotic jumble of streets and patches of green that is London seen from the air. But the president did not look down. And not just because of his vertigo. It was also that he'd had quite enough of the annoying little country falling away beneath him and was glad to see the last of it for some time. Royalty and pageantry and all that to-do about nothing, he thought.

He had endured a stiff and formal afternoon at Downing Street, followed by a stiff and informal dinner at the prime minister's country residence, and a night on a stiff and intractable mattress in a room that made him feel claustrophobic. And, of course, he had endured the stiff and boring prime minister, whose snobbery and reserve he found almost unendurable. Even the loutish, inebriated over-familiarity of the Russian president was preferable to that.

And as for the breakfast he had been served! President Bradshawe reached into his pocket for his Rolaids but then remembered he had eaten the last of them that morning. He rang the bell for the flight attendant.

Sitting several feet behind the president, in the corner of the large flying office, James Fenton was quietly confident that things were well in hand. Based on the information Angela Baines had given him, he had decided to heed Larry's warning. He had alerted only those who needed to know about the change in destination, and even then, he had waited until a few moments before Air Force One took off from Heathrow to make the necessary arrangements. The plane's pilots and the American security men in Moscow were the only ones told of the change. Even the president himself was not yet aware that the plane would be landing at Domodedovo. Not that Fenton thought it would make much difference to him. As long as there was a camera where he was heading, he would go.

Just outside the office, in what looked more like a spacious lounge than the inside of a plane, sat Bud Hays. He was also feeling pleased with himself. He had enjoyed Angela's favors a second time after dinner last night and was anticipating more of the same during their stay in Moscow. He watched her now, her body swaying as she walked across the floor to the bathroom. She really was a beauty; there was no doubt about that.

Poor Bud, Angela thought, looking back and smiling at her boss: He had no idea of what was about to happen.

The Kremlin, Moscow
10:00 hours

Vladimir Ivanovich Konyigin loved television. On the second floor of what used to be the Supreme Soviet Building, in a lavish office decorated for Andropov many years back, when the chairman of the communist party was God, Konyigin and his top advisers were reviewing videotapes of the British news broadcasts describing the American president's visit to Downing Street.

Fascinated, Konyigin watched every move, every gesture the American president made. Already, in his mind, he was rehearsing the signing of the treaty tomorrow. He knew this would be his biggest public relations coup ever. It would be a chance for him to bolster his failing popularity in preparation for the elections later in the year, his chance to show the Russian people and the world that he was a man of actions, not just words, that he could get things done.

He also knew what really mattered to his people was not the treaty itself but the influx of foreign investment and the gigantic American aid package which was Bradshawe's bribe to him for getting this thing done.

He wanted to be sure that nothing could go wrong. He had already been briefed by Gregorin, his security chief and the head of the Presidential Guard, who was now sitting next to him in the conference room. He had a clear image of the day's events mapped out in his mind. He could see it all now: the crowd of reporters and television crews at Sheremetyevo Airport as the president's plane came in, the drive in the limousine, the reception with the Guard of Honor at the Kremlin, the signing of the treaty, the handshakes, the slaps on the back, the smiles of friendship . . . this would be for all the world to see.

Next to him, the security chief's mobile phone rang almost unheard. Gregorin took the device out of the holster hanging from his belt and pressed it to his ear. After he had spoken and listened to the caller for a few minutes, he put the phone away and took a deep breath. He knew what he had to say to President Konyigin would not go down well.

"We've just heard from the American Secret Service. They want to change the arrival point to Domodedovo."

"What!" thundered Konyigin. "Out of the question! All our arrangements have been made. They must stand."

"The Americans say there is a security risk at Sheremetyevo," the security chief said apologetically.

"But the airport is protected by the army," snarled Konyigin. "How dare they question my authority? Tell them the arrangements stand."

Gregorin cleared his throat. "I'm afraid they won't listen, Vladimir Ivanovich. They have presented this as an ultimatum: Domodedovo, or they stay at home."

Almost beside himself with fury, President Konyigin slammed his fist on the arm of his chair, causing a little cloud of dust to rise. "The arrogant bastards! Let them stay home, then." He sat in silence, his face contorted by an angry frown.

The security chief waited. He knew the signs: Within ten minutes Konyigin would have calmed down, within fifteen he would agree to the change, and within half an hour he would once again be boring everyone with boyish, enthusiastic praise of all things American. It was only a matter of time.

Outside the Kremlin
10:11 hours

Ten army trucks were approaching the Kremlin walls. They were moving at a slow pace, keeping a uniform distance between them. After entering the inner yard they came to a stop, lining up outside the yellow four-story building of the old armory. As the soldiers disembarked, Sokolov gathered the senior officers around him and gave them a brief address. This, he knew, was the most important speech of his career, and he was giving it to soldiers who believed they were there to make a movie. What an irony, he thought.

"Now I know this is only a movie," he said, "but I want you all to behave at all times as though you were on active service, in a normal operation. The main film crew will arrive shortly. We will get into position in a moment. You are to instruct your men to refrain from talking to anyone but me. If anyone approaches them, for whatever reason, they are to get their weapons in a ready position and appear to be ready to shoot. It must look real, is that clear?"

They all nodded, smiling to one another. Sokolov had never seen officers and soldiers of the former Soviet Union comb their hair as much as this unit he had received from the Ukraine. It was as though every last one of them believed he would be discovered and taken to Hollywood, to live in Beverly Hills and sleep with all the movie stars.

"The Kremlin," he continued, "must look occupied. We are also using hidden cameras, so it is important that appearances be kept up. Is that understood?"

They all nodded again. "Very well," he said, "carry on."

The soldiers formed three ragged rows of ten by their respective trucks. Each truck also carried a sergeant who now ordered the troops to stand to attention.

"At ease," came the shouted command, and the men moved as one. "Attention!" came the order again, cutting through the cold air like a sharp blade. "By the right—form!" Each man now extended his right arm and placed his fist against the shoulder of the man next to him, shuffling his feet in small steps to bring him to the correct distance. Now the ranks were in orderly parade-like position.

While this was going on, Sokolov made his way to the building that was known as the Supreme Soviet. He knew it was now called something else, but since it was still the same building with its large gold insignia of the shield with the hammer and sickle in a laurel crown, it didn't much matter. The soldier in the dark blue uniform of the Kremlin Guard stood in his path.

"Sir!" the guard said, chin out, Kalashnikov held closely to his chest.

"I'm here to see the chief of Kremlin security."

The guard moved to the side like a well-oiled robot and pointed to a tall door in the whitewashed wall of the building. "Through there, sir."

"I will show you in, sir," said a second guard, walking toward the door. Sokolov was escorted to the office of Colonel Denisov, who looked at him with a complicitous smile. "Good morning, Colonel Sokolov. It is good to see you. Is everything proceeding according to plan?"

"Yes, indeed. Our men are assembling in the square outside. You may dismiss the Kremlin Guard immediately."

"Very good," said Denisov. The two men left the

office together. At the door, Denisov seized Sokolov by the arm and said in a low voice, "Today will be a great day for Russia, my friend."

"Indeed it will," replied Sokolov.

"I will see that your men are in position," the officer said, beginning to walk faster.

Sokolov stopped in his tracks. "Wait," he said. "You get your men out of the Kremlin, I will put my men in. When you are done, wait for me in your office."

"I thought we would—" began Denisov, but Sokolov cut him off. "I'm working on direct instructions from General Rogov. Do you have a problem with that?"

"No, not at all. I will meet you back in my office as soon as I have instructed the men to return to barracks."

Outside, the Ukrainians had formed as one large block in the center of the square, thirty ranks of ten men each. Under Sokolov's instructions, each group of ten men was marched by its sergeant to a predetermined location within the Kremlin walls. Once he was satisfied that the Kremlin Guard had been replaced by his Ukrainian stand-ins, Sokolov returned to the office.

Denisov was waiting for him. "Is everything in order, sir?"

"I believe it is. One question: We are expecting no resistance, but should anything unexpected happen, I would like our men to be fully prepared. Do you have any antitank rockets available?"

"Indeed we do," said Denisov. "Come with me."

They walked to the armory. Denisov unlocked the door. Inside was a considerable stock of assault rifles and grenade and rocket launchers, including the deadly RPGs. As they headed for the door, Sokolov, walking behind Denisov, clipped a silencer to his pistol. A few feet from the door, he called on the man walking before him. "Colonel Denisov."

Denisov turned quickly, eager to please. Then he saw the bore of the gun facing him.

"Colonel Denisov," Sokolov said, "you are under arrest on a charge of treason."

Denisov smiled—an involuntary facial reaction that rapidly changed to an expression of shock when he realized that Sokolov was serious. He reached for his gun, but before he had time to fire, Sokolov put a bullet in his chest. A shocked expression was still on his face as he slid to the floor.

"I was hoping that would not be necessary," Sokolov said, looking at the dead body, "but somehow I knew it would be."

One side of the armory had a small office, where Sokolov stowed Denisov's body. Locking the door behind him, he returned to Denisov's office and sat at the desk in his place. He took the telephone and dialed the number of the presidential bodyguard.

Ten minutes later, Gregorin hurried into the office, flushed and smiling apologetically. "Sorry to keep you—a slight emergency. The Americans have decided at the last minute they want to land at Domodedovo instead."

Sokolov did his best to look surprised. "Really? And will they?"

"We are still discussing it. I'll let you know what is

arranged," said Gregorin. "Now, how are things on the ground?"

"The Elite Corps is in position," said Sokolov.

"Good," said the security chief. Then he went back upstairs to try to placate President Konyigin.

CHAPTER 35

Everything was ready. A convoy of trucks, armored cars, and tanks was arranged in formation in the parking area of the bunker. Among them was a van specially fitted with sound and video equipment, from which the new ruler of Russia would show his face for the first time. General Rogov's men were waiting for the order to close the iron fist that already held all of Russia in its grasp.

The telephone call came through right on schedule. The only problem was, it came from the wrong place. General Rogov had been expecting to hear that his elite commando corps was securely in position in and around the Kremlin. Now here was their commanding officer, phoning in from Vnukovo Airport. After apologizing for not landing in Gorky because of technical difficulties, he declared that he was awaiting further instructions.

The general personally got on the line. "Who instructed you to divert course?"

"I received instructions from Blaze Delta Fox, sir," said the puzzled officer on the other end. "He said I should keep radio silence, sir, I know. But since we couldn't land in Gorky, I thought I should call in."

"Well done," the general said. As it turned out, he thought, destiny was on his side. No one could stop him now. It wasn't only Moscow that was at his feet; soon it would be the entire world. And without the arrogant Americans to disturb it, it would be a better world indeed.

"So it's Sokolov," the general whispered as he looked at his code list. "He's the culprit." Had he not the proof that Sokolov's code name was used to divert the Ilyushins, he could scarcely have credited the earnest, methodical colonel with the initiative or guts to be a traitor—or could it be that he had misjudged him? Too late to worry about that now. Peter had only one option.

"Wait there," he told the officer on the other end. "I will join you at Vnukovo and together we will take the Kremlin by force if we have to. They will not defeat us with a little trick like this."

Peter went down to the control room. "Get me the ICBM site at Svirt," he commanded.

"Svirt on the line, sir," said the radio operator.

Peter picked up the microphone. "Nine nine four gamma nine. Begin the countdown now. Alpha, alpha two five five nine Peter."

"Initiation confirmed," came the voice over the speakers. "Targeting one o nine." A red circle lit up next to the city of New York on the world map, then another number was called and a circle lit up next to Washington, D.C. Then it was Los Angeles, then Chicago. Within five minutes the entire United States was covered with tiny, ominous circles. Then came the voice again. "Countdown initiated, Svirt, over."

On the map, white lines splayed out westward from a point north of Moscow. Somewhere above the Atlantic Ocean, each dotted line split into several more, which spread out and finally linked with the little red circles. In the corner of the screen, white digits began to turn. One showed tenths of a second, moving too fast for the eye to see clearly. The other digits showed seconds, minutes, and hours. At this point the digits showed three hours, fifty-nine minutes and forty-five, four, three, two seconds.

Satisfied that all was now in order, Peter made his final preparations to depart. Everyone in the bunker knew their orders. He gave Colonel Mirsk, who was in charge of the array, a final briefing, and bid farewell to Major Androva, who was disappointed that she would not accompany the general on his triumphal journey to the Kremlin.

"When all is done, my dear," he promised her, "you shall be the tsarina of all Russia." Rogov got into his mobile media van and the convoy moved out of the bunker compound.

A half a mile away, on the other side of the valley, Edward watched the convoy leave. As soon as the last truck was out of sight, he sent his men on foot down through the woods in the trough of the valley. Their task was to get as close as possible to the bunker without being seen. Edward threw the crossbow into the back of the Jeep Cherokee and got behind the wheel. According to what Sokolov had told him, there was a road a couple of miles away that passed within a few hundred yards of the bunker's mouth. More important, it passed a point uphill from the bunker itself, which meant that he should be able to approach unobserved. He was to look for a bend in the road by a large craggy boulder. Forty yards uphill from there was a flat area beside the road where he could park the jeep. He would then be separated from the bunker by about five hundred yards of inhospitable rocks and wilderness.

It took him about twenty minutes to drive around to the point Sokolov had described, by which time he hoped that his men would be in position. He left the jeep and struck out across a jumble of rocky terrain to the right. He made slow progress through the rocky scrub, feeling somewhat encumbered by his assault rifle and grenades, as well as the heavy crossbow.

He had moved perhaps three hundred yards when he felt the ground begin to slope more sharply downward. Rounding a rocky outcrop, he caught a flicker of movement below. He froze and watched, counting the seconds as they passed. Nothing happened until, seconds later, the same flicker caught his eye. He realized it was the helmet of the sentry as he passed on his rounds below.

Moving as stealthily as he knew how across the rugged terrain, Edward got within twenty yards of the sentry. He knew, from previous observation and the information

Sokolov had given him, that behind the personnel door at the side of the bunker's mouth, a second armed sentry would have his eye to the narrow horizontal observation slit. In addition, the front of the bunker was surveyed by two video cameras, one stationary and one moving. Positioned above the rolling garage doors, they provided between them a panoramic view of the entire frontal approach. Through binoculars from the other side of the valley, Edward had painstakingly observed the movement of the camera and the sentry. Marching back and forth from one side of the bunker's mouth to the other, the sentry was in view of the cameras at all times, except for a few seconds when, every third or fourth time he reached the left-hand side, the moving camera was pointing away to the right. The video monitors were deep inside the bunker, in the control room. If anything untoward were to appear on them, the alarm would be raised, and the surprise factor, on which the success of Edward's plan depended, would be lost.

He had to get closer. The land here was smoother, providing little or no cover. On the other hand, he was well above eye level, so as long as the sentry didn't lift his sight above the top of the garage doors, Edward was safe.

Crawling on his stomach, Edward got to within a few yards of where the trapezium-shaped section cut into the surface of the hill. Keeping his head as low as possible, he positioned himself directly behind the moving video camera. He could just see its nose protruding from the bunker's mouth as it swept across the grounds below. He also could see the helmet of the sentry as he slowly made his way from one side to the other.

Edward took a wad of putty from his pocket and began to knead it between his thumb and fingers. It softened with the rhythmic movement of his hand, which calmed his nerves. He knew the timing for this operation had to be impeccable. He calculated that on the next sweep, the camera would be pointing to the right just as the sentry reached the leftmost end of his path. He positioned the crossbow, dislodging a pebble that fell to the ground in front of the garage. The sentry stopped and turned around. Edward cursed silently. The sentry, deciding that the sound of the pebble was nothing to worry about, continued marching. But now the sequence of his movements was different, and as he reached the end of his beat, the camera was following him.

Edward had to wait until they got out of phase again. At least now, though, the crossbow was in position. Edward was able to check his aim twice as the sentry turned. Beneath him, Edward saw the nose of the camera as it swung. This was going to be it. At precisely the right moment, Edward let fly with the crossbow.

Domodedovo Airport, Moscow
11:40 hours

The media were getting impatient. They had found out just in time that the president was to land here instead of at Sheremetyevo, and they had rushed over as fast as their cars and vans could carry them. Now they wanted to see some action, but the president's plane was apparently in a holding pattern above the airport and would not be landing for another ten minutes.

The presidential limousines were also waiting. The Secret Service men inside had to do some fairly fancy footwork to get here in time. They all had to get past the Russian troops guarding the airport, whose tanks were stationed at various points, surrounding the runway where the plane was due to land. And more of them were moving in from the surrounding hills.

"I would rather have them pointing in the other direction," one of the Secret Service men said as a pair of T-72 tanks sped in the direction of the terminal, one on each side of the runway.

"What do you want?" said his friend, leaning on the limousine. "They need to show they're in charge. How would you feel if you were on the losing side of the war and then they let you keep some of your toys?"

"Yeah, I guess you're right, but I tell you, I'd still rather have them move a little further down. If they are here to protect us, they should do that."

Somewhere to the north of Moscow, President Bradshawe was getting ready to brace himself for the landing. Right now, it was the only thing he could think about. He was told that the airport had been changed at the last minute for security reasons, and he was assured that the media were informed and in waiting below. It was just going to take a little longer, Fenton said. He was not going to approve the landing until he got confirmation from the ground that all was well, he told the president, and the president knew the security chief was working within his authority and guidelines. There was no point in arguing, so he might as well sit back and try to relax for a while.

At long last, the media people saw the big plane coming in. Cameras turned and microphones were switched on, recording the exact moment when the wheels touched the ground, leaving a puff of white smoke as the brakes locked and the engines crunched into reverse with a deafening roar.

"A historic moment," "a perfect landing," said the reporters, eager to extract maximum footage from the rather commonplace event of a plane touching down. As it got closer, the large "United States of America" inscribed on the side of the fuselage came into sight, as did the Stars and Stripes on the tail, which rose some eight floors off the ground. The presidential seal signified where the door was, and the light blue stripe gave the ungainly whale some style.

After reaching what seemed to be the end of the runway, the big gleaming bird came to a halt. Turning slowly, it started the long taxi back toward the terminal. The Secret Service men were in their cars, already heading for the point designated as the final stop, at the end of a long red carpet which stretched from the entrance to the terminal building to the side of the tarmac, where a battery of microphones were ready to take in whatever the president decided to say.

"Why are they doing that?" asked the Secret Service

man as they approached the microphones. More of the tanks were converging in their direction.

"Fuck if I know. Something doesn't look right." He grabbed the radio and called for his team leader, who was in the first black limo forty feet away.

"I can see them," said the unit commander. "I don't know, I think they're trying to impress us. I'm going to talk to their boss. Stay put."

The unit commander got out of the limousine and walked over to the military command car which stood several feet away, its officer busy giving orders to his troops over the radio.

"Get those tanks out of my face," the Secret Service man said. The tanks were now moving in closer, some of them turning on to the runway behind Air Force One, which was now just about at its contact point by the red carpet.

The Russian officer ignored the Secret Service man, who started to speak in Russian. That got the officer's attention. "What do you think you're doing?"

"Who are you?" the Russian asked.

"I'm head of the president's Secret Service detachment in Moscow."

By now the reporters were coming closer as they, too, began to realize something was not quite right.

"One minute, please," the officer in the command car said. Then he got out of the car and fired a flare gun into the air. The tanks closed in on the presidential plane.

"Here," the Russian officer said to the Secret Service commander, pointing a pistol to his head. "This is for you." Before he could fire, he was hit by a bullet that came from the direction of the Secret Service car. The officer fell to the ground. Most of the reporters, except for a few cameramen who stayed in place as if they were not at all part of the scene, fled toward the terminal building, only to be cut off by an advancing line of Russian soldiers. The Secret Service men joined what seemed certain to be a losing battle, their backs to Air Force One, protecting their president with their own bodies.

Almost lost in the gunfire was the ominous beat of the three Mi-8 helicopters that appeared as if out of nowhere. The beached whale around which the battle raged was trapped in a ring of armor and steel. The Mi-8s, with their twin circular jet intake openings above the cockpit and their extended angular tails, looked like some exotic breed of insect. But no insect could unleash the destructive power of an Mi-8. On each side, under the small wing-like protuberance that carried the fuel tanks, was a cluster of missiles.

Yazarinsky, in the middle chopper of the three, had his eyes fixed on the words he loathed, "United States of America," marked along the side of the aircraft. It was there that he had instructed his men to aim.

Something came in over the radio and the Secret Service unit commander called his men to retreat.

"Back up, back up," he shouted, directing them into their armored limousines. He was pushing as many reporters into the cars as he could, while bullets flew all around them. Some of his men were wounded and two were already dead. The media people were screaming in fear. A cameraman stood on the tarmac, taking pictures of the oncoming troops as if he were in the middle of a movie shoot. He was tossed to the ground by a fast-moving T-72 that went on to grind the man and his camera into a pulp.

"No way, I'm not leaving my post," one of the Secret Service men shouted back at the unit commander.

"We need to regroup. We're good for nothing if we're dead. Get over here, you jerk." They finally retreated into their armored limousines and started moving away from the plane, leaving it at the mercy of the tanks and helicopters. The unit commander could only hope none of the tanks decided to take him out. There was nothing he could do against them. About then, Yazarinsky gave the signal.

From each of the three helicopters, there was a burst of white-hot fire as the missiles were released. Leaving a trail of smoke behind them, the missiles zeroed in on their target: the exposed flank of the 747. The plane exploded in a mass of fire and smoke.

More explosions followed as the fuel tanks ignited. The destruction of the plane was complete.

The scene around the small podium was utter chaos. The red carpet was burning, the battery of microphones now half-melted, and the people who had not escaped into the limousines lay dead on the tarmac.

Inside the limousines, the media people were at first too stunned to speak. Then they began a confused babble of shock and outrage, trying to put into words the incomprehensible event they had just witnessed.

"The president is dead!"

"The president has been assassinated. Air Force One has been destroyed!"

But to no avail. The viewers in America who were watching the live CNN broadcast had been disappointed when, just as the plane was about to touch down, there was a break in transmission and a card appeared on the screen, preprogrammed to fill the space in case of an emergency, with the words "Temporary Fault" in yellow lettering across the top. A few moments later a confused anchorman came on the screen, saying that satellite communication with Moscow had been temporarily interrupted but they would be returning to coverage of the president's Russian visit as soon as possible. Meanwhile, in other news . . .

The communication array had seen its first use.

CHAPTER 36

CG Command Bunker, outside Moscow
12:00 hours

Without waiting to see if his arrow had found its mark, Edward leaped down on the concrete in front of the garage doors. He had six seconds to do what he had to do before the camera picked him up and someone raised the alarm. The pin was out of the grenade even before Edward was on his feet. Keeping low to remain out of sight from the stationary camera, which was pointed horizontally, Edward ran to the personnel door and, pressing the grenade to the wad of putty, stuck it near the handle on the metal door. Then he took cover around the side of the bunker.

The sentry lay on the ground. The arrow had sliced through his neck, piercing the jugular, and he was not long for this world. The last thing he was conscious of was the explosion as the grenade blew the lock off the bunker door.

As soon as he heard the detonation, Edward fired two bursts from his Kalashnikov, one at each camera, rendering them junk. By the time he had kicked the door open, his men were with him. Jean-Pierre tossed in a stun grenade. Containing a large charge of magnesium, it produced not a violent blast but a loud noise and a blinding flash of white light. Within, any personnel in the vicinity of the bunker's doors would now be temporarily but effectively blinded.

Edward's men charged through the open personnel door. They found themselves inside a large area like an underground parking lot, the oil-stained floor of which testified to the fact that until recently the area had housed a large number of heavy motor vehicles. Against the far side, two parked jeeps were all that was left behind after Rogov's convoy had left.

Dazzled and confused by the magnesium grenades, the soldiers in the parking lot fell quickly under the platoon's assault rifles. The gunfire, amplified by the echo from the concrete walls, gave the impression of a much larger contingent than was actually there. Led by Edward and Tom Murphy, the platoon rushed toward the doorways at the far end. One doorway gave into two spiral staircases, one going up and one going down.

"Which way?" Tom asked.

"Down," Edward said, and he threw a flash grenade down the stairwell. They both backed up, backs to the wall, until the flash died down. Even though they had released the genie of surprise out of the proverbial bottle, they all knew there were still armed men in the facility who were not aware of what was going on. They ran down the stairs, trying to be as quiet as they could with all their gear and extra weaponry. When they came across a live target they fired a short burst to change his status, then moved on. Edward knew speed was everything. At the third level they reached a hallway, from which someone was firing indiscriminately into the stairwell.

Realizing whoever it was had not actually identified a target, Edward stopped his men and waited a moment. He put out his hand, and someone behind him handed him a grenade, pin already removed. He held on to the lever. The firing ceased while the shooter changed magazine clips. Edward released the lever, waited for a full two seconds, and tossed it through the opening on the landing. He leaned away, leaving the grenade to do its work.

There was silence. They slowly walked down toward the landing. Stepping over the torn body, they cautiously looked down the corridor. At the end of the hall there was a large metal door with an inscription in red Cyrillic letters.

"Vanya," Edward shouted. "Is Vanya still alive?"

"Da, da. I'm fine, why you suddenly care about me?" The Russian came forward, stepping over the body and into the long hall. Edward pointed at the door. "Can you read that?"

"Central Information Center, or something like that."

"Good, now get back. Valdez?"

"Yes, sir?"

"Would you please open that door for me?"

Chico Valdez drew a small package from his pouch. "Everybody back into the staircase," he said, heading for the metal door. Edward stayed behind to cover him in case some creep showed up from somewhere unexpected and tried to hit his man.

"Let's get the hell out of here," Valdez shouted, running back toward Edward. As they cleared the hall, the blast shook the entire bunker. "What did you put in there?" Edward asked as a cloud of smoke and dust filled the hall and stairwell.

"Just your everyday plastic."

"Let's go! Let's go!" Edward shouted. And they all ran down the hall. The room that opened through the smoke before them was huge. There were screens on all the walls. The chatter of calling radios went unanswered. Then came a burst of gunfire from behind one of the consoles. Tom silently fell to the ground. Edward knelt by him. He couldn't feel a pulse. Valdez helped him pull the big man out of the room and lean him against the wall. They checked his pulse again but he was dead.

They heard the thud of an attack grenade in the control room. There were several short bursts of fire. Then there was silence.

"It's clear," came the French-accented voice of the Canadian. They walked back inside. Jean-Pierre and Doug Findley had killed three of the five men who were in the control center, and two more were wounded and under guard. Edward sent five of his men to survey the entire bunker and ensure that there were no remaining pockets of resistance.

Colonel Mirsk had been wounded in the fray, whereupon he had surrendered immediately. He now sat on the floor with his back against the wall, the front of his uniform soaked in blood, a couple of Kalashnikovs aimed in his direction. Around him, the illuminated maps and computer monitors continued to wink and glow. Edward bent quickly and examined the prisoner's wounds.

"Get Vanya in here, quick," he said. Someone went off to look for him.

Vanya was in the parking lot, smoking and assessing the damage to the bunker. He was just thinking what a useful resource a place like this could be to Yuri's organization, when someone called him into the control room.

"Tell this man that unless he receives medical attention quickly, he will probably die," said Edward, pointing at Colonel Mirsk. "He will obtain that medical attention as soon as he answers all my questions truthfully." Vanya looked a little blank, but when Edward repeated the order he nodded in understanding. He spoke in Russian to the prisoner.

All the fight had gone out of Colonel Mirsk. He was suddenly very clear about two things: one was that the Black Ghosts had been defeated; the other was that he didn't want to die. In answer, he gave a tight nod.

"Ask him to tell us what these mean," said Edward, pointing at the illuminated maps on the wall.

The wounded man replied slowly, painstakingly,

beads of sweat on his forehead. In halting English, Vanya began to translate.

"Red, Rogov's troops, yesterday. Now go to Moscow."

"How many troops?"

"Many thousands. Tanks too."

Edward had Vanya write on a notepad the disposition and movements of the troops in the Moscow area as Mirsk described them. It seemed that Rogov was intending to throw the full weight of his considerable forces at the Russian capital.

"Hey, have a look at this, boss," said Doug Findley, pointing at one of the computer monitors. "Looks like a countdown. D'you reckon the place is going to blow up?"

Edward looked at the screen with the white digits dancing in the corner. The dotted white lines that fanned out from Russia to North America looked awfully like missile trajectories.

"Tell him to explain this," Edward said to Vanya. While the question and answer were being translated, Edward sat at the computer console and experimentally pressed a couple of keys. The image on the screen changed: Now it showed the interior of a rocket silo. The foreground of the picture was filled with the rounded nose cone of an intercontinental ballistic missile. In the background, the curved dome of the silo was beginning to open.

Vanya was now ready with Mirsk's reply. "Nobody can stop. Only Rogov."

"What do you mean?" asked Edward.

"Personal order. From him only. Or else no stop."

The full situation now became clear to Edward.

Rogov was going to unleash—had unleashed—a nuclear inferno that would destroy one-half of the Earth. Unless something could be done to halt that countdown, North America was about to become twelve million square miles of scorched wasteland.

"Where is Rogov now?"

"To Vnukovo."

"To Vnukovo? Why there?"

"Many soldiers there. Then to Kremlin."

To the Kremlin . . . Edward stood there for a moment, speechless with anger. After all they had done, the bastard still had the upper hand. Was this it? Was there nothing more they could do?

"Find me a phone that works," he snarled.

The Kremlin, Moscow
12:30 hours

Seated at the desk that had until recently been occupied by Denisov, the telephone to his ear, Colonel Sokolov listened attentively to what Edward had to say. By the time the American had finished, Sokolov was shaking his head.

"There is a problem. I cannot order troops into action that are not under my command. These people think they are making a movie, for God's sake." He paused. "Yes, I know they are real soldiers, but they are not my soldiers. We need them to be activated and the only one who can do that is the Ukrainian president." He paused again. "I can't go to the president because I don't know how many people around that ape are loyal to Rogov. If we show our cards now, we're lost."

Sokolov listened again. "No," he said, "very few people in the organization know what he looks like."

He listened for a few more minutes. "Very well," he said, and hung up. He went out of the office to where the commanding officer of the Ukrainians was waiting.

"I want every officer you have in here immediately," he said.

Within ten minutes, the captains and lieutenants of the Ukrainian units were assembled in the office.

"Thank you for being here, for collaborating in this project," began Sokolov. "You are fine soldiers, and a fine soldier always does what is expected of him to the best of his ability, whatever the circumstances. You were brought here on the understanding that you were extras in a film production. Unfortunately, the situation has suddenly become much more complicated than that. We have just received word that a military coup is being attempted. A large military force is on its way to the Kremlin at this moment. Moscow is surrounded by rebel forces. The whole of Russia is in danger of falling into the hands of a military dictatorship."

Sokolov paused to let this information sink in. The officers were looking at one another with astonishment. This was not at all what they had expected.

"Very good plot," said Major Ostinov. "I like it." The others, thinking as he did, started nodding and smiling again.

"No." Sokolov stood up. "This is not a movie, this is bloody real. I need hardly say what a Russian coup would mean to you, loyal citizens of Ukraine. An expansionist, militaristic regime in the Kremlin would give you two options: slavery or war. And it would not be a war that you would find easy to win." Again he paused, looking around the room at the expressions of shock and perplexity on the men's faces.

"We must cut this attempted coup off at the root, before it can gain strength and grow. We are presently engaged in communications with your president. We are requesting the authorization to put you on active service immediately. When that authorization comes through, I expect you all to be ready for battle. Are there any questions?"

"How will we receive the authorization?" asked Major Ostinov.

"I'm afraid that is one of our other problems," said Sokolov. "The enemy has managed to suppress all radio communication. Here, within the Kremlin, we must rely on telephone communications or word of mouth."

"When are the rebel forces expected to arrive here?"

Sokolov looked at his watch. "In one hour at the most."

"I will have to give my people the option of fighting or walking away," the Ukrainian officer said.

"What are you talking about?"

"We are free people, we no longer have the heavy boot of the Kremlin on our throats. I agree that if there were to be a military coup in Russia, we would be next in line. And as we can see in Bosnia and other places, the world will not necessarily do very much to help us. I am willing to help you, but because this is not the Ukraine, I will have to ask my men to volunteer."

Sokolov was not happy with what he heard, but he had no other options. He had thought of trying to reach the real Kremlin Guard in its barracks but then discounted that notion, remembering how many of them had passed on information to the CG over the last few months.

There were some more questions, and then Sokolov sent the officers to their posts to explain the situation to their men, await the presidential authorization, and prepare for battle.

Sokolov strode outside into the bright sunlight. He could not believe the calmness of the place. He was aware of the cloud on the horizon, but no one else could possibly know about it. The feeling of walking on a battlefield before the battle was fought was very eerie.

He climbed into the jeep and drove to where the media vehicles were parked in the corner of the square. He stopped by the van that bore the Cyrillic symbols for NTV, Russia's largest independent commercial TV channel.

"Who is your senior staff member?"

A bald, plump-faced man came forth. "I am," he said. He didn't like soldiers, never had, and this one looked as angry and domineering as any he had ever seen.

"You will come with me," said Sokolov. The bald man and his crew exchanged nervous glances. Was he being arrested?

"On what grounds . . . ?" began the man, but Sokolov cut him off with an angry wave of his hand.

"I'm not arresting you. I need your help—urgently."

"Help? What for?" The man was still doubtful.

"For Russia, for democracy!" shouted Sokolov. "Now get in here."

The bald man got in the jeep with Sokolov and nearly fell over backward as the vehicle accelerated away.

CHAPTER 37

The convoy moved in a majestic procession along the Bolshaya Ordynka, the tank chains chewing up the cobblestones with a loud grind. General Peter Rogov sat in the passenger seat of his armor-plated media truck. Behind him were monitor screens, video cameras, microphones, and other radio and television equipment. The screens were on but presently blank. Two of them monitored the truck's video cameras, which for the time being were idle. The third was hooked up to the array in the bunker. It monitored whatever was being transmitted by the array, which was also idle at this point. Originally the general had wanted to have marches of the Red Orchestra played over the dead airwaves, but he decided against it, as it might tip off the enemy to the fact that there was a military coup in process. The array was now merely suppressing all other broadcasting without transmitting anything in its place. Peter was not ready to make his broadcast; the Kremlin was not yet his, and besides, he needed the phone link between Major Denisov's office and the bunker to transmit his broadcast to the array and from there to the world.

Rogov wished the convoy would move a little faster. Every second that passed meant that the forces occupying the Kremlin—whoever they were—would have time to prepare their defense. He had decided not to attempt an entry via the Troitskaya Tower, which would likely be heavily guarded. Instead, he would approach from Red Square and use cannons, rockets, and grenades to puncture two holes in the Kremlin walls, one on either side of Lenin's Mausoleum. He would then invade the grounds in a two-pronged attack. Infantry and armored personnel carriers would enter near the Nikolskaya Tower, between the former Arsenal Building and the building of the Council of Ministers, while he would enter behind the tanks, which would burst in near the Savior Tower. The name of the tower was so appropriate, he thought, and since he was making history, all the details had to be properly planned.

The convoy moved across the Pyatnitskaya Bridge. Nothing stood between him and the Kremlin: Whatever Sokolov had been able to muster he would undoubtedly handle in a wink. He, General Rogov, had armies at his command. He had no doubt that there was a scramble in Washington and most of the world's capitals to try to understand what had taken place on the tarmac at Domodedovo Airport. The vice president of the United States was probably being sworn in at that very moment somewhere in Washington—most likely in a bunker. By the time the swearing-in ceremony was complete, he would not have a country to be president of. Now there was only this hemisphere, only one great power, and Peter was about to become its ruler.

Among the cars moving along the Moskvoretskaya Embankment below, to the right of the military convoy, was a pale brown Mercedes, also heading for the onion-shaped spires of the Cathedral of the Intercession in Red Square.

Moskvoretskaya Embankment, Moscow
13:30 hours

Sparky Houston was worried. He had spent the morn-ing at the television station, in communication via radio with Air Force One. He had also been watching on the television monitor the scene at Domodedovo Airport, as the 747 had approached touchdown. Then all commu-nication had been cut—the radio link and the television picture had failed at precisely the same moment, as if a blanket had been thrown over them. Sparky knew about the array and could only assume that it had caused this blackout. But he didn't like it. He felt as though he were in the dark—not a feeling he enjoyed. It reminded him too strongly of the months of darkness he had spent liv-ing on the streets of New York City.

Shortly afterward, two of Sokolov's men had come to get him. Without a word of explanation—not that he could have understood anyway, having no Russian—they had hustled him downstairs and into a pale brown Mercedes, which was now driving at full speed along the Moskvoretskaya Embankment. He wondered where they were taking him, and why.

Ahead of them was the Pyatnitskaya Bridge, crossing from Bolshaya Ordynka Street to the foot of Red Square. As they passed under the bridge, Sparky could see a large military convoy moving north above them. The Mercedes continued along the Kremlevsakya Embankment, turning right on Bol'saja Poljanka, then right again on Maneznaja. They were now in front of the Troitskaya Tower gate of the Kremlin. The gate was guarded by numerous troops. However, rather than attempting to stop them, they waved cheerily as the Mercedes drove past and into the square.

They were met by two men from the presidential bodyguard, who escorted them to the office now occupied by Sokolov. The bald man from NTV was sitting there, still wondering what was going on, watched over by another member of the presidential bodyguard.

As Sparky entered, a tall, slim man in a well-tailored uniform, who had been explaining something to the bald man, broke off to greet him by name.

"You must be Sparky," Sokolov said with a big smile. Sparky could sense the fear behind the smile. It was something he had picked up on the street. You become very sensitized to people's feelings and expressions when that is all they have left in the world. "I'm Sokolov, a friend of Edward's. I am very glad to see you."

"So they have the array working?"

"Yes, it's a long story, but they're on the way here and we have a lot of work to do."

"When you say 'they,' do you mean the convoy I just passed on the way here?"

"Wait," Sokolov said, and he called in the Ukrainian officers. "They are almost here," he said to them.

"We're all with you," said Major Ostinov. "All our men have volunteered."

"I want you to know we really don't stand much of a chance," Sokolov said. "What we might gain is maybe a few minutes."

"We are free people," said the major. "Believe me, that is a good feeling, worth dying for. We choose to fight."

They got as much information as Sparky had about what was heading their way, and the major left the office to get his men ready to take their stand. It was then that Peter's tanks first opened fire.

CG Command Bunker, outside Moscow
13:40 hours

Edward stared as if hypnotized by the digits that were counting down the minutes and seconds on the monitor. You did not have to be a rocket scientist, he thought grimly, to know what they signified. In thirty-four minutes and nine seconds, the missiles would be launched. And once that happened, there was not much anyone could do to halt the destruction of America. It was possible to retaliate but not to stop something that was already on its way. "Come on," he said aloud, "what's keeping you?"

Major Mirsk's wound had been patched up, stopping the flow of blood. He now sat next to Edward at the computer console, watched over by Vanya, who seemed to enjoy pointing an assault rifle at a former member of the KGB. The gleam in his eye said he would enjoy it even more if the prisoner gave him the slightest excuse to open fire.

The telephone rang and Edward grabbed it.

"Sokolov?" he said. "Finally! All set?" Then he handed the phone to Vanya.

Vanya reeled off the names and locations of the Black Ghosts' forces around Moscow. Then he handed back the phone.

"Is Sparky there?" said Edward. "Put him on."

For several minutes there was furious activity in the control room, as Sparky asked questions and gave instructions. Edward answered and obeyed when he could, otherwise Sparky's request would be translated by Vanya, for Mirsk to answer.

Finally, everything was set. This is it, thought Edward, it's now or never. He looked again at the white digits of the countdown.

The Kremlin, Moscow
14:00 hours

Around the Kremlin walls the battle raged. Plumes of smoke rose from the inner yards as bullets spattered off the thick walls the czars had built, which gradually gave way to the constant barrage of exploding shells fired at almost point-blank range by the sea of tanks moving from side to side like giant fire-spitting turtles. The Council of Ministers Building was ablaze. The earth shook as mortar shells exploded between the tanks. Every so often a soldier of the Ukrainian unit would come out from behind a smoldering vehicle and run under fire for a better position. Then he would fire a single antitank missile at the oncoming, seemingly endless waves of T-72s, blowing off one of the low turrets, turning the killer turtle into a burning, exploding heap of scrap iron. Another tank that followed would get the soldier in its sights and blow him and whatever he was hiding behind to smithereens. But gradually there were more and more of the smoldering heaps that used to be tanks, and the Ukrainians kept popping up. Rogov's infantrymen were also running into trouble from the snipers who were picking them off from every direction. The Savior Tower was on fire, sending flames high into the air.

Around the corner, in the lee of the Tsar's Tower, Peter sat in his truck, protected from the heat of the battle by heavy armor plating and the Kremlin walls. He was confident that within a matter of minutes his troops would have secured the Kremlin and he would be able to make a triumphant entry. He could feel the blood pounding in his veins. This was his great moment. The defenders of the Kremlin only made his victory taste better. There is nothing as sweet as a military victory against a brave foe, and whoever they were, they were brave. But in and around Moscow, Peter had as many brigades as he could want. He had tanks, armored troop carriers, and more tanks. Nothing could stop him.

Abruptly the monitor in the truck lit up, and a hiss of static came over the audio system. Peter stared incomprehensibly at the screen. "What the hell is this?" he shouted at the technician seated by the console. Then a bald, plump-faced man appeared on the screen. He seemed nervous, looking to the side as if he wasn't sure what he was supposed to do. Peter leaned closer to the screen. He wanted to hear what the man who couldn't be was saying.

"We are expecting an announcement," the red face said. He paused and someone handed him a note. He read from the note. "There will shortly be an address to the people of Russia by General Peter Rogov, the leader of the CG."

"How can this be?" Peter roared. This unscheduled broadcast was going out over the array! That fool Mirsk. Somehow, the man had allowed himself to be tricked.

Peter leaned out the window and shouted an order at the soldier whose head stuck out the top hatch of an armored car. The car ground into motion, heading for the breach in the wall, followed by Peter's truck. He had to get to a phone line and stop this madness.

Inside the wall, a narrow track ran from the breach by the Savior Tower along the back wall of the Supreme Soviet Building. At the far corner of the building stood one of Peter's tanks, its cannon pointing across the square. There was a crunch of thunder as the cannon fired.

The armored car edged along the track, with the truck close behind. A burst of machine-gun fire from the trees opposite strafed the vehicles. An armor-piercing bullet managed to make it in. Some of the equipment in the back of the truck was damaged, but no one was injured. About halfway along, Peter called a halt. In the wall of the Supreme Soviet Building there was a back door, now level with and protected by the dark green bulk of the armored car.

"Open the door," yelled Peter. There was more fire from the trees, quickly silenced by a return volley from the armored car escorting the truck. The first soldier out of the truck had been hit and fell painfully to his knees. The tank fired again, there was more fire from the armored car, and a second soldier began to disembark.

Across the square, two Ukrainian soldiers were preparing to launch an RPG. The rockets had so far proved highly effective: Scores of tanks were destroyed. The disadvantage of the RPG is that the user needs to expose himself to his target for a short time. But that disadvantage was undermined by the bravery of the Ukrainian soldiers, who kept popping up like poison mushrooms after the rain. Nevertheless, numerous tanks remained, including one positioned at the corner of the Supreme Soviet Building.

A soldier held the launcher on his shoulder, setting the tank's center in his sights. The tank commander saw him and frantically tried to turn the turret so he could blow the man away. In the meantime, he opened the top hatch and started to fire the Gurianov machine gun, raising clouds of dust around the soldier, who didn't move. The bullets hit the wall behind him. Finally the cannon was on target. Each fired at the same time and neither was around to witness the destruction of the other.

The loss of the tank was the least of Peter's worries. In the back of the truck the one television screen that was still functional lit up again. Peter was enraged to see the face of Sokolov appearing and his voice saying, "To all divisions of the Black Ghosts, this is your commander, General Peter Rogov, speaking."

"Impostor!" yelled Peter, beside himself with fury. Then he stuck his head out the armored truck window. "Move! Get that bloody door open, now, now!"

The second soldier reached the door and, attaching a small explosive pack near the lock, blew it off its hinges. Peter jumped out of the truck and, huddled between the technician and two more soldiers from the armored car, rushed inside the building.

They were met with a burst of fire from a group of soldiers at the far end of the corridor. While his men returned the fire, Peter opened a door at random. There was a staircase. Without hesitating, Peter ran up the stairs and into the first floor corridor. There was no one in sight here, but there were also no other doors. Peter ran to the end of the corridor and peeped around the corner, where he saw two soldiers standing guard outside an ornate double door.

Peter recognized the place. He knew they were guarding President Konyigin.

The president, seated on a large sofa, wished he had a drink. Everything had been going so well—the Elite Guard in position, the Americans' plane just coming in to land. Then the television screen had unaccountably gone blank. Worse still, Gregorin's mobile phone had stopped working, cutting them off from all but a handful of the Presidential Guard. There had been shouted orders and hurried movements of soldiers in the square below. In Red Square, visible across the Kremlin walls from the upper floors of the Supreme Soviet Building, heavily armed troops had appeared. Then the shooting had started. Something was obviously very wrong.

Konyigin seethed with impotent anger. He felt like an innocent bystander, watching but not directly involved in the battle going on all around him. But he knew that whatever happened, it would involve him soon enough.

He drew some comfort from the presence of Gregorin, his security chief. Solid, reliable Gregorin—he would not let anything happen to his president, would he?

Outside in the corridor, Peter again peeped around the corner at the two soldiers standing guard. He was alone again. Deep inside, he had always known he would have to do things himself. The men guarding the president should have been his men, and the president should have been dead by now. Peter couldn't trust anyone. He would have to finish the job himself. He drew his pistol.

Then, walking tall, he stepped into the corridor. The two soldiers stared at the general in his glorious uniform, with stripes and ribbons and rows of medals. They froze, just long enough for him to fire twice from the hip.

That was all it took. The two guards crumpled in a heap. Peter was at the door in a second. Pistol in hand, he opened it and walked inside.

"Good afternoon, gentlemen," he said.

CHAPTER 38

CG Command Bunker, outside Moscow
14:10 hours

Even though he could not understand the language the man on the screen was speaking, Edward knew what was being said. The tone of voice was calm, reassuring, serene. Not only that, Edward had told Sokolov exactly what to say only a few minutes earlier.

"I repeat, this is General Peter Rogov, commander-in-chief of the Black Ghosts. Blaze Alpha Alpha Two Five Five Nine Peter. In the best interests of Russia, our glorious motherland, I hereby issue the following decree: Suspend all hostilities. Return to your barracks. We have won our victory. All hostilities will cease immediately.

"To Svirt, nine nine four gamma nine. Stop count-down, return clock to zero, now. All orders to launch ICBMs are rescinded. There will be no nuclear strike. I repeat, suspend all hostilities, return to your barracks . . ."

So far, the link that Sparky had patched through from

the mobile television van in the Kremlin, via phone line to the array in the bunker, was performing flawlessly. Observing the monitor in the bunker's control room, Edward could see and hear Sokolov as clearly as if the man were sitting opposite him. The same signal was being broadcast throughout Russia, to every radio and television that was switched on. Now Edward could only hope that whoever controlled the missile in the silo visible on the other monitor was also watching Sokolov's broadcast.

The countdown was still running. It had reached one minute and eight seconds.

As Sokolov's voice continued, Edward's eyes were on the white digits. Thirty seconds, twenty-nine, twenty-eight . . . and then, twenty-eight. Twenty-eight! The countdown was halted with twenty-eight seconds left. On screen, the curved dome of the missile silo could be seen moving slowly into the closed position. Edward started breathing again.

The Kremlin, Moscow
14:15 hours

The news came through by phone. A jubilant Edward told Sparky that disaster had been averted: The missile countdown had been halted. Sparky gave the signal and Sokolov wound up his broadcast. Once he was off the air, the colonel took the phone out of Sparky's hands.

"We did it!" Edward could barely contain his joy.

"Not quite," said Sokolov, and Edward could hear the explosions in the background. "We've still got a battle going on here."

"What is the signal for stopping hostilities?"

"The general said that in the battle we would stop fighting only when the other side was dead or waved the white flag of surrender."

"Well, what the hell are you waiting for? We'll blow up the array here, and you wave the bloody white flag."

"Good idea." Edward could hear Sokolov shouting orders in Russian. "They're putting a flag up now. Let's hope it works."

"Get the Russian president on the air," said Edward. "Have him tell the people that everything's under control."

"We'll do it over the regular broadcasting system, the moment you disable the array."

The battle for the Kremlin had lessened in fury but was not yet over. The Ukrainians had performed superbly, and despite heavy casualties, they had been able to contain the Black Ghosts' onslaught. But Peter's infantrymen were still active and several tanks were still operational.

Soon after the white flag went up, the fighting ceased. Sokolov, still wearing the general's coat he had used for the television broadcast, walked into the inner courtyard. He had the Ukrainian officers with him as he approached the commander of the armored column that they had been battling.

"We have won," he said to the colonel who had stepped down from the rear of a T-72 tank to greet him. The colonel saluted smartly. "What now, general?"

"Assemble your men at the Askanskia Stadium. Clear the Kremlin, the fighting is over. Russia is in our hands." Sokolov knew he had to be convincing. Now with the array about to go off-line, if the Black Ghosts' soldiers suspected anything it would be very easy for them to reassemble. He had to get them out of the way until he could be sure the general was taken care of. And he had no idea where Rogov might be.

Nor did anyone know where the Russian president was. All Sokolov knew was that he was under guard in an upstairs room of the Supreme Soviet Building. Accompanied by a half dozen men, Sokolov went looking for him.

Of all the Kremlin buildings, the Supreme Soviet had been the worst hit in the battle. The west wing was almost entirely destroyed, and smoke was rising from several of the broken windows of the east wing. Only the central block was fairly free of damage.

They made straight for the room where the president was last seen. The bodies of the two guards outside were not a good sign. The ornate doors were hanging open. Two of Sokolov's men went in first, guns ready. Sokolov followed. Inside, Gregorin lay dead, the victim of Peter's first bullet. Two other personnel of the presidential bodyguard were wounded, one seriously. Peter himself was sitting in a chair, his eyes wide open, the back of his head missing. President Konyigin was weeping softly.

Domodedovo Airport, Moscow
15:00 hours

"We have raised Domodedovo control tower," the pilot said over the internal speakers in Air Force One. President Bradshawe breathed a sigh of relief, even though they were still in the air.

For the last three hours they had been in a holding pattern above Moscow, circling round and round, cut off from the ground by a complete failure of radio transmission, not knowing whether or when it would be safe for them to land. Fenton, wanting to cut away and leave the area, was locked in an ongoing argument with the president.

"I'm not turning tail," Bradshawe said. "We stay until we start running out of fuel. And then—and only then—will we divert to another airport."

"But sir, what's the point? For all we know, there might not be a Russia down there, and surely not the one we were coming to visit."

"We will leave when we know, and that's that."

Now, at last, radio communication had been reestablished and they had been given permission to land at Domodedovo Airport. Fenton managed to open a channel to his people on the ground, who gave him the full picture. They had already been contacted by the Russian president, who wanted to talk to President Bradshawe. They were going to set up the link, then they would decide what to do. An endless stream of calls were coming in from the White House, where the vice president was about to be sworn in.

"What the hell is going on?" asked Bradshawe. "They all think we were killed? What are they talking about?"

On the ground, the media crews were in a state of utter confusion. Having seen with their own eyes the destruction of Air Force One a few hours earlier, they had now been told the president's plane would be landing shortly.

To insure that no red tape would trip up the valiant soldiers of the Ukrainian army, Sokolov had informed President Konyigin that the authorization to protect him came directly from the Ukrainian president. When Konyigin called the Ukrainian president and informed him of the heroism of his men, he was surprised, to say the least. But having the big Russian brother in his debt was not something he was going to argue about. He would worry about what had really happened later; for now, he decided to make the most of this unexpected Russian goodwill.

"I would be honored if you and the American president would be our guests here in Kiev. We will also request authorization to sign the treaty and join in your heroic effort for world peace and democracy." So it was settled.

Accordingly, an Mi-8 helicopter was sent to the Kremlin to pick up President Konyigin and his bodyguard and take them to Domodedovo Airport. Sokolov was among the party. Edward had set out by road from the bunker and was to meet them there. The Russian president would board Air Force One, which would then fly on to the Ukrainian capital.

Edward sat in the cab of the old army lorry, on the tarmac at Domodedovo. He was watching the sky. First to land was the Mi-8, which came down not far from where he was parked. He could see the presidential bodyguard escort Konyigin to the waiting car, which drove him to a secure area. Then he saw Sokolov, whom by now he regarded as an old friend, alight from the helicopter to wander around close by it, stretching his legs. Edward jumped down from the cab and went over to greet him. They shook hands and embraced warmly. Standing in the shade of the helicopter gunship, they turned their eyes once again toward the sky.

Edward's men were slowly coming off the truck, tired and jaded with the events of the last twenty-four hours. They had taken some casualties: one dead and several injured, mainly with flesh wounds. They had learned the fate of their specially painted 747 when they arrived at Domodedovo, adding two more dead to their list—the pilots who had flown the false Air Force One into the airport. Still, they realized they had come out fairly well from what had basically been a suicide mission.

President Bradshawe had already heard about their feat from Fenton, who filled him in on what Larry had said and on other information regarding Edward and his men.

The president felt a lurch in his stomach as Air Force One lost altitude. This was it: Now they were definitely going down. He closed his eyes and grabbed hard on the armrests, as he always did.

Air Force One was now visible from the ground as it made a wide sweep around the airport before banking into its final turn. As Edward and Sokolov watched the growing spot on the horizon line up with the runway, they heard the rhythmic sound of a chopper taking flight. The sound got louder, and then, like a bad dream, it rose over the treeline across the tarmac. Not four hundred feet from them, the black helicopter gunship came into view, a cluster of rockets under each wing. Edward and Sokolov looked at each other. There was no doubt what the thumping wasp had in mind: It was hovering slowly toward the end of the runway, pointing itself at the incoming jet.

Inside the hovering gunship, Yazarinsky's eyes fixed unblinkingly on the distant incoming plane. He had heard the broadcast by the supposed leader of the Black Ghosts and had dismissed it as a futile gesture. It was true that no one apart from the core personnel at the bunker knew what Rogov looked like, but Yazarinsky refused to believe they would be swayed by such an obvious trick. And even if they were, was not Rogov himself still at large, eager to continue the battle?

Yazarinsky did not know. What he did know was that he had been ordered to destroy Air Force One, and he had apparently failed in that task. Now he was being given a second chance. Let it never be said, thought the little man, that he had failed in his duty. He readied the gunship's rocket launcher. The black dot got bigger, gradually taking on the shape of Air Force One.

"Do you know who that is?" Edward asked.

"I don't have any choppers," Sokolov answered. "I believe this one is a CG. It's going to go for the plane."

It felt as if time had stopped. Everyone was staring at the chopper and then at the incoming plane. Everybody realized what was about to happen, but no one did anything. As he ran back toward the truck, Edward shouted: "Mario, shoot the bastard down!"

Mario heard him and turned to grab the first weapon he could lay his hands on, which was an RPG antitank missile. The distance was at the limit of the weapon's range, and the target was moving faster than a tank, but it was the best he could do. He aimed ahead of the chopper and fired.

The roar of the approaching jumbo jet mingled with the pounding of the helicopter's blades. Yazarinsky was in the position he wanted. He put his finger on the rockets' firing button.

Before Yazarinsky could press the button, the RPG—almost at the end of its run but still as potent as ever—contacted the nose of the chopper. The gunship exploded.

Air Force One touched the ground, bounced up, touched down again, and taxied to a halt. The media people began to clap and cheer. The president and several of his entourage disembarked and were escorted to a private lounge in the terminal building.

Once all the explanations had been given and President Bradshawe at last got the full picture, realizing just what he had been through—and what he had missed—over the last few hours, he asked to meet Edward in person.

"It seems I have a lot to thank you for," said Bradshawe. "You saved my life—twice—and you also saved that of the Russian president. Quite an achievement."

"I had a lot of help from a lot of good people," Edward said.

"I'm sure you did," said the president. "That trick with the phony Air Force One plane—that must have taken quite a bit of planning and cooperation."

"It sure did," Edward assured him. Not to mention, he thought, lying, fraud, and theft.

"I can promise you," said the president, "that what you and your men have done will not be forgotten."

"I'm sorry to say I have a problem believing that, Mr. President," Edward said.

The president looked surprised. "Why do you say that?"

"Because, sir, we did it before, and you people up there on the Hill forgot all about us. Why not again?"

"Because of what you and your men have done. Why don't you join me, and make sure? I can always use a good man around the White House."

"It's not for me, sir," Edward replied. "But if you really mean it, I know someone we all trust." He was thinking of Joe Falco. The man could use a break, and this would be a big one.

"You got yourself a deal, my man. Now get your people aboard the plane and let's get you home."

The president turned to the other members of his party who had also disembarked—his friend Richard Townes and the corporate financier Hubert Austin—and gestured that they should all get back on board the plane. At that moment, several of the Secret Service men came through the lounge, escorting a handcuffed Bud Hays into a waiting car.

"What makes a man do that?" the president asked, his face saddened.

As they headed to the lounge's exit door, a voice rang out over the terminal speakers. It was not the customary airport announcer. It was a woman's voice, and it spoke in English. "Mr. Singleton, I know who you are. You owe me." Edward felt a shiver go through his body. There was no mistaking it: It was Natalie's voice.

"What was that about?" the president asked. The members of his entourage all shrugged. But Edward could have sworn he saw a nervous twitch pass across the face of Hubert Austin.

What did she mean? he wondered. He would probably never know.

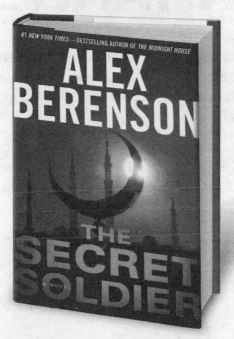